The Régime Change Man

By the same author

The Régime Change Man (The Long Version)

The Populist

The Plutocrat

Rory Harden

THE RÉGIME CHANGE MAN

Black Spike Books

www.regimechangemanbook.com
www.roryharden.com

Published by Black Spike Books

US First Edition

Version 1.00

ISBN 978-1-910665-07-7

Cover photo of lion in South Africa by Nancy Crockett.

For Nancy Crockett

"My belief is we will, in fact, be greeted as liberators."

- A famous warmonger.

CHAPTER 1

It was the safest town in Africa. And the oddest place in Namibia. It was a little German town that had strayed from its origins — and from the nineteenth century — and had anchored itself to the scoured-empty Atlantic coast of southern Africa.

It was a town of salt roads and sea fog, with cool, damp mornings and German street names — most of which had survived a general and recurrent mood to Africanize them.

It was a town of Bavarian gables and Teutonic brick, where you could hear German spoken on the street and where you now saw Volkswagens where once there had been ox wagons.

It was a town alone, menaced by a giant and relentless neighbor, the great Namib Desert, that sent its hummock dune infiltrators into the town's southern and south-eastern outskirts and wanted to suck the moisture from them.

It was a town where you could escape the beaten-down heat of the interior, or of the capital; where you could park without difficulty most of the time; and where you could enjoy a beer and a pizza at very reasonable prices.

It was a vacation town, created and maintained — like its vast and ancient companion — by the uncaring and unpredictable Benguela current, which pumped cold Antarctic water by the cubic kilometer up to the African coast and fluctuated according to its own concerns.

You could dip your toe in the Atlantic here; you wouldn't keep it there for long.

You could explore the dunes, in an environmentally tactful way and in a Land Rover, and marvel at their complex ecology.

You could admire the salt works.

You could motor, if you drove carefully and with your lights on — count the little shrines by the roadside — south to the modern and uncharacterful port town of Walvis Bay, once a strategic enclave of the old South Africa and, before that, a possession of the British Empire. If you were young, had travelled little, and had exhausted the local possibilities, you might think it worthwhile.

You could drive north, if you chose, to a lonely and downbeat resort village.

You could take the salt road to the north-east, heading for Damaraland and its famous prehistoric rock paintings, and lose yourself in the desert. Your tire tracks might be visible for years.

The town was called Swakopmund because it lay at the mouth of the Swakop river. The river, in accordance with Namibian custom, flowed rarely. But when it did — when the annual rains, if any, reached the interior — it was forceful, a brown torrent full of debris.

Mund is the German word for "mouth". Swakop means "rubbish" or, some say, "shit".

A new bridge had been built, some years before, at what had seemed to the town's citizens great expense.

It was the safest town in Africa and it was the town to which George Fischer had chosen to retire after a life and valiant career, as some would have it, in some of the continent's least safe.

His neighbors probably thought him a gentle, patient little tub of a man, if reserved. They couldn't have known that he lived every day in the grim conviction that his past was out to get him.

George, who Anglicized his first name but not his last, was the owner of George's Desert Garden Hotel. It was a sound business, but one whose fortunes varied — in a way that depressed his fellow hoteliers — with the pattern of events hundreds or even thousands of kilometers distant.

Tonight, George had ten rooms and six guests. Three couples. He provided breakfast and, if asked in advance, a simple evening meal. Today, no one had asked.

The walled compound at the back of the hotel, that served partly to deflect the encroaching dunes, had been secured; the guests' rental cars were safe.

His garden had been watered. As far as he knew — and this was an issue that excited him — he had the only green lawn, with pond, of any hotel in town. And it was the end of the dry season, too.

Roberta, his part-time assistant manager, had tidied the bar-restaurant area and the lounge and had retired to her tiny office to catch up on the day's paperwork. Her light was on and her door was half-open. She leaned forward at her desk, face hidden. Her hair flowed over the back of her chair. She had her strong, thin calves hooked around the chair legs, her plastic sandals about to fall off.

As he watched, the left sandal fell, and then the right, taking her foot with it. He almost laughed out loud. She wouldn't have been offended, but he stifled the impulse anyway. He'd paid for the artificial foot out of his own money, which back then, of course, had been burning one hole in his pocket and another in his heart. It was the best to be obtained in Hamburg in 1983.

He listened. Her worn-down fingers tapped at the worn-away keyboard and the worn-out printer slogged its way through the month-to-date expenses. George's admiration was boundless. Next year he would buy a new computer, if business held up.

"You don't have to finish that tonight," he said. "It's not necessary."

But she didn't seem to hear.

Normally his guests returned from dinner at about ten or ten-thirty. It wasn't a late-night town. This particular group of six all seemed to know each other; they might want a drink before bedtime.

Later, he would go into the bar and loiter, just in case.

Meanwhile, he would relax here in the lounge and watch a little TV. Since most of his guests were German, he kept the satellite system on a German-language news or entertainment channel. He left it on most of the time, with the sound turned down low.

He settled down in front of the TV. From here he could also survey the lobby, the spot-lit garden and the main gate.

A movement at the edge of his vision startled him. What was it? There: A large, white four-wheel-drive, parked in the street with its front passenger window aligned perfectly with the hotel's iron gate. The street was dark; he couldn't see the driver. High walls either side of the gate hid the rest of the vehicle.

Was that a shadow, or was the driver still in the car? It looked new, expensive — too expensive for a local. And even here, no one would park such a vehicle in the street overnight. Just visiting someone, perhaps.

The printer choked to a halt and buzzed as if in pain. Roberta cursed. George heard her shake and slap the machine in a way that suggested she'd done so before. It got the message and went back to work.

The white car was still there. Perhaps he should take a look...

There was a movement inside the car — a hand raised from lap to chest and then lowered again, like a man checking that he had remembered to stow his wallet in his jacket.

He strode over to the office.

"Roberta. The front gate is locked?"

"Yes, of course."

"The guests have a key?"

"Yes, they do. They have the blue key."

"The blue key."

"On the blue key chain."

"Yes. Thank you."

He went outside and stood on the door-step, hands on his hips, the conscientious property-owner checking that all in the garden was as it should be.

It began with a scuffling, a sudden hubbub and a mob scene at the gate: The guests. A woman's laughter like an adolescent hyena. The scraping of key in lock. A second attempt. The offering of advice. The gate flung open and swinging back against the wall with a force sure to weaken the hinges — except that he'd reinforced them.

Welcome home, he ought to be saying. Trust you had a pleasant evening. One at a time, please. But something kept him from speech.

The gate was narrow, deliberately so. Nevertheless, the guests approached in pairs. A commotion of squeezing and bumping, mock embarrassment.

Six of them. No, not six — seven. At the back, a powerfully-sized man, a little older than his oblivious new companions, moving with contrasting caution. A

3

heavy and voluminous jacket, possibly suede. Short wiry hair and a belligerent moustache.

George slipped back into the house.

"Roberta. The guests are back. They are going to make some noise, I think. They are still in the party mood. Let me close the office door for you."

He closed it, went back out into the garden and held open the door for the guests.

"Welcome home! Please! Did you all have a good time? Did you see what night life we have here?"

One English couple; two German. They seemed to have met on the road, or at another lodge, and had obviously forged a lifelong alliance. Unsurprisingly, they all spoke English.

"Yes! We see the night life!"

This from the elder German male, who had assumed the role of patrician and was bringing up the rear, or so he thought.

An advance party — the rotund and predictably sunburnt but otherwise pretty Englishwoman and the younger German girl, blonde and short-haired as customary — negotiated George's twisty garden path, picking their way between the spotlights, elbows entwined for mutual support. The rest of the pack swayed along behind, a tableau of bleary gratitude. Some shushing, some fingers on lips. They were trying to keep the noise down.

Normally he would have been concerned for his pond. Tonight, he was concerned for his life.

Arnie Muller had come to see him.

*

A rnie Muller was big, loud, and full of ridiculous stories; he was George's dumbest, greatest friend from the good old times in the bad old days. No, don't ask, George told the guests, you'll embarrass him! Arnie hadn't seen his best chum in years, and now here he was — just think of it!

And Arnie Muller was a performer. He was shocking, he was funny. He was an old campaigner — one end of the continent to the other since he was *this* high. He'd seen everything, George, hadn't he? First time for these nice people? African virgins! Ask him anything! The guests couldn't believe their luck.

George avoided looking at Arnie. Instead, he watched the guests. Would Arnie fool them?

Visitors to southern Africa from the more comfortable parts of the common European home, encountering the white South African male of a certain age, outside his home country, often felt ill at ease. At least, the more thoughtful ones did. They saw men who looked like Arnie and who worked for the big safari companies in remote spots in Zambia, Botswana or Namibia — and they wondered. Could they tell that these were men who used to be estate managers or farmers or special forces? Now they were writing eco-audits for young graduates in Johannesburg and serving afternoon tea. You didn't need to ask them what they thought of their home country these days; they let you know. You didn't need to scratch to smell the resentment.

4

Of course, Arnie was a special case; he had a brutal talent for opportunity. And tonight he had George's guests entranced and they loved him. He had bush-glamor and tales to tell.

"George! Come along with the drinks here. We're all getting thirsty."

Arnie giving orders again. Hasn't lost the taste.

"What are you looking at over there? Some bad guys trying to break in?"

They're already here, George thought.

"Don't listen to him," he told his guests. "When he was young, he was in the South African security forces. The stories he could tell. If he was allowed to."

Did Arnie find that provocative? No, he was enjoying himself too much.

The guests took their drinks from the tray. George caught Arnie's gaze for the first time. Two decades later, and those eyes had changed. More patient? Perhaps. Softer? No.

"We were comrades," Arnie said. "But that was a long time ago."

"So Arnie, what did you get up to in the security forces? Sort of SAS stuff, was it?"

A diffident inquiry from the English girl's paunchy, tight-shirted husband or boyfriend, who was trying to look like someone who might have joined up himself if he hadn't had other priorities. If he only knew what he was asking. And who.

"Two things," Arnie said, with gravity. "Security. And force."

They took this for wit, and smiled accordingly.

Arnie's not happy, George thought. He's wants them out of here. Roberta? Keeping still and quiet, in her little den.

"Are any of you people flying up to the Skeleton Coast?"

They wanted to, but it was too expensive.

"Ah, but you must!"

Then, for a full twenty minutes, the story of the wartime fliers who crashed on the coast and their improbable rescue.

Impressed by Arnie's sweeping narrative and his grasp of African history, the younger German couple — they'd been debating this on their own account, it seemed — had a question for him.

"Why must there always be so much war in Africa?"

Good girl. Asking the right man.

The blonde girl propped her chin on her fists and peered wistfully up at the once and future mercenary. Her boyfriend slipped his arm around her waist and played with his drink.

"You must know the answer, I think," she added.

Now they're asking, George thought. Arnie doesn't know. Doesn't care. He's just thankful for it. Tell them about Angola, Arnie.

A flicker of something — but not shame and not disgust — on Arnie's face. Was he going to give them his whole bloody tailgate philosophy? Let's hope not, George thought; they don't deserve it.

"It's tribal," Arnie said. "They can't help it."

Liar. Coward. No money in tribal, Arnie, you bastard.

The guests signaled for another bottle of wine. Arnie left them, shambled up to the bar and helped himself to another beer. He spoke quietly.

"There's a job for you, if you're not stupid. I need you. They're running me ragged. Good money," he said, sighing.

A shimmer of the old Arnie: Self-pity and aggression.

"I already have a job."

"How much can you make out of idiots like these?"

"It's enough. The exchange rate —"

"That's rubbish. You want dollars, George? They're going around with suitcases. Suitcases. It's true. Why are you bothering with this nonsense? Why do you want to live here?"

"That must be obvious."

"Come back. It's different now. They have new people in charge. Everyone knows what they're supposed to do. They run it like a business. It *is* a business. You will have an executive role. You can call yourself a consultant."

"I'm a hotel owner."

"You don't own it. The bank does."

"Leave me to my business, Arnie. I have nothing to offer you."

"What about your friends?"

"What friends?"

"Your friends in Windhoek and Luanda. Your SWAPO guys, and all the others. Your bush buddies. Some of them are big men, now."

"Don't call them that."

"We know you talk to them. You can talk to them for us. You think they'd even look at me? And you can supervise transactions. It's a white-collar job. Very clean, if that's what you're worried about. Lots of paperwork."

George said nothing.

Arnie glanced over at the guests, who were taking photographs of one another.

"What did you do with all the money, by the way? Did you spend it? Invest it? Buy a villa in Marbella for your ageing and devoted parents? Donate it to Amnesty International? Or did you give it all to that black girl?"

George said nothing.

"George, you've got to help us."

"I can't."

"We had a guy in Jo'burg, but he had to step down. Now they're recruiting an idiot Englishman in London who thinks there's a place for him in the master race. Don't quote me on that. But he's just handling the finance and I think he's only temporary. Disposable. Name's Vickery. He's only been to Africa once. On vacation. With his bloody awful wife."

George uncorked the wine.

"Have you talked to your SWAPO chums recently? Ask them about Pasquale."

Pasquale, the Angolan oil minister until a month ago. Sliced in two inside his Mercedes, which was supposed to be bomb-proof.

"Ask them about Muñoz."

Hector Muñoz, economic advisor to the Angolan government, whose recent and cogently-argued report had recommended against liberalization of the oil industry. Found in a tree.

George delivered the wine to the guests, finding a hushed debate raging in German. The blonde girl was agitated, flushed. The patrician looked concerned.

6

The English girl leaned back in her chair with her eyes closed. Her boyfriend looked at the floor.

"George."

Arnie summoned him back to the bar.

"They're going to push the Chinese out of Luanda once and for all," he said. "What passes for a régime up there? It's gone. I know what you're thinking. All that bloody investment! But they'll all be better off, trust me. The MPLA is corrupt as hell. You, of all people, know that. They're all buying themselves Mercedes and private bankers while the food rots in the warehouses. There's no access to information, no free enterprise. It's your stinking Marxist bureaucracy."

So this is it, George thought. Arnie's persuaded the CIA, the Pentagon and the military-industrial complex to overthrow the legal government of Angola. Or thinks he has. He's going to be a big wheel in the Transitional Authority or the Provisional Administration. Why not? He has at least one conviction for fraud. One hand on the tiller, the other in the till, to use an English expression. Of course, there's as much Marxism in Angola as there was poison in Iraq. But there's oil. And since when has Arnie been interested in free enterprise — as opposed to free loot?

The guests had abandoned their drinks and were shuffling towards the exit.

"I don't want to know," George said.

"You don't want to know. So that's your attitude these days. You don't want to know about me. You don't want to know about the future. You don't want to know about your own past. Perhaps you don't want to know about your American friends, Mr. and Mrs. Ellis, either? Bill and Elaine? You remember? But how could you could forget?"

How indeed. George said nothing. The guests had gone — without their complimentary schnapps, without the friendly good-night from their host to which they were entitled. George started after them.

"Now there's a family beset by tragedy," Arnie said, grabbing George by the arm and holding him back.

"I need to —"

"Don't you remember?"

Yes, he remembered.

He saw the dirt track, the bridge over the stream, the shattered culvert. He saw the Jeep with its wheels on fire, the splintered trees, dripping blood.

No, he thought, don't replay it now; this is not the time.

Arnie was talking. But George didn't hear. Instead, he heard his own voice describing the scene.

There's me, lying in the ditch, holding my knee together. Over there, on the other side of the track, that's Roberta sitting up working on her foot, or what's left of it; she's seen this happen to other people. Here come Bill and Elaine and the others, running up from the second Jeep, which is unharmed. What's that mess in the front seat of our Jeep? That's the Ellis girl.

And here comes Mr. Moreland. What does he have to say? This is his expedition.

Arnie was waiting for him.

"What's happened to them?" George said.

"Nothing yet, but it's any day now. They'll be detained for helping terrorists."

"What are you talking about? There are no terrorists in Windhoek. In Namibia. It's absurd. Bill's the ambassador."

"You are completely out of touch, George. They are everywhere. If you don't take that seriously, it's as good as helping them. Your friend Bill may have assisted a proscribed organization."

"What organization?"

"My personal opinion, his wife put him up to it. She has a vendetta against Douglas Moreland. And we all know her political views. They're going to pay the price. It's very sad."

Arnie gripped George by the wrist.

"Go up to Luanda. Talk to your old chums. Find out who's in and who's out. You can make two lists."

"Let go of me, Arnie."

Arnie twisted George's wrist.

"Tell them the new administration will require their services. We're not going to purge the whole lot of them."

"You will start another war. Another twenty-five years."

"And then go to Windhoek. Tell them if they know what's good for them they won't interfere. Make a contribution to SWAPO funds for the next election. Find out if there are any hard-nuts left."

Arnie released George's wrist and pushed him back from the bar. George stumbled.

"If they want a guerrilla war, they can have one. It won't matter. They won't have the Russians to help them. Or the Cubans. The Chinese won't fight. Once we move in, we stay."

George was silent. Arnie turned his head as if he'd heard a noise somewhere.

"Is there someone else here?"

"No."

Arnie stepped away from the bar.

"I have only so much time, George. I will have to cut this short."

"Get out."

"I can't believe you don't want to help your friends Bill and Elaine. After what they did for you."

"I know what they did."

"You owe them, George. Where's your new-found honor?"

Bill and Elaine, George was thinking — spiriting their Mr. Fischer away, with their daughter's blood all over him. And Moreland thinking he was a spy for the Cubans.

Now Moreland was back to kick Angola again.

"So George. Are you going to help them or not?"

"No."

Arnie rubbed his rings.

"You never told them, did you? Bill and Elaine?"

"Told them what?"

"How it came to be there. On that particular day. That particular landmine. Of all the landmines in Africa."

There was nothing to say, nothing to think. He was hollow, he was a shadow, he was nothing. If he could, he would stand here until the dunes covered the town and obliterated him. He should never have come to Africa. He should never have existed.

Arnie smiled.

"So. Let me ask you again. Don't you want to know if there's anything you can do to help?" he said.

George nodded.

"Come with me."

He followed Arnie into the lobby.

"Give me the key. Wait here."

Arnie went out to the four-wheel-drive and returned with a shopping bag. Inside were a mass of cables, two small black boxes and a satellite phone.

"Sat-phone," Arnie said. "Keep it charged up, keep it on. Brand new, top model, very expensive. But don't worry — you don't have to pay for the calls. Very private. They can't even break it at Fort Meade, not that they'll be trying. If it rings, you answer. Are you with me?"

George nodded.

"It works best outside."

"I know."

"Good. Now, if you don't mind, I'll leave you to entertain your bloody guests yourself."

He glanced pointedly over George's shoulder at the door to the office. Then he slapped George across the shoulders and walked out.

George watched him drive away, then dropped the phone on the floor and went back to the bar. It was empty; the guests hadn't returned.

He felt Roberta's hands on his shoulders.

"Don't worry," he said. "I will not do this. I will not be involved in this. I just wanted to get rid of him."

She looked back at the shopping bag in the hallway and then put her arms around his waist and hugged him.

CHAPTER 2

Dale Summers couldn't figure out whether he'd just had a good day — or a really, really bad day. He was a junior diplomat at the US embassy in Windhoek, Namibia. Or a senior gopher, as it more often seemed. His job was supposed to be economic development, not that many people back in Washington took *that* seriously these days.

But the point was this: It wasn't *his job* to deal with hostages.

That would be *Jay's* job. But Jay hadn't been around. And Ambassador Bill, for some reason, had picked on Dale.

No one had expected that the kidnapped New York banker – her name, Jennifer Ross Lenehan, now firmly imprinted on Dale's fevered consciousness — would be dumped on the Embassy's doorstep that very morning by persons unknown. That kind of shit never happened. And, if it did, it was Jay's job to take care of it.

The newly-freed hostage had not been in poor condition, luckily. Dale had organized a medical check-up and later, at Ms. Lenehan's insistence and with an armed escort, he'd accompanied her on a trip to Independence Avenue to buy new clothes.

Now, she was safely installed, under Bill and Elaine's supervision, at the residence. Dale had bid her goodnight and sleep well, and had then mentioned that he was going home to his wife.

But he had lied like a dog. He hadn't gone home. And he needed to get his head straight before Jay found him.

Thus here he was, perched at the expansive and, by local standards, expensive, curved bar of the Quiver Tree Brewhouse and Restaurant. He often came here to admire and, occasionally, to shoot the breeze with the beautiful, dreadlocked manager of the bar. The locals still referred to her as "manageress", amazingly. Namibia — so beautifully, politely behind the times. He hadn't quite mastered her name yet. Began with a "K". But, after eighteen months in Windhoek, he was proud of his growing and sophisticated appreciation for the subtleties of African customs and culture. Not bad for a Southern boy.

11

His secondary purpose was to delay, for a few hours, his return to Sheryl and the apartment. (His rank at the embassy, modest as it was, ought to have brought him a small house, but rising rents in Windhoek and rising paranoia — security, Dale! — in Washington had dictated otherwise.) This reluctance was shameful. But he had to forgive himself; nobody could say he wasn't trying his hot-damn best there.

And, besides, what if Jay were waiting for him there?

As for Ms. Lenehan, the former hostage, he had to ask himself why he was so taken with her. It wasn't just Sheryl, with her gloomy eyes and jittery fingers, dropping things around the house and cursing under her breath — whatever all that was about. Ms. Lenehan was like a cool breath of wind, in this hot city, from some different place.

He'd only been to New York once. The people there had seemed to him confident and assertive. Kind of loud. Maybe arrogant. Not particularly polite, unlike in the South, where he'd grown up, and here in Africa.

In New York, he'd gone to Central Park and seen an open-air play — his girlfriend at time (just her and then Sheryl; not much of a record) being an English major and adventurous. In the play, a girl had washed up on a beach — shipwrecked, probably, after having been exiled, or something bad. And of course, she's of noble birth, and has to hide the fact. Why? Well, it didn't matter. She just did. And look — here's Ms. Lenehan washing up in Windhoek, out of the blue, all kind of noble and not really as arrogant as all that. Did this make any sense? How many beers had he had?

He was alone but for a bottle of Windhoek lager — his third, he calculated. An early evening bustle had subsided. The city crowd — professionals, government workers and what passed for the local media — had gone, and only the jet-weary tourists remained, mostly German and on a hot bus to Etosha tomorrow.

With a grimace of calculated vulnerability and an exaggerated gesture, he asked the manager for a small bottle of water. She gave him a lustrous smile and brought it over.

He had placed his embassy-supplied phone on the counter; it rang as he was in mid-chug. Startled, he spilt half the bottle down his shirt.

Elaine Ellis. Wife of ambassador Bill. What the hell did she want? He let it ring.

Probably setting up another boozy soirée with the girls. Doesn't want to drive. Not at night, alone. Wants me to go round and pick them all up. And then take them all home after midnight. No way. Or else she's going to bitch about something I did or didn't do, or said or didn't say, regarding Ms. Lenehan. Because there's something political going on there, and they're both totally on edge. Give me a break. The ringing went on much longer than he thought it would.

She's steamed about something tonight.

A hand fell his shoulder and almost rocked him off his stool.

"Dale, my man!"

"Jesus, Jay, don't do that!"

Jay Percival, who, with typical perversity, wore raggedy bush clothing with shiny black dress shoes; who walked around like a cat on the prowl with a ferocious smile; whose tangled black hair always seemed to have dust in it; and who was the most mysterious man at the embassy — to those unfortunates who didn't know that he was all the CIA could spare for this threadbare and unthreatening corner of the globe — had materialized and, very unusually, had decided to inflict himself on Dale.

"Hey. Come outside. I want to talk to you. You paid your tab?"

Without waiting for an answer, Jay threw some South African rand on the bar, about enough for five beers. The manager gave him the same smile she had given Dale.

Outside, Jay opened the passenger door of his over-sized, white pickup. It was a new vehicle. Jay had a reputation as a reckless driver. The truck had been blasted with dust: It was cemented into the gaps around the lights; sculpted over the fenders and the running boards; blown into a miniature dunescape in the back. He'd been out of the city on the gravel roads, probably going way over the semi-official embassy speed limit of eighty k's.

So he'd been out of town, missed the fun, and come hammering back to get a play-by-play from Dale. Well, let's keep it short here. Tell him Sheryl's not well and, you know, *major shit storm* if you're not home in, oh, twenty minutes. Don't want to be running errands for mister spy-man. Bad enough with Elaine and Bill.

"Uh, Jay, Sheryl's not too good, and —"

"Sheryl's not too good and you're sitting in a bar? Listen up, Dale. Where is she?"

"In the apartment."

"Not Sheryl. Lenehan. Jennifer R. Lenehan. The Union Bank woman."

"At the residence. But they're shipping her out tonight."

"Where to?"

"Don't know. Ask Bill."

"Who's doing the shipping?"

"Got me."

"Sure you don't know? You hear anything? I know you hear stuff."

"Nope."

Jay gave his lip-sucking, peeved look — generally the alternative to the cat-grin. Dale stuck his hands in his pockets and rocked his weight from one foot to the other.

"Okay, Dale. So *you* were doing my job today. I want to see how good you did. Get up here."

Dale climbed up, grudgingly. Jay got into the driver's seat and started the engine.

"Shut the door."

Dale shut the door, too hard.

"Hey, hey, cool it. And buckle up."

Actually, that would be a smart move. Seeing who was driving.

They drove — slowly and calmly, to Dale's puzzlement — out of the restaurant parking lot and through the commercial center of the city, past the neat but slightly gaudy little office blocks favored by the local business elite. There was little traffic. They cruised along Sam Nujoma and Nelson Mandela, slowing in advance at intersections.

Jay said nothing, his jaw slack with concentration, both hands on the wheel. He was looking in the rear-view too much. Threat of remedial driver's ed? No more trucks for you, if you trash this one? Or just the usual paranoia with these guys, when they're left to their own tricks?

On the fringe of the government district, they parked outside a pizza restaurant. Inside, a smart black couple were about to finish their meal. Just in view, at the end of the street, on the left, was the corner behind which the US embassy crouched. Jay turned off the lights and killed the engine.

"So Dale. Did you see what happened? This morning?"

Now right here, Dale had a problem. He *had* seen what had happened. There he was, sitting at his desk, staring out of the window, wondering if Sheryl would let up on the What Do You Like So Much About This Place Anyway theme if only he could get them a house instead of the apartment. And he had seen it all. Like a movie. On the other hand, he had been at the back of the crowd when everyone went outside to fetch her in.

So he could just tell Jay that, until Ambassador Bill had picked on *him* to take care of her, all he'd gotten was the back-row view of a mob scene.

Plausible deniability. Keep out of the cat's clutches.

But overriding all this was one growing conviction: Ms. Lenehan was in trouble. The best thing to do was to play dumb and hedge, until Jay revealed his angle.

But be careful — this guy's a pro.

"Uh, some, I guess." A poor start.

"So you're sitting at your desk, looking out of the window and you see the whole thing."

Shit!

"Well, kind of, yeah."

"All righty. Tell me what you saw."

So much for subterfuge.

"Okay, sure, fine. But look — Ms. Lenehan, is she in trouble?"

"What do you think?"

"I think she is."

"You're damn right. Want to tell me what you saw now?"

So he spilled the whole deal — the white Nissan; Ms. Lenehan in the trunk; the two men, with their faces hidden; how he, Dale, had untied her wrists and ankles; how she was all scratched-up physically but pretty cool mentally; how her co-worker was still in captivity and in bad shape; how they hadn't blindfolded or hooded her — which had struck him as weird; and how he'd tried to comfort and reassure her.

They were disturbed by the owner of the pizza parlor, who banged on Jay's window and offered to present them with a take-out menu. Jay accepted it with grace and pretended to study it.

Dale moved on to the doctor's visit and the clothes-shopping trip, elaborating his tale, as he became more confident, with observations on Ms. Lenehan's character and personality, which — he didn't mind if Jay knew it — he generally admired. He proceeded to speculate about why the terrorists, intimidated by her obvious resilience, had been forced to dump her.

But Jay interrupted.

14

"The Nissan. What model was it?"

"Maxima. Old one."

"Thank you."

"Welcome."

"Okay. Now, let me ask you this: What instructions — exactly — did Bill give you about whether or not you were to say anything to anyone outside the embassy about what happened today?"

"Talk to nobody. You know, until the appropriate channels — all that crap."

"And you talked to nobody?"

"Nobody. Absolutely nobody." He tensed. "Except Karl."

Jay sat up straight.

"Who's Karl?"

"Guy from the radio station. You know — *heat on the street*. He was at the Quiver Tree."

"*Beat on the street*. You talked to Karl from the radio station."

"Yes. Yes. I did."

A leopard-sized smirk spread across Jay's face.

"Thank you, Dale. Thank you again. Such a pleasure doing business with you."

Why he was so pleased wasn't clear. But, relieved, Dale figured he must have done the right thing.

The pizza man came back to pitch for an order, but Jay waved him away and started the truck.

They drove around Robert Mugabe until they reached the intersection with Hilltop Road. Jay parked the truck half up on the sidewalk, under a jacaranda tree.

"Welcome to spy school, Dale," Jay said. "We're going to sit quietly and watch. This is your free introductory lesson."

They waited for about an hour and a half.

At eleven-forty, Dale saw two black Chevrolet Blazers exit from Hilltop Road and turn right, heading south. Jay started the truck and followed, driving very gently, using only his parking lights, and at what seemed to Dale an impractical distance. They followed the two Chevys until they saw the cars turn left on to the highway that led to the airport.

"Definitely trouble," Jay said. "Think we should help her?"

"Yes." Very much so.

"Think we should follow them out to the airport?"

"Yes."

"Wrong answer. Going to play the long game, Dale. Time to take you home."

Jay then drove smoothly to Dale's apartment building and stopped outside. Dale could see that the lights in the apartment were all out, except for the nightlight in the hallway. But the knot in his stomach he would normally have felt in this situation was absent.

He was half out of the truck when he felt Jay's grip on his arm. The man just loved to grab you.

"So I think we have an understanding, you and I. Is that right?"

"That's right." Frankly, he wasn't sure.

"Good. And I can rely on you?"

15

"You can."

"Perfect. Come around to the back of the truck."

While Dale peered up at his bedroom window, looking for a shadow or a twitch of the shades, Jay unhooked and lowered the tailgate. Tied down with string at the rear of the dusty but otherwise empty truck bed was a small object wrapped in a mass of sacking. Jay eased himself up into the back of the truck. He untied the string and shuffled the object back on to the tailgate in front of Dale.

"Take a look at that."

Dale groped inside the sacking and withdrew a small metallic cylinder, colored yellow. It was finely grooved or scored along its length. At one end two rings had been painted: Black and red.

"What is it?"

"It's a cluster bomb. I beg your pardon, bomblet."

"Jesus fucking Christ, Jay —"

"Don't worry, it's okay. Just don't drop it. Now, my question to you, Dale, is this: What could possibly be the connection between *that* and your heroic lady banker Ms. Jennifer Ross Lenehan?"

CHAPTER 3

Alan Michael Vickery was annoyed, bloody annoyed. One phone call had done it. His wife Mariella, the well-known interior designer (not *decorator*, Alan — don't you know the difference?), had hit the buffers on all five of her bloody credit cards during her current side-jaunt to Manhattan, a stop-over habit she'd taken up after triumphing in her campaign to force him to buy into bloody HotJets, whose posh private planes couldn't fly non-stop from bloody London to bloody Barbados.

Now it cost him three times as much.

His daughter Sara, the well-known financial liability, had finally left Cambridge — save some cash there, hopefully! — but was demanding a job at the bloody BBC, which she seemed to think he was duty-bound to provide. Oh and, by the way, she now wanted to be known as Zara with a "Z". Not Sara. This vital upgrade deriving from the considered advice of an unnamed "major player" (field of expertise also unspecified) and he and her mother were just going to have to lump it. No offence, Daddy — honest.

And, as if that wasn't enough, the Conservative Party, that well-known gang of twerps and losers, had sent back his bloody check. What were things coming to when you couldn't bung a quick half-million to the Party of Business? (Ah, but maybe he was in the right place now!) Bloody note had come back with the check, according to Mariella: Sorry, Alan — love the cash, it's the Caribbean banking we have a bit of an issue with. Or words to that effect.

He'd been in the men's room (remember not to call it a *toilet*, Alan), in mid-pee, when his mobile had rung. He wouldn't have answered it except that he was expecting a call from Phyllis Ann Curtin, the woman herself, in person, and he wouldn't have missed that for anything. That was why he'd made this bloody pilgrimage all the way to bloody Philadelphia.

So he'd stood there at the urinal, unzipped, phone in his left hand, listening to all this bloody nonsense from his wife, who had called him from New York on her British bloody mobile with its monstrous roaming charges. Ever heard of a payphone, darling?

17

He slouched out of the men's room back into the ballroom. His annoyance faded in the glow of the splendor before him. The swanky Sheffield Park Hotel — a member of the Something Whatsit Group — in Center-City Philadelphia obviously knew a thing or two about ballrooms. They had three of them. This wasn't even the biggest. Nevertheless, there were at least a hundred large, round tables, set for between twelve and twenty people each. Three thousand dollars a plate; work it out for yourself.

There were probably five hundred people here already and it was only six-thirty; kick-off at seven-fifteen. A little more than half were standing and yakking; the rest, sitting and whispering. To Vickery's watery eye, they seemed to divide neatly into three distinct demographic groups: Smart, old and rich; smart, middle-aged and rich; smart, young and rich. But, despite this diversity, Vickery got the impression that they were all talking about the same thing. Something to do with Africa? What was so important about Africa?

And there were flags everywhere. American flags, of course. Someone was making a bloody bundle.

Oh, but what had he just gone and forgotten? It pained him to realize that he hadn't washed his hands. Bloody Mariella. Well, once wouldn't matter. With maximum furtiveness, he wiped his right hand against the back of his trouser-leg. Thus cleansed, he strode confidently back towards his table.

A thick place-card, fetchingly embossed with a union jack and stuck on the top of a thing that looked like a brass candlestick, described him to his peers as the representative of the Atlantic Affairs Institute of London.

Actually, he was more than a mere representative. He owned the thing, lock stock. All paid for out of his own hard-earned. More or less.

He parked himself back on the gilt and velvet, nodded graciously at his neighbors, and then he noticed a funny thing.

Wending its way between the tables, provoking waves of laughter, snorts, whoops, yahoos, and what he thought he would have to describe to Mariella later as bloody animal noises, was a strange procession.

A small group dressed in orange jump-suits, like prisoners, wearing huge polystyrene heads like gargoyles, and generally done out like a chain-gang — not real chains, of course — was being driven from table to table, with mock ferocity, by two girls with long blonde ponytails, who were togged up like US marines. The girls were carrying buckets — with flags on, naturally, of course — and the punters were chucking hundred-dollar bills into them. Vickery didn't recognize any of the big-headed caricatures, but the words stenciled on the back of each jump-suit gave him a clue: "Liberal Media".

The troupe homed in on a table of little old ladies. Much joy and hooting. Out came the cash — but slowly. Can't find their purses when they're young; can't even see 'em when they're old. One veteran aimed her walking stick — that's right, give her a little help there, please — at the lead criminal. He cowered. He shook. He pleaded. He begged. Blam. No mercy.

Vickery's neighbor, Zarnoff, elbowed him.

"Got any euros, Alan?"

Very funny.

"Don't you worry, Paul, I've got some real money."

He'd been told that Paul Zarnoff was a wit, a top-table socializer, a financial genius, a great guy and a Leading Free-Market Thinker. What he saw sitting next to him was a croaking, seventy-five-year-old gnome.

"You know what, Alan?"

"No, Paul, what?"

"The trouble with the old Soviet Union was..."

Zarnoff paused for effect, gunning for Vickery's chest with both index fingers.

"Rubbish economy?" Vickery prompted, helpfully. "Too much vodka in the ranks?"

"Communism." Triumphant beam from Zarnoff.

No, really? What a turn-up. Vickery nodded in agreement. Slow and serious, that's it.

"You understand what I'm saying — correct?"

"With you all the way, Paul. Wouldn't disagree. Listen, Phyllis is definitely coming tonight, isn't she?"

"She's the introductory speaker. I imagine she'll show. That's hilarious."

"What?"

"Liberal media."

"Oh, right, ha-ha. Saw it coming out of the gents," he said, improvising. "If I wasn't already empty, I..."

Zarnoff was giving him a look. Suspicious.

"So you know Phyllis?"

"Yes. Not personally, I mean. Through contacts. I'm supposed to meet her tonight. In the flesh. Great, great honor." He hoped that last bit sounded sincere.

"I've known her for fifty-two years. It's all a question of command and control."

"Is it? What is?"

"The Soviet economy. Under communism, they had command and control. They just didn't have the right command and control."

"No, no, I see that. Stands to reason. About Phyllis. I was just wondering... Did you have any dealings with her? A connection? Business, I mean."

"Well, since you ask, we did have a relationship at one time, but don't think I'm going to —"

"No, business. *Business.*"

"Oh, I see. Hmm. Well, we always took the view that while business should under all circumstances be free — entirely free, mark you — to pursue its legitimate aims, ultimately it must be enjoined to support the power of the state. At least in foreign policy."

This was getting exasperating.

"I'm all for that, Paul. Just tell me one thing."

"Anything for you, my young friend."

"Can Phyllis, can she..."

Zarnoff was giving him a nasty but encouraging look, rather like a gnome who, having recognized a fellow spirit, was prepared to lend him his fishing pole.

"Can she get me in to where — where they make the arrangements? I'm talking about the sort of —"

"I know what you're talking about."

"Is she the right person to —"

19

"She's hooked up with the best of them, my boy."

A mountainous figure subsided into the empty chair to Vickery's left. Wheezing and creaking — Vickery thought the creaking was probably the chair — it passed its chubby right hand, in one movement, from brow (moist) to hair (oily) to Vickery's left shoulder (new suit).

"Alan!"

"Hello, Bryce. Wondered where you'd got to. Saw something you fancied?"

Bryce Kellerman: Vickery's main contact and, according to the extra-special, blue-edged ID badge on a string around his neck, the leading cheese with Kellerman Associates, purveyors of Corporate Communications and Public Policy Consulting.

"So how's the loan-sharking?" Kellerman said.

Tiresome. Does it every time. Playing to the bloody gallery.

"Pretty good at the moment, although, as you are well aware, I am a responsible and fully-licensed credit provider of the highest standing."

"And the time-shares?"

"The market for quality shared-ownership vacation residences is, sad to say, a bit slow, Bryce. With this economy, what do you expect?"

"And, ah, what was the other thing?"

Here it comes.

"Rats. Right, the rats. How're the rats?"

"Environmental health services. Growth area, believe me."

"So you're smokin' 'em out and you're huntin' 'em down?" Big laugh from Kellerman; quite offensive, really.

"Spot on."

All a bit rich this, coming from a former S&L bandit, junk-bond kingpin, dot-com plugger, sub-prime scammer, serial intern-fancier and Democratic Party chuck-out.

"Okay, great to hear you're still king of the financial jungle, and everything's sweet. Now here's the good news. Alan, you want to meet with Phyllis, right? You come all the way over the pond, you pay three thousand bucks to sit... Oh, didn't see you there, Paul, I'm sorry. How's it hanging? Alan?"

"As I recall, you promised —"

"Not a promise, Alan. But, as it happens, thanks to me, you lucked out. She's holed up on the fourteenth floor, with some people — you'll really like them, trust me — and I'm authorized to bring you up and introduce you. Now. So let's move it. You're gonna get fifteen minutes, twenty max."

Suddenly energized, Vickery hopped out of his seat with a quick nod to Zarnoff, who replied with one of his best conspiratorial smirks, and trotted along in Kellerman's wake as he steamed across the ballroom towards the elevators.

Predictably, on reflection, the Something Whatsit Group had neglected to install an official thirteenth floor, so Vickery found himself yanked out of the elevator prematurely into an oak-paneled hallway of stirringly-named "plutonium senior suites". No, hang on, his error — platinum. Freudian, you call that.

"We're looking for Excellence and Achievement," Kellerman announced, skirting Ethics and Responsibility and bypassing Leadership and Integrity.

Is he sending me up? Never mind. We're off to see the wizard. Or, in this case, wizard-ess. Or should that be witch?

They marched on. The suite names came in a swirly italic script, which was hard to read. Vickery saw it first.

"Is this it?"

Kellerman licked his lips.

"Yeah, this is it. Ready?"

"Ready."

Kellerman buzzed. They were instantly admitted by a threateningly tall young man in a gray suit, crew cut, yellow tie and ear-piece, who must have been stationed behind the door.

Kellerman tapped his ID badge, respectfully.

The tall young man directed them across a lobby full of urns to what turned out to be a kind of conference-room-cum-den. The blinds were down and the lights were on.

Phyllis sat poker-straight at a round table with two fifty-something business types: One fat, one thin, both balding. Vickery found himself flicking his glossy mane, like a nervous racehorse.

In the corner of the room was a leather sofa, occupied by a youngish man with long hair, a turtleneck sweater, leather trousers, an ear-piece and a MacBook Pro. He paid no attention either to Kellerman or to Vickery, but poked methodically at his computer. As he poked, he shifted in his seat, which was a little low for comfort. The result was a soft squeaking of leather upon leather, which made Vickery cringe — though he could see that Kellerman was trying not to laugh.

Phyllis herself was as advertised: Stiff high-collar suit, in deep raspberry; rigid hair, in perma-frost; regulation pearls; cappuccino tan; petite. But the really eerie thing was her skin. Perhaps it was just the light in the room, but Vickery didn't think so. She had to be almost as old as Zarnoff, yet she possessed the barely-crinkled outer wrapping of a forty-year-old. It was like a science-fiction movie.

"Sir Alan, please..."

She nodded towards the one empty chair at the table. Vickery sat.

"Actually, I'm not quite —"

"It's any day now — right, Alan?" Kellerman managed to crash land on the sofa without disturbing Leather Man.

"Any day," Vickery lied.

In fact, he'd been blacklisted for a *Sir* by that bitch Christine Sharp, Member of Parliament for Bitchington North (Labor, old, very), and Chairperson of the House of Commons Committee on Business Ethics and Corporate Governance. Her words might have been seared into his soul, had he been the sort of person susceptible to soul-searing.

Mr. Vickery has demonstrated beyond doubt his dedication to the tax avoidance industry; however, one struggles to uncover evidence of a similar commitment to the British economy or to society at large.

So no chance until the next election, if then.

"We'll go with Sir Alan. I'm sure it's a foregone conclusion. And I think the title will work well for us. This is Raymond Priles..."

21

The fat one. Call him Ray.

"...and this is Martin Bazon."

The thin one. Marty.

"We've all read your excellent reports from the AAI."

Ray and Marty nodded, without enthusiasm.

As well they might. The Atlantic Affairs Institute consisted of Vickery himself; the two girls at the office, in sophisticated Paddington; a brace of hired profs, paid by the hour; one spotty youth for the web site; Mariella, when she was in a good mood; and an intermittent supply of Sara's dumb, aristo boyfriends. Sorry — Zara.

"Hullo," he said. "Great to meet you. Glad you like the stuff. We take a lot of pride. Uncompromising. Forthright."

Wait a minute. Priles and Bazon — those names were familiar. The top cashers-in, if he wasn't mistaken, in the last big corporate bust but — what, twenty maybe? He studied the mug-shots. It was them all right. What an honor.

Ray and Marty gave him a nod each, not unfriendly, but not wholly welcoming either.

"We may have to cut this short," Phyllis went on, "so, if you don't mind, I'll say my piece, and then, I believe, Raymond and Martin have a proposal for you."

"Right-ho."

What was the name of that company that Priles and Bazon had driven down a mineshaft, having pawned the silver beforehand? One of those snappy monikers that sounds nifty but means bugger-all. MoroNet? RipCo?

"At the Liberty Club, our *mission* — like yours — is to bring to the halls of public policy debate the *finest* distilled wisdom of all of the best minds in the fields of free-market economics, libertarian philosophy and the New Democratic Consensus."

Okay on the first two. What was the New Democratic Consensus?

"So it is not *unnatural* that we should have developed, over a long period, many valued and esteemed *relationships* at the highest levels, both inside and outside of government. As I'm sure you have."

That would be an exaggeration, but was truer than many people might suppose. Was it PonziTech? FiberCon?

"Now *Bryce*," Phyllis continued, with an impertinent flick of the wrist towards Kellerman, "persuades us that you and your *organization* may possess the requisite intellectual firepower, financial resources, and other capabilities to make possible a new and exciting international partnership."

Kellerman appeared to be inspecting his knuckles.

"We *envisage*," Phyllis said, "a *coalition* of the best and the brightest, drawn from the Liberty Club itself, from among our *friends* in government, the corporate sector, academia and the churches... And *you*. Some of the *best* people are already working — so *very* hard! — in our cause; it is now time for us to bring our message of liberty to your... Your island."

"Great idea," Vickery said. "Perfect. Lot of potential over there, hardly made a start." ScamGen?

"Now, of course —"

22

Phyllis put her elbows on the table and raised her hands to her temples, as if to screen from her vision some imaginary awfulness.

"— the *nuts* and *bolts* of all this are not my *domain*. That I leave to my wonderful Bryce. I believe he knows of some *projects*."

Down went the hands. Up went the intensity of the gaze.

"But I want to ask you *this*, Sir Alan: Are you a *believer?*"

Crikey.

CHAPTER 4

Vickery bit his lip with great shrewdness. A *believer?* "What in?" he almost said. Careful, now: Wrong answer here and it's game over, nul points. Kellerman should have warned him.

What to say? Mariella had a stab at Buddhism, once. Any good? No, not religious enough. Say something. He opened his mouth to speak, but inspiration did not descend.

"He's an Anglican," Kellerman said, shrugging.

Phyllis sniffed and studied the ceiling for a moment. Then, with a puzzled shake of the head and a great sigh of what could well have been spiritual fortitude, she appeared to dismiss the issue. She rose — with the possible assistance of hidden machinery — to her feet, and held out her right hand.

Vickery stood, began to reach for the handshake, and then, recalling with a jolt his dreadful sin of omission on exiting the bathroom, froze — all of him, that is, except for the vile, polluted hand itself, which trembled and — it seemed to him in his panic and his horror — glowed green. It was one of those two-second intervals that seem to last minutes. On one side of his field of vision, he saw the first blush of doubt on the faces of Ray and Marty. On the other side, he saw Kellerman's eyes begin to bulge. And, right ahead, he thought he saw the tiniest frown begin to form on Phyllis's porcelain forehead. His once-in-a-lifetime opportunity swung in the balance. The drawbridge was about to fly up and toss him in the moat. There was nothing for it.

He shook.

"I'm sure this marks the start of something *very* special," she said, and then shuffled off to berate Leather Man, probably about the squeaking.

Vickery sat.

For a moment he felt a little off-balance, queasy. These people took everything so seriously. Well, all right, it's business, it's politics, it's serious, but — well, there's life, too, isn't there?

And he wasn't quite sure what he'd agreed to. A *coalition?* Did that mean he was going to be ordered about? Then again, any partnership with Phyllis Ann

Curtin and her mob counted as an entrée. Even if Kellerman gave him some dirty jobs, which was likely. Got to *pay to play* — as Kellerman liked to say, often.

"Hey Alan, great web site. Neat layout, quality content. My wife loves it — oh my Lord, does she. Especially the cartoons," Ray said, in high musical tones that didn't sit well with his girth.

Cartoons? News to Vickery, but worth an extra tenner in young spotty's pay packet.

"Great," he said, weakly.

"So you heard about TechStar, huh?" Marty said, having ceded the pleasantries to Ray.

That was the name. TechStar. Mundane, as it turned out. Marty was leering at him in a predatory sort of way.

"Read about it in The Economist," Vickery said, half-lying.

Marty's face, red to begin with, empurpled.

"Don't believe what you read. Bullshit. Fucking smart-ass lying bullshit. There's one reason we went down. One. You want to know, I'll tell you. Those fuckers at Union Bank. They're looking at a couple of these structured things we did, and suddenly it's like, oh — I think this looks like a loan, let's tell fucking Moody's. Moody's fucks our rating, Union cuts our fucking lines, the market fucks our stock and by this point TechStar is totally fucked."

He paused for breath. Vickery saw Ray and Kellerman turn to see how Phyllis was taking this. But Phyllis and Leather Man had absconded into a kitchenette and shut the door.

"Okay, we made some arrangements with the stock options, on a personal level. But the company is still — is still screwed, okay? Why? Why is Union doing this to us? This is the fucking question. Here's why. They got a sweet IPO deal with that fucker Tom Lester at Giraffe Corp, who just happens to be our fucking competitor, and sold us the fuck out. Take a look at your friends of fucking Tom at Union, see how much they made on that fucking deal. And his ex-wife is screwing the CEO. Did you read *that* in the fucking Economist?"

Vickery looked at Ray. Ray looked at Kellerman.

"Well, Alan," Kellerman said, from his now even lower seat on the sofa, "let me explain what Marty just said. Okay with you, Marty?"

No answer.

"TechStar had a banking relationship with Union Bank of New York. For reasons which are still — pardon me, Marty — in dispute, the bank woke up one day and decided that TechStar was a whole lot riskier than they thought the day before. And this led to an unfortunate series of events culminating in our old friend, chapter eleven. And an SEC investigation, not that that matters. Okay so far?"

Vickery nodded.

"Now Marty feels that this whole thing was cooked up by the bank in conspiracy — conspiracy, right, Marty? — with this little software company called Giraffe, which was a competitor with TechStar but also a favored customer of the bank. Marty further believes that executives at the bank profited fraudulently. Tom Lester is the guy who owns Giraffe, or most of it. And he bought your software division for pennies, didn't he, Marty?"

No answer.

"Ray?"

"I'd say that's pretty close."

"Alan?"

"Must have been awful, what a shame. Can't trust anyone, can you? Not banks, anyway. What's it to me?"

"We want you to buy Giraffe," Ray said.

This was unexpected.

"But I don't want to buy any software companies."

Ray seemed disappointed. Marty had slouched down in his chair and was drawing patterns on the table-top with his index finger, in some kind of funk. The room was feeling warmer.

"Never been in that business. Don't understand it. All too airy-fairy," Vickery said, ramming the point home. "Wouldn't touch one with a non-stick barge-pole," he said, clinching it.

A little victory, he thought. Important to make them understand there are limits.

Kellerman stirred awkwardly in his nest, and mopped his brow.

"I think you *do* want to buy this company, Alan. Let me tell you why."

This should be interesting.

"First, it's a great business. You don't know software, so I'll tell you. Marty's software was a crock, he'd be the first to admit it — but he had a couple of good guys and now Tom Lester's got them."

"What happened to the others?"

"Who knows, they're on the street. Now, Giraffe's code is shit-hot. Lester knows what he's doing, he sticks to his stuff, and he doesn't have to buy three companies a month to keep up his earnings. Hey, Marty?"

No response from Marty.

"He has this thing, it's amazing. You hook it up to your funds transfer, you hook it up to your accounting, you hook it up to your back office."

Ray was sitting up straight, a vacant beam on his face, as if he were dreaming an insider-dream.

"It comes back and it says, hey — look what's going on here. You got your insider trading, you got your market manipulation, you got your suspicious trading patterns, you got your regulatory infractions, you got your capital inadequacy, you got your terrorist finance networks, you got your money-laundering —"

Money-laundering! Shiver down the spine, as they say. There but for the grace.

"— and so on."

"And it actually works?" Vickery said, with dismay.

"Pattern-matching," Kellerman said. "Can't beat it."

Ray was now beaming directly at Vickery, clasping his hands together in a sinister gesture of piety and incipient joy, and generally looking as if he'd found a long-lost son. Marty had given up doodling and was rubbing his eyes.

"Well, that's — that's absolutely fascinating. Technology, I dunno... I mean, the things they can do these... But, honestly, it's not my thing, probably ruin it. Probably couldn't raise the cash, anyway."

"No problem, Alan. Two reasons. First, you're going to get it cheap. In fact, it's not going to cost you a penny. Second, you don't have to raise any cash. Ray and Marty will provide the funding."

"We prefer to keep a low profile," Ray said. "It's the right thing to do."

So that was it. Time put your foot down. Throw a little tantrum, if necessary.

"No, I'm sorry, it's not for me. Wish you every success, and so on, but no. Can't do it. To be perfectly blunt, I don't like the sound of the bloody thing at all. Sorry, Ray, but there it is."

There followed a pause for reflection.

"First thing we do," Marty said, rising from the depths, "change the fucking name."

Another awkward moment.

"Alan," Kellerman said, "why do you think Ray and Marty are here? Now? With Phyllis? On this auspicious occasion?"

"Opportunism?"

"It's more than that. This software has huge, huge applications in national security. Homeland security, if you will. Lester won't and can't sell it to the Federal Government. There's some mistrust there; it goes back aways. But Ray and Marty can. What I'm saying is, with Phyllis's help, they can. And if you've got a contract with the Defense Department, then hey..."

They had him. No deal with Ray and Marty, no deal with Phyllis. Pay to play.

"Second thing," Marty said, "kill the fucking aid program."

"What?" Vickery said, distracted.

"Oh, our guy Tom Lester thinks he's a philanthropist", Kellerman said. "Gives money to Africa. Forget it, it's not important. Oh, one more thing Alan. We have a kind of a feeling — a pretty strong feeling, if you really want to know — that Lester's stock price is going take a hit. Maybe several hits."

"That's always the problem with these personality-led companies," Ray said. "Think of poor old Lehman."

"Well, well, well," Vickery said, "this is interesting. So very interesting. My lucky day. So glad I came. What would you have me do?"

"Just your usual, Alan, please," Kellerman said. "One of your layered offshore deals. Have your offshore entities buy some little do-nothing companies over here and start accumulating Giraffe stock. Watch for the price hits. Don't go over the threshold until we're ready to make a play. Ray and Marty will fund you. They'll do some swaps or some structured notes, whatever."

"Should I be writing this down?"

"No need. Ray?"

Ray produced a folder from his briefcase and gave it to Vickery.

"Make sure you zap it when you're done. You look like a man with a shredder. Now, are you happy? You got your political ambitions, that's nice, we all agree with that. And you got a share in a deal that will make you rich. Richer."

Well, there was always that. A point to emphasize vis-à-vis Mariella.

"It's so good to be doing this with you," Ray said. "Are you ever in Fort Lauderdale? We're building a house there. You should come visit with us. And a golf course."

Ray was smiling at him. So was Kellerman. Feebly, he smiled back.

Marty's mood, perversely, seemed to have worsened; he was kicking the legs of the table. Vickery began to wonder if there was more to come. But then Phyllis and Leather Man emerged once more from the kitchenette in a flurry. Leather Man, revoltingly, had his finger in his ear.

"It's the General. He's in the building. He's got new information. The word is they've been found."

Vickery was, all at once, off the agenda.

"Who?" he asked Kellerman.

"The General. The candidate. General Fricke. Come on, Alan, time to go."

"Who's been found?"

"Who do you think? Come on."

Phyllis and the TechStar twins went into a huddle. Leather Man urgently wound down his MacBook Pro. Like two unwanted guests at a wedding, Vickery and Kellerman slipped out of the conference room, glided across the urn room and, finding the door already held open for them, landed effortlessly on the hallway carpet, leaving Excellence and Achievement behind, at least for now.

Vickery trudged back to the elevators, folder under arm, behind Kellerman.

It had been satisfactory, on the whole, if you didn't count the ambush. Perhaps he could string them along and weasel out later. But there were a few points he wanted to clarify now.

"Do you think Ray and Marty can come up with the cash?"

"Just because they're bankrupt, doesn't mean they're not rich, Alan. You should know that."

"Who's Mr. Squeaky on the sofa? Is that her son?"

"No, that's her gigolo. Or toy boy, I think you say."

"You're joking."

"No, really. I mean, I don't think they do anything, it's just for show. She gives him stuff to do, you know — unimportant stuff. She's got a whole staff for the really important things."

"Who's General Freaky?"

"Fricke. Frick-ee. General Wallace Fricke. Or Friggin' Wallace, as he's known to our young men and women in uniform. He's our candidate for senator. You must have heard of him."

"So he's getting my three thousand dollars?"

Kellerman pulled up short and turned on Vickery. He held up his right hand level with his head, like an old-fashioned policeman directing traffic, or a corporate executive about to take the fifth.

"No, he is not. Listen carefully, Alan. You, as a foreign national, are prohibited by federal law from contributing campaign funds to any federal candidate. Got it? Plus, this event tonight is not for Fricke. It's for Phyllis's Liberty Club foundation. Okay? That's why it's in Philly. Fricke just happens to be the main guest speaker. And the Liberty Club is non-partisan, don't forget."

They started walking again.

"You know, really, Alan — you got to be a bit careful about what you say. I know you've got your ironic bent —"

"Bent?"

"Bent. And your sense of humor, and all that. But this is serious. If you screw up with Phyllis you're going to be in deep shit, forget Ray and Marty. Okay?"

"Okay."

Point taken. Worth thinking about.

"Wait a minute. General Thingy. Wasn't he the one who —"

"Yeah, that's right, he's the one. I thought you'd remember."

"Seems to be doing all right, though."

"Yeah."

"Is he going to win?"

"Yeah, he's cruising."

"Got enough money?"

"Five times as much as the other guy."

"He was the one who blew up —"

"Yeah, yeah. You obviously know the story. So he took out the village, sure, and there just happened to be a small number of villagers left inside. He gave them time to get out. They didn't get out. Either they didn't want to leave, or they weren't allowed to. That's unfortunate. What're you going to do?"

"There's a saying..."

"Destroy it in order to save it, yeah, I know. Point is, it happens to be true sometimes. I know some of your guys over there nearly blew a fuse. But more and more people are coming to understand. Really. You know?"

Vickery said nothing.

"Oh, Alan — my fee, right? Same arrangements as usual. Only this time, not Bermuda. Make it, oh, make it Saint Vincent. Okay? You're welcome."

In silence, they made their way back to the ballroom.

The table was now full, but for Vickery and Kellerman. They sat. Zarnoff appeared to have nodded off. Kellerman took out a tiny tablet computer and began scrolling and tapping.

"Oh, shit!" he said.

"What?" Vickery asked.

"The General's going to make an announcement. You know what that means."

"No. What?"

"Don't you read the papers? Oh — that's right, you read The Economist. Forget it, Alan. It's bad news but it's nothing to do with you."

"If you say so."

Vickery brooded. Software nuts, money-laundering, golf courses, stock scams, plague of the neo-con zombies, expletive-prone executives, gigolos, that handshake: How to make a coherent narrative out of all this for Mariella's benefit? Simple: Show her the money. But this intuition brought down a great weariness upon him; what a way to make a living, eh?

Phyllis was wheeled on stage, literally. Some hoots and cheers, but mostly polite applause. Zarnoff, not asleep after all, leaned over to Vickery.

"Her legs give out after about six-thirty," he said.

Vickery gave him a blank look.

Zarnoff opened his mouth to add something, but changed his mind. Instead, he turned to the stage, rapt. He tried to make a little tent or church with his fingers, but failed and meekly put his hands in his lap.

Vickery fell into a reverie of Caribbean beaches, post office boxes, glass-bottomed boats, bikini girls, sea-shells, shell corporations, currency regulations, accommodation addresses, government officials, swimming pools, encrypted communications, lobster dinners and bearer bonds.

During this he was intermittently aware of Phyllis's address — duty, honor, morality, the stock market, charity, war, sealing the borders, godliness, the flat tax, education vouchers, Islamofascism, socialized medicine, that shameful woman Diane Pennyman who wanted to restore the death tax, school text books, the European Union, stem cells, Chinese aggression, hedge fund regulation; pretty much the normal stuff.

Then she was off and the General was on, in a suit.

Uproar. A band — somewhere — started playing. Not Hail to the Chief, but a ditty of similar intent. Shrieks, whistles, blonde marine girls jumping up and down.

But the General looked serious. He held a small piece of paper.

Eventually, the crowd got the message and a hush fell.

The General looked at the floor, scratched his eyebrow, looked up.

"I have just received some information," he said, pausing to let this sink in and to build up tension. "You will all be aware of the two bankers from New York..."

He looked at the paper.

"...from Union Bank... Charles A. Barclay..."

Another glance down.

"...and Jennifer R. Lenehan..."

A solemn pan from one side of the ballroom to the other.

"...who were abducted at gunpoint in Africa six weeks ago."

He lowered the paper.

"I now have to tell you... That they have been found. They did not survive."

A general gasp. A wail of anguish from the back.

Vickery felt a tug in his stomach. That's awful. Truly awful. Whatever your views on banks, when it comes down to it, they're only human, aren't they? Shame he has to start his speech that way. Wait a minute. Which bank was that?

He turned to his left, but Kellerman had vanished.

To his right, Zarnoff scowled like a gnome whose worst fears had just been confirmed.

"Which bank?" Vickery said, as softly as he could.

"Some big Wall Street — oh, Union Bank, Union Bank of New York," Zarnoff said.

How curious.

31

CHAPTER 5

Dale Summers sat in his wife's Toyota, with the motor running and the air blasting, half up on the sidewalk at the foot of the hill upon which Ambassador Bill had leased his castle.

His hair was still wet from the shower — he'd wanted to get out of the apartment before Sheryl got up — and he was trying to dry it out in front of the air vents. (His own car, an old Cherokee, might have done a better job but Jay had asked to borrow it, and he hadn't been in the frame of mind to refuse.) He was chilling the heck out of his head and the car smelt of damp and peach — from Sheryl's shampoo.

But at the same time he was fuming and fretting, something bad.

His fingers, despite the scrub-fest in the shower, still stank, he felt sure, of that bomb or grenade or whatever the hell it was that Jay had tricked him into picking up. Dale couldn't smell it himself, but there were machines, weren't there? Everywhere, these days. What if he set off an alarm? As for Jay, the guy got off on that kind of stuff; he was a menace, one of your new-style, unbuttoned, unhinged, *humint* menaces. And what's human intelligence now? Trucks, guns, drones, and boots on the ground. Or shiny wingtips, in Jay's case.

A laundry truck drove past and started to labor up the hill. He ducked down and pretended to be looking for something under the seat. Getting kind of paranoid, hey Dale?

But here was the thing: Bill had told him — told everybody — not to talk about Ms. Lenehan. Not inside the embassy, not outside, not at home. *If you please, people* (meaning: That's an order).

And he, Dale, had gone and told Karl.

He'd had this, well, exciting kind of day, he'd had a couple of beers, he'd wanted to talk to someone — Sheryl not being an option at that point — and Karl was a friend, an okay guy. It wasn't like he was the Voice of Namibia or something, or a news anchor, or even a journalist — he was just a drive-time DJ who did traffic segments and read some of the ads himself. So why should he, Dale, feel so bad? Worst case, it was a technical infraction; Bill would understand. All the same...

Okay, let's be honest: What was eating him most was the way Jay had taken the Karl thing. He'd been pleased. More than pleased. Why, exactly? Didn't say, did he? Same old arrogance: we know all this incredible stuff, and you never will, because we run everything out of the back of the store and you're just something we put in the window. Public diplomacy and bilateral trade relations — yours to run on a dollar a day.

So maybe Jay was going to tell Bill and get Dale fired. But why should Jay care? That didn't make sense. Dale and Jay hardly knew each other. And it was widely understood that Bill and Jay kept way apart. Bill wasn't dumb.

And why was Jay so stuck on Ms. Lenehan? (Unless for the same reason that he, Dale Summers, a mid-level foreign service bureaucrat with marital issues, was.) Why had they driven all over the city and then staked out Bill's house?

And, really, come on — what was all that shit with the bomb?

Well, there was really only one theory that met the case. It all had to do with the great, epochal régime-change. The War in Heaven. The humiliation, purgation and resurrection of the CIA.

It went like this.

The old guys were out of the game now, and they knew it, and they were spitting about it. First, they lost their wonderful old KGB, and all that Cold War glamour stuff. Huge old peace dividend. Didn't see it coming. You can bet that was like bad news in the mail for them.

And then, second, all this new shit comes along, and the War Zones, and people are going crazy and it's like: Why are you spying on these people, why don't you just kill them? But that's not so cool. That's just... Murder. The old guys don't want to do that. Most of them. So out they go.

In comes the new generation. Young. Educated. High-tech. Motivated. Ideological. Violent. Like Jay. They get a couple of months' training — because, hey, what's to know? — and they're let loose. So then this happens: A lot of freelance fun and screwing around, meaning nothing to them but a pain in the ass for everybody else.

His hair was dry now, more or less. But, like his mood today, it was kind of spiky. He turned the air down.

So the issue, now he'd really gotten to it, was this: Go confess to Bill, or sit it out and hope nothing happened?

Better confess.

He jammed the car into first gear and lurched up the hill.

The guys on the gate recognized him but didn't make fun of the car, as he'd been expecting. In fact, they seemed pretty downbeat.

The main door to the house was open. He tip-toed in, aiming to avoid Elaine and the inevitable harangue on the subject of having embassy-supplied cell phones and not answering them.

He peeked into each of the main rooms on the ground floor. Nobody around. Elaine still sleeping it off, most probably.

It was still early, but getting hotter by the minute. He swung by the main kitchen. Nobody there either, surprisingly. Somebody, though, had left a milk carton open on the counter. There were pots on the floor. In fact, the kitchen was a mess. Elaine making her views known again, probably, after a night on the bottle.

He wandered out to the veranda at the rear of the house. There was an empty wine bottle on one of the tables. The terrace hadn't been swept; it was covered with petals, leaves, bits of twig.

He scanned the garden. At first he could see no one. Then he saw a narrow figure emerge from the shadows at the near edge of the pool and swim slowly and deliberately toward the far end: Ambassador Bill doing his morning laps.

Maybe he should come back later. No, get it over with.

He put his shades on and ambled awkwardly down to the pool.

Bill reached the sunny end, stopped briefly to take a breath, turned and struck out again for the shaded end. And if there were any embassy employees standing by the side of the pool, dressed in suit and tie, and trying to attract his attention by hopping from foot to foot and flapping their hands against their empty jacket pockets then, well, the ambassador must have decided not to notice them immediately.

Discouraged, Dale took off his shades and stood still.

Bill swam back to the sunny end and stopped. He stood with his back to Dale, breathing deeply.

This didn't look too great.

Then he turned and waded over so that he stood in front of Dale, about a yard away from the edge. There was something reduced or affronted in his normally magisterial demeanor, as if someone had taken his empire away and given him this pool instead. He waved at Dale to come closer.

Dale crept up to the edge of the pool and hunkered down on his heels. He couldn't resist dipping his hand in the water. Kind of cold; not heated. The lapping of the water filled his ears. Sunlight, reflecting off the surface, almost blinded him. A whiff of chlorine made him think of the kitchen in their obsessively-cleaned apartment and Sheryl sitting down alone with her cup of coffee, not reading the newspaper.

"Um, I thought I ought to —"

"I was just trying to think."

"Yes."

"I didn't mean to ignore you."

"No."

"I suppose you know they've taken her?"

"Well..."

"There was nothing I could do."

"Ah."

"Nothing anybody could do."

"No."

"Not even Jay."

Dale said nothing.

"You haven't seen him?"

"Jay? No."

"He's no good. I never trusted him."

"No."

35

"We need to worry about ourselves now."

"Do we?"

"Yes. Yes, we do."

The ambassador looked down at the water for a moment. Then he held his hand out to Dale.

"So. We in this together?" he said. "What do you think, Dale?"

For a moment he thought the old man was going to pull him in. Then he saw that the droplets under the old guy's eyes weren't pool water, but tears.

*

S o Dale Summers didn't confess to Ambassador Bill, after all. Given the old man's condition, it didn't seem appropriate, or wise.

Furthermore, Bill seemed to have gotten the story all wrong, and this was a worry. But Dale wasn't ready to contradict him — not yet. Despite appearances, the old guy was pretty sharp, and Dale wasn't sure that he trusted this hitherto unadvertised emotionalism.

Dale knew his boss, after all. The US Ambassador to Namibia had spent a third of his life in Africa. He had labored on the logistics of progress and humanity, on the State Department's payroll if not always in its good books; he had lived within the sound of guns during the Great Power proxy wars of the 70s and 80s, with only a desk and a typewriter for protection; he had not been political enough to rise beyond Africa — he had been too interested in Africans; he was seen to be crusty on the outside and deemed to be even crustier on the inside. But now progress and humanity were forgotten and Freedom and Democracy were what you got, whether you liked it or not. And old Bill was going to pieces in front of him.

So, like a fire-tender trailing an obsolescent liner on its final approach into port, Dale tacked cautiously along behind his boss on the short voyage back to the house.

He had a developing intuition that Jennifer Lenehan, though assertive and smart and able, he suspected, to see right through him — and maybe also a little touchy, he would have to say — *was* an innocent in play. Two sides contested her. One side was hostile to her. The other... He didn't know. Which side was Bill on? Which side was Jay on, if not merely his own, as usual? Could he find out what the contest was? He already knew which side he was on.

"Washington says they still don't know who took them," Bill said.

He was repeating himself. This had been his refrain as he'd limped and dripped and muttered to himself, from the pool to the pool-house, and all the way back to the main kitchen, with a pink towel over his shoulders and Dale in tow.

"That's bad enough. They say they don't know who took them."

Dale didn't know either, Jay's insinuations notwithstanding, so he'd said nothing. Plus, after Karl, extra prudence was called for.

"They say they don't know why. That's bad. They say it's just terrorism, what else do you need to know? That's worse. But it's not the worst. Want to know what is?"

They were sitting at a large table normally used for food preparation. A box of fresh vegetables, the day's delivery, sat untouched at one end. Dale noticed that the kitchen had that almost imperceptible film of uncleanliness that you got when you skipped a day in a place that was cleaned all the time. Like the Summers family home in Greenville, but not like the apartment; Sheryl cleaned too much — she was wearing the place away.

Bill was drinking Irish whiskey out of a tea-cup. Elaine had still not appeared. This was not their normal routine, Dale felt.

"They say — are you listening? They say that she was abducted twice. *Twice*. What do you make of that?"

"That's not right. Can't be." Unless you counted last night.

"They say she and Mr. Barclay were taken in Johannesburg, and it was just another one of these attacks. You know — there have been so many. But in *North* Africa, not there. And this attack is not typical. This is obvious even to me. It's too targeted, too quiet; there's no video. There isn't even a web site. Are you following me?"

"Think so."

"Oh and publicly, it's the same as usual: We won't rest until the freedom-haters are brought to justice; we expect total cooperation from the South Africans. With most countries, that means we threaten to cut off their money or their guns and then we wait to see if that encourages them. This time, so I hear, the word is *back off and leave it to us*. What do you take from that?"

"Not sure as I know."

"No. Nor me. But then after six weeks Ms. Lenehan is delivered to our door by taxi and they don't even stop for the fare. What's going on? Well, she tells us. She tells *you. You* get the story. *You* are in a position to make a judgment. Responsibility falls on *you*."

Dale felt his face begin to color. Bill sipped his whiskey.

"But sometimes the foolish are fortunate. At the beginning, at least."

Another sip.

"Lucky for you our military friends were in a hurry last night. Might have come looking for you. Out somewhere on your own, were you?"

"At the Quiver Tree. I just — it's kind of a good place to keep up with all the local —"

"She was abducted twice, Washington says. There's a second group. Takes her from the first group. Gives her back to us. We need to find these people, they say. To give them a reward, I say, a vote of thanks from Congress, a Presidential commendation? No, they say. These people are a threat. We need to find them. Is this making sense to you?"

"Well, no. Because —"

"They don't care about the first group. But they've got their hair on fire — those are their exact words — about the second. That's what they're all fussed about."

"They are? But there's only one group... You know, she told me —"

"Have you picked up on the missing issue here, Dale?"

"Do they think that someone —"

"What about Mr. Charles Barclay of New Jersey? Doesn't anyone care about him? Where is he? Is he still alive? How come he doesn't check in here in the company of Ms. Lenehan? Was she able to explain that to you? Why does Douglas Moreland insist that Mr. Barclay is dead?"

"I guess he might —"

"Why does Douglas Moreland tell his staff to tell the news media that *both of them* are dead — the day before one of them washes up here in, as far as I can tell, perfect working order?"

Time to show solidarity. First name terms.

"Ah. You know, Bill, I agree with you — this all sounds pretty screwy."

True. The story had gotten all twisted up. He ought to say something. Not that Douglas Moreland was talking out of his ass, even though this was a perennial and popular view among the lower ranks at the embassy and throughout the tiny diplomatic community in Windhoek — even including the Brits, after a couple of beers at the Quiver Tree.

Nor should he say that Jennifer had told him, while the two of them were on their emergency clothes-shopping trip to Mr. Price, and she was measuring herself up against a pair of slim-fit, boot-cut jeans and waiting (provocatively?) for his opinion, that he *wasn't exactly what she'd been led to expect.* He'd homed in on that give-away word, of course, being a sharper cookie than some people, including Bill, appeared to think. *Led.* She had been told to expect somebody. But not Dale. How about somebody slick and sly, somebody pickled in conspiracy? How about somebody like Jay?

Bill looked mournful.

"Dale," he said — and then made one of those chewing noises that old people use to signify distaste. "Do you know where in hell Jay has been of late?"

The old coot was reading his mind. But what could Dale tell him about Jay? How about this.

Jay's been out in the desert, degrading embassy transportation again. And he's been up north, probably in the old bandit country in the Caprivi, probably close to the Angolan border. There's something going on up there and now he thinks that's where they took her. The place is so piled-high with advanced munitions that he figures he can steal one without the bad guys noticing. Assuming they are bad guys — all a matter of politics, these days, as everybody knows but daren't say. Lots more terrorists than freedom-fighters. All depending on which way the wind blows in Washington. And Jay gets so excited he doesn't make it back to Windhoek in time.

But who told him he needed to be back here? Good question, Bill, huh? And then he fakes me out by pretending he thinks she's some kind of arms smuggler. Which he knows she's not. Wants to make sure I'm not one of the people he suspects are reporting back on him. And he's happy about the Karl thing — oh, you still don't know about that, do you, Bill? And he and I know — because we saw the cars and she's not here any more — that Moreland's people have shipped her out (abducted a third time, must be getting sick of it!) to an undisclosed location, probably military, and she's not going to like it. So, to answer your question, Bill...

"Not really," he said. "Don't want to know, to tell the truth."

"You *have* seen him. When?"

How come everybody could read his thoughts, including Sheryl?

"Last night. At the Quiver Tree. Think I saw him there. In passing."

"In passing? Come on, Dale — he never goes there. He was looking for you. What did he say? Speak up."

"Well, ah, he thinks she's in trouble."

"You could have told him that. Is he already involved in this?"

"He's making out like he's interested in it."

"Actively interested?"

"I guess. I mean he was acting like he was. But he's so full of — he's what everybody says he is."

"And does he know more about this than we do?"

"He gave me that impression."

"Is he the reason that she was dumped here? Or part of it?"

"Didn't say."

"What do you think?"

"It's possible."

"Well then we're finished. Thank you."

And it seemed to Dale at that moment that Bill descended into a state of fist-clenching defeat, looking like he was going to crack up right there or start blubbing. Something big and nasty must have gone down the night before while Dale was joy-riding with Jay. Jay brought trouble. He went around in the night and broke things. In the morning other people got the blame. Whatever happened now, Dale felt inclined to blame Jay, no further evidence necessary.

All the same, he wanted to keep the story — her story — straight and uncontaminated.

"No, look, Bill — she wasn't rescued. She wasn't abducted twice. There wasn't any second group. The people that took her — they just wanted to dump her. It's not political. They could have killed her, but they didn't want a search-and-destroy coming down on them. Apaches at dawn or drones in the night, no thanks. They just wanted the guy, Barclay. He works for a bank. It's a financial thing. It's just crime. Money. She told me."

Bill was looking at him with a disconcerting compassion.

"Moreland and his people were here," he said, sniffing. "They took her away. They're all convinced there was a rescue operation. You know — organized. Wanted to know who did it. Asked me if I did anything. Said there had to be a reason they brought her *here*."

"Jay."

"Jay's involved in financial crime?"

"Why not?"

Bill laughed.

"Even if he is, doesn't help us. Or her."

"Why?"

"Because Moreland's the man we need to worry about. You and I. He has an appetite for retribution; and a talent for it. Didn't you know?"

Bill had finished his whiskey but was still playing with the cup, tapping it against the table.

Well, this was stupid. A whole lot of good it was going to do anybody — Bill sitting in his kitchen, drinking whiskey, dripping on the floor, wearing a bathrobe that was too short for him, worrying about Douglas Moreland.

"Somehow it was on the local radio," Bill said. "Moreland knew before I did. You can imagine how he played that. So anyway, they killed it before it got on South African Broadcasting. Or, God help us, the BBC."

"They killed it?"

"Yes, the story."

The story, not Karl.

Bill studied the bottom of his teacup, as if contemplating a further slug.

"So don't worry, Dale. I'm sure it wasn't you. I declare myself completely satisfied on that point."

"Okay. I won't worry."

Here comes the conspiratorial bit, he thought. We're in this together, Dale. Because Bill's got Jay running wild, and he's got Douglas Moreland on his case, and there's something pretty bad going on with Elaine--that was for sure.

"I don't think Moreland is going to do anything — anything he shouldn't do. Anything extreme. I don't--I really don't believe he would do that."

Do what, exactly? Dale waited for the rest.

"Let me tell you what happened last night."

Again there was a pause, as Bill put his teacup down and contemplated it from, as it were, a distance.

"Dale, get me some more whiskey--would you mind?"

"Sure. No problem."

He took Bill's cup and began the hunt for the bottle.

"You know that Moreland and I worked together on Angola, back during the war. You were aware of that?"

Dale was aware; it was common knowledge — though nobody he knew had ever cared much about the details. More important was the obvious fact that Bill had wound up running a bottom-rung embassy with budget cuts, whereas Moreland had risen to a position of eminence on the National Security Council and a series of off-balance-sheet juntas, all of which were Special and trafficked in Strategy, Plans, Operations and so on, and whose budgets were either black or invisible, or both, but unlimited in any case.

"Angola? Uh-huh. Something happen last night?"

Where did Bill get the booze from? Where was the bottle?

"I don't know that we can be proud of everything we did. We were there because the Soviets were there. The Soviets were there because they were afraid to leave Africa to us. And the Cubans were there because we were there and because the Soviets were willing to pay them. So the Angolans trade their oil and diamonds for money and guns, kill each other, wreck their country — which is as beautiful as any in Africa, by the way — sow the place with landmines and wipe out their wildlife."

"Bill, I can't find —"

"You arrive with the idea that there is an enemy, and that all necessary solutions to all problems flow from the defeat of that enemy. The enemy never changes and never has any desires other than the ones you deem him to have.

So we air-freight cash to that thug Savimbi and we help the South Africans drive SWAPO out of the bush."

"Do you keep your liquor in —"

"Next thing, the Soviet Union is gone like a bad dream. So are the old South Africans and their hired guns. The head of SWAPO is the President of Namibia. I come here. Douglas Moreland goes into private industry. Savimbi reneges on the peace deal when he loses the election and the war comes back. But there's no money in it, and no one cares any more."

"Bill?"

"Someone gets Savimbi in the end. For a while there's hope. Then the Chinese come along and — Lord be praised! — they want to invest!"

Dale gave up on the whiskey. Bill sent his cup skittering across the table.

"But now Douglas Moreland is back and he's finding new enemies."

"Here?"

"The whole of southern Africa. You think he would limit himself?"

Bill got up and slopped over to what Dale had taken to be a janitor's closet, but which apparently doubled as a wet-bar. He located a new bottle.

"Actually, this belongs to Elaine. So, anyway, we acted too much of the time according to this ideology of enmity, of evil. It's so simple — all you have to do is stamp it out, you see? And I thought it had gone. I thought Douglas Moreland had gone. We should have gotten over the ideology. We had a ten-year break to do it in. We could have reflected on the mistakes. Later on, it's easier to see the mistakes. You can say, well, we'll do that differently next time. But you have to remember. Takes effort. I remember. George remembers. But I don't think Douglas does."

"George?"

"George Fischer. Worked for the South Africans."

Bill refilled his cup.

Was this going somewhere? Why was he all so worked up about Angola? How about last night?

"Ah, Bill--did something happen last night?"

"Yes. Yes, this is really the point."

Dale watched while Bill drank the whole cup.

"Mary Barclay called the embassy," Bill said.

Dale waited.

"She's the wife. Of the other hostage. She wanted to know, was her husband here. Said she'd talked to Miss Lenehan directly. Said she knew Miss Lenehan was here."

Dale stared at Bill but the ambassador had closed his eyes and was acting like he was addressing some imaginary third person.

"So the folks at the embassy told her, as they were supposed to, you know — we can't give you any information. They say it over and over. At this point Mrs. Barclay gets upset. I guess I would. She says she was told, just that morning, that her husband and Miss Lenehan were both dead."

Dead? Jay hadn't told him that. Had he known but kept it back? She's in trouble — oh, big-time, Dale! And she's in the bomb business, and all the time, back home, she's dead already. Everybody's lying about her. She's lying about herself. And, guess what — now it's going to be your turn.

Bill was waiting for a reaction. Dale picked the stopper up off the floor and eased it back into the bottle. Then he returned the bottle to the closet. The old man was still waiting.

Give him something, he thought. You're shocked, you're taken aback. Just try it.

"Oh man! Man, that's bad. I mean, how..."

Bill wasn't buying it. He turned away, as if in contempt.

"Dale, I don't know exactly how it happened. It doesn't matter how it happened. Sometimes the cruel and the embarrassing... Coincide. Sometimes it's simple incompetence. You might instead care to ask yourself why."

Bill paused for a moment, breathing deeply. The cold water, the exertion, the alcohol and perhaps also his sickly reminiscences were getting to him.

"In the end they had to hang up on her. Moreland was here in the residence while all this was going on. I think he arranged for some people to go around to her house. Jersey, I believe. All the time they've got Miss Lenehan in — in one of the bedrooms upstairs. They drugged her, Dale. Come here."

They drugged her? And people? People going to Mary Barclay's house?

Dale came back to the table and stood next to Bill. The old man was trembling from his eyelids to his fingertips.

"So the new line is this," Bill said. "Miss Lenehan was never here. We never saw her. You didn't talk to her. She and Mr. Barclay are now only *reported* dead. By someone or other. Not us. We are seeking confirmation. Urgently, we are allowed to say. Mrs. Barclay is either mistaken — she's been under stress — or she is the victim of a hoax call over a poor-quality, transcontinental line. We do not know Miss Lenehan and we never will."

Dale could have put his hands on the old man's shoulders and shaken him. He could have fetched the whiskey bottle and smashed it on the table. He could have torn the phone from its wall fixture, he could have slammed it down in front of his boss, he could have demanded that he make the call. But what call, Dale?

So instead, he just bent down so that his mouth was a spit away from the old man's left ear.

"But she was here. She's not dead. This is bullshit. You can't go along with that — you can't."

"No choice."

"Why not? The hell you have no choice. What do you mean?"

No answer.

"But how did Mary Barclay know Jennifer was here?"

He'd called her Jennifer in front of his boss. But so what?

"Ask *her.*"

Bill nodded towards the doorway. Elaine stood there, mostly upright, giving off a kind of drowsy defiance. She was smartly dressed in white pants and sleeveless shirt. But she hadn't done her hair or her face.

She walked up to Dale and pushed him gently away from her husband.

"Sit," she said.

Dale sat. She stood behind him.

"I gave her my phone," she said. "Funny thing is, it rang while Douglas and his friends were here. It was out by the pool. They brought it in, but of course they wouldn't let me answer it. They just counted the number of times it rang, and wrote down poor Mrs. Barclay's number every time. Bastards. Aren't they?" She gave Dale a little poke at the base of the neck with her knuckles.

Dale put his elbows on the table, his face in his hands, rubbed his eyes.

"So, Dale," Bill said. "Now you see how we're in this together, correct?"

"What's Moreland going to do?"

"You're concerned for her. Nothing wrong with that. Fact is, it's normal. It's admirable. Elaine and I feel the same. Personally, I believe she — she'll be just fine. You want some assurance from me. Well I can't give it. She's involved in something, that's clear. What is it? I don't know. You may have a better idea than me..."

I *do* have a better idea than you, Bill.

"...but it comes down to a question of trust in the system. Not in Douglas Moreland, Elaine. There's a system. In this case there's obviously an issue of timing. Do you want to just throw it all out there and see who gets hurt? How do you know who else is involved? Maybe they're trying to stop another bloody disaster like Nairobi. How do you know? By what —"

"Stop it, Bill," Elaine said.

Dale stopped rubbing his eyes, opened them and looked up at Elaine.

"What's Moreland going to do with her?"

"We don't know," Elaine said. "We just know what he's done in the past. Right, Bill?"

"This is an American citizen we're talking about. There's only so much..."

"Elizabeth was an American citizen," Elaine said. "As I recall."

Bill sat up straight. He opened his mouth as if to speak, but said nothing. His eyes — watery again — were full of a kind of childlike rage, but also panic. He got up and stumbled out into the garden.

"Tell him what he has to do," he said.

Then he was gone.

"Elizabeth would have been her age," Elaine said, too quietly for her husband to hear. She gave Dale's shoulders a rub and then flopped down in her husband's chair.

"He's going to swim some more. Then he'll be okay."

Dale waited.

"Doesn't usually drink tea in the morning. Probably trying to calm his nerves. What a joke."

Dale felt an urge to ask who Elizabeth was. But he didn't really want to hear the answer. He was pretty sure he knew. She was a girl in an old photograph with a white dog. Their dead daughter.

"What do I have to do?" he said.

She laughed.

"What you have to do is nothing," she said. "That's what he means. Because if you go out there and you bust up this — whatever this thing is, then we'll be destroyed. Really. You know, it's not like we've been in a very strong position. He's proud of his record in the service. He has a right to be. But, like a lot else,

43

it's been reinterpreted. You know? So, in his way, he's asking for your help. He wants you to spare us."

"What about her?"

"She might be okay. It might depend how she handles herself. You know something, don't you?"

"No."

She laughed again, but a little less easily.

"Look Dale, we're finished here, the two of us, pretty much. Doesn't matter. Career's already over. You're not in any better shape––in case you didn't know. Moreland knows you talked to her. To Jennifer."

She paused for a moment, picked up her husband's cup and put it on the counter. Then she sat down again, reached across the table and put her hands on top of his. He couldn't help noticing how mottled and unhealthy her skin looked.

"If you want to do something," she said, "go see George."

"George Fischer?"

"Uh huh. You know him?"

"No. Bill just said something."

She gave him a long look, then seemed to make a decision.

"He lives on the coast. Swakopmund. He's got a hotel or guesthouse or something. It's named for him – George's whatever-it-is. You can have a nice weekend at the beach. Get away from the heat. With Sheryl."

"I'll think about it."

"Sure."

He hesitated. A little more detail about George might be useful. But she didn't look like she wanted to talk any more. Maybe he could just ask...

"Well, I think you could go now," she said.

So that was it. He got up, walked through into the hallway and looked back. She was watching him. He made a little bye-bye gesture with his left hand. She didn't respond.

He went out and got in his wife's car. The steering wheel was too hot to touch.

CHAPTER 6

When he got back to the apartment, which was located in what many people at the embassy — quite seriously — referred to as the "US Compound" and which wasn't much more than a small, flat-roofed block with a chain-link fence and a padlock for security, Dale saw his Cherokee in the parking lot. It was covered with dust, and someone's finger had written "Thank U!" on the back.

Hoping that Jay had simply left the keys with Sheryl and gone, he stalked across the barren yard to the stairwell, avoiding the cement path, which would be too hot to walk on in thin-soled shoes. As usual, dogs were barking in the neighboring yard. Then he cursed when he saw Jay's truck parked under a tree, with a new scrape across the driver's door.

What was Jay up to now? He'd borrowed Dale's Cherokee the night before, had done something unspeakable with it — Dale didn't want to know and wouldn't ask — and had brought it back, dirtied-up as expected, while Dale had been at the Ellises". Then he must have gone away, fetched his own vehicle, and returned. Why?

He climbed the steps. For no particular reason, he became exercised by the weeds that were growing through cracks in the cement and scuffed at them with the heel of his shoe. You didn't know the gaps were there until things started growing; they took hold and after that you could never get rid of them. And right here, too, was the smell; it never went away. However hot and dry it got, the stairwell always gave off an odour of mildew and drains. He liked to pretend it was kind of exotic — hey, it's Africa! — but he knew Sheryl didn't agree, and the truth was it was just bad plumbing. That really was the truth of it. No question.

Why the hesitation, Dale? Oh, surely now — you know you shouldn't think those things.

The apartment door wasn't locked, like it should have been. He turned the handle and gave it a gentle push. The door had barely cracked open and he'd hardly taken a breath of the cold, stale atmosphere before he knew everything was wrong. It was something about the taste of the air — some scent of distress — but he couldn't say exactly what. The door swung wide open on its own.

45

Here came the shock; why did it feel like he was expecting it?

The place had been wrecked.

He stood in the doorway, unable to move until his presentiments settled. For a moment he heard nothing — he only saw: Books, papers on the floor; drawers pulled out; chair cushions scattered; closets open, clothes in heaps; broken glass. Then everything shut down — he didn't hear, he didn't see. A cold terror overwhelmed him, even as the sun burned the side of his face.

Robbers in southern Africa... This wasn't Carolina; the whole calculus was different here.

In his imagination he saw Sheryl — and he couldn't move. He wanted to call to her and hear her answer. He didn't want to find her; he didn't want to go room by room until... He wanted her to come to him. But he couldn't speak. His eyes began to moisten with the pity of it all. Then, angry and ashamed, he took one frightful step into the apartment.

A man came out of the bedroom.

"Dale, it's okay. Sheryl's okay. Come on in."

Jay.

"Dale, you look terrible, man. Come on."

The panic ebbed away. It left behind it the stain of a more familiar emotion: Guilt. But he was grateful. Not to providence, and certainly not to Jay. To Africa. For not betraying him.

He stepped inside, stood in the middle of the living room and made out like he was surveying his shattered domain. But nothing registered: Not the enlarged prints, now torn, from their honeymoon in Maui (where's the hurt in a old photograph?); not Sheryl's clothes, but none of his, spread all over the floor (you just wash them, they're fine); not the address book with pages torn out (just information; easily obtained).

Jay shut the door and locked it.

"Dale?" he said.

Dale looked up. Jay made a gun-shape with his hand and pointed meaningfully at the bedroom door.

She was lying on the bed, face down, dressed in jeans and a white top, with her eyes closed but not asleep. No shoes; dirty feet. He stood beside her, rubbed her shoulder and ran his hand through her hair — which she had cut short because of the heat and, she said, because there was no one to see it. He turned her chin, and brushed back her bangs to reveal her eyes. She rolled over on her back and looked up at him, saying nothing. That she looked at him — that was enough.

"Jay says you're okay?" he said.

She nodded, tried to smile, almost made it.

He ran his finger down the ridge of her nose: One of his old tricks and one that she understood. That cute little ski-jump you got there, oh my...

She smiled.

"You didn't get hurt?"

She shook her head. He knew she wouldn't want to talk with Jay there. She had one of those voices that, well, gave everything away. And her face wasn't so hard to read, either. She was okay, for now.

"I better talk to him," he said.

She nodded again.

He kissed her on the top of her head, and went back out to the living room.

Jay had replaced the cushions in the leather swivel chair and was sitting there, swiveling hard, with his legs crossed, apparently studying the tip of his shoe.

"The first thing I think I should point out, because it'll save us some time is, this happened at my place, also," he said.

"Was she here?" Dale said. "Was she here when it happened?"

"Yeah. Yeah, she was."

Dale stared at him. Jay shifted in his seat.

"They didn't hurt her. They just shut her in the bathroom. That's where I found her. But she was scared. Of course she was. But, as you probably know, I have some training."

"When did you get here?"

"About a half-hour ago."

"When did it happen?"

"Sounds like about twenty minutes after you left."

Dale stepped around a pile of papers and magazines and picked up a photograph in a frame. Mom and Dad and his two sisters about to step up into a second-hand RV and head for the Outer Banks. Dad with his camera gear, that cost him so much and which he never really understood. The girls about twelve and fourteen and, as ever, at least two years his senior. Mom with an extravagant sun hat. Himself with a junior football, but also a map. A first trip into the wilderness, or close enough. There was the tiniest crack in the corner of the glass.

"It's pretty obvious," Jay said. "In fact, it's insultingly obvious. No class, in this new era of ours. Style is out of style."

The guy was raving again. Dale put the picture back up on the bookshelf.

"What?" he said.

"Nothing stolen, nothing damaged — well, you know, unless it's all kind of deliberate. So it's a message. Goes like this. Please be frightened. Be afraid. We would like for you to feel a little shit-scared at this point."

Oh, we're scared, Jay. We just don't know what scares us the most. Maybe it's you.

"So you know what we have to do," Jay said.

"The hell are you talking about?"

"You've just been over at the Ellis place?"

"Yes."

"Then you know."

"I don't know anything. Who did this?"

"Aw, come on. Relax. You don't have to be too scared, my friend. It's not life and death. Not for you. Not yet, anyhow."

Jay got up out of the chair and walked over to the apartment door. He rooted around in a plastic shopping bag and took out a flat, rectangular object, wrapped in sacking. He held it out to Dale.

"Here. Take it."

What was it with the man?

"No. What the — what is this, Jay? I don't want your bombs, I don't want your spy crap. If you know who did this, then for God's sake tell me. Otherwise..."

"It's the plates from your Jeep," Jay said. "You're going to want to put them back on."

Dale stared.

"Unwrap them," he said.

Jay unwrapped the plates and held them up, one in each hand. Dale took them. Then Jay went back to his shopping bag — Mr. Price, Dale noted — and brought out a DVD.

"Now, this is the important thing," Jay said, removing the disk from its sleeve. "Where's your DVD player? You still have one? Oh, there it is."

Dale cleared a space on the floor and sat. He started to sort through a heap of papers and magazines. Jay fiddled with the machine, muttering as if talking himself through its intricacies.

"Okay, here it is. Dale, please look at this."

It was a jumpy time-lapse recording, taken from a high angle, of the inside of a clothing store. Racks of clothes, a checkout counter at the top, windows and glass doors to the right. The checkout clerk was writing out something on a pad. A couple of girls were shopping for jeans.

"Keep watching," Jay said.

The doors on the right opened. Two people entered. Jay hit the pause on the front of the machine.

"Do you know where the remote is?" he said.

Dale ignored him. He got up on to his knees and crawled closer to the screen.

"Oh, oh, oh!" Jay said. "That's you. Look. And that's her."

Dale peered at the screen. It was a pretty clear picture of the two of them together. You couldn't mistake it. He was holding the door open for her. She was going in first. He had his hand between her shoulder blades. She was wearing the clothes she'd arrived in. They'd borrowed some sneakers for her. She looked tired, maybe frightened. At the time, she hadn't let him see that.

"So I got the security video from the store," Jay said. "I told them I was you. I think it'll work out better that way."

He restarted the video. Dale watched. He and Jennifer moved between the racks. She seemed to know what she wanted and she went straight for it. He saw himself tagging along behind, nervous, looking around whenever anyone came into the store. Sometimes they went out of view.

"Only got one camera that works." Jay said. "You see the date and time at the bottom there? Could fake that, not a hard thing to do."

"This is all real. It's not a fake."

"Absolutely. All the more reason you need to get it out now."

"Me?"

"You're in it. That's credibility. I can't do it. You're the guy. I'm assuming you've got the nerve."

"To do what?"

"Take it to SABC. Or the BBC. Not Karl, okay? Karl's a bust. Don't know why you thought you could rely on him."

Jay took the disk out of the machine.

"That was just —"

Jay held the disk up in front of Dale's face.

"Take it, Dale. I want to see it on the nightly news. I want to see you and the dead lady. The dead lady who's shopping for clothes. I think she has good taste, by the way. I want to see you explaining how you took her to the store, and how happy she was, and how you saw her driven away from Bill's house, in a convoy, under cover of darkness, all the way out to the airport, against her will--that's a stretch, I know, but it doesn't matter--and how you have no idea where she is now."

"No, listen, Jay —"

"Shut up. I want to hear your boss up in the State Department tell Wolf or Brent or Jane or Flint or Al the weatherman how come this woman's buying jeans in a mall when their best information is that she's floating in a river with a hole in her head up in the Caprivi. Or wherever the hell they took her. And now don't forget poor old Charlie Barclay. Remember him? Make sure you mention his name. Are you worried for him? I am. Here."

Dale took the disk. Jay gave him a poke on the shoulder.

"You're a good guy, Dale. I knew I could trust you. Do the right thing. That's a neat saying, I always liked it."

He's raving, he's wild, he's out there. Worse than ever. Jesus, get him out of here. But first...

"Jay, *was* she in the Caprivi? Who took her?"

"Yeah, I'm thinking so. Or maybe further west. Second question, still don't know. Wouldn't tell you if I did. You, my man, are in enough trouble already, don't you think?"

"Then who got her out? Is that what this is about?"

Jay gave one of his feline smirks, went to the door and picked up his bag.

"See you on TV. Lock the door."

"Jay, wait..."

Jay turned and looked at him, turning his head slightly to one side as if in warning.

"Yes, Dale?"

"You know who they are, don't you? Those two guys."

"What two guys, Dale?"

"The two guys who brought her to the embassy."

Jay turned his back and was gone, shutting the door gently.

Dale threw the disk on the couch and listened to Jay's metal-studded heels banging slowly down the cement steps. And then, as he waited for the frantic roar of Jay's truck, his gaze fell into their tiny, cheap bathroom. Sheryl's Lion King robe, bought back when the excitement of their impending departure for Africa was still fresh, had fallen from the hook on the back of the door and lay in a heap on the floor. On the window ledge above the toilet, two flower jars from a street stall in Okahandja and an ornamental cat had been knocked over. One of the curtains was half torn-down from its track. How long had she been in there?

Then he felt Sheryl's arms around his waist. And then her forehead against the back of his neck, where Elaine had stuck her bony knuckle.

He was married to an innocent. A twenty-eight-year-old innocent who spent half the day cleaning the apartment and the other half on her computer and was afraid to go out. A girlish English tutor who had been so excited to dump her bratty and overfed underachievers and their stressed-out moms and absent dads, for the picturesque peoples, the vibrant cultures, and the enchanted animals of Africa.

So much more real than Charlotte or Washington! Even if the people are poor — perhaps even *because!* We'll be enlightened; we'll learn the languages. There'll be so much to do and discover. Money will be okay if we're careful. It will bind us, it surely will. We'll grow up together.

But she knew nothing — nothing at all — about politics.

And, he felt, she hadn't grown with him — unless there was something he was missing. She remained an innocent and she wanted to go home. He didn't love her any the less. No, he was confident about that.

"I don't understand what you-all are talking about," she said.

But that voice... It always gave him the shivers when she used it.

"There's nothing to understand. It's Jay. We need to clean the place up."

"He's making you do things."

"No, he can't make me do anything."

"He shouldn't make you do things, just because..."

"Because what?"

"Don't do what he says," she said, barely audible.

"No," he said, taking her hand. "He's crazy. They're all crazy. I don't know what we're going to do. Come on, let's clean the house up."

He picked up the disk and slipped it carefully back in its sleeve.

CHAPTER 7

A lan Vickery was feeling — let's be honest about it, shall we? — a little down. Not his usual self. No vim. His return to base camp in New York had gone to plan; no surprises.

Well, except for the change of hotel, thank you darling. Not the St Regis, not the Pierre, not the Waldorf, not even the bloody Ramada Inn Times Square — but some ghastly designer boutique hotel on Thirty-Second Street, where they gave you a little user guide with a translucent cover to help you understand the signage and the bathroom. And where the walls in the public areas were apt to change color or take in a movie.

Never mind.

A stack of quality purchases — mainly shoes, if he was any judge (and he was) — awaited transportation home on Mariella's behalf. Heavy lifting, Alan's job. Plus the customary bills to pay and accounts to settle; nothing out of the ordinary. By now she'd have been received unto the gentle sands, idyllic grounds and exquisitely-designed interior of the front-line beach residence known as The Vickeries (local joke, pun on Valkyries, whatever they were), that the local real estate crowd took delight in describing as "nestling amid lush tropical vegetation on the favored and romantic west coast of Barbados, the British-flavored jewel of the Caribbean." She'd be ordering taxis and complaining about the scum in the pool. Especially if they happened to be Derek and Ronnie from the club.

All that was normal and, indeed, reassuring.

The problem was, you see, he still felt an outsider over here — an alien, to use the dread word. He'd hobnobbed with Zarnoff, laughed it up with Kellerman, been blessed by Phyllis and had even gotten to shake General Fricke's hand, eventually (wait on line please, one shake per customer). But then he'd allowed himself to get suckered into Ray and Marty's lunatic revenge take-over scheme, a sort of low-budget Barbarians at the Gate, with psychos instead of Barbarians. Imagine inviting that man Marty Bazon around to tea with Mariella. *Hello fucking Mariella, nice to fucking meet you.* And he was sure Kellerman still had something deliciously appalling lined up for him. Would it ever be worth it?

No vim, and not a hell of a lot of vigor. Well, do us all a favor and try to make the most of it.

He'd been invited to a party.

The evening's entertainment was to be provided at the pleasure of one Bradford Urquist. There was probably a middle initial, but Vickery had given up on those. His presence had been requested by — who else? — Kellerman. Bradford! Where did they get these names? Bradford City nil, Leeds United one. Call him Brad, for God's sake, and then you won't be thinking about football all night.

According to Kellerman, Urquist had inherited a fortune built, way back in the early twentieth century, from real estate speculation. Now, he presided over an empire that was entirely financial. Widely admired and often seen on the covers of business magazines, he patronized think tanks and built weirder-looking art galleries than any of his rivals.

Urquist's residence was an apartment on, no surprise, the Upper East Side. It was accessed — though doubtless only by the few — via private elevator from an upper lobby. Inside, preliminary analysis revealed the atmosphere to be composed of furniture polish, odor of orchid (or possibly lily — Mariella would have known), partisan jollity, cigar smoke (the whiff of liberty!) and, to Vickery's increasingly cynical nose, the nitrogen of complacency and the oxygen of ambition.

There might have been a hundred people. Black tie and pearls. Low lighting, and lots of it. High-toned buzz of conversation. Luscious hair. Fantastic teeth. Enough accessories to fill a wheelbarrow. Elegance on legs, as Marie-Thérèse, Mariella's best friend, had once said.

Vickery was in his second-best business suit; as usual, Kellerman hadn't warned him. Making up for this, however, was a hand-made silk tie, picked out by Mariella on a trip to Piccadilly, that carried a sharp and aristocratic motif. He hadn't a clue what it meant, and it felt vaguely fraudulent, but right now he'd take any boost he could get.

His first stop was the bathroom. Again. Prostate problem? Surely a bit young for that, wasn't he?

The apartment was not a flat. Not as he understood flats, anyway — and he'd lived in a few. This was more like a country mansion (Connecticut, probably) which had been dismantled on the instructions of the owner, trucked into the city, knocked into a single floor and then slotted into a browny-green skyscraper, about six floors down from the top.

Urquist was a successful investor, according to Kellerman, and a Movement guy. Precisely which Movement, Vickery hadn't had time to establish. But it wasn't hard to guess. And, come to think of it, in all his trips to the States, he'd never met an *unsuccessful* investor. How did you explain that? He would have to ask someone.

On exiting a bathroom the size of a three-car garage, hands all clean and dainty, Vickery ran into his host, a young man about three inches shorter than Vickery's own barely adequate five feet and ten.

Urquist looked about twenty-six. He was fair-haired, rounded and plump — but in a toned sort of way. Unlike his guests, he was dressed with flair, humor and individuality, in baggy shorts with too many pockets, and in a T-shirt endorsed by the editors of the Weekly Consensus. It looked like he was still on one shave a week.

They exchanged compliments, cursed Kellerman on a number of jovial pretexts and then, stuck for small-talk, Vickery asked Urquist how the investments were going.

"Oh boy. You know, I'd really have to ask my managers. I know we're placed with Goldhurst Capital and Black Heath Partners and Oak Creek Asset Management, but I couldn't really tell you what strategies they're following. I guess it's kind of a mix of regulatory arbitrage, pro-cyclical yield curve plays, private equity, a bunch of those synthetic index options they're all doing in the Far East, you know — just the obvious things. It's a tough market. And everyone's buying volatility — I mean, that's a no-brainer. What're you doing?"

"Oh, well like you were saying, just the obvious things. I always think the obvious ones are the best. Very dodgy market, in my opinion."

Got to remember to have a word with Fat Phil the accountant. Find out where to get our hands on some volatility. No brains required, right up his alley.

"Bryce says you have your own little financial empire over there," Urquist said.

"Yes, that's right. In a manner of speaking," Vickery said.

But the empire had suffered of late from a spot of restlessness amongst the natives, according to Phil. Problem with one particular hundred grand loan, case in point. Had to refer the matter to the Pinton brothers of Walthamstow. And, by extension, their Ukrainian associates. Always an occasion of the greatest regret. A dreadful duty, in fact, that he earnestly wished to transcend, one day, and not something he would care to explain to the present company (or Mariella). Imagine.

"Of course, we operate extensively offshore. High-end. Caribbean, primarily," he said, as much to himself as to Urquist.

"Uh-huh. That's good. That's cool," Urquist said, managing to look both up and down his nose at the same time, and drifting off towards a clutch of young women who, though noticeably taller than their host, nevertheless became excited at his approach. "I can appreciate that. Enjoy..."

He felt small, a little dirty.

But then he rebelled at the smell of his own self-pity. You play the games you have to play. You start with what you start with. Never mind the rest. Never mind the bollocks, as they say. The hard knocks, you've done that. Made you what you are. You are you, you idiot. And don't you forget it.

A bit of straight talk, nothing like it. More bracing than the kind of instruction he got from Mariella as a rule.

Self-reliance, Alan! Beats privilege every time.

He grabbed at a glass of champagne from a passing waiter, almost missing, and spilt a puddle on his shoe. Discreetly, he shook his foot, but the liquid merely dribbled down to his toe and fizzed with a pointless exuberance.

He slurped recklessly and wandered.

Somewhere out of sight in an adjacent room a piano started up. Gershwin? Or the theme from that film about the maid who became President?

A couple went out on to the balcony. The male pointed up and down the river with great animation while the female nodded and sipped.

Vickery eased his way through the mob, looking for a quiet spot or, preferably, somewhere to sit down. Snippets of conversation caught his ear.

"You used to be able to see the planes going into La Guardia from here..."

"It ought to go up. It *has* to go up. This is the greatest economy in the world, the greatest country in the world. Don't tell me that's not worth twenty percent a year!"

"I had no idea you could get insurance for that..."

"Well, *I* don't know anyone who believes the Chinese economy is *that* big. *Of course* they're going to lie about the figures."

"The problem with the UN was just, like, this basic structural flaw — it was always going to be a hundred ninety to one. How fair is that?"

"Is that really Paul Zarnoff — he looks so old!"

"Have you read *Atlas Shrugged?* I've read it like nine times. I've heard they're coming out with the video game. It rocks, I'm telling you..."

"I can recommend you, but I can't promise anything. What kind of dog is it?"

"Alan! Alan! Over here."

It was Kellerman, huge and glowing as usual, summoning him like a dog or waiter to a corner of the room near the window.

Smiling, but with gloom in his heart, he made his way across.

Alongside Kellerman was a sixty-something, overbuilt man with a ginger moustache, a large wristwatch and as much gold and jewelry as his knuckles could stand.

"Alan, this is Arnie Muller, a friend of ours from South Africa. Say how d'you do."

"How do you do, Bryce. No, don't answer that, I know exactly how you're doing. Nice to meet you, Arnie."

"You and Arnie are going to be working together. I talked to Phyllis's people, they're giving you the green light. Are you happy?"

"Have you ever been to South Africa, Alan? It's a great country," Muller said, with a slight tone of challenge.

Mariella had wanted to go to Sun City once, long ago — until she found out that apartheid was still in effect, actually, and recalled that some of her dearest friends were sensitive on such matters. Subsequently, of course, Mandela had been one of her heroes. Elegance on legs.

"Of course I have my home in London, now," Muller said, not waiting for Vickery's reply. "St John's Wood. Are you familiar?"

"My wife has some friends there."

"Okay Alan, here's what we're going to do — uh, did you meet Bradford yet?" Kellerman said.

"Brad? Yes, had quite a nice little chat. Volatility."

"Don't call him that. He likes to be called Bradford. Volatility, what's that about?"

"Nothing. What is it we're going to do?"

"We're going to Queens."

"Bryce, I've only just got here. This is my first drink."

"Don't worry, we can come back after. Drink up. Where's Bradford?" Kellerman reared up on his toes and peered over the throng, like a bear in a corn patch.

Urquist's girls had been joined by a gang of strong-chinned boys who looked like catalog models.

"See that bunch of kids?" Vickery said. "He's in there somewhere."

Kellerman squinted. The boys and girls swayed merrily in unison. There came a flash of shin, plump and fluffy, and Kellerman surged off. A scuff of tux, a brush of pearls, and he was upon his prey. The young people — neophyte investors all, no doubt — were reluctant to yield up their asset. They put up a fight, bless them. But Kellerman wasn't having any of it.

"So Arnie, what sort of business are you in?" Vickery asked, to pass the time while Kellerman performed the extraction.

"The logistics business."

Clear. Succinct. Entertainingly vague.

"What, warehouses, distribution, lorries, track your own parcel on the web — that sort of thing?"

Muller broke into a lop-sided little grin. Fellow soul, perhaps?

"We don't, as a rule, track our consignments on the web, Alan. Our customers tend to be in remote locations. Internet access is not always available."

"Very specialized service, is it? Customized?"

"Oh, very much so, Alan. Our clients are very demanding. Especially our American clients. One must strive very hard to meet their requirements..."

I bet one must.

"ISO 9000 and all that?"

"...but they are generally very good about payment. As long as they are completely satisfied."

Kellerman burst back upon them, herding Urquist in front of him like a scout returning to the stockade with the captured son of the local Indian chief.

"Let's move it, gentlemen. The car service is waiting."

Urquist didn't seem put out to be dragged away from his fan club. Quite right, son: Always leave them wanting more. In fact, he had a happy sort of gleam in his eye.

As they descended in the elevator through the building's sedimentary layers of opportunity and enterprise, Vickery mused on Mr. Muller's profession.

Exactly which flavor of smuggling or trafficking did Arnie go in for? Let's see. What comes out of sub-Saharan Africa? Diamonds, ivory. A possibility. Dollars, of course. Looks a bit too, well, *horny-handed* for that, our Arnie. Dictators, when the Yanks are finished with them. Failed coup-leaders. Rhino horn, for the insatiable Chinese market? Uranium? Definitely not that, one earnestly hopes. Bushmeat? Don't be ridiculous. What goes in? Drugs. Grow their own, mostly, don't they? Tiny market for the expensive stuff. Fake CDs? All those people in Angola and Zambia listening to Sting. People? Hardly. Terrorists. Don't think they want Arnie's help. Hmm. Only leaves one thing, really, doesn't it?

Waiting for them at the curb side was one of those big, black Town Car limos, all red on the inside, that always made him think of sex and death at the same time. He felt a horrible little shudder.

Urquist went in first. Kellerman sat next to him, in the rear-facing seat. Muller insisted Vickery go in before him.

55

The car took off and rocketed down Second Avenue. As it rebounded from each dip in the pavement, Kellerman rose in his seat and brushed his over-tended locks against the upholstered roof, leaving a smear.

The Queensboro Bridge at Fifty-ninth Street was snarled up on account of another terror-plot scare, so they continued downtown.

Muller seemed to be sizing Vickery up, from behind his moustache, in a vaguely approving way.

"So Alan, what do you think of the current political situation?" he said.

"Alan's a supporter of the New Democratic Consensus," Kellerman said.

Muller snorted with laughter.

"Is he? Are you, Alan? Well, I must say I'm honored to meet one at long last."

"Thanks, Arnie. As a matter of fact, I don't have a clue what the bloody —"

"Alan was with us in Philly," Kellerman said, with a sideways glance at Urquist. "Met the General."

"Now there's a man who knows how to take command of a situation," Muller said. "That is what we have to do in Africa. I was glad to see you sent Douglas Moreland out to Pretoria," he said, talking to Kellerman. "Those ANC guys, they're not all bad — but you've got to be firm with them."

He looked at Vickery.

"Or, failing that, you've got to buy them."

The car heaved through a yellow light. Much blaring of horns. Kellerman hit the roof.

"We got any Diet Coke in this car?" Urquist said.

Kellerman pretended to look for Diet Coke.

"The thing with Africa is this," he said. "Secure the resources and stabilize the threats. But it has to be done..."

He gave Urquist a sorry-no-Coke-pal shrug.

"...in a less obvious way than in certain other, uh, theatres. Middle East, Central Asia. East Asia. Central America. South America."

"The military's over-stretched," Muller said. "There's only so much they can do. They're tied up in North Africa and East Africa. Meanwhile, the Chinese —"

"You need a vigorous and forceful foreign policy," Kellerman said. "You need a new, hard-ass school of diplomacy. And you got the military option — your drones, and so on. But then, in between, you got —"

"An opportunity for the private sector," Muller said.

"This is not making me happy, if you really want to know," Urquist said, slumping even lower.

"He means the Coke," Kellerman confided to Muller.

The car took an abrupt left. Vickery was flung against Muller, who reached out his right hand to steady himself. The man had scars under his rings.

They bowled over the Brooklyn Bridge. Looking down to the right, Vickery could see the string of empty barges that, temporarily and for the foreseeable future, guarded the East River.

"I hope Alan isn't going to be squeamish about this," Muller said.

The shudder returned for an encore.

CHAPTER 8

T he car hurtled down into Brooklyn, past a fortified building that looked like a courthouse, and made a left on to a wide, straight thoroughfare called Atlantic Ave. They cruised in silence for some time, past self-storage warehouses, auto repair shops and flag-and-razor-wire used car lots.

At length, Kellerman turned to Vickery and whispered in his ear.

"Queens," he said, authoritatively.

Soon afterward, they took a left up a narrow street just past a car wash and a White Castle restaurant.

Urquist came back to life. He buzzed the window down and leaned out. The driver eased the car past a sagging, brown LeBaron and swung right on to the top of a downward-sloping ramp that was blocked at the bottom by a heavy roller shutter. His small frame half out of the window, Urquist tapped out eight digits on a keypad. Up whirred the shutter and they barreled on in.

The car wallowed to a halt in a boxed zone of yellow lines claimed by the fire department. Muller and Kellerman were silent; Urquist seemed to be humming to himself. The driver unlocked the doors but stayed put. Urquist bounded out and led the way.

They were in a large, empty loading bay or parking area. It was underground; there were no windows. Two fluorescent strips lit the whole place. The walls, floors and ceiling were all of concrete and exuded a uniform dankness. Small pools of water, or perhaps oil, broke up the landscape. It was chilly. Didn't that boy feel the cold?

Urquist scooted across to a large pair of sliding steel doors. With Muller's help, he got them open. The second space continued the theme of the first but was larger.

They advanced.

Arranged in a single line before them were about twenty wooden trestle tables. On the tables were guns. Lots of them. Big, small and family-sized. Vickery stared. The thing was beautiful, in a horrible way — sort of like a wedding buffet. Delicate rifles with skeletal butts. Bashful machine guns on tripods, with multiple barrels. Self-absorbed two-man jobs with bulbous, high-tech sights. Brawny belt-fed numbers with, it appeared, optional truck mountings. A selection box of rockets, artfully decked out like a hamper at Harrods. Some of those tube things — what were they called? Mortars? All laid out like a regular trade fair, minus the free bottled water and the long-haired models.

There was a smell of oil and sawdust.

Vickery congratulated himself on his prescience. Alan, you wise old bird. Spotted it straight off, didn't you?

Kellerman was giving him an uneasy grin.

"You okay there, Alan? Just wait here with me a moment."

"I'm fine, thanks, Bryce. Who's that?"

Urquist and Muller had approached a thin, dark man in blue jeans and a bulky, gray bomber jacket who was attaching an enormous sight to what Vickery guessed was probably a rocket launcher. Urquist hung back as Muller edged forward. The thin man ignored them both until he had completed his task. Finally, in his own time, he stood and shook hands — first with Urquist, stiffly, and afterward with Muller, in more comradely mode. Then he started into a conversation with Muller while Urquist sauntered off to inspect the weaponry.

"That gentleman is Mr. Harlan Petty," Kellerman said. "He's one of our top boots-on-the-ground guys in southern Africa. So they tell me. He's got a new mission."

Vickery thought he heard something in Kellerman's tone. A note of asperity there? Not quite the full vote of confidence?

"Are those Arnie's guns?"

"That's right. Samples. Harlan's going to pick out what he wants."

It's a bloody Tupperware party.

"What's Brad's angle?"

"Bradford. He provides the money. And enthusiasm."

"And what's mine?"

"You handle the financial arrangements."

Well, well, well — I'm a bloody arms dealer now, Vickery thought. What a laugh. Arms to Africa. How to put this, with maximum delicacy, to Mariella? Let's see. Emphasize stylishness and fashionability of weaponry? Black is very in, this year. Really, Alan? Everyone's using RPGs these days. Oh, I know. This season the best people won't be seen dead without a — let's see if we can read the card from here — recoilless rifle made in Hungary to a German design under license from a well-known British manufacturer. They weren't serious about all this, were they?

Vickery watched Urquist pick up the merchandise and play with it. Kid in a toy shop. Muller was keeping an eye on the boy, he noticed. A certain queasiness came over him.

"Bryce..." he said, nudging Kellerman. "These guns. Not loaded are they?"

"Just demo stuff. Arnie's not dumb. Worried about Night Vision Boy?"

"Frankly, yes."

"Don't be. He's just a harmless gun nut."

Harmless?

"A harmless, supply-side gun nut. Get his name right, flatter his little idées, and he's not a problem."

"What does Phyllis think of this?"

"Aw, come on, Alan. Phyllis? This is like the nuts and bolts she doesn't do. This is not the plane she operates on. She's up here," Kellerman said, making an eye-level gesture with the flat of his hand. "And we're..."

He pondered for a moment.

"We're in a fucking basement in Queens. She wants to export freedom and democracy. This is how we do it."

Doesn't want to get her hands dirty, you might say.

Muller and Petty, having caught up on the gossip, concluded their chat with a little back-slapping, shoulder-punching finale. Ignoring Urquist, who was fiddling with something that looked like a Frisbee, they marched to the portion of the spread where the smaller items were arrayed. Petty picked up a heavy pistol, noted the price tag, and began to toss it from one hand to the other, in an appreciative sort of way. Muller got out a notebook and started to write.

He's taking the order.

"What's Harlan going to do — start a war?" Vickery said.

"Yeah."

Well, you asked.

There was a sudden bang and clatter. Vickery flinched; they all flinched — he saw it distinctly. Urquist had thrown the Frisbee up in the air and failed to catch it. He'd made a leap, flopped, and was sitting on the oily cement floor, wiping his hands on his T-shirt and thus also across the condescending smile of the Consensus's star opinion-former.

"Sorry, I guess..." he said, smirking.

No comment from the grown-ups.

Vickery bit his lip. Someone ought to have a word with the boy's parents. No one could say he and Mariella — well, Vickery, at least — hadn't taken the time with Sara. Zara notwithstanding.

Kellerman fastened on to Vickery's elbow and led him over to the middle of the armaments display. Muller was in the throes of demonstrating to Petty how a light machine gun, manufactured in the Czech Republic to an original Soviet specification, had been modified to accept NATO-standard ammunition. Gun of the Month Club selection, quite possibly. Or a special deal from the Warmongers' Clearinghouse.

Kellerman kept a tight grip on Vickery's arm, as if he felt he might have to withdraw him at short notice from harm's way.

Petty slapped a huge magazine into the machine gun, with a casual and precise violence that made Vickery blink. Muller seemed to appreciate it — he puffed up his cheeks and nodded. Petty lowered the gun to waist level and turned to Kellerman.

"So this is the guy."

More of an acceptance than a question. Not too friendly, either.

"Yeah, this is him."

Kellerman's customary ebullience seemed to have deserted him. Petty gave Vickery the quick up-and-down.

"This is Alan Vickery," Kellerman said. "He's going to take over the, uh, financial administration. He's going to run it out of London. They don't want it run out of here any more. Not until all the shit with Union's squared away. Maybe not even then. I don't know. Their decision, what can I tell you?"

Petty didn't seem convinced.

"I thought the money went through London anyway."

"Yeah, yeah — it did," Kellerman said, letting go of Vickery's elbow and swinging his arms in a kind of nervous frustration. "But it was *controlled* from New York. All your commands, your messages, your emails, whatever — it all came out of here. That's how they tapped into it, Tom Lester and that guy at Union. You see what I'm saying, Harlan? It's computer stuff, it's complicated. That's why we need Alan."

He paused, looking for a reaction from Petty.

"Alan's a good guy," he said, not getting one.

Petty tossed the Czech machine gun back to Muller, who set it carefully back into position on the table. Urquist wandered over to take a look, but backed off when Petty leaned across the table at him.

"Harlan, if you don't mind me saying," Vickery said, trying to jolly things up a little bit, "you've got absolutely nothing to worry about. We know what we're doing over there. Not that you don't here, of course, ha-ha. What I mean is, it's all voluntary, isn't it? Voluntary. Self-regulation. We regulate ourselves. Best way, really. All based on tradition, I expect."

This wasn't working; he was losing his audience. Get to the point.

"Never had a problem. Know the Caribbean like the back of my —"

"You're a computer expert?" Petty said.

"Me? Oh, no, no, no. Got someone to do all that. *He's* an expert. I can fix the printer, but..."

Petty sucked his cheeks in. Vickery had never seen anyone suck their cheeks in so menacingly.

"It's the money, isn't it?" Vickery said, his sense of desperation mounting. "It's getting it from A to B. Isn't it? Without anybody *see-ing*, as it were, ha-ha."

Petty opened his mouth to speak.

"He's very good at it, Harlan," Kellerman said. "Really."

Petty folded his arms.

"You've done this before?" he said, with a nod to the travelling gun show.

Vickery took a long glance at the equipment. Back down at the gas-and-grenade end, Urquist was grinning, standing on one leg and talking on his mobile. Muller was pretending to care for his stock, while in fact listening with concern. The smell of oil and sawdust, augmented by leather and something else — rust? — had begun to condense in Vickery's nostrils. Kellerman, still agitated, was watching him.

"Oh yes," he said. Might be a lie, might not be. Lots of times he made a point of not asking what the money was buying. Client confidentiality, serious matter.

There was a pause. Petty turned to Kellerman.

"Bryce, my people are professionals. If they don't get paid, they don't work. If we have another interruption, they will lose confidence. Confidence is very important."

"Arnie — tell him, please," Kellerman said, turning his back on Petty and Vickery.

"Harlan..." Muller said, indicating to Petty that a stroll to the far end of the table was in order.

Vickery brooded; he was definitely picking up on something here. There seemed to be a — what do you call it? — a trust or credibility gap between Kellerman and Petty. You had to be alert to these subtle dynamics when you ventured into the corridors — or basements — of power politics.

"Bryce," he said, in a soft and encouraging way. "Want to tell me about it?"

Kellerman, for a moment, was distracted by Urquist, who had removed his shirt — a pitiful sight — and replaced it with a kind of bandolier full of large bullets or shells with silver tips. He was leering in an expectant sort of way towards the entrance.

"Alan, my old friend," Kellerman said, "this is all I'm going to say to you, okay? You're listening? Okay, good. Be careful with that guy. Just be careful. Let Arnie handle him, if possible. Keep your yap shut. Stay out of the way. And none of your humor, okay? What was all that shit about your printer?"

"Well, he —"

"Never mind. Oh shit, what's this..."

It was the boys and girls of Urquist's fan club. They shimmied in through the sliding doors in droves, laughing and waving, dancing around the filmy puddles in their party clothes. The boys appeared to be fired-up with alcohol. The girls were clutching themselves against the cold. Urquist brandished a rifle above his head in a gesture of triumph, or *full-spectrum dominance*, to use the current slang. Obviously, he'd summoned them on his phone, with a view to impressing them with his arsenal. Fantastic American technology, Vickery thought — phones that worked in basements! Or Korean, possibly.

The kids swarmed around Urquist and, as before, he disappeared from view. Only the rifle remained visible. Muller and Petty appeared transfixed, but not in a good way. Muller's mouth was open.

Though they'd only been apart for an hour or two and, obviously, had not been out of radio communication, the bright young things appeared to have a great deal of news to pass on to the young plutocrat. The noise was fearsome.

Vickery could only guess at its import; it was another world. At Urquist's age, he would reliably impress a girl with a borrowed Ford. He looked on in bemusement, and everything seemed to go a little fuzzy.

We're going to start a war. Why? It's the fashion. Make the world a better place; don't know why nobody thought of it before. Bryce doesn't seem to want to, but he's been overruled. It's going to be in Africa; don't know where yet, exactly. Good place for wars, Africa: Low real estate values, no one gets hurt. Well, no one who matters.

Harlan's in charge of the troops — ordinarily valiant fellows, no doubt — whose confidence is in question, alas. Brad's paying for it, and he can afford it — though what he's getting out of it isn't entirely clear. If he just wanted to play with guns, he could do that at home, couldn't he? Or out on Phyllis's ranch in Wyoming that they all keep talking about.

And Arnie's a respectable South African businessman who lives in London but loves his homeland to death. And Bryce, who is devoted to Phyllis and loves the General, has qualms about Petty — although not about much else.

And these boys and girls are going to parachute into the battle zone, plant their boots on the ground, degrade and diminish the terrorist forces, and then take back their capital city, block by block. And this is all for the sake of freedom and democracy — or *stability*, at least — and, when it's over (by Christmas, of course), Phyllis will invite me to afternoon tea. And Mariella, too.

Kellerman poked him in the ribs.

"I do not believe this."

The boys had removed their jackets, rolled up their sleeves and started in on the guns, ignoring Muller, Petty, Kellerman and Vickery. Muller looked furious. The boys called out to the girls to join them and, like a small herd of particularly thin and curious antelope, they edged towards the table, noses out ahead as if to smell danger.

The lead girl, an almost weightless creature dressed in salmon-pink tissue paper, applying both hands, picked up the very same pistol that Petty had chucked about. She raised it up in front of her face and peered down the barrel, examining it in the same way that Vickery had once seen Mariella study a ruby bracelet of dubious but exciting origin.

Mariella, she looked right down the barrel! Yes! No, of course it wasn't loaded, but, well, would you? It's as if they have no sense of personal danger — they pay people to do all that for them. And no, I don't remember what she was wearing.

One of the boys came to take a peek.

This was too much for Muller. He strode over and snatched the gun away. The boy jumped with fright — he'd been completely oblivious to Muller's presence. Then the pink girl noticed the black smears on her hands and, arms outstretched, skittered back over to Urquist, who picked up his shirt and tossed it to her.

Another black mark against the Consensus.

Petty had wandered off into a dark corner and turned his back. Muller attempted to remonstrate with Urquist. But Urquist smiled a regal smile and revolved slowly as the boys and girls tried to snatch the rifle away from him. Probably a game they played all the time.

"Little fat fuck..." Kellerman said, with understandable emphasis on the little.

Better stand back, Vickery thought — he's beginning to lose it.

"You have no fucking idea, Alan. Old man Urquist..."

A rubbery thundering sound — like Wellington boots tumbling down a concrete staircase — came from the entrance. The doorway darkened. Someone kicked the steel doors wide open. Thin, red laser lights cut across the space. One drew a circle on Vickery's breast pocket.

Kellerman moaned.

"Oh, Jesus. That fucking little..."

There came a barrage of yelling, almost incomprehensible.

"What?" Vickery shouted.

Kellerman screamed back at him, inaudibly, shaking with apparent rage and pointing at Urquist.

In the doorway were perhaps a dozen men, all kitted out in trendy black, looking like martial skateboarders in knee-pads, elbow-pads, helmets and super-sized, Hollywood-style assault rifles.

The yelling began to make sense, sort of.

All present were required to *freeze*, and also, in contradiction, to *get down*.

He chose to get down, lying flat on his stomach with his tie adrift on an oily pool. Kellerman flopped down alongside, cursing, flapping his pudgy hands and looking like an elephant seal taking a break on its way back to the ocean.

"You know what this is?" he hissed at Vickery. "Stupid fuck sat on his panic button. Jesus!"

It made perfect sense: Urquist, while juggling a landmine, had landed on his arse and inadvertently set off some kind of personal alarm contraption. The cops — or these chaps, at least — had come running. Though you couldn't help noticing that the boys and girls had got here first.

They, too, were obliged to lie down in the muck, although, unlike Muller and Petty, they weren't extended the encouragement of a boot in the small of the back.

Urquist was scooped up by two men — though one would surely have sufficed — and whisked out of sight, legs pumping in empty space like those of a pesky cartoon character.

The yelling subsided. Vickery could hear the young ones sniggering. What was so funny?

"Uh, excuse me! Excuse me!" Kellerman was saying. He was having trouble getting air into his lungs, but had been able to extract yet another laminated ID card from his jacket pocket and was waving it, pathetically, at what appeared, from the extra detailing on his helmet, to be the officer in charge.

"Police?" Vickery asked.

"Shit, no. Not cops — not NYPD anyhow. TRU."

"What's that?"

"Uh, I said, excuse me! Over here! Ow, fuck!"

The chief walked over, put his boot on Kellerman's shoulder and took the card. He studied the front, then the back, then the front again before summoning a subordinate.

"Check this out."

Vickery relaxed a little. If Kellerman didn't have a string to pull, no one did. Then it was simply a matter of explaining the guns, and perhaps also the boys and girls. What was the TRU?

"Who are you?"

He was being addressed.

"He's with —" Kellerman said, before having his speech curtailed by boot pressure.

"I said, who are you?"

The rifle barrel swung in front of Vickery's nose. His tie was sinking.

"Um, Alan Vickery, actually. Atlantic Affairs Institute. I'm with —"

"Where're you from?"

"London?"

"Foreign?"

"I suppose..."

The chief walked away.

"Check this one for weapons and ID."

Vickery felt himself massaged and prodded. His passport, conscientiously carried at all times, as required, was ripped — along with his reading specs and some embarrassing business cards — from his inside pocket.

"Hang on in there, Alan," Kellerman whispered, giving Vickery a look as odd as it was sorrowful.

It looked like Muller was getting the same treatment. Petty, however, was on his feet and talking to two of the men in black. It was a conversation that involved a lot of slow hand gestures on Petty's part, which seemed in keeping with his personal style. His interlocutors did him the honor of raising their visors.

Perhaps Urquist had gotten word back. The girls were patted down thoroughly and unnecessarily and then shooed out. The boys were allowed to follow.

Muller was on his feet, helping the cops with their enquiries concerning the arsenal. Petty butted in from time to time with a languorous gesture. Muller offered paperwork for inspection. It was flipped through and returned with indifference. A small blue book, probably a passport, was swiped across a portable device, with results of no consequence. Muller was dismissed and went off to huddle with Petty.

Vickery's breastbone began to ache.

Now Kellerman was hauled, wheezing, to his feet and given his ID back. The chief approached, muttered something inaudible yet sinister to Kellerman and glanced down at Vickery.

"No, no, it's okay, fuck it," he heard Kellerman say. "I understand. You gotta do what... Shit, look at my suit!"

A pair of pointy, black boots with suspiciously tall heels splashed down in front of Vickery's face, pretty much giving the coup de grâce to his Jermyn Street tie. It was Petty.

"Bad luck, Mr. Alan Vickery of London. We'll be seeing you around."

Bad luck?

"Okay, Alan. Come on. You can get up now," Kellerman said, offering his hand in a limp and useless fashion.

Vickery got up unassisted.

"So... Is everything sorted out?" he said.

"Oh yeah. Kind of. You just need to go with our friends here, and, uh... It's just a bureaucratic thing. You know how it is these days. Should have you out in a day or two."

"Out? Out of what?"

"Don't get excited. They'll treat you nice. Harlan here told them what the deal is."

"Out of what?"

"The processing center."

"The what?"

"Don't worry. We won't forget about you. It's nothing. It's a database thing."

"What about Arnie?"

"US passport."

"But he's —"

"Cool it, Alan."

Vickery felt his arms yanked behind him and something thin and plastic tightened around his wrists.

He saw Kellerman and Muller look away.

And he saw Petty give him a little wave.

A drop of dirty water fell from his tie and ran down the front of his trousers.

CHAPTER 9

S tuff, Dale felt, was crowding in on him. The Ellises had vanished. In Windhoek, the embassy was running on automatic, with shields up. Jay wouldn't leave him alone. Sheryl was freaking out one moment then creepy-quiet the next. Karl had been kind of brutal with him. And Ms. Lenehan, the cause of all this (though he still had little idea why) had become a — well, a cause.

Everything was up in the air. And now, so was he.

It was early in the morning and he was looking down on Johannesburg just as the sun rose above it. Sheryl slept in the window seat with Dale's coat over her. Couldn't leave her behind on her own. Not after what had happened. Plus he felt a little braver, paradoxically, with her at his side.

The plane banked to give him a view of the city. He'd been through here so many times, but had never bothered to look down. It struck him that the city was easy to read. The main highways stood out. There was the Central Business District, once faded and dangerous, now recovering. Over here were the industrial areas. In the north, the hotels, malls and apartment buildings of upscale Sandton. And with their twisty roads, tiled roofs, lawns, driveways and pools, the residential neighborhoods were a cinch to spot. Major roads demarcated these distinct zones.

But what, then, were these large brown patches? He kind of knew the answer, but he couldn't make it fit. No roads in there, but a grid-like pattern all the same. Hundreds of little boxes. An occasional metallic flash as the plane turned and the sun caught. Containers, sheds, huts? Houses? But look at the size — compared to the suburbs...

Okay, Dale, he told himself. You're looking at the townships and you know it. Tell Sheryl.

He nudged his wife gently.

"Look," he said. "Down there."

Sheryl rubbed her eyes and looked at him.

"No — down there. Look," he said.

She looked.

"See?" he said. Then, lowering his voice: "the townships. Still there."

Sheryl slumped down in her seat and pulled Dale's coat up over her face.

Well, he thought, maybe not. Maybe not what everybody wants at this time in the morning. He, on the other hand, didn't mind going about with his eyes open. Most of the time.

In a briefcase in the overhead bin above him was a DVD. Two, in fact. He'd made a copy. To tell the truth, he'd made six copies. Sure, Jay probably had copies, too. But who wanted to rely on him? Today, he's on one side of this morass; tomorrow...

In addition to making copies, he'd transferred the whole thing on to Sheryl's PC. And then he'd tried emailing it to his Gmail account. That hadn't worked. So he'd made another DVD and mailed it to his grandmother in Winston-Salem. He felt a little guilty about that, but it was probably okay. Who was going to mess with her? She had a dog and a rifle.

The plane banked again and started to descend in earnest, rendering the townships invisible.

Despite what he knew, he still felt a shock at seeing the truth laid out so plainly below him. "Graphic" was the word you always heard people use about development reports. *Graphic* picture of poverty. *Graphic* insight into whatever. But the reports were just words. What counted was seeing. And he had a video.

Karl had used his media contacts to come up with a name. Someone who would, most likely, be receptive. This had taken a while and caused a lot of frustration because Karl didn't really have any media contacts and was upset about being hassled by Jay (it sounded like Jay from Karl's description) and two other men (who remained mysterious and a concern). But the result was a name: Some guy called Brian Callaghan who was Irish and worked for the BBC in Johannesburg.

Brian Callaghan, according to Karl, was well-known as one of those guys who went into war zones, spoke to the victims in their own language and got the news out first. Back in the day, that is, when such things were possible. Before war zones were The War Zones. Before any westerner was a dead hostage walking. Obviously not a young guy. But he went in on his own, or with a guide, and *not* with a backup convoy and the camera always on him. Karl said he'd talked to a friend whose brother-in-law had worked as an accountant at the BBC and who swore that this guy — Callaghan — was okay.

Dale had never heard of him. But he had his address.

Callaghan rented an apartment in a new building next to a mall that was even newer. Sheryl was thirsty so they parked in the mall and found a coffee shop.

As he sat watching the shoppers go about their languid business a sense of disorientation crept over him. The glass store-fronts were spotless and enticing. A friendly jangle of underwater music and gentle laughter filled his ears and soothed his soul. The air was cool and fragrant, the lighting soft, natural and indirect. He began to relax, to drift. Inside the coffee shop there was the clinking of cups and the hiss of steam; and the aroma. Outside, the tinkling of a fountain and the chiming of helpful announcements. What could be wrong with any of this?

"I'd better eat something," Sheryl said. "You want anything?"

"No. Thanks."

She left the table. Her half-empty cup was removed.

So much marble, so much glass, so much to buy. What could there be in such a place to be afraid of? He, Dale, wasn't a threat to anyone. Nor was he about to turn the world upside down. He would do his little bit and that would be that. Forget about Jay's obsessions, which, as usual, were obscure. Give this guy Callaghan the video and say: "Look — that's me, that's her, check the date. See?" Perhaps it doesn't even get on the air. It's just one person; with everything else that was going on...

So, anyhow, word gets around and they have to produce her. Habeas corpus, right? And it's "Oh, say people, look — here's Ms. Lenehan, not dead after all, sorry about the mistake, don't know how that happened, time to move on'. And then, whatever else they do to her, it has to happen in the open. With lawyers.

This last thought was a comfort. Get the lawyers involved, yes sir. Where would we be without them? Where she is, probably.

And he and Sheryl would have to leave Africa now. So it didn't matter whether Bill's successor fired him or sent him home. At least they wouldn't have to pay for relocation.

There it is, he told himself — you see? Sit in the mall here for twenty minutes and it doesn't seem so bad. You get a perspective.

Then he remembered the view from the air.

Sheryl returned with a muffin.

"So what are you going to say to this guy?"

"Oh, I don't know," he said.

But, of course, he had been rehearsing a little speech. It went something like this: "My name is Dale Summers and I work in the US Embassy in Windhoek, Namibia and this video proves that on October 27 I was shopping with the kidnapped banker Jennifer Ross Lenehan and she was alive, not dead, as you have been told, and I don't know what's happened to her but our government does, and if you show the video they'll have to let her go."

It didn't sound very persuasive, and he knew the first question would be "Who are *they?*" Who were they? His answer would be: "Please. Just look at the video. I don't know what's happening to her. Show the video, so they know they can't go any further."

He was afraid that Callaghan would want to interrogate him, record him, point a camera at him. If this happened, who knew what stuff he would blurt out? But then maybe Callaghan would just tell him to get lost. That would be worse. What then?

"Let's go do it," he said.

They left their rental car under armed guard in the parking lot of the mini-mall and walked the short distance to Callaghan's building in ten minutes, alone in the sunshine. A security guard noted Dale's briefcase, but waved them through.

Callaghan's apartment was on the third floor. Dale knocked. The door opened immediately. A blowsy, florid man in tight, faded jeans and a voluminous, white, dress shirt filled up the doorway.

"Oh, all right. It's you," he said. "Bloody hell. Come on. Oh, you as well? Right. Come on in, the pair of you."

They were shooed in like two sheep late for a party.

Dale expected to find the apartment full of newspapers, dirty clothes and whisky bottles. This turned out to be naïve. It was remarkably tidy — as was its occupant, except for his straggly, gray hair. The kitchen was well-organized, the counter-tops clean. In the bathroom, towels were neatly stacked. There was an ironing board, folded up but ready for action; and a sinister device he'd seen once in a hotel in London — a trouser press.

"You must be Sheryl. Have a seat. Want some tea? I'm Brian."

So he was expecting them. Jay? Karl?

Sheryl got some tea, even though she hadn't asked for any.

"Dale, hullo, hullo," Callaghan said, shaking Dale's hand with a grip that seemed too soft for such a large man. "Got a video for me, then?"

They sat at a small, circular dining table. Sheryl watched from a couch.

"Well, I guess you probably know what's on it," Dale said, happy to have an eager interlocutor and not a hostile one.

"Yes, yes, I do. Who's on it is the important thing."

"Just me and her."

"Exactly."

"Want to see it?"

Callaghan thought for a moment, sparing a quick, encouraging glance for Sheryl as he did so.

"Why not, why not?"

He took the video from Dale's briefcase and set it running on a small TV on the kitchen counter. After thirty seconds or so of concentrated viewing he muted the sound and turned back to Dale.

"Brave man. All I can say. Now then."

Callaghan leaned forward on the table like a doctor about to break the bad news.

"Have you considered your next step?"

His next step? Dale flashed back to the scene in his apartment — Sheryl in a state of shock; Jay hollering and bullying, ordering him about; his own sense of helplessness. This was supposed to be it. There wasn't supposed to be a next step. The only next step was on to a plane to Charlotte — or, to be realistic, Atlanta — just himself and Sheryl; followed by the rental of a modest two-bedroom in a nice area, with Africa left behind and no more spies and no more politics.

What next step?

"So are you planning on broadcasting it?" he asked, cautiously.

"Definitely."

"Well, that's all I — I mean we..."

"Ah." Callaghan said, tapping the table with his notably well-manicured fingers.

Dale was struck by the sudden suspicion that Jay — or someone — had given Callaghan more of a lead-on than was justified by the circumstances. And was Callaghan a TV journalist? He didn't look like one. Didn't sound Irish either. Was this really Callaghan, or...

"So you're not really Irish," he said, trying not to sound accusatory.

"No," Callaghan said, looking puzzled. "No. Come from Southend."

There was no way of verifying this, whatever it meant — but it had the dull ring of truth.

"Can we just go, Dale, please?" Sheryl said.

Callaghan was looking at his watch.

"Sheryl. Sheryl," he said, as if repeating her name was enough to convince her of some unspoken proposition. "Know you want to get going. But I really need, really need to have a little chat with your husband."

Dale didn't want any little chats — this was shaping up like the afternoon-tea version of Jay.

"Brian, I'm sorry. We got to make tracks now. You got the video. That's all I came for. Shit, I could have mailed it."

"No, you couldn't. Listen to me."

"Sorry, Brian, we're going."

He got up from the table and offered his hand to Sheryl.

"I know you want to help her," Callaghan said. "Very noble. Completely innocent, you know."

Dale thought of Jay and the bomb. Innocence turned, by degrees, into foolishness, which mutated in time into guilt. Theory number one. Or you could believe theory number two, the current doctrine — all that black-and-white stuff — but, if you did, you found yourself demonstrating, one day or another, the validity of theory number one. What mattered was what he had felt the first time he saw her. She was innocent, no question.

Sheryl had the door open.

"We have an appointment, you see," Callaghan said. "Running a bit late, as it happens. I was expecting you earlier. Did you get lost on the way from the airport?"

They had indeed lost their way. Dale felt his resolution weakening.

"What appointment?"

"But the problem is, they've sent me a new assistant. Not that I need one, last one was useless. And I've got to pick her up from her pad. Doesn't know her way around. *I'm* assisting *her*. Daft, isn't it?"

"Is it? But what —"

"Lives in Bryanston, apparently. Know where that is, do you? Bryanston? North-west, isn't it? I'll drive. You can have the map."

"What is this appointment?"

"What we'll do is, we'll drop the video off on the way, and my friendly editor will make sure it gets shoved out on the air right after the sport. And then the Southern Africa correspondent — nice chap — will come on and say this poses an awkward dilemma for the American administration. Sound okay to you?"

"This is Jay, isn't it?"

"Him? No, no. Then it'll be "Well, what do we know about this plump, young chap who doesn't mind standing around holding coat-hangers during office hours?" No offence. Following me?"

Sheryl closed the door again.

"Who are we going to see?" she asked, quietly.

"Ever heard of a chap called George Fischer?"

Dale hesitated.

"No," Sheryl said.

"What about Walter Gabo?"

"No," they said together.

Callaghan gave his chin a two-fingered tap, as if weighing the evidence.

"Heard of SWAPO, of course?"

"Sure," Dale said.

"Well, it's Walter we're going to see. He's a lawyer. I think he can help you."

A lawyer...

"But first," Callaghan said, with a flutter of irritation, "we have to collect Miss Zara Vickery."

CHAPTER 10

allaghan made a face — as if someone had given him the wrong story. "This doesn't look right." He had drawn his weathered, green Land Rover up to the electric gates of a fake-French mini-château.

A gravel drive led past stripy lawns to a turning-circle graced by a fountain in the shape of two mermaids with their tails entangled. The shuttered and turreted house looked down on its visitors with bleached condescension. To the side of the mansion a well-kept tennis court could be seen through a screen of trees. Discreetly attached to the gates was a security company plaque. Dale wondered why people who wanted to live in France had built their house in Johannesburg.

"Supposed to be a penniless graduate."

Callaghan pulled out a scrap of paper from his back pocket and studied it. "Nope, this is it."

He turned around to Dale and Sheryl, who sat uncomfortably in Callaghan's recently-shampooed back seat.

"How much do you think *this* costs?" Callaghan asked, jerking his thumb.

Dale was thinking about the video. He'd seen Callaghan toss it on to the receptionist's desk and trot back out with hardly a word spoken.

"You got me," he said, drawling facetiously. "Ain't nothing like this in Windhoek."

"Got to be at least forty thousand rand a month," Callaghan said. "What's that in dollars?"

The answer was alarming. They sat contemplating it for a moment.

"Better see if she's at home," Callaghan said. "In residence." He jumped out of the car and strode up to a communication panel in the perimeter wall.

"Check out that fountain," Sheryl said.

"Yeah, really." It was hard to say which predominated — the eroticism or the fishiness.

Callaghan bounced back into the car.

"She'll only be ten minutes. Don't know why I'm bothering with this. Don't like keeping Walter waiting. Don't like it at all."

"So who is this Walter guy, exactly?" Sheryl asked.

Dale had been struggling to understand something odd about his wife's behavior today. Gone was the fearfulness, the edginess, the terrifying quietude. She seemed grounded, confident, assertive even. Why the change?

Callaghan was talking on his cell phone and rubbing the back of his head. Dale wondered why his hair was the only untidy thing about him. Because it was the only thing he couldn't keep an eye on?

"Oh really?"

Callaghan had been repeating this phrase into his phone and snorting to himself, in mock-grim satisfaction.

"Walter?" he said, turning the phone off. "One of our leading statesmen that nobody's heard of. Not in London or Washington, anyway. Started out as a harmless trouble-maker and trainee freedom-fighter. Worked his way up to international guerrilla chief. Had a bash at Truth and Reconciliation — quite successfully, by all accounts. Now he's a legal eagle, government advisor, article-writer and stalwart of Broad-Based Black Economic Empowerment. Busy lad. Answer your question? Ah — look!"

The front doors to the château had parted and a tall young woman stood poised on the threshold.

"Must be her. Behold Miss Zara Vickery," Callaghan said.

To Dale, she looked exotic. She was dressed all in pale-blue denim, but it was the kind of dress-down, designer outfit that had to have cost a ton of money. Her pale, blonde hair was done up in a ponytail that came half-way down her back and was artfully threaded through the hole in the back of her velvety, pink golf-cap. On the front of the cap were the letters "TG", which meant nothing to him. She had a front-of-the-queue assurance about her — Dale had the sense that this was someone who never had to get in line for much — and an incuriosity about her surroundings: she was checking herself out with a self-concern that wasn't self-awareness, and ignoring the world about her, including Callaghan's car and all within it.

The girl fumbled in her bag and extracted a pair of gold-rimmed sunglasses. Dale noted with awe that she was wearing more jewelry than Sheryl possessed in her entire collection. And it looked real, too.

Callaghan seemed to have picked up on the jewels. He was muttering something under his breath. It might have been "Where does she think she is?"

The girl tossed her hair back and strode towards them without quite seeming to acknowledge their presence. Her boots slipped about on the gravel but she ignored this. A pair of black hands closed the doors behind her.

"So TG — what's that?" Sheryl asked.

"Dunno. Tory Girl?" Callaghan said.

"What?"

"Well, I think I know who owns this house. Chap called Aylsham. Jeremy Aylsham. Don't suppose you've heard of him. Part-time British politician of the Conservative variety. Supposedly retired. Got caught in a spot of sanctions-busting. Used to be a Sir. Got stripped. A right piece of work."

The girl was trying to figure out how to operate the electric gates. Suddenly they slid open on their own, startling her.

"So she's his daughter? Or his niece?"

"No. No, I don't think so…"

"What then?"

Callaghan seemed distracted.

"I don't think we want her around while we're talking to Walter," he said slowly. "What do you think?"

But Zara had arrived and was climbing into Callaghan's front passenger seat without waiting for the official invite.

By some strange instinct, she turned immediately to Dale and stuck her hand over the back of the seat.

"Hiya, I'm Zara. Really nice to meet you, Brian. Mrs. Brian?"

Dale shook her hand. It felt ridiculously soft. "Hi there. I'm Dale. This is Sheryl. That's Brian."

Zara retreated gracefully.

"Oh! Okay… Brian!"

"Hullo, hullo. Lovely to see you at last, my dear. Do all the intro stuff later, okay? We're a bit behind."

Callaghan started the car and took off, smartly.

"Nice place your uncle's got."

"My uncle?"

"Sir Jeremy."

"Oh, Jerry. No, he's just a friend of the family, you know. Well, actually, my dad, really. They're absolutely, well, you know."

"Mm."

The car swept on to the N1 and joined the traffic swarming south.

In the Central Business District, Callaghan negotiated his way past minibuses and street traders into a zone of early twentieth-century office blocks and skyscrapers. Dale couldn't quite gauge the neighborhood: some buildings were shabby; others had been renovated. On Commissioner Street, Callaghan slowed and pointed out one particular building.

"See that? The Corner House. It's a famous building."

The building was a solid, grand affair of nine stories or so, with classical ornamentation, bronzed bay windows and little bridges at the uppermost floor to link the building's two sections. It had a dome. Impressive — and surprising.

"Built in 1904. Tallest building in southern Africa. Whole country was pretty much run out of here. *Randlords*, they were called. Now there's a hotel and apartments. Walter lives here."

They left the car in a parking garage and ventured into the marble lobby of Walter's abode. Callaghan pinched Dale's sleeve and held him back while Sheryl and Zara walked ahead.

"I'm just going to pop upstairs and have a chat with Walter," he said. "Keep Miss Vickery amused. Don't say anything in front of her about you-know-who. Have a whisper in your wife's ear. *Pas devant l'enfant* and so on. I'd send her on an errand, but it's probably a bit unwise. Back shortly."

Dale watched Callaghan bound up the stairs, ignoring the elevators. Sheryl wasn't going to say anything in front of the girl; she was pretty damn sharp today.

In fact, chances were that she'd have a better take than he did on what the deal with Walter was; he didn't get it, that was for sure. He should go ask her, that's what he should do.

But Sheryl was listening to Zara talk about how she hadn't really been looking for a job, but a friend had mentioned her name to another friend and blah-blah-blah; and Jerry was just one of those people who would always help one out if he could; and she really just intended using the BBC as a stepping-stone to something better; and more blah. It looked like Sheryl was kind of tied up.

Why was Callaghan suspicious of the girl? She looked harmless. Okay, so she was upper-crust. So what? Maybe Callaghan was just a paranoid old lefty. But no, that wasn't it. Despite his manner — what would you call it in British-speak, chummy? — he was hard and cynical. There was a reason for his suspicion, but his act was the kind of stuff that he and Sheryl couldn't fake and couldn't entirely trust. They had better hope that he was truly on their team; they were in his hands — and maybe now Walter's, too.

Callaghan was back, whispering in Dale's ear.

"Walter is of the opinion that I am A, a paranoid old hack and B, not prepared to have a bit of fun now and again. I am neither, of course. Anyway, upshot is, everyone's invited. Up we go."

Walter's apartment was large, dimly-lit and simply but elegantly furnished. In the center of the living room, two sofas had been arranged in an L-shape. An oblong coffee table had been positioned in front of one of these, and in front of the table, pointing at the sofa, was a video camera on a tripod. On the wall behind the sofa were framed photographs of Thabo Mbeki and Nelson Mandela, the latter positioned two inches higher. No picture of Jacob Zuma — perhaps in another room?

Both Mandela and Mbeki were shaking hands with the same short, stocky man with wide shoulders, a large head, short, frizzy hair, John Lennon glasses and a gray-white beard. This man now emerged from a kitchen carrying glasses and bottles of water on a tray. He set the tray, a little unsteadily, on the table. Dale figured he was at least seventy-five years old.

"Brian..." Walter said, gesturing at the camera.

"Right," Callaghan said. "Zara, love — know how to work a camera, do you?"

Zara looked doubtful.

"Nothing to it. Come over here. Walter, this is Miss Zara Vickery and she's my, um, assistant. Aren't you, Zara?"

Zara was inspecting the camera.

This is the bit of fun, Dale thought. Or the start of it.

"Now, Mr. and Mrs. Summers, I am very honored to meet you. Would you please sit..." Walter indicated the hot seat. "...and I will join you."

Callaghan sat on the other sofa, out of shot.

"Red button, Zara, love," he said. "But not 'til I say so."

Dale looked at Sheryl. She seemed composed; in fact, she was adjusting her hair.

"I don't know about this..." he said.

"I think it's okay."

"Don't worry, Mr. Summers," Walter said. "We are not making a public broadcast. This is for insurance only."

"In case someone puts the screws on the Beeb," Callaghan said. "Our fearless BBC. Has been known."

Walter touched Dale on the arm.

"But let me ask you something first, please, Mr. Summers. Where are my old friends Bill and Elaine Ellis? I am unable to contact them."

"All I know is, they're gone from the residence and the place is locked down."

"I heard they had gone to Djibouti. Why would they go there?"

Sheryl looked up and said something under her breath. Callaghan was listening intently, with a small notepad on his knee and a pencil behind his ear. Dale felt a sudden cramp in his stomach. Djibouti, he thought. The bases. Neat location for one of those new military intelligence fuck-ups. Was *she* there?

Something distracted him — a red light on the camera. He straightened instinctively.

"No, no, no, Zara," Callaghan said. "Not yet. Delete that bit, there's a good girl."

Dale saw the flash of humiliation on the girl's face. If Callaghan did, he pretended not to.

"Well, we must hope for the best," Walter said. "Now let me say plainly that I am not a member of, nor an employee of the government of South Africa. But I try to make myself useful and they do listen to me from time to time."

He paused to take a sip of water.

"They also ask me for favors." He looked pointedly at Callaghan, who nodded in response.

"The government is very much opposed to mercenary activity involving the territory of South Africa or the citizens or foreign residents of the country. And they have made laws against this type of behavior. I'm sure you can understand why. And I know that Bill and Elaine would understand only too well."

"What if you don't call them mercenaries," Callaghan said. "What if you call them private military companies?"

Walter smiled, sourly.

"Flexible approach," Callaghan said. "Tried and tested in the UK and other leading nations."

"We don't want any of it," Walter said. "It is one more disease we wish to eradicate from our continent."

"Right ho." Callaghan leaned back and folded his arms in response to Walter's frown.

"Mr. Summers. You met a lady called Miss Jennifer Ross Lenehan. And this happened in Windhoek just last week."

"Yes."

"And this is the same lady who was kidnapped here in Johannesburg — up in Sandton — eight weeks ago."

"Yes."

"Do you know why?"

"No."

"We think that she and her companion, Mr. Barclay, were following a trail of laundered money. We think that this money is to pay for mercenaries. We would like to know who they are and what they intend to do."

Walter took another sip of water and waited. It had to be something like this, Dale thought. It explained Jay's bomb — though not quite the vehemence or personal character of his interest. And what of the Ellises? What was going down in Djibouti?

"Why did they say she was dead?" he asked Walter.

Callaghan took a huge sigh. Zara looked confused and jumpy; she was looking up at the ceiling, mouth open, as if trying to memorize something.

"They were going to get rid of her," Sheryl said.

There was a moment of stillness.

"Who was?" Callaghan asked. But Walter held up his hand; no one spoke.

She said it out loud, Dale thought. We're on a new track. She's leading the way. Something's going to happen.

Walter was rubbing his hands together like a businessman about to make a difficult pitch.

"Mr. Summers. How long have you been working under Bill Ellis in Namibia?"

"Couple of years."

"And did you get to know him very well?"

Dale thought of the scene by the pool and its sequel in the kitchen.

"Not that well, I guess."

"He and his wife have spent half of their lives in Africa."

This was uncontroversial.

"Mr. Callaghan here would probably tell you that they went native," Walter said, giving Callaghan another severe look. "But then he often speaks in outmoded language, and this is not, in fact, the case." He turned back to Dale.

"Do you know their history?"

There was something about Angola, wasn't there? And the daughter?

"Not that much."

"Namibia achieved independence from South Africa in 1990. But SWAPO — the South-West Africa People's Organization — was formed in 1960 — by Mr. Nujoma, and Mr. Pohamba, among others. They were resistance fighters. There was a long struggle. Eventually, each became President of Namibia. In 2014, the Namibian people elected a third President. Also from SWAPO."

"Sure."

"Angola became independent from Portugal in 1975. But there was civil war until 2002—except for two short interludes, one for the conduct of elections and another for a brief visit from the UN. The MPLA, the Angolan liberation movement, fought against Jonas Savimbi and Unita. The Soviet Union and Cuba backed the MPLA. The United States and South Africa backed Savimbi. Savimbi was a monster, by the way."

"Right." These old guys loved their history lessons.

"In South Africa, we had majority rule in 1994. After nearly a century of resistance."

"Yes."

"And this was our life. So it became for Bill and Elaine. To the extent that they could, they adopted it. The struggle. They were working for your State Department. But whereas we knew which side we were on, they were obliged to make a constant... Recalibration, in response to the pressures on them."

"Balancing act," Callaghan said.

"Sometimes they miscalculated, but they survived," Walter said. A cloud seemed to cross his face. "Well, the two of them survived. And we had hoped that those days were over. But it appears they may not be."

"This time they got screwed," Callaghan said. "No balance of power any more."

What was Callaghan talking about? Why the history lesson from Walter? And Sheryl looked grim — what was she thinking?

"Have you ever heard the name George Fischer?" Walter said.

That name — it kept on coming back.

"People keep asking me if I've heard of him," he said, glancing at Callaghan, who didn't react.

Zara, who had been standing on one leg, looking bored, said: "Who?" They all looked at her.

"Someone needs to pay George a visit," Callaghan said. "Before he gets swept up into anything. Right, Walter?"

"Thank you, Brian — I was coming to that point." Walter paused, as if gathering his thoughts. Zara looked angry, Dale thought. Didn't like being ignored?

Sheryl leaned across Dale to look Walter in the face.

"They had a daughter. The Ellises had a daughter."

Walter looked pained.

"Yes, they did. She was killed. Up north in the Caprivi."

Dale blinked. Sheryl was amazing him today. And she hadn't finished with Walter yet.

"I was there," Walter said. "So was George."

"What was her name?"

"Elizabeth."

Sheryl sat back. Walter coughed; he seemed to want to move on.

"George can help us all," he said. "By virtue of his particular contacts in Namibia and Angola — and his relationship with Bill and Elaine. But we must explain the situation to him. And we must do so before — before others do."

"Ever been to Swakopmund?" Callaghan asked, looking at Dale.

A weird little seaside town on the Atlantic coast. People went there to get away from the heat of Windhoek.

"Couple of times."

"Know what to expect, then."

"You will have the support and backing of the South African government," Walter said. "But it will be indirect. Through me. The security services are very competent — especially in regard to mercenaries — but there are always leaks, and we suspect our adversaries have many resources. Is that not correct, Brian?"

Callaghan nodded.

"We will mention this in our interview for the camera," Walter continued.

Another mission, Dale thought. But he'd already fulfilled his assignment for Jay. This was too much. He'd brought the video. The video would be shown on

TV — of course it would. Jennifer would be released. Everybody could go home. Not to Swakopmund. Was this really just part of Jay's scheme all along?

"Is this Jay's deal?" he asked, sounding a little too plaintive and looking from face to face, including Zara's, for an honest answer.

"That's what we'd like to know, Dale," Callaghan said.

"So what do we say to George?" Sheryl said.

There she went again.

"We can't do this," he said. "We're out of our depth, we don't know what we're doing. I — we just wanted to help Jennifer. She didn't do anything, and..."

He wasn't sure what else he meant to say. "Why can't you just go get your mercenaries?" he said. "Arrest them. Throw them in jail."

"We don't know who they are," Walter said. "We know only that large amounts of money have been coming into our country and passing through some very dirty hands. This is what Mr. Barclay discovered. We cannot even be sure that he told Miss Lenehan. But we would like to know what they know."

"Send somebody else."

"It's important that it be you. You met Miss Lenehan. You know the Ellises. You have certain other qualities. There is no one else. It is perfectly reasonable that Mr. and Mrs. Summers should wish to take a short holiday by the coast."

Callaghan had budged forward on to the edge of his seat; he was giving his chin the two-fingered tap again — a gesture that Dale now began to find annoying and unsettling. Callaghan realized Dale was staring at him.

"Zara," he said, turning away, "come and sit down. We're not ready yet. Give your legs a rest."

Zara scowled and sat.

"We must help Bill and Elaine," Walter said, his voice tightening. "George is essential."

Sheryl took Dale's hand.

"We'll go, won't we?"

He wanted to ask her what the heck had come over her since the break-in at the apartment, but all he could do was sit back and breathe out slowly.

"Time for the in-depth political background," Callaghan said. "From Your Own Correspondent. Zara — do me a favor, love, see if there's a beer in the fridge..."

The girl looked at Callaghan as if he'd asked her to take off her shirt.

"I believe there is," Walter said.

Zara slouched her way into the kitchen, almost upsetting the camera.

Sheryl gave Callaghan a look that reminded Dale of those he often received on his return from the Quiver Tree — except it was more curious than censorious. He wanted to pursue the Swakopmund issue — this was evidently where the legendary George lived — but Callaghan seemed to be cranking up some kind of oration.

"Africa," Callaghan said. "Big place, lot of problems. No need to go through the list — you know what they are and I'm not some pompous, fat-headed, western politician talking to a bunch of bankers in Switzerland."

Walter seemed to find that amusing.

"But what," Callaghan continued, "is the single biggest impediment to progress down here below the Sahara?"

"Dysfunctional governance," Walter said.

"Thank you, Walter. Correct answer. And which country is therefore the most important country in Africa and quite possibly the world?"

"This one. South Africa."

"Right again, Walter." Callaghan frowned at Sheryl and Dale as if to make sure they were paying attention. "Now, for your bonus point, Walter, explain why that might be so."

"Because we have a good government, an economy that is strong and growing; and because we have advanced political institutions and a true multiracial society."

"And...?"

"And we may be able to transfer these benefits to our neighbors without invading them."

"Good answer, Walter, and — because I like you so much — I'll gloss over the arms procurement scandals, the peccadilloes of certain ANC top brass, white disengagement, the scandalous treatment of mineworkers, and sundry other little embarrassments. Your point stands."

Zara shuffled back with a bottle of what appeared to be premium German beer. She thrust the bottle, unopened, at Callaghan, who produced a handkerchief from his front pocket and wrenched off the bottle-top with one twist.

"Thank you, Zara. Very nice. Walter, you're getting a little decadent in your old age."

"George introduced me to it."

"Ah. Where were we? Right. You've got your African Union, your New Partnership for Africa's Development, growth on the up in sub-Saharan Africa, Chinese investment and so on, and you're going to lead the continent out of poverty. Fabulous. But what is the last thing you need?"

"Recolonization."

"Is there a danger of that?"

"Yes."

"Why would anyone want to recolonize you?"

"Natural resources and strategic security. Particularly in respect of China."

"In other words..."

"Oil and military bases."

"Where's the oil?"

"In the Gulf of Guinea."

"And where are the military?"

"The Americans have set up a *Command* for Africa. They call it *Africom*. It's everywhere. Egypt, Tunisia, Algeria, Mali, Mauritania, Morocco, Niger, Chad, Nigeria, Kenya, Uganda, Djibouti, of course."

"What about Angola?"

"What indeed."

Callaghan focused on Dale.

"Namibia will be affected if anything happens to Angola. And Botswana, probably."

He switched to Sheryl.

"Angola needs decades to recover. Walter and his people need to be allowed to get on with what they're doing. Walter?"

Walter shifted in his seat and rubbed his eyes.

"There was a series of meetings in Pretoria. Just recently. It appears that we have been insufficiently supportive of American policy in our region. We were warned not to intervene in events — in our region. There was a gentleman by the name of Douglas Moreland. George and I knew him thirty-odd years ago in Angola. So did Bill and Elaine. I have no idea what his official position is now."

"What did he say, Walter?" Callaghan asked.

"He said we were not to stand in the way of freedom. If we did, we would face consequences."

"What did he mean?"

"We don't know."

"It's Angola, isn't it?"

"We think so."

Callaghan put down his beer and got to his feet.

"How's it going to happen?"

"We must follow the money," Walter said. "That is to say, someone must. *We* have been warned."

"George is the man. And you, Dale and Sheryl, lovely people that you undoubtedly are, are on a mission to Swakopmund. That's where he lives."

Callaghan checked his watch.

"But now, it's time for the news. Where's your TV, Walter?"

"Over there."

"Zara, love," Callaghan said, "channel four hundred, if you wouldn't mind."

As if numbed by the preceding conversation, Zara obeyed. They sat listlessly through sport, weather and the latest War Zone statistics — and then there she was.

Sheryl sat up straight. Walter adjusted his glasses. Callaghan took a slow draw on his beer. Dale felt the Central Business District heave under his feet.

Weaving between the rails, picking at T-shirts, scrutinizing labels, holding up a sweater to check the size, smiling at her nervous companion: a trim, assertive woman, wearing an intelligent but tired expression, moving with deliberation and assurance.

Zara made a face.

"So like who the hell is *she*?" she said.

CHAPTER 11

Alan Vickery had bought his house in Chelsea, using cash of the hard-earned persuasion, in the summer of 1994, on the basis of three iron convictions: First, that, however nauseating the architecture or the neighbors, snobby London property was a no-lose proposition; second, that there was a decent boozer just across the river in Battersea (now a tapas bar, alas); and third, that Mariella refused to live anywhere else.

In respect of this last consideration, he reflected as he slouched alone in his home theatre watching Argentinian football on Sky Sports and trying to decide if all ten speakers were actually working, it was highly ironical that she was never to be found in the bloody place. According to Danesha (Danuska? Danusia?), the maid from Poland (Slovenia? Slovakia?), *Mrs. Vickery go to Zurich.* All gnomes and chocolate, wasn't it, Zurich? Must have discovered curtains suddenly. Or maybe a marble crisis had flared up and an appeal had gone out for expert assistance.

Speaker number eight was the one he didn't trust: The smack of the ball hitting the net in the last goal but one should have sounded a lot crisper. This was the trouble, and it was typical of his life these days: With money came responsibilities. *Onerous*, was the word.

Or it might be number nine.

What he needed was entertainment and relaxation. Football wasn't doing it for him and neither was Argentina — not that he had anything against the country; war all forgotten, best steaks in the world and so on. He needed to get out of the house. He had, after all, suffered extreme privation during his brief period of detention at the pleasure of the Terrorist Response Unit. Had to hand it to the Yanks, though; they certainly knew how to lock someone up.

And, if that someone was an important foreign businessman from a crucial ally nation, with links to all the top movers and shakers in the New Democratic what's-it, then they knew how to let him go bloody sharp as well. Had to be something to do with Market Forces, which were well-known to be the authors of all happy endings. All the same, there had been some unpleasant people in the slammer with him and he had thus been, as Mariella would say, *totally stressed-out, darling.*

But there was a reason why he was reluctant to venture out, in his habitually carefree and airy way, for a brisk one down the King's Road.

Someone was watching him. A man on a motorcycle.

Who could it be?

Mariella? Checking up on him while she was ripping out cuckoo-clocks or recoiling at the fondue in — it was alleged — Zurich? Hoping to tail him to, say, a fragrant flat above a Lebanese grocer's near Marble Arch?

Her Maj's Revenue and Customs? Hoping to catch him renting out his spare bedroom? Aylsham claimed that if his lot ever seized power, they'd abolish all tax collectors and replace them with something voluntary. What a joke.

Arnie Muller? One of Arnie's special-forces chums, down on his luck, willing to do a bit of freelance nosing around to make sure that Arnie's new partner was on the level? Faintly insulting, of course — of all the hundreds of people that he, Alan, knew intimately, he couldn't think of anyone more trustworthy than himself.

That bloke Petty? Harlan Petty — the name had a ring to it, but not a nice one. This was scary. The man was seriously into guns — not just the honest and gratifying profits to be made from them, but the nasty bits of metal themselves. Trying to cut Vickery out of the deal? Looking for an angle? And why the hostility at the gun show? Petty had clearly enjoyed the spectacle of Vickery being dragged away by the cops. Well, some people were like that. And another thing — why were the cops more interested in Vickery than the guns? Oh well — put it all down to Market Forces.

Speaking of which, what about Ray and Marty? Now Ray, the fat one, seemed like an agreeable chap, if a stock or two short of a full portfolio. He was doubtless far too preoccupied with building his golf course to go around hiring leather-clad snoopers. Marty, the thin one, on the other hand, was a true psycho who would probably stop at nothing in pursuit of his nutty revenge buy-out scheme. But what if, as they had insinuated preposterously, they really did have a pack of trained moles digging away at the Pentagon in search of military gold? Wouldn't that mean laser-beams bouncing off his windows, satellites swooping overhead and drones patrolling Mariella's Italianate terrace? And not a lonely greaser on a moped?

And then there was Phyllis...

But this was silly.

It dawned on him that the number of individuals, organizations, pressure groups, government departments, muck-raking publications, lefty trouble-makers, disgruntled former employees, quasi-criminal syndicates, financial regulators and people who had lent money to Sara — Zara! — who might want to spy on him was actually quite large.

This depressing thought led him to flick through the news channels on the TV, hoping for a funny animal story or a Botox scare in Switzerland. But what was the point, he thought, of having eight news channels if they all showed the same story at the same time? Then he noticed what the story was. It was the tale of the murdered bankers, as rendered so movingly by General Freaky. Except they weren't murdered after all — or one of them wasn't, at least. Why, with all the stuff that was going on in the world — the dollar, the endless terror-plot alerts, the security restrictions, the economic crisis, the War Zones and so on — why was this important?

But it was then that inspiration descended. The answer to the problem of the man on the motorcycle was Aylsham. Tedious, pompous git he might be, but he had one big advantage. The boys at MI5 — cognizant of Aylsham's predilection for interfering in other people's countries; for getting up the noses of UN inspectors; and for generally embarrassing Her Majesty — kept him under constant surveillance, and didn't make a secret of it. And, if you were in his company, then James Bond himself would be certain to see off any pretenders.

Ordinarily, the prospect of an evening with Jerry Aylsham would not have been thrilling. But tonight was different.

He picked up the phone.

*

"**A**lan, you're looking particularly moldy this evening. What on Earth have you been doing to yourself?"

Aylsham was one of those lanky, upper-class types who seemed to be constructed entirely of weird angles and non-standard components (no doubt the result of centuries of inbreeding, port-guzzling and horse-riding), and yet his clothes always fitted him perfectly. It was a puzzle. His eyes were restless, his hands thin and menacing, his posture taut. You always felt he was contemplating acts of unspeakable violence — or Vickery did, at least. Aylsham's hair, although not a patch on Vickery's glossy luxuriance, was sleek, fair and schoolboy-floppy. Combined with that vicious little curl of the lip (did they train them to do that?), his tapering chin and his baby-smooth, millpond brow, the overall effect was of a very well brought-up gangster.

"Jet-lag, I expect," Vickery said. "Been across the pond doing deals and cementing alliances."

"Looks to me more like the aftermath of a night in Marble Arch," Aylsham said, brutally.

They sat in a plush and crepuscular restaurant somewhere in darkest Vauxhall. Aylsham's ageing and decrepit Rolls-Royce ("It's a classic, Alan") had collected Vickery from Chelsea and deposited him at this secretive and underground eatery. Now, the equally aged driver had taken the car off to have its grommets chamfered, or something. Vickery had looked for the tail, but these MI5 blokes were good — very good. The absence of motorcycles spoke to their prowess.

To judge by the menu, the restaurant was French with an American twist, a very curious confluence. Aylsham leaned over and whispered in Vickery's ear.

"Steps from the embassy, Alan. Merely steps."

Well, yes — except for the *moat* that the Yanks had cunningly installed to protect their new diplomatic fortress. But was he supposed to infer something from that? Probably not. Aylsham was always hinting at intrigues and conspiracies. Trouble was, one time out of ten, he really *was* up to something, and it invariably blew up in his face. In fact, it was a mystery to Vickery where

Aylsham's apparently copious funds came from. His elder brother had blown the inheritance on a web site for domestic servants — tactfully named skivvies.com.

"And where is the beauteous Mariella?" Aylsham asked.

There was nothing to worry about — it was just the way he talked.

"Zurich."

Aylsham's face fell and two deep, vertical lines appeared at the top of his nose.

"Those Swiss bastards. Did I tell you what they did to me?"

"Yes, Jerry, you did."

Aylsham had learned the hard way that banking secrecy was not a service you could order up à la carte.

"Jerry," Vickery said, anxious to change the subject, "where is he? Your MI5 man? Is he under that table over there, or is he hanging out in the kitchen, hoping for a free bash at the sole meunière?"

"You do talk rubbish sometimes, Alan. It's called the Security Service, and you'd think they'd have better things to do than persecute honest citizens whose only crime is a selfless sense of patriotism. It's pure harassment. You don't know how vindictive these socialist types can be."

Yes, he did. Exhibit A: Ms. Christine Sharp, MP.

"We have to take complete control, before it's too late," Aylsham said, sighing.

"You keep saying that," Vickery said. "But the other side keeps stopping you. I tried to make a donation to your lot but they wouldn't take it. It's lunacy."

"People are too bloody comfortable," Aylsham said. "What we need is a war."

"I thought we'd had several."

"No, I mean a real war. Then people would realize."

"Realize what?"

"Alan, you're being particularly obtuse tonight. Anyway, even when our side is hamstrung or out of office, it doesn't necessarily follow that we're out of power. Do you understand me?"

"Of course." Well, sort of.

Aylsham lowered his voice.

"If I could tell you, I would, Alan. Let me just say that a group of us have hit upon a little scheme of our own, whose ramifications, were we to be successful, would change the face of politics in this country."

This sounded familiar.

"What are you going to do?"

Aylsham waved his index finger in front of his mouth; the waiter was approaching.

"The Château Haut-Brion, I think, don't you, Alan?"

"That's a good one, yeah."

Aylsham proceeded to order half the menu. Where did he put it all? Vickery ordered something he believed would turn out to be steak and chips.

"Ah!" Aylsham said, as the waiter retreated. "I meant to tell you something. Got your girl Sara a job."

"Really? She's been pestering me like — wait, this isn't your *scheme*, is it?"

"No, no, no. Nothing like that. No, she wanted a job at the Beeb. So I got her one."

"What, just like that?"

"I happen to know someone on the new independent board."

"Well, Jerry, I don't know what to say... Really grateful, actually."

Never in a million years would he, Alan Vickery, be able to pull off a stunt like that, however rich he became. But Aylsham...

"What's she doing?"

"Well, she's just a dogsbody, of course. But..."

Aylsham leaned across the table.

"...it's rather interesting, actually. They've got this terrible lefty chap in South Africa. Callaghan, I think his name is. Been trying to get rid of him for ages. So they've sent your Sara over there as his assistant. I think the understanding is, she'll report back if there's, you know, anything to report back."

Bloody Aylsham. There was always an angle.

"Well, it's what she wanted." And South Africa was a long way away.

"By the way, Jerry, she calls herself Zara now. Zara with a zed."

"Why?"

"I don't know."

The wine arrived. They drank in silent contemplation for about a minute.

"So Alan," Aylsham said, pausing to lick his lips suggestively, "did they welcome you into the bosom of the Republic?"

"Yes, they did. Had a fantastic time." If Aylsham had somehow heard about the incident with the cops he would just have to laugh it off.

"And did you get to meet Phyllis?"

"Got on like a church on fire."

"Remarkable woman. If only we had something like the Liberty Club here. Think what a difference it would make."

"Ah!"

"Ah what?"

"As it happens, I persuaded Phyllis to invest in the Atlantic Affairs Institute. We're —"

"Your bijou little think-tank in Paddington, you mean?"

"Yes. We're going to expand. We're going to be promoting the New Democratic thingy. For a UK audience, as it were."

"Consensus."

"What?"

"New Democratic Consensus."

"Is that what it is?"

"Yes."

Vickery paused while Aylsham's initial courses were delivered on a fleet of trolleys. Aylsham plunged directly into something that looked like a bird's nest in a puddle. Perhaps this was the moment he'd been waiting for?

"Jerry," he said, narrowing his eyes for extra insouciance, "if you don't mind my asking, what exactly is the New Democratic Consensus? I know it's free markets and liberty and all that stuff, but... What is it *really?*"

Aylsham sat back and dabbed his face with his napkin.

"Well, Alan," he said, demonstrating that horse-boxes full of money on haughtiness lessons hadn't been spent in vain, "it's a state of mind, a philosophy, a movement."

"Yes, and..."

"It's the result of the great changes we have witnessed in the world since we defeated Communism."

It was hard to picture Aylsham defeating Communism; when animal protesters invaded his farm he locked himself in the bathroom.

"And what changes are those, exactly?"

"I thought you knew your history, Alan. Your reports are full of NDC theory."

"Don't write 'em myself, you know."

"No. Well, those of us who keep up with the cutting edge of the intellectual debate consider it axiomatic that liberal Democracy is approaching its final and most perfect form, having triumphed in the Cold War, and —"

"What about the financial crash?"

"Creative destruction, Alan. The system has proved its resilience."

"Has it?"

"Of course it has. Are *you* richer than you were before the crash?"

"Yes."

"There you are, then. Thus we may say that a final settlement is possible and imminent."

Final settlement sounded a little ominous. And there was a glaring flaw in Aylsham's analysis.

"But your bunch can't win elections."

"I don't mean here! That's why we — you and I and others — have to pull our bloody socks up."

Things were getting only slightly clearer.

"But what about the Consensus bit, Jerry? What does that mean?"

"It means that we're all agreed."

"Are we?"

"Yes. Of course we are."

"What about the people who don't agree?"

"There aren't any."

Vickery thought back to Phyllis's speech in Philadelphia.

"I think there might be."

Aylsham attacked his brie and buffalo soufflé with a steak knife.

"Only enemies of freedom, Alan. Only enemies of freedom."

"Ah, right."

Vickery's food arrived. It comprised some small medallions of gray fish, in green sauce, complemented by a pyramid of exotic berries and julienne vegetables.

"Oh, excellent choice, Alan!"

Bugger, he thought. Could he send it back? Not in a place like this. Where were Market Forces when you needed them?

"Fish! Mariella told me she was working on your diet."

Well, there had to be a kebab shop somewhere between Vauxhall and Chelsea — probably in Victoria — but would he dare ask Aylsham's driver to stop?

The evening, so far, had been less fun than he'd hoped. But Aylsham had hinted at some entertainment to follow dinner. It wouldn't be Soho — Aylsham might invest in porn shows, but he'd never visit one — it would be some private club, known only to people who named their dogs after great military leaders and discreet enough for two upstanding members of the New Democratic Consensus.

He took a bite of the fish. It tasted of... Well, nothing really. Was he missing something? Was it genetic? Or was it — as it so often turned out to be, in his experience — a load of total bollocks?

Aylsham was absorbed, almost literally, in his food. Vickery waited until the plates had been cleared, then he popped the question.

"So, um, where are we going?"

"The Glue Factory."

The Glue Factory!

CHAPTER 12

T he Glue Factory turned out to be an art gallery in Bethnal Green. "Aren't you excited to be back in the East End, Alan?" Actually no, Jerry. Not really.

Aylsham was beside himself with glee. The Rolls-Royce, whose grommets sounded, if anything, worse than before, dumped them in front of the flaky, wooden gates of a brick-and-iron industrial building of the mid-nineteenth century.

"Just look at this, Alan!"

He'd seen it before. Before it was hosed down. Before it acquired window-boxes.

"Look! A cobbled street!"

Yes, but not original. No loose ones. No dog shit.

"And these houses — look how low they are! So tiny! Amazing that they escaped the bombing."

No, a pity. And as for the faux-authentic delights of the East End, he was with Mariella on that one.

"Fabulous texture. So earthy. So real. Imagine how it used to be — vibrant, teeming!"

Vickery didn't need to imagine. He could still smell it. As for the vibration — that was just the railway.

"These places go for a tidy sum now."

Vickery scanned the street for the tell-tale. Yes, there they were: The craft shop with its whimsical watering cans; the pub with NO football; and, inevitably, the tapas bar.

"You know Marie-Thérèse, of course?"

One of Mariella's chums. But which?

"Is she the one with the hats?"

"That's her. This is her gallery. It's the opening night, ticket only. We're very privileged."

Privileged? The word spun around in Vickery's brain until it lost all meaning.

"The artist is called Aldi and the title of the show is 'Transubstantiations: Images of War and Beauty.'"

Aldi? Wasn't that a cheap supermarket?

"Oh, don't look so glum, Alan. There'll be plenty of champagne. And Mariella's friends are always so delightful."

Aylsham lowered his voice.

"And — whatever you think of it — there's money to be made in contemporary art. Just take my lead. Come along."

Ah, Market Forces again, back on the job. Something to cling on to.

A gigantic, pink sombrero loomed behind the filthy gates. Why didn't they clean them or paint them? There had to be a reason.

"Jeremy! So glad, so glad!"

Marie-Thérèse was upon them.

The gates swung open to reveal a cobbled yard (in Vickery's memory, the yard had always been dirt and coal dust, but never mind), occupied by five piles of rusty, scrap metal. The price tag on the nearest pile was £2,995.

"Alan, if you're looking for a gift for Mariella, I have something much more suitable inside."

The image in Vickery's mind was of Marty's Pentagon drone pin-pointing the artwork on Mariella's terrace and launching a pre-emptive missile strike.

"What is it — a monkey with a bazooka?"

Marie-Thérèse studied the object.

"No, I don't think so. Alan, Jerry — come inside and meet everyone."

"Was this really a glue factory?" Vickery asked, maliciously.

"Well, of course." Marie-Thérèse led them into a whitewashed hall full of champagne and haircuts.

"Checked, have you? Historical research? Asked the locals?"

"Unfortunately, most records were destroyed in the war."

"But you're in no doubt?"

"Oh, no. You only have to look at the place."

"Jolly well smells like one," Aylsham said.

That's the hair gel, Vickery thought.

"Well, I'm sure you know what you're about," he said.

With a glance at once wounded and fretful from underneath her ample, pink brim, Marie-Thérèse steered Aylsham away from Vickery and towards a posse of art-lovers in black T-shirts and thick-framed spectacles.

Should he tell Marie-Thérèse flat-out that he knew this building to have been nothing more exciting than a coal merchant's lock-up, and subsequently a potato store for the chippy around the corner, or should he torment her a bit more? The latter seemed like the best choice. He'd been hoping for entertainment, after all.

Searching for the bar, he remembered the party at young Brad Urquist's apartment. At least here he could enjoy a sense of superiority. And there was little chance of his being trampled into a puddle or cast into a dungeon. It did rankle that Urquist had done nothing to save him from the goon squad and that it had taken several calls from Kellerman to Phyllis's squeaky assistant before Phyllis herself had got on the blower to someone Kellerman insisted on calling a "senior administration official". Only then had the word gone out: "Free Vickery — he's one of us". To be fair, the cops had been apologetic; they'd given him a T-shirt. He was wearing it now, underneath his dress shirt. It featured a badge-like logo in the form of an angry eagle sitting at a computer, with the legend "Joint Internal Security" above and "Honor Bound To Screen Your Ass" below. He assumed it wasn't official merchandise.

Kellerman, it went without saying, *charged* him for the calls, once again illustrating the prevalence of Market Forces.

Noting with satisfaction that the pink sombrero had instituted a personal *cordon sanitaire* — if that was the phrase — with Alan at its center, Vickery sidled up to the bar, where he found a man in a tight, black suit, with a shaven head and the build of an ex-boxer or skip operator.

"Hullo," he said. "Any chance of a brown ale, or is it champagne only?"

The skip operator looked at him suspiciously. Something popped and bubbled in the depths of Vickery's memory.

"Just joking, mate," he said. "Are you the, er..."

"The barman? No, I'm the artist. Help yourself." This came in an odd, strangled accent. Wait a minute...

"No, you're not," Vickery said, sternly.

"What do you mean, I'm not?"

"You're Fat Phil's bleeding nephew. Sean, isn't it?"

"Alan? Alan Vickery?"

"The same. Blimey," he said, relapsing into the ancestral tongue, "how long have you been out?"

"For fuck's sake, Alan!"

"It's all right — this lot, they'll love that sort of thing."

"No they won't. Look, don't bugger it all up for me. I've got an effing mortgage."

"A mortgage? Why didn't you come to me? I'd —"

"Give me a break, Alan. I'm trying to go legit."

"Why are you calling yourself Aldi, then?"

"You're supposed to be a businessman. It's marketing. I thought it was funny."

"Did *you* tell them this was a glue factory?"

"No."

"Did you?"

"No. Not really. I mean, they were dead keen on a factory, and there aren't any sodding factories left. They're all flats. You know that. So I just said, well, it looked a bit like a factory, and, you know, maybe at some point it might have been used as a sort of —"

"What about the glue?"

"They just made that up."

Well, this was a turn-up. Did Aylsham know?

"Sean, you see that floppy-haired git over there? Is he in on this?"

"Him? No way. He's just a tasty punter. I mean customer. I mean collector."

"Where do you get all the junk from?"

"Skips, mostly."

"Do you make all the stuff yourself?"

"Yes. No. Yes. Yes, of course I do. Look, Alan, even bleeding Leonardo subcontracted."

Vickery considered this eloquent rebuttal.

"But... It is all a scam, isn't it?"

"No. Well, yes. Well, no. No, actually it isn't."

"You really are an artist?"

"Of course I'm a sodding artist."

"All right, keep your hair... What happened to it, by the way?"

"Image, Alan."

"Speaking of images, what's all this War and Beauty crap?"

"It's what's selling, that's what it is."

Vickery suddenly saw what he should have seen all along.

"Oh! Oh! Sean, old son, I'm afraid I underestimated you. Was it Phil's idea, by any —"

"It was *my* idea, Alan."

"Bloody good one, too. Look, I need a good laugh — show me your War and Beauty. More scrap, is it?"

"No. It's photomontage."

"Photo what?"

"Get yourself a drink, and I'll show you. But if you say a bleeding word out of line, so help me, I'll —"

"Not to worry, Sean — sorry, Aldi — I'm on your side, matey. Thank you, Jerry, you daft old ponce."

"What?"

"Nothing. Let's go."

As they made for the start of the prime exhibit, the haircuts parting in deference to the artist known as Aldi, Vickery's mobile rang. Some smart-arse — he didn't know who but he was going to find out — had reprogrammed it to play the theme from *The Godfather*. The haircuts smirked. According to the phone, "Warthog" was on the line.

"Alan, it's Arnie. Arnie Muller. We have to talk. Where are you?"

"Hullo, Arnie. I'm in The Glue Factory."

Trotting after Sean, Vickery took a huge swig of champagne and descended into what used to be the spud vaults.

"A glue factory? What in heaven's name are you doing in a glue factory?"

"Getting *stuck in*, ha-ha."

"Alan, a very serious emergency has arisen. This is no time for your English levity."

"Sorry, Arnie — it was a *tacky* remark."

"What? Never mind. Listen. Everything is being moved up. The schedule has changed."

"Then I expect I'll have to *adhere to* the new schedule."

"What? Yes, of course you will."

Sean had taken up a position by the first picture, arms folded, waiting for Vickery. A gang of haircuts had dropped anchor a short distance away, hoping to catch a pearl or two from the Master.

"Alan, our friend from Alabama needs his merchandise. All the vendors are ready and waiting. You must get the money to them as soon as possible. And also the money for — for you-know-where. That is even more important. Have you been in touch with Bradford?"

"We've formed a *permanent bond*."

"Forget about your glue! Forget about your factories! Please tell me where you are."

Vickery told him.

"But that is in the — oh, never mind. I will see you in ten minutes."

Must be in the City, Vickery thought. Or at the dog track.

"War and *frnngh* Beauty!" Sean announced, a little too loudly and without entirely swallowing the seditious adjective. The haircuts pretended not to notice.

"Sorry, Sea— Aldi, old son. Pray begin."

Sean gave Vickery a threatening look. Vickery lifted another glass of champagne from a passing haircut. "Ta, mate."

"What we are to see in these images," Sean began, struggling, Vickery noticed, to keep up the accent, "is a juxtaposition neither post-ironic nor yet normative; a conflation not simply paradoxical; but a rhetoric of brutality and transcendence — a new mythology of war and beauty."

The boy had clearly been putting in the hours. And he wasn't getting any of this from his uncle.

"What does Transubstantiations mean?" Vickery asked, putting on a frown of curiosity. He noticed Sean's right hand form itself into a fist.

"It means one thing changing, in essence, into another."

"Sounds a bit religious to me."

"Could be."

But the cut-and-thrust of artistic debate was stilled by the dolorous tinkling of Vickery's phone.

This time it was "Lardboy".

"Hullo, Bryce. And before you ask, the check's in the post. How's things in Vegas?"

"I wouldn't know, I'm freezing my ass off in jolly old London. I just blew over on a major shit-storm. Listen, Alan, where are you? We gotta talk."

Vickery filled him in.

"The fuck are you doing out there? Okay. Give me twenty minutes."

Shit-storms were a common meteorological feature of Bryce Kellerman's world — but this one sounded serious.

"Maybe you'd prefer to buy the show guide, Alan," Sean said, through gritted teeth.

"No, no, no," Vickery said, "not with the horse's mouth right here. Oh, no. What's this one about then?"

The pictures all seemed to be composed of snapshots from the War Zones — in black-and-white for enhanced poignancy — combined with color cut-outs from women's glamor magazines and celebrity rags. Picture number one featured a tank in the grounds of a burnt-out hotel knocking over a line of starlets like skittles in a bowling alley.

Sean grabbed Vickery by the lapel and pulled him close.

"See that?" he hissed in Vickery's ear. "That's War. And that —"

The Godfather theme beeped out again, this time heralding "Princess M".

"Ignore it, please, everyone! Just ignore it!" Vickery said, making a mental note to check his voicemail at the first opportunity.

"What was the second thing?"

But Sean had stalked off, scattering the haircuts and leaving them awed and bobbing in his wake. Typical temperamental artist, Vickery thought. But before he could slope off for a pre-voicemail refill he found himself cornered by Aylsham and Marie-Thérèse.

"What did you just say to him?" she demanded, biffing him obliviously on the forehead with her millinery.

"Nothing. Just discussing how he suffers for his art, and stuff."

"I hope you haven't upset him, Alan. There's a lot of money riding on this show."

"Really? How much?"

"A lot." She lowered her brim, and her voice.

"I know it's a load of old tosh, but Aldi is scorching hot right now —"

Aylsham made a witty *tsss* noise and tapped Vickery on the chest with his forefinger.

"— and I want to shift this lot before the market tumbles."

"You think the Aldi market might tumble?"

"There's a girl from Ipswich who cuts up her own pajamas."

Aylsham was nodding, in a sagacious way.

"Ah."

It seemed as though Market Forces would not be smiling upon Sean for very long.

The Godfather returned for another sequel, with "The Fat One" in the lead role.

"Hullo, Ray," Vickery said. "Don't tell me — there's a sudden crisis and you're on your way over."

"Oh my, Mr. Vickery! You took the words right out of my mouth, I'm sure. I was just saying to Marty, "Marty," I said, "I'm sure our good friend Alan would want to hear about this right away. It's only fair." Now, I was out on the eleventh fairway when I heard the news — I don't think they've got it right, you know, they've got the bunker too close to the water. Oh, dear me. You'll see when you visit. Anyway —"

"Ray. Please. What are you trying to tell me?"

"Well. We need to see you. Now, I'm afraid. That's all it really is, you see."

"But I'm at this place in East —"

"Yes, yes, we know. We'll be there in twenty-five minutes. This is just a courtesy call, you see. Manners are so important."

"We?"

"Did I say we? Oh, but you see I can't leave Fort Lauderdale. Oh, dear me, no. I'm sure you understand. No, Marty is on his way. He had some business with your Financial Conduct Authority. I do hope he calms down."

How did they know where he was? Was it the drones, after all? All Vickery needed now was the man on the motorcycle. He sauntered out into the yard for some much-needed reflection.

An outbreak of shouting, swearing and gate-rattling turned out to be Muller negotiating admission with Marie-Thérèse.

"*Very* nice friends you have, Alan," she said, storming past him back into the gallery and holding on to her hat.

"Alan," Aylsham said, trying to appear shrewd but looking devious instead, "you're a financial wizard. What do you call it when you buy something at a low price in one place whilst simultaneously selling it at a higher price somewhere else?"

"Arbitrage." Market Forces at their best.

"Ah, yes. Thank you. Very good."

He wandered off after Marie-Thérèse, singing something to himself about pajamas and fiddling with his mobile.

"Who in hell's name is that madwoman, Alan?"

Muller seemed a little out of breath, like a warthog which had just been surprised by an overdressed hyena.

"Don't worry about her," Vickery said, "she's got pajama issues."

"Pajamas? Issues? No wonder you lost your bloody empire. Now listen, please. Harlan needs his equipment." Muller produced a sheaf of papers from his cashmere overcoat. "Here is the inventory. You must go to Amsterdam, Prague and Budapest to check the merchandise and execute payment. Then call me and I will give you the shipping arrangements."

"I can't check the merchandise — I don't know the first thing —"

"You will have to learn. I have to be in Namibia tomorrow."

"Where?"

"Have you set up your Caribbean entities?"

"Not yet. I'll have to go there, as well."

"It seems to me that you had better get moving, then."

"Oh, I will."

There was a pause, in which they pursed their lips at each other.

"I don't see you moving."

"First thing tomorrow."

"Alan, do you really understand what you are involved with here?"

"Oh, absolutely. It's just that I'm waiting for Bryce Kellerman and Marty Bazon and a man on a motorcycle."

"Well, hear this, Alan. Whatever they want, your priority is to..."

Muller seemed taken with something he could see over Vickery's shoulder.

"Is that a monkey with a bazooka?"

"Opinion is divided."

"So will you be if you are not in Amsterdam tomorrow."

The look on Muller's face told Vickery that Muller was a man whose threats, however ill-expressed, probably meant something.

"All right. Don't worry. Oh, look — here's Bryce."

The cobbled street went into full eclipse momentarily as Kellerman billowed into the yard. The look on his face was one of incredulity and disgust.

"What is it with you limeys and your crummy Victorian shit-holes? Why don't you just nuke it and build something nice?"

"Bryce, if it was up to me..."

But Kellerman had seen Muller.

"Oh. Hey there, Arnie. Thanks for the *heads-up*, Alan. Shit! Harlan here too?"

"No," Muller said. "Mr. Petty is now on site preparing for operations. Without much of the equipment that he has been promised."

Kellerman looked relieved, and yet pensive.

"Better get your ass in gear, Alan. You're going to be a busy boy. We got a major news management scenario. Put your top guys on it, your best media performers — from your dork squad, whatever the fuck it's called."

"The Atlantic Affairs Institute."

Top guys? The hired profs didn't take kindly to sudden demands, especially if the demands interrupted their preferred pursuit of academic infighting, which was usually the case. And few of them were fit to be seen on TV before the kids went to bed. The Institute's other main resources — Sara's tweedy boyfriends — were likely to prove reluctant in the absence of the adored one. And Mariella, the organization's one true star, would have to be enticed home before she made it to the slopes. Or — more problematic — the après-ski.

"He means you must take control of the news agenda, Alan," Muller said, "before *they* do."

But what news was it that he was supposed to control? The economic crisis and the War Zones had already been spun to death.

"We got a bunch of hot-shots from the Liberty Club on the way over," Kellerman said. "They'll feed stuff to your beautiful right-wing press. Kind of prime the pump for our dweebs back home. They can stay at your house — right, Alan?"

"I suppose so. Can't they afford a hotel? I thought the Liberty Club was rolling in it."

Kellerman shrugged his mighty shoulders — not easy for someone with no neck.

"They're hard-core, Alan. True believers. Friggin' wing-nuts. Not like you and me. They upset people. Keep 'em on a short leash, okay? No red meat. No women. No men."

A light rain had begun to fall. And, just like in the old times, it had an oily sheen.

"So can we go inside, now, please?" Kellerman said. "What is this dump, anyhow? It looks like a friggin' junkyard."

"Come this way," Vickery said. "And I will show you War and I will show you Beauty. You too, Arnie."

Muller and Kellerman exchanged glances.

Vickery led his skeptical little troupe of opinion-molders into the exhibition hall. Over by the bar, Aylsham and Marie-Thérèse seemed to have fallen out. Some aesthetic dispute, no doubt. Marie-Thérèse was flapping her arms with considerable emotion, while Aylsham appeared cool — almost smug, in fact. Meanwhile, Sean had girded himself about with a shield of haircuts and, catching Vickery's gaze, gave him a stare familiar in exercise yards the world over.

"So what's up then, Bryce?" Vickery said, guiding Kellerman and Muller away from Sean and towards the potato vaults. "Why the sudden propaganda offensive? Phyllis had a brain-wave or something?"

Muller and Kellerman swapped glances again. They were turning into a double-act.

"Don't you watch the news?" Muller said.

"Yes, but it's the same old —"

"What about today?"

"Well, it's all about this banker woman. I mean, I have eight news channels and —"

"Banker woman!" Kellerman said. Then he and Muller did the glance thing again, which was really one time too many.

"What? What?" Vickery said, feeling that he still hadn't got to the crux of the matter.

"Don't you know what this means?"

Muller was becoming agitated and, unused to the confines of an East End fake-factory art gallery, as opposed to the open expanse of the veldt, was bumping into people and spilling their drinks.

"This woman —"

"Hey, hey, hey!" Kellerman said, turning on Muller and breaking up what had seemed a promising partnership. "Keep it down, will you? Alan, is there some place we can talk?"

"Yes. Down here."

The potato vaults, home to the War and Beauty exhibit, were empty. It was a strange thing with these art-lovers: No matter how much they loved the stuff, they didn't care to look at it much. They preferred to go off somewhere and talk about it. Muller and Kellerman scanned the walls in silence.

"Would you like me to explain?" Vickery asked. "The artist's a pal of mine. Now, you see that tank? That represents —"

"The artist's a pal of yours?" Kellerman said. "A *pal* of yours?"

"Yes. Old Aldi and I —"

"Alan," Kellerman said, getting quite steamed now, "do you know what would happen if Phyllis heard about this? This is fucking commie art. What are you doing here? Jesus!"

"I came with Jerry."

"Who?"

"Jerry Aylsham."

Kellerman seemed to go off the boil.

"Oh. Him. Okay. Shit. Look, Alan, I know he's one of the good guys and all — but he's also a nut, okay? He's some kind of private-adventurer doofus. You wanna be careful there."

"The guy is an amateur," Muller said. "He is living in the past. Too cocky. He puts us all in danger. Keep away from him, Alan."

Perhaps they had a point. Poor Jerry. Mariella had it in for him as well. Something to do with fake Dutch miniatures.

"But what about this woman — the banker?" he asked. "Isn't it good that she's alive and free? Remember how General Freaky —"

"Fricke."

"— General thingy said that she represented everything we hold dear?"

There was an icy pause.

"Did he say that, Alan?" Muller asked.

"I think so."

Kellerman went up to picture number two — night-time bombing with superimposed fireworks — and inspected it closely. Muller watched him.

"So what's the problem?" Vickery said. "I mean, it's a shame about her friend. But at least one of them..."

Kellerman dismissed picture number two and moved on to number three, which featured a wedding party and a lot of blood. Muller began stubbing his toe against the brick floor.

Vickery sensed hostility. Had he said something to upset them? Best to shut up for now and let Kellerman take the lead.

"Should have done it while they had the chance," Muller growled.

Kellerman, now on to picture number four, a kaleidoscope of bombs and bejeweled body parts, shook his head slowly.

"Bingo! There you are, Alan!"

Aylsham leered down at them with a kind of smarmy triumphalism from the top of the steps.

"Look, I'm all done here. Splendid result. I'll be waiting for you in the car. All right? Don't be long. We'll get a night-cap at the club to celebrate. Pajamas, Alan! Pajamas!"

Then, with an indifferent glance towards Muller and Kellerman, he was gone. Muller spat on the floor. Kellerman shook his head.

"Okay, Alan," he said. "Here it is. Let's assume that, like many millions of people, you were paying attention to the news. What would you have seen?"

"Cheering crowds? Weeping relatives? I dunno."

"No. First off, you see this crappy video. And it's her, okay? She's buying friggin' clothes. After she's supposedly dead, okay?"

"Doesn't surprise me. Mariella —"

"So why did the Vice President, the Secretary of State, General Fricke and everyone else on down say she was dead?"

"Got me."

"Because there was a covert operation to rescue the Barclay guy and they were using disinformation to put the bad guys on the wrong foot. Do you buy that?"

"Not really."

"Well, you're a smart guy. Plenty of ordinary folks will buy it. That's fine. But here's the problem. She's not on our side. She is what we call a hostile element."

"She could wreck everything," Muller said. "They say she was very uncooperative."

"And here's how it affects you," Kellerman said. "You're building us a new financing network to southern Africa. Correct?"

"Am I?"

"Yes. But your network replaces the old network — that got trashed by this bitch and her pal."

"How?"

"Fucking computer shit, Alan."

Vickery shivered; if there was one thing that made his skin crawl it was computers sneaking up on you.

"Hate 'em. Prefer paper any time."

"Yeah. We don't know if she knows the whole ball of crap. But if she does... Think about it, Alan. If she follows the old network back far enough, she gets to the point where it meets yours, probably in New York. Then she follows it forward, to you. Or back, to the source."

And the source was... What? Urquist? Phyllis? Someone or something else?

"Can she do that?"

"Maybe."

"But... So what if she did?"

"As you know, Alan, money is the root of all evil. If you follow the money, where do you suppose it leads?"

"It leads somewhere?"

"Sure it does."

"Somewhere important?"

"You bet."

"And would she follow it?"

"She might. Like I said, she's on the other team."

"What other team?"

"Come on, Alan. The people who hate freedom."

"Is she? Does she?"

"People need to know that. We have to get the word out."

"Can't they stop her talking?"

Muller and Kellerman looked at each other again. Infuriating.

"You got yourself a very interesting question, right there, Alan," Kellerman said. "Arnie, what's the answer?"

"I would say that there is a short-term solution and a longer-term solution."

A longer-term solution?

"You, Alan, are part of the short-term solution," Kellerman said. "The guys from Liberty will help you. The world needs to know what an evil, twisted, perverted, amoral, godless, pinko-liberal piece of shit this woman is. Who she screwed, who she betrayed, who paid her off, and so on. Got it? Let's create some realities on the ground."

"Yes, but why me?"

"Because she's here. Now."

"Here?"

"In London."

"But how?"

"Alan, it's pretty weird stuff," Kellerman said with a serene smile. "We may never know the whole truth."

"But what's she doing here?"

"Story is, this is where they hid her. Where they've been protecting her. Can you believe that?"

No, he couldn't. Furthermore, he couldn't believe she was what Kellerman and Muller said she was. And he couldn't believe that they expected him to help make a monster of her and to make people hate her. This wasn't what he'd signed up for. Was it?

"But, Bryce," he said, "I haven't got time to go around creating realities — I've got to go to Amsterdam and Prague and Budapest. Haven't I, Arnie?"

Muller was stroking his moustache, as though it were an aid to concentration.

"No, this takes priority. There is no point going anywhere until we have this woman under control."

"So, Alan," Kellerman said. "First thing tomorrow at your Institute, with your people and the Liberty guys. Where is it, again?"

"Paddington."

"Paddington?"

"It's an up-and-coming area. Handy for the trains." Some of the profs didn't drive. Some of them didn't wash, either.

"Sure. See you there. You better come too, Arnie. Jesus and Mary! I am so fucking out of here."

Kellerman indulged himself in a final viewing of picture number five, a fiery scene in a school-room, ripping it from the wall and smashing it on the floor. Then he stormed up the steps and, pausing briefly to topple something broad and pink, vanished into the night.

With a sour grunt of farewell, Muller followed, reaching the top of the steps at the same moment that Marie-Thérèse regained her composure. She must have been miffed about something because she tried to bar Muller's path — a mistake, as Vickery could have told her. Muller, in the manner of a warthog with a bad day ahead in its diary, shouldered her aside and stalked off. Down she went again. War and Beauty, Vickery thought — it's everywhere.

"Alan! Alan! I want a bloody word with you, you absolute bastard!"

Vickery took his chance, vaulting up the steps two at a time and sprinting out into the glistening yard. What he saw there surprised him.

Or, rather, it didn't. He saw Marty Bazon, morose as ever, advancing on him, accompanied by a phalanx of, oh, maybe a dozen or so broad-shouldered, bristle-haired men wearing razor-sharp suits and carrying briefcases. Bloody hell, he thought — lawyers! Actually, there were only three of them; it was just a popular fallacy that they always came in twelve-packs. Out in the street, a long, black limo contended for cobble-space with Aylsham's Roller.

"Um, hullo, Marty. Lovely to see you."

"Uh-huh," Bazon said, miserably.

Vickery gestured at the yard and its contents.

"Sorry about the, er..."

The chief lawyer — usually the one with the biggest wristwatch, in Vickery's experience — stepped forward and thrust a thin folder at him.

"Fucking Switzerland," Bazon said.

"What? Is it? Who is?"

"Fucker Lester's making a fucking speech."

"Is he? What about? Who again?"

It was so difficult holding a conversation with this man.

"Could screw the whole fucking Giraffe deal."

"Could it? How?"

"Fuck him before he fucks us."

"All in favor of that, as a rule, Marty, but why —"

"Fucking woman."

"Is he? You mean —"

"Get out there or we're fucked."

"Where, Marty?"

"Fucking Switzerland, where'd you fucking think? Are you fucking listening?"

"Perhaps if I called Ray —"

"Just read the fucking papers."

The lawyer held the folder up in front of Vickery's face, like a hungry prosecutor flaunting the bloody glove. Vickery took it.

"Nice fucking seeing you again," Bazon said.

And with that, the entire crew filed back into the limo, which started rolling the moment the last lawyer got a foothold — much to the disdain of Aylsham's driver, who was making use of down-time to polish the Roller's hood ornament.

Vickery glanced inside the folder. There was some kind of schedule, apparently printed from the Internet, with one particular item highlighted. "A speech by Tom Lester, CEO of Giraffe Software," he read, "on the subject of adaptive algorithms, financial networks and money-laundering, with illustrations from a current case..."

Money laundering! Algorithms?

And Marty thought this speech was going to blow up the take-over scheme? How? What was he supposed to do about it? Didn't he have enough to do, what with the character assassination and pampering Arnie's gun-peddlers? Plus anything to do with computers and money-laundering made his head throb.

He was all at once overwhelmed with a desire to peel himself away from the Glue Factory and seek solace in the nearest pub — even one with no football.

But at that moment he heard footsteps behind him — size fourteen footsteps.

Sean had emerged from the exhibition hall, his face sculpted into what Vickery took to be a murderous snarl of rage. Considered as a rendition of War and Beauty, it drew heavily on the former and very little, if at all, on the latter.

"Vickery!" he yelled, kicking over the monkey with the bazooka. "Come here!"

Vickery couldn't help but recall a few of the colorful terms employed by the Judge in his summing of up Sean's case. "Mindless thuggery untrammeled by conscience or by common sense," was one. Not strictly necessary to remember the others, he decided. The thing was to reduce the distance — in a nonchalant and non-provocative manner — between himself and Aylsham's car, while at the same time increasing the distance...

"They've all gone," Sean said, in the hurt, wondering tones of a prison-movie inmate whose pet birds had just been confiscated by the warden.

"Who's gone, Sean?" Vickery said, playing for time.

"The buyers. They've buggered off."

"Have they? What a shame. No accounting for taste, is there?"

"Somebody told them."

"I never said a word, Sean, honest," Vickery said, backing away and hoping desperately that Aylsham would fling the car door open for him at the opportune moment. Sean was advancing on him, fists clenched.

"Somebody bleeding well told them."

"Told them what, Sean?"

"About this stupid girl and her fucking pajamas."

Bloody Aylsham!

"Now they don't want to buy my sodding work. Marie-Thérèse is *absolutely livid!*"

At this point Sean froze, and a quizzical look passed over his face, as though he were suddenly compelled to question where his epithets were coming from. But then the mood passed and normal service — as detailed earlier by the Judge — was resumed.

"But what do they want pajamas for, when they've got War and Beauty?" Vickery said, stepping up his retreat.

"They don't know anything about Beauty, the bastards!"

The Rolls was now within striking distance, docked outside the gates with Aylsham lolling happily in the back. Vickery risked a quick glance and made the universally-understood wind-your-bloody-window-down gesture, supplementing it with vivid mime. Aylsham looked baffled.

"They've never been in a bloody war!"

"Well, be fair, Sean. You haven't been in a war, either. And you're not exactly an oil —"

"I AM AN ARTIST!"

Since this was not an assertion that could be fruitfully contested, Vickery turned and fled. Pummeling on Aylsham's window was, he found, the most effective way of conveying his requirements.

"Get this crate shifting, Jerry," he said, slamming the door and locking it. "Aldi's gone mental."

Aylsham gave the driver an all-but-imperceptible nod.

"Arbitrage is a wonderful thing, Alan. I had Marie-Thérèse over a barrel on War and Beauty and a trust fund in New York with no clue about pajamas."

Vickery pictured what he might do with Aylsham were any barrels suddenly to make themselves available.

"And you blamed me for the leak, did you?"

Aylsham looked sheepish.

"I bought you dinner, old chap. Be fair."

By now, they should have been gliding elegantly across the cobbles. But they weren't.

The starter motor whirred and clunked. And whirred and clunked. And clunked. All in the most tastefully muted tones, of course. The driver turned his doleful countenance to them.

"Sorry, Sir Jeremy. She's had one of her turns."

"For fuck's sake, Jerry — why don't you get a proper car? He's going to murder us. He's Sean Penrose and he didn't acquire his bloody metal-working skills at art school. Call the police."

Sean had reached the Rolls and was patrolling its perimeter like an angry bear looking for a claw-hold. The car's exquisite sound-proofing protected their ears from whatever it was he was screaming as he flailed at the car's bonnet with the monkey's bazooka.

For an agonizing minute or so this continued, Vickery wondering all the while when Sean's newly-cultivated intellect would lead him to turn his bazooka on the windows.

A flash of pink and a rattling of chains indicated that Marie-Thérèse had, prudently, shut up shop for the night.

But then, whether from divine intervention or distaste for Sean's language, the car's engine harrumphed into life.

"Oh, good work," Aylsham said. "Off we go then."

The car surged across the cobbles, casting Sean aside like an unworthy peasant, and swept around the corner on to a pot-holed section of tarmac. As they passed an alley on the left, Vickery spotted a black van with a metal grill over its windscreen.

"Jerry? You know when I said call the cops... Did you somehow —"

The Rolls lurched and skidded gracefully to a halt as a second black, armored police van shot out from the left and blocked the street. Van number one, the clever one, nipped out behind them and sealed the road to their rear.

"Whatever this is, Jerry, I blame you," Vickery said, as hordes of eager policemen in riot gear piled out on to the street.

In these situations, Vickery reflected, policemen always felt an overriding urge to make a terrible amount of noise and to shout orders that were incomprehensible, or contradictory, or physically implausible. Was it the training? The uniform? The excitement of the moment — the rest of the afternoon having been spent crammed in a van with one's sweaty comrades? Who could say?

But he knew what was coming next.

Sure enough, in short order, he found himself face-down in a puddle with a boot between his shoulder blades. Out of the corner of his eye, he could see Aylsham, left hand on hip, wagging his finger in the face of the top cop. It had to be something genetic, it really did.

"Alan Michael Vickery, you are being detained on suspicion of potential accusations of possible terrorism support or sympathy-related activities."

Not arrested, but detained. How curious. As for the rest of it — it was impossible to parse.

"Jerry! Do something!" he managed to call out before his lungs succumbed to boot-pressure.

"Do you have anything to say?"

He did indeed; he just didn't have the breath to say it with.

"Refusing to talk, are we? We'll see about that."

Above the clomping of boots and Aylsham's rising, nasal whine, he heard the dying stutter of a motorcycle engine, followed by the insolent clacking of metal-studded heels.

A shadow loomed over him. There came an unbidden hush on the part of the cops — although not from Aylsham, whose bleatings persisted.

Twisting his neck, Vickery saw a leather-clad figure in a full-face helmet standing at his side in a stylish and provocative pose.

Slowly and deliberately, the creature unzipped its jacket. Underneath was a white T-shirt bearing a familiar design — two zeroes and a seven shaped like a fancy gun. The creature gave Vickery a little wave with its mitten, and he fancied he spied a mocking grin behind its smoky visor.

Then it was back on its steed and farting its way between the potholes into the sunset, or possibly the junction with the Commercial Road.

105

What could this apparition possibly signify? Was it the same fiend that had been stalking him since his return from New York? Was it Aylsham's spook? Were they one and the same? It was perplexing.

And was it dungeon time again? If so, then surely his Liberty Club pedigree would be enough to spring him. They really ought to hand out cards that you could keep in your wallet. But, failing that, it was a given that Aylsham knew someone on some board, panel, committee, bench or throne.

Unless, of course, it was really serious this time.

He prevailed upon the leaden-footed cop to relent via the simple expedient of turning blue in the face.

Some urgent squawking noises from police van number one told him that Aylsham had accepted alternative transport. This was not encouraging. But then, as he pondered Kellerman's likely fee for liberating him twice in one week, his field of vision became occluded by a stout pair of shoes. And they didn't look like any police boots he'd ever seen.

They were stumpy, white high-heels with squared-off and slightly scuffed toes — the sort of shoes that brought rare color to Mariella's cheeks. He tried to peer up, curious as to what type or manner of policeman this might be.

Thin ankles led to thin calves, which disappeared up into a long, thin, gray skirt on a long, thin frame. Higher up, one encountered a brief, snowy slope before coming upon a craggy summit of windblown, gray granite.

It was the beaky, desolate formation known as Ms. Christine Sharp, Member of Parliament for some squalid, Labor-voting, enterprise-deficient, northern hole. Unusually, she looked happy — but you had to be an expert to know.

"I expect you're sorry now," she said, cheerfully.

"Not really," he said, gasping. "My friend Jeremy can explain everything."

"He'll be explaining all right."

"That's what I just said."

This seemed to throw her for a moment. But she came back strongly.

"Did you really think you could get away with it?"

What did she mean? Aylsham's manipulation of the art market? The Roller's unroadworthiness?

"But I haven't got away with anything."

Once again, he had her stymied.

"No, but... Oh, you think you're so clever. But you can't buy your way out this time. No one's going to help you now."

Oh no? Her intelligence was obviously out of date.

"Ever heard of a lady called Phyllis Ann Curtin?"

That knocked the stuffing out of her. She sniffed and clicked her fingers. He could see her toes twitching inside their simulated-leather holsters. But she wasn't about to let him go quietly.

"People like you disgust me. All you care about is profit. Dirty, filthy profit. You swan around the world, pillaging its resources, poisoning its seas and forests, building dams and sweatshops and motorways and airports and fast-food outlets; oppressing women, children and the elderly; destroying indigenous cultures; turning simple, native villages into glitzy resorts; undermining autonomous community-level neighborhood partnership development initiatives; ramming your vicious capitalist dogma down the throats of the poor; kicking the homeless off the steps of your opera houses; stealing our pensions to play in your stinking capitalist casino..."

He thought he saw where she was going with this. Had he stolen any pensions? He tried to remember.

"...vomiting your putrid class-based hatred on to our airwaves..."

Hatred? That was unfair. There truly was little that he hated. He might make an exception for Ms. Sharp.

"...selling girls as young as..."

"No, really — she was thinking of someone else there.

"...filling our schools with drugs and sex and sugary drinks..."

He was going to explain to her that he was merely a slave of Market Forces — a willing one, admittedly — and it wasn't fair to blame him, personally, for all the harm that money did in the world. But it was then that things got a little out of hand.

The cops, a somewhat more relaxed bunch than their New York mentors, were too taken with Ms. Sharp's acute and wide-ranging indictment to bother cuffing him. He reached for Ms. Sharp's ankle — merely to gain her attention, of course.

The last thing he saw before he fell into a whirling, phantasmagorical pit was the blunt end of a scuffed, white ankle-breaker coming his way.

CHAPTER 13

"**I** want that bloody woman locked up!" But it was no use. No matter how many times, following his return from the whirling pit, Alan Vickery had submitted this simple, reasonable request, and however eloquent he became — and he outdid himself on this occasion — the proposition failed to gain traction.

Indeed, it was he who spent a lonely, quiet night in super-secure Paddington Green police station — a notorious West End tower-blot, bearded terrorist types a specialty. Aylsham, of course, had done his usual bloody vanishing trick. The man had so many strings to pull he could have knitted a bloody sweater.

But, with a bruise on his forehead the size of a snooker ball and an official ration of two paracetamols until the morning, Vickery had been grateful for this rough repose. It was eerily quiet. He presumed they didn't do drunks at this station — and the bearded ones were probably too busy praying to make a racket. For it would have been bloody loud here, he speculated, were it not that the Marylebone flyover — looming outside his window — had been off the menu since the rocket attack. The station still looked a little scorched around the edges, but had otherwise brushed up quite nicely — all at the bloody tax-payers' expense, of course.

And what would those same tax-payers have thought if they could have witnessed the enormous waste of police resources that had gone into ambushing Vickery en route between Glue Factory and kebab house, dragging him from Aylsham's roller, and practically pinning him to the ground while that hard-left harridan, Ms. Christine Sharp, danced on his face in hobnailed boots?

People read about these things in the paper. But they didn't believe it until it happened to them.

He hadn't been allowed to call anyone, which he would have said, ordinarily, was a bit of a no-no. But during his stomach-churning struggle out of the pit, as he rolled on the floor of the van and tried to stop his eyeballs from spinning, he gathered from the voices floating above him that some politician or other — not Ms. Sharp, he was coming to her later — was determined to protect the public from him and he could therefore forget about civil rights or phone calls or any

109

namby-pamby nonsense of that sort. He should think himself lucky he was being indefinitely detained in a civilized country.

Sleep, like Aylsham, had fled from him. He was wasted and hungry and sitting on the floor, there being no bed. They'd taken his watch and phone — the latter presumably already downloaded to the Pentagon and its contents picked over by Ray and Marty. And there was, of course, at least one unsampled voicemail from Mariella; he preferred to keep on top of those, as a rule.

It seemed to be morning. Perhaps they would feed him soon. He hadn't had his kebab. The kebab he'd promised himself. The kebab he'd so carefully incorporated into his plans for the rest of the evening. Possibly the best kebab of his life. He'd been looking forward to it.

But, kebabs aside, it was necessary to review his situation. His leading theory, now that he could think straight, was this. The matter was blindingly obvious.

Aylsham, up to his neck in another of his stupid schemes, had been rumbled. Christine Sharp, having had it in for Vickery for many moons, had used his innocent friendship with Aylsham as a pretext for getting him banged up. Aylsham had done the dirty on him, possibly assuming that as a leading Consensuser — would that be the word? Consensual? — he could look after himself. Well, he could, of course. So long as he could get Kellerman on the blower. Kellerman, to use a couple of the big guy's favorite expressions, would immediately get himself all *lawyered-up*, go *ballistic* on the appropriate party's *butt*, and bingo.

But Vickery was a man of well-tempered resources and deep perspectives. He could cope with these little vicissitudes. What he deplored was the malice. That Sharp woman, for instance. Not a trace of humanity in her. One shuddered at the horror of it.

And then, as he shuddered, things started happening. The cell door opened and a greasy, shirt-sleeved copper invited him downstairs for a chat with what he called "a gentleman from the Security Service".

Security Service, Vickery thought. Real name, MI5. Now we're getting somewhere.

Down in the basement, Vickery found himself in what appeared to be an interview room. It didn't seem to have been redecorated in a while. That's good, he thought. Saving the public purse.

A young man in what looked like a tracksuit came and sat on the other side of the table. He was wearing some kind of audio device — one of those silver things with ear-plugs. His chopped-up hair was glued back like a kind of macho tiara. He wore a logo-laden sweat-shirt from one of those Oxford Street shops that gave Mariella the shivers. Poor complexion, Vickery thought. Nicks, razor-burn. Doesn't look like he moisturizes. Where's our spy?

The kid tossed a ratty folder on the table. Vickery noted a wine-glass stain.

"Hullo," he said. "I'm Alan Vickery. I haven't had any breakfast. How about grabbing me something while I'm waiting? I prefer fresh-squeezed, but I'm not fussy."

This friendly proposition brought no response. The kid seemed sunk in gloom or despondency. Probably a spat with the girlfriend. Vickery strummed his fingernails slowly on the table. The kid glared at him.

"I was just saying," Vickery said, "that while I'm waiting, I wouldn't mind a spot of breakfast. Whatever you've got."

"Waiting? What do you think you're waiting for?"

"MI5. They need my help, apparently."

The kid snorted and made an insolent gesture, jabbing his thumb towards his chest, then folding his arms and rolling his eyes.

"You?" Vickery said. "No. You're having a laugh. All right, let's see. How about this. Listen. Where's Smiley?"

"What?"

"Where's Smiley?" Vickery repeated, wittily.

The kid stared at him. Vickery beamed back.

"Bring me Smiley — or I won't talk!"

He waited for a response, but the kid's face was blank.

"Smiley!"

Still nothing — just the same dumb-arsed scowl.

"I said —"

But he didn't say. The terrible truth crowded in on him. Talk about disillusionment. It was the death of romance; Aylsham must have felt this way when that Swiss bank manager wouldn't take his envelope. The suave and laconic spies of Vickery's imagination — where were they? Were they a figment? How could it be? Then he remembered the creature on the motorcycle. Definitely something not right there. And now the defense of the realm was in the sticky hands of this scruffy little turd? And no breakfast? It was almost more than he could bear.

"You are Alan Michael Vickery?" the kid said.

"Just told you I was. Who are you?"

The kid sighed.

"And are you an expert in international law, Mr. Vickery?"

Odd question, he thought. *International law?* He was pretty sure Zarnoff and the others at the Liberty Club had had something to say about International Law, but he couldn't remember what it was. Best to bluff.

"I try to keep up."

"Oh, you try to keep up, do you?"

"Yes. I do."

Vickery began to wonder if what he'd been reading in the papers about educational standards was actually true. You had to tell this twerp everything twice. Probably selected for his job by computer on the basis of two O-levels, or whatever they called them these days. Different in the old days, of course. Draw them aside, that's what they did. Draw them aside after the rowing match or the college debate or whatever. Some old toff — sort of like Aylsham, but with ethics — would draw the young recruit aside. Having sussed him out completely beforehand, naturally. A quiet word with the parents, tea with the headmaster — that sort of thing. They didn't get paid much, but then they didn't need the money, did they? And loyalty wasn't an issue because they were all descended from William the Conqueror and thus English through and through.

And it had come to this.

Normally, Vickery considered himself one of the upper classes' sternest critics. But they had their uses.

"This so-called Atlantic Affairs Institute of yours. It's a front, isn't it?"

Tread carefully, he thought. He never washed any cash through the institute, but if they thought he did, it should be possible to brazen it out.

"It's at the *forefront*, if that's what you mean. You haven't told me your name."

"The forefront of what, exactly?"

"Atlantic Affairs. What did you think, sonny?"

The kid blushed, in spite of himself, and flicked open his grubby folder.

"It's Redpath."

A made-up name, if ever he'd heard one. The talent had to be out there. Why couldn't they find it? Zara (getting the hang of it now!), for example, had deceit and manipulation down to a fine art.

"Armed subversion, Mr. Vickery. Assassination, Mr. Vickery. Weapons smuggling, Mr. Vickery. Violation of United Nations sanctions, Mr. Vickery. Violation of the Geneva Conventions..."

Now, the Geneva stuff he knew to be bogus. Everyone at Urquist's party had agreed it was obsolete.

"...Mercenary activities, Mr. Vickery. The violent overthrow of a friendly government, Mr. Vickery. Conspiracy to facilitate acts of a terroristic nature, Mr. Vickery."

Redpath paused while he riffled through the papers in his folder.

Vickery considered the evidence so far. It sounded very much as if Aylsham had bought into another hopeless coup. The greedy git was pushing his luck — one failed coup and the world raises its eyebrows; two failed coups and, well, you know...

"Oh, and then there's the tax evasion, the extortion and the money-laundering," Redpath said irritably.

Vickery stiffened in his chair.

"Looks like you're going to need all that knowledge of international law," Redpath said in a sneery sort of way.

But there wasn't time to take offense; this nonsense had to be straightened out right now.

"Look here, Mr. Redpath, it's not me you want, it's Aylsham. He's the one. He can't say no. It's like he's addicted. Coup crazy, if you want to put it that way. I've got his address, if you need it. Jeremy Aylsham. He's your man."

"No, he isn't."

"Yes, he is. He told me only yesterday he was working on a secret scheme."

"We keep Mr. Aylsham under constant surveillance. You wouldn't understand — it's very high-tech. He's not working on any secret schemes."

"He's *always* working on a secret scheme!"

"We're talking about *your* plot to overthrow the legal government of Angola, Mr. Vickery. The government takes a very dim view."

"Where?"

"The Foreign Secretary himself, as you may or may not be aware, has vowed to stamp out this kind of illegality..."

"Where was that again?"

"...and there will be no mercy for the likes of you."

"Overthrow what government?"

"You're going to be going away for a very long time, Mr. Vickery."

"No, hang on a moment —"

"Unless you choose to cooperate..."

Unless you choose to cooperate...

Those were the words. The words dreaded by any self-respecting entrepreneur who'd started with nothing and been forced to cut a few corners on the way up.

How many times in his life had he feared he was about to hear them? You never lost the fear. Never quite exorcised it, however successful you became. Sometimes, usually after a hearty dinner, he would wake in the middle of the night, drenched and shivering, with the nightmare still bright and intact and echoing in his mind.

And those were the words he heard.

Here, in the dream, smiling behind the teak desk, was the bank executive who had recorded their conversation; over there, avoiding his gaze, the girl who had gone through his pockets while he nipped to the gents; and, all around, shrugging and shuffling their feet, were the trusted associates who'd all reluctantly concluded they had no choice but to shop him. And there, at the foot of the bed, Mariella and Sara stood in their night-clothes, crying.

But this wasn't a dream. He really was expected to cooperate. Yet there was so much still to be achieved in his life! Had the evil hour truly come so soon?

Thus Alan Vickery felt himself on the edge — the edge of despair. He hated to admit it, and it wasn't like him at all, but if there was one thing he prided himself on — apart from his hair, an admittedly lesser attribute — it was his fearless ability to face up to the truth.

The kid Redpath was sulking in a corner, mumbling into his mobile. Probably explaining to his mum why he hadn't cleaned his room or done the laundry. That Vickery's downfall should come at the hands of a pup like this was — what was the word? Galling. Galling was the word.

Overthrowing the legal government of Angola? Was that what Arnie and Harlan were up to? Despite current circumstances, you had to be impressed. Such ambition, such enterprise. But he couldn't remember them spelling it out for him quite that way. Had he not, for once, been paying attention? Urquist and his circle had been a bit of a distraction.

Angola, of course, was some place in Africa. He wasn't sure, but something made him think Angola was quite a big place — and thus way out of Aylsham's league. It was a big enough deal, in all probability, to make even Phyllis think twice about plucking Vickery from the maw of socialist spite (also known as Christine Sharp, MP).

He felt a tremor of remorse for having tried to finger Aylsham. But only a small one; the old toad was definitely working on something. No, Christine bloody Sharp was clearly the villain of the piece. No doubt she and her comrades were crowing about it even now in the wine bars of Islington. Meanwhile he, Vickery, faced political persecution and indefinite detention. He was beginning to see what the bearded blokes were getting so huffy about.

But wait. Urquist and Arnie and Harlan — and Kellerman, for that matter — were all operating under the auspices of the Liberty Club and thus in the greater service of the New Democratic Consensus. And if the wise minds of the NDC had given Angola the once-over and deemed a spot of régime change *de rigeur*, so to speak, then it had to be, basically, okay. What this meant was that, although you might not get your top politicians coming out in public and saying, for example, "Angola? Yes, what a brilliant idea! Bloody hell, let's have a bash at Angola!", in private, in the halls of power, it was all nod-and-a-wink stuff. Whispering in each other's ears, marking each other's cards, crawling up each other's... Well, you got the general idea. Riff-raff like Christine Sharp didn't operate at this level; your top leaders were realists — they knew better.

From this shrewd analysis, it was immediately evident to Vickery that his predicament was not as hopeless as at first it had appeared. Leaving aside, for a moment, Redpath's throwaway lines about, you know, tax and stuff, what you were left with was politics, pure and simple. And in politics, all that really mattered was power. In other words, who you were allied with. Who was on your side. And who, he asked himself, was on Alan's side? He began to unbutton his dress shirt.

Redpath had finished his phone call and was looking miserable, as if his mum had threatened to shove his PlayStation on eBay. He resumed his seat but said nothing and avoided Vickery's gaze.

"Problems at home?" Vickery asked, sympathetically.

Redpath seethed.

"Shut up and wait."

"So we're back to waiting, are we?"

No answer.

"Who're we waiting for this time?"

No answer.

"I said, who are —"

"Bloody SIS. Now shut up, will you?"

"Right-ho. No need to be unpleasant about it."

SIS, he thought. Which lot was that? Aylsham had explained British Intelligence to him once, at length, but the picture he had sketched perplexed then and it perplexed now. And if you thought that was bad, Aylsham had contended, look at the Yanks. They had about fifteen spy outfits, and half the time they were spying on each other. They appointed one supremo after another, but it only got worse. The Brits might have a garden-shed operation, but at least they knew who the enemy was. And who, exactly, Vickery had wanted to know, was that? Ah well, that all depends, Aylsham had said, in an offhand and mysterious way.

Something now caught Redpath's attention; he was on his feet. Vickery saw two men in suits enter the interview room. The first was tall, sleek and well-dressed, with natty cufflinks, blond, wavy hair and the persistent hint of a smile. He was about fifty and looked, in other words, like a posh TV doctor from about twenty years ago. The second man was slight and neat and unremarkable except for his obvious addiction to after-shave or — could it be? — perfume, and his apparent inclination to touch people — even Redpath.

The first man ignored Redpath; the second, tapping him on the shoulder and propelling him by the forearm, whispered something in his ear that caused Redpath to flee without a word, banging the door behind him.

Now a strange little scene played itself out. Two men, one chair. A deferred to B. B deferred to A. A offered to stand. B wouldn't hear of it. A exited in search of additional furniture. B approached Vickery and sat down.

These must be spies of a different order, Vickery thought. Potty, but different.

"Well, Alan! Does rather look like they've been putting you through it, doesn't it? Trust you're holding up all right. My name's Richard. Had breakfast, have you?"

The friendly tone, Vickery felt, was welcome — sincere or not. He was, after all, a prominent businessman, entrepreneur and patriot; and not one, as the monstrous Redpath had alleged, given to facilitating acts of a terroristic nature. Redpath, the poor fool, lacked the mental wherewithal to distinguish between a properly-thought-out régime change and, well, just blowing people up.

"Hullo Richard. It's been trying, I'll say that. And no, I haven't had breakfast. I did ask."

"When Jason gets back, I'll pop out and see what I can rustle up."

Jason, Vickery thought. That sounded more like it. Possibly the last of the drawn-aside generation. And as for Richard, the very tone of his voice suggested nothing less than the rustling-up of smoked salmon or Belgian waffles.

Jason returned with a wheeled, reclining, leather office chair, which he offered to Richard. Richard made a fuss of declining, but then changed his mind. Jason helped him adjust the seat.

Marvelous, Vickery thought.

"All set?" Jason said.

"Perfect," Richard said.

"Shall we?"

"Of course."

"Would you like to...?"

"No, no. You first."

"Are you sure?"

"Oh, quite."

"Okay then..."

"Ah! Breakfast! Almost forgot. You start — I'll be right back."

Richard scooted from the room; Jason peered after him.

"Down to business, then," Jason said, still watching Richard but also signaling that the Alan Ayckbourn stuff was over and something more gritty about to start.

"First of all, Alan, I think perhaps I should apologize if anyone here has been a little too, shall we say, *over-eager* or *injudicious* with respect to certain *occurrences* and *events* and the interpretation of those occurrences and events; and, indeed, if anyone has *suggested* that your knowledge of or proximity to certain, ah, *developments* should or could be construed as in any way *injurious* to your reputation or legal standing."

"You're calling off the hounds, you mean?"

"If you want to put it that way."

"No mercy one minute, not guilty the next."

"It *is* a little embarrassing."

"I expect I could sue. I'll sue that Sharp woman."

"Christine Sharp?" Jason permitted himself a fruity chuckle. "Not one of your admirers, is she? Well, you can sue if you want, of course, Alan. Free country. But you'd be wasting your money, she's practically penniless. And — I don't suppose you've heard this yet — she's resigned."

"Resigned? Not voluntarily, surely?"

"Of course. Her party leader ordered her to resign voluntarily. They'll force her out of the party, too. I'll give her boss about a week."

"What happened?"

"She said some unwise things. Someone — I can't imagine how they managed to do it — recorded her."

"Money, was it? Couldn't have been sex."

"There *was* money involved. If you believe the recordings."

Vickery had the sense that things were going his way. But there was something slippery about this Jason. There had to be a catch.

Richard returned with coffee, orange juice and pastries from Starbucks.

"Terribly sorry, Alan — best I could do at short notice."

"No, no," Vickery said with magnanimity. "Perfectly acceptable under the circumstances. Where were we?"

"This Angola business," Richard said. "Amazing how these things pop up out of nowhere, isn't it?"

"Disconcerting," Jason said. "Makes you feel at a disadvantage."

"No one wants to be at a disadvantage, these days," Richard said. "It can be awfully disappointing to discover that you're not quite in the swim."

"Not up with the latest, because..."

"...someone didn't think to..."

"...drop a hint or mention the possibility..."

They were looking at Vickery as if they expected him to understand. After a moment, they exchanged a glance. Vickery flashed back to the scene with Muller and Kellerman in the Glue Factory; this looked like another double-act in the making.

Richard leaned back in his chair — a little too far, perhaps; he'd hadn't had time to master the thing.

"Put it this way, Alan," he said. "We would value your input. Value it enormously. What do you say?"

In the vaults of Vickery's folk-memory, alarm bells rang, buzzers buzzed and sirens wailed. He felt instinctively for his wallet. Useless, of course, because it had been confiscated.

"Input? Are you asking for... A *contribution?*"

Richard catapulted forward in his chair.

"No, no, no," he said. "Dear me, no. I'm not making myself clear. Oh dear. Jason?"

"Alan. You are — and I don't think anyone here will deny it — a sophisticated observer of the world. You know that the world runs on information. Take your institute, for example. We understand that it's tied into some very impressive networks. And you've been expanding recently, have you not?"

"That's right. Just done a deal with the Liberty Club. There's this thing called the New Democratic Consensus. You probably haven't heard of it yet. We're going to be promoting it."

"Of course you are. And this Angola thing — that's sort of connected, isn't it?"

Vickery knew when he was being pumped. He took a ruminative bite at a croissant.

"Lots of things are connected, Jason."

"Exactly. We just want you to join the dots for us. As you see fit. On an ongoing basis. Starting about now."

Vickery must have looked skeptical; Richard leaned forward.

"We're asking you to step up and help your country," Richard said.

"Ah!" Vickery said. "I get it. The old draw-aside. You're drawing me aside."

The two of them exchanged a puzzled glance. What was it with people?

"Yes," Richard said. "We're drawing you aside. That's a good way of putting it. We're drawing you *this* way..." Here he made a shooing gesture with his hands. "...in order that you should avoid being drawn *that* way..."

Jason picked up Redpath's mangy folder and flipped through it.

"Tax evasion?" he said. "Richard, can you believe that anyone would bother Mr. Vickery with something as petty as that?"

"Surely not."

"Hard to credit, isn't it?"

"Very. But then — please correct me if I'm mistaken — didn't they get Al Capone on tax evasion?"

"You know, I believe they did. Amazing, isn't it? All it takes is one zealous official, however misguided..."

"All right," Vickery said. "Spare me. I get it. What do you want to know?"

"We just want to know what's happening," Richard said. "It's not too much to ask, is it?"

"Apparently, it is," Jason muttered to himself, brushing off a dark look from Richard.

"We'll give you a nice little phone," Richard said. "Go about your business and call in whenever you get a chance. Simple as that."

"You mean..."

"Go and buy your guns, wash your cash, play your little stock market games — whatever you want. Just keep us in the loop. You know what a loop is, don't you? And don't, for heaven's sake, say a word about this to Mr. Aylsham. Or the fragrant Mariella."

Look who's talking, Vickery thought. And how did they know so much about Mariella?

"What about Redpath?"

"Who? Oh, him. Sad little fellow. Forget about him."

Well, well, well, he thought. Alan the spy. Not exactly the outcome he had anticipated, but seemingly the best deal on offer. It appeared he would have to consider himself recruited. He would be spying for England, of course, a noble calling and quite an honor in fact — but who was he spying on?

"Well," Richard said, "I think we can all feel pretty satisfied. We've saved the Prime Minister from the most terrible embarrassment. Camp David beckons anew."

If Vickery's mind hadn't been racing, he might have sought clarification of this remark; but it was, so he didn't.

"By the way, Alan," Jason said, pointing at the grumpy, data-processing eagle on Vickery's screen-your-ass T-shirt. "Funny shirt. Honor bound, ha-ha. Just don't flash it around a lot."

"All right. Can I go now?"

"Of course," Richard said. "Toddle off to your institute. They're all waiting for you. There's just one thing."

The catch!

"What?"

"Well… Don't you want to finish your breakfast?"

CHAPTER 14

Alan Vickery's spy-phone was pink. Jason, apologetic but business-like, had admitted, when pressed, that it was the ladies' model. Someone, apparently, had mis-ordered.

Vickery had felt taken aback and — if he were to be honest with himself, which of course he always was — a little perked up to learn that there was such a thing as a British lady spy. Your Russians and your Germans — they used women, obviously. Notoriously short on scruples and such-like. French too, probably. But surely subterfuge did not sit well with the English rose? (Unless she happened to be Zara.) And how did the old draw-aside work with girls? Interesting question. He would have to come back to it later.

Jason had demonstrated the phone. It had extra encryption, or something, and you couldn't use it to call any five-quid-a-minute oh-nine-hundred numbers. Jason had programmed in his own number, to save Vickery the trouble. Otherwise, the phone seemed ordinary.

Vickery was to call Jason — not Richard — if anything interesting came to Vickery's attention. What counted as interesting? That was entirely up to Vickery. Richard and Jason had complete confidence in him. No detail should be considered too trivial. National security, they told him, depended upon apparently meaningless arcana. Arcana, Jason had subsequently explained, were mysterious, secret, esoteric things. Vickery was to watch out for them. Jason hadn't explained what esoteric meant, but Vickery got the message anyway: Be on the lookout for anything dodgy or fishy.

The first thing he would probably spy on, he mused as he set out on foot to make the short journey south-west from Paddington Green to the railway station and the headquarters of the Atlantic Affairs Institute, was Aylsham. Once Jason was apprised of Aylsham's secret scheme, whatever it turned out to be, the fool Redpath would stand exposed as a charlatan and an incompetent.

Reflecting on his dramatic change of fortune — from contemplating the anguish of visiting day with Mariella to anticipating the thrill and glamor of espionage — Vickery arrived at two subtle conclusions.

119

Firstly, there was a big difference between the two main spy outfits — and he knew which one he preferred. One was the pitiless tool of state oppression; the other took a broader and more sophisticated view.

Secondly, the fact remained that Richard and Jason, while drawing his attention on the one hand to the gruesome fate of Al Capone (an unspoken threat, of course), had also, on the other hand, encouraged him to indulge unstintingly in the very same armed subversion and so on that Redpath had been so unpleasantly snotty about.

What this all meant was that something very deep was going on. This was often the case in international espionage. Shady deeds were done for reasons that could never be revealed. It was all a matter of the greater good. The public, lacking the aforementioned sophistication, had to be kept in the dark for their own sake. He, Vickery, could take all this in his stride. The need-to-know principle held no fears for him.

All the same, he'd rather got the impression — and it was one of those niggling impressions — that all Richard and Jason thought he needed to know was how to work his girly spy-phone. Well, he'd show them. Perhaps he should have asked how to change the ring-tone, though. Currently it played a tune from some drippy film — he couldn't recall which. He hummed the melody to himself as he walked. Later, no doubt, he'd remember the title.

As he approached Paddington Station, he loitered for a moment to admire the shiny, new office buildings that had shot up around the canal basin. Modern, thrusting, outward-looking, uncompromising — just like himself. Perhaps, if Phyllis came through with the dosh as expected, he would be able to shovel the Institute into more fitting surroundings. Currently, it occupied the top two floors of a building whose other tenants were a Turkish restaurant (mediocre kebabs, alas) and one of those schools that taught English cheaply to foreigners. The contrast with the Liberty Club's sprawling campus in Oklahoma was cruel.

In his new spirit of selfless and patriotic dedication, he peered into the restaurant — just in case there was anything to spy on. But all he saw was old Mehmet with his feet up on a table reading some foreign rag. Probably totally innocent, but he'd mention it to Jason and let him decide.

The language school, as usual, was reciting pleasantries to itself. *How are you today?* Not bad, he thought, considering. *What is the time, please?* Time to start making money, he thought. Time to kick arse. (Yes, yes, he knew it was *ass*; he could make up his own slogan, couldn't he?) Time to shake the world up; time to step up to the next level, to the top table; time to demonstrate to people like Jeremy Aylsham and Christine Sharp and Bryce Kellerman — who had crawled their way to power and influence or been born to it — what true, native talent could achieve; time to put in his claim; time to turn the tables; time to live up to the ideals of the Vickerys — ideals that he himself had established, in lieu of inheriting any from the old man — ideals of valor, pride, and not letting the bastards take it away from you once you'd got it.

The door to the Institute was ajar. Inside, to judge by the noise, all was in uproar. No one seemed to notice him enter.

The door to his private office was closed; a sign saying "meeting in progress' hung on the door-handle. Someone had some cheek.

Half a dozen or so of the profs had made it into town. Instead of parking their raincoats (why raincoats on a sunny day like this?) in the cloakroom they had thrown them on the floor. They were sitting around the conference table arguing over the newspapers and drinking hot liquids — possibly soup — from thermos flasks. He felt a flash of irritation. There was a perfectly good espresso machine in the kitchen; these scruffs were letting the side down. The academics who worked for the Liberty Club were always spotlessly turned-out; they shaved and they didn't eat chocolate biscuits in public.

A shaking of the floor indicated that Kellerman was on the premises. Sure enough, Vickery heard him shouting down a phone. This was how you dealt with shit-storms. You shouted down a phone.

He peeked into the library. There was Aylsham, red-faced and full of himself as usual, lecturing to a rowdy bunch of supporters on the subject of Why Christine Sharp Represents Everything That Is Wrong With This Country And Where We Go From Here. Backing Aylsham up were two men Vickery hadn't seen before: A mallet-headed giant and some porky git with nasty, raked-back ringlets.

Scanning the room, he caught a glimpse of a girl who looked like Zara. But it couldn't be — she was in South Africa. Aylsham was too impassioned to spot Vickery at the door. He was ranting about something he called "our decapitation strategy". If *this* was his secret scheme it wouldn't be secret for long. Worth a mention to Jason if only to put Aylsham's name in play, as it were.

Stepping back from the library door, Vickery bumped into something solid and musky. It turned out to be Muller. He looked anxious.

"Alan, thank God you are here at last. The place is in chaos. Where have you been? No one could find you."

"Don't you worry, Arnie. I'm here now. And I'm in the mood for a spot of arse-kicking, as it happens. Didn't Jerry tell you where I was?"

"He said you were arrested."

"I was. Detained, to be precise."

"We didn't believe him."

"So was he — detained I mean. Wheedled his way out, as usual, didn't he? Leaving me in the —"

"What were you arrested for?"

"More or less everything."

"Everything?"

"Facilitating acts of a terroristic nature — that was my favorite."

"What!"

"Acts of a —"

"What did you tell them? Why did they let you go?"

Muller looked like a warthog on the verge of a nervous breakdown. Vickery took him by the elbow.

"Arnie. Calm down. It's all right. I handled the situation. I turned the tables. And now I have the upper hand. Let's have a little talk, all right? Come into my office."

Muller held back.

"We can't go in there."

"Of course we can."

"No, Alan. Look. You can see the sign on the door."

"It's *my* sign, Arnie. It's *my* door. It's *my* office. It's *my* bleeding Institute."

"You don't understand. The Liberty guys are in there."

"Who?"

"The guys Phyllis sent. Remember? Bryce said —"

"Well, they can go in the kitchen or somewhere. What are they doing in there?"

"They're praying, Alan."

"Praying?"

"Yes. You can't disturb them. Bryce said —"

Vickery gave up.

"Oh, well, in that case..."

"Alan," Muller said, urgently. "What did you tell the police?"

"Nothing," Vickery said, regaining his cool. "Absolutely nothing."

"But didn't they..."

"Didn't they what?"

Muller squinted at him.

"Apply certain approved methods?"

"This is England, Arnie. Never forget that."

Muller seemed unpersuaded; hard for him to understand, no doubt.

"Why did they let you go?"

"No evidence. Simple as that. All trumped up by that Sharp woman. Thanks to me, she's history."

Muller frowned. His undisguised skepticism was becoming irksome.

"Then perhaps there is no harm done," he said. "And, by the way, I think you will find that Ms. Sharp's fate is the work of your friend Jeremy."

"Jerry Aylsham?"

"Yes. Look, Alan — is there nowhere we can talk in private?"

Vickery sighed.

"They're really praying in there?"

"Yes."

"And how long —"

"They've been in there twenty-five minutes."

"All right, Arnie. Come with me."

Next to the media center was a supply room that contained a photocopier and doubled as Mariella's office. Vickery locked the door behind them and sat on the photocopier.

"It's all under control, Arnie," he said. "We can go ahead as planned. I'll be in Amsterdam tomorrow."

"What about the police?"

"They can't touch me. I've got protection."

"Where from?"

"From the highest level. Seriously, Arnie. I think someone wants us to succeed."

Muller stroked his moustache; Vickery's calm, understated confidence had clearly moved him.

"Well, that might explain a few things," Muller said after a pause.

"There you are, then."

"I suppose so. We are all on the same side."

"Exactly," Vickery said. "It's straight on to victory. The game's afoot, whatever that means. By the way, why didn't you tell me we were toppling?"

"Toppling?"

"Toppling the brutal tyrant who rules Angola, whoever he may be — though I can't say I've ever heard of him myself."

Muller gave Vickery a shifty smile.

"It's not quite like that, Alan. There isn't a single all-powerful dictator or anything like that. It's more a question of corruption and security and foreign interference."

"We're foreign interference."

"No, we're not. It doesn't work like that. Not when you're installing a proper democratic government."

Vickery wondered if Muller's idea of a proper democratic government had evolved since his early career in apartheid South Africa. But that was a side-issue.

"Toppling," he said. "Installing. Why not? Someone's got to do it. I mean, what sort of state would the world be in if they didn't?"

"Alan, if you don't mind my saying, you are a bit of an odd character. But I like you."

"Same here, Arnie, old mate. Now then. Where's Bryce?"

Nothing like taking command, Vickery thought. You wouldn't have believed that a tough old bruiser like Muller would have gone wobbly, but there you were. Vickery had bucked him up. Muller had been impressed with his performance under duress; awed, possibly. What Vickery had to do next was sort out Kellerman re: this daft character assassination job on the banker woman. For one thing, it wasn't fitting work for a valuable intelligence asset like himself. Oh, and there was a third thing, wasn't there? Something to do with Switzerland?

The Bible boys were still bashing away at it in his office so he sent the warthog off to task Charlotte or Zoë with booking his flights to the gun-running capitals of Europe. This accomplished, he went in search of Kellerman.

He found Lardboy in Mariella's office, crammed into the delicate Regency armchair that Marie-Thérèse had given Mariella as a make-up gift after they had fallen out over some hat-related incident. Kellerman had stopped shouting. In fact, he was eerily quiet.

"Hey there, Alan," he said, with none of his usual exuberance.

"Hullo Bryce. What's the matter? Someone not paid their bill? Why are there Jehovah's Witnesses in my office?"

"They're not Jehovah's Witnesses, they're — I don't know what the crap they are, I can't keep up with all this religious shit, Alan. It's like killing me, you know? They're intense. The arguments — they never end. Too much is more than enough, you know what I'm saying? They're fucking fundamentalists, what can I tell you? Nice kids, though."

It was clear that, like Muller, Kellerman had been feeling the strain. Another spot of bucking-up was in order.

"Bryce, you will be delighted to hear that not only have I demolished a vicious leftist conspiracy, but I have gained allies in high places. Influential allies."

"That's great."

"I got rid of that Sharp woman. Quite a triumph. What's the matter?"

"Problems, Alan, problems. General Fricke, okay? One lesbian daughter, we can manage. We know about it up front, we can spin it. Family values, compassion, crap like that. Two lesbian daughters, we got a problem. The base gets confused. They start looking things up in their fucking Bibles. Jesus! Why didn't he tell us?"

"Two? Really?" Highly unusual, but oddly intriguing.

"Yeah. And that's not all..."

"You don't mean..."

Kellerman gave him a mournful look.

"Ah. Well, I'm sure you'll think of something, Bryce. I know I will. But where do we stand? What about us?"

"Yeah. Oh, and just for your information, Alan — this Sharp woman? That wasn't you. That was your pal Aylsham, along with Flint and that sleazoid Nigel guy, plus a bunch of folks with some very big computers. You with me?"

"Who's Flint?"

"That guy from FNN. Head like a mallet."

"Oh, right." And presumably the porker was Nigel.

"They recorded some phone conversations. Made it sound like Christine Sharp and her boss practically sold themselves to the Chinese. It was sweet, Alan. Plus she dissed the Commander-in-Chief, and you don't get away with that."

Vickery's intelligence antennae began to twitch.

"You mean they were in league with the Chinese commies?"

"Yeah, and I'm in league with the Dallas Cowboys. Computers, Alan. We can create our own reality."

This was an unnerving thought. But you couldn't argue with the results.

"Speaking of creating realities, Bryce —"

"Yeah, well that's the other problem."

"But we're all ready to launch the campaign. If you still think it's really necessary. My people..." And here Kellerman gave him a sour and ungrateful look. "...are here. Your people are here. I suppose Jerry and his lot could lend a hand. That Nigel bloke — is he a journalist?"

"Have you seen his hair? Of course he's a journalist."

"So what's the problem?"

Kellerman squeezed out of Mariella's chair and shut the door.

"There's no problem with the media campaign. Especially now we got Flint and Nigel on board."

Vickery sensed they were moving into deeper, dirtier waters.

"Then what?"

"Alan, I hate to put this on you."

"What?"

"You're committed to what we're trying to do, right? You want to see the project succeed?"

"Very much so. You mean the Angola thing."

"Yeah, and the New Democratic Consensus and the global triumph of freedom and democracy in the wider, non-Euro-defeatist sense. The whole deal. You're all signed up to that?"

"Can't get enough of it."

"And you understand that sacrifices have to be made."

"Goes without saying."

"Sure does."

"Never any question about it."

Kellerman picked up a photograph from Mariella's desk. It showed Mariella and Marie-Thérèse, in swimsuits, sitting on a yacht, laughing and drinking with some leather-tanned, paunchy bloke in a captain's hat.

"You bet. And some people gotta get their hands dirty."

Vickery saw the trend of Kellerman's argument. And he didn't like it.

"Who, exactly?"

Kellerman replaced the photograph. Then he picked up an antique paper-knife and began to toy with it.

"In your early career, Alan, you must have known a few guys who didn't get too cut-up about getting their hands dirty."

"Not any more. What makes you such an expert on my early career?"

"Hey, don't be so defensive. You got nothing to be ashamed about."

"No. Nothing."

"You can't help where you start out from. Some guys would have done the same. Other guys, maybe not. But where would *they* be, now?"

"Nowhere."

"Exactly. Give yourself a break."

"Thanks. I will."

There was a pause. Kellerman put the knife down.

"So. Do you know anyone?"

Burning humiliation. That's what he felt. And there was nothing he could do about it. It didn't matter about the house in Chelsea, or the one in Barbados, or Mariella, or his beautiful if wayward daughter, or his string of companies, or the photographs in his hall of himself with Margaret Thatcher and Dan Quayle and that bloke who refused to accept euros in his electrical shops, or his financial achievements, or his Institute, or his name on the door of the new gym at Sara's old school, or his blessing from Phyllis, or his new rôle in British Intelligence — not that Kellerman knew about that, of course — or his posh suits or even his incomparable hair. When people like Kellerman — or Aylsham — looked at him they saw a thug in a tie. It made him want to cry.

And he wanted to cry all the more because, much as he resisted, the image of Sean Penrose materialized before his eyes. Sean Penrose — not with an artist's brush in his hand, but a baseball bat. Vickery saw that what he'd done — laughing at Sean and sending him up — had been a crime of sorts. They came from the same place, he and Sean. Why hadn't he seen it at the time? Too late now, of course. And the real fault was Aylsham's. If Sean gave up art and returned to — well, to his former profession, then Aylsham had a lot to answer for. Why was it so hard to change the system? Why did people have to be trapped like this? Wasn't the whole story of his life a struggle for the simplicities of freedom and respect? Wasn't everyone entitled to those? Why, after so much slogging and so much effort to rid himself of the tyranny of vile expectations, was it so easy for someone like Kellerman or Aylsham to knock him back into the mire? Just a flick, that's all it took.

So, what should he say? Kellerman was looking him as if he were a workman hired to do something unpleasant with the pipes.

"No. I don't know anyone."

"Oh, come on..."

"Is this your idea, Bryce? Your fucking stupid idea? What do you want to do to her?"

"Hey, cool it, Alan. No, it's not my idea, as it happens. No way. I don't make the policy, I just get to implement it."

"Then who —"

"You know I'm not gonna to tell you. So why'd you bother asking? Huh? Huh?"

"What do you — *they* — want done to her?"

"No, no, Alan. We don't do it like that. I am not telling you what to do. You find a guy, you tell him she's been causing trouble and she just needs a little persuasion so she can shut up and start minding her own business. You let the guy interpret that in his own way."

"No."

"She could blow the whole deal. A lot of important people are gonna be real cross — cross with *you*, Alan. Because it'll get back. It always does."

"No."

"Oh, like you're so pure now. You think this is so terrible. Wait 'til —"

Kellerman stopped.

"Pardon me, Alan. I know this seems kind of ugly to you. But it's necessary. It just is. This is a war we're in. The battlefield is everywhere. Think about it."

"I'm going home. And I don't want those religious nuts in my house."

"Okay. You had a rough night. Go relax. We'll talk later."

Vickery stumbled out of the office. He was trembling — not with fear or rage but shame. A novel, bitter, frustrated shame. Another one to add to his collection.

Passing the library, he saw his daughter with Charlotte and Zoë. He stopped. The girls looked up and saw him. He wanted to ask Sara why she was back from Africa. And he wanted to ask the other two why in hell's name they weren't busy booking his flights. He opened his mouth to speak but said nothing. The girls stared at him.

At this moment the spy-phone rang. He took it out of his pocket and examined it. Yes, it was Jason calling. Perhaps to ask for Vickery's maiden report. That would be it. Or maybe Jason had some spy-tips he had forgotten about earlier and wanted to pass on.

And now he remembered the name of the tune. It was "Nobody Does It Better", from that film with what's-his-name, Roger somebody. The thought crossed his mind that Richard and Jason were having a laugh at his expense, but he dismissed it. Sara and the girls, on the other hand, *were* having a laugh at his expense.

But he was used to that.

Without a word, he left the Institute and closed the door behind him.

CHAPTER 15

"**S**top the car. Please stop the car." Sheryl did what she was told, pulling the car to the edge of the road, skidding in the gravel and crunching to a halt.

Dust rose in the headlights. With an effort, she hauled on the parking brake; she was wrung-out. She left the engine running and kept her hands, both of them, on the wheel.

"You're too tired," he said.

She was still looking through the windshield, as if gravel drifts, potholes and stray kudu or ostrich might yet be a threat to a stationary vehicle. There were no animals here, but the gravel could be deadly. She had been driving at eight-five kilometers per hour — too fast.

"Sheryl?"

Was she squinting at the fuel gauge? You had to watch your gas out here. They didn't have a spare can.

"Sheryl? Turn the engine off."

He had been struggling to stay awake. He'd driven hundreds of kilometers today. Walter wouldn't let them fly. Walter didn't want them anywhere near Windhoek. Walter sent Callaghan out to rent them a different car. Callaghan returned with a white Toyota Condor, a kind of small minibus. It was good for game viewing, he said, although privately Dale disagreed. Everyone would think they were going to Etosha.

They had driven west from Johannesburg and had crossed the border into Namibia just beyond the dust-blown town of Rietfontein. Sheryl slept. Then they rattled for a hundred sixty-eight kilometers through desert along the C16 gravel road to the oasis of Keetmanshoop, a lonely stretch. Here, they turned north, taking Namibia's only major road, the B1. Sheryl drove this section. To avoid Windhoek, as instructed, they took a left at Mariental on to the C19. At Maltahöhe, they forked right on to the C14, a minor gravel road. Here, Dale took charge again.

Heading north-west, they drove for over two hundred kilometers, traversing the Naukluft Mountains and their deep ravines of dark limestone. Then, finally, they descended from the central escarpment into the northern Namib desert, crossing the Tsondab — one of those Namibian rivers that, from time to time, flows down into the Namib and dries up in the middle of nowhere.

Twelve kilometers later, at the one-house, one-store, one-gas station, desert town of Solitaire, they stopped, ate and refueled.

By the time they reached the Kuiseb Bridge — the river was dry, as expected — it was dark and cold and Dale was exhausted. Sheryl took over. She drove for fifty kilometers before Dale told her to stop.

Here, in the northern reaches of the Namib desert, beyond the great dunes of the south, the landscape was rock and more rock, changing gradually as they sped along from a choppy, alien sea of rugged, empty canyons to a flat ocean of gravel plains, after which the road ran almost straight to the coast and the port town of Walvis Bay.

From there, the B2, a well-maintained, surfaced road, would take them north to Swakopmund, and the home of George Fischer, the designated but as yet unpersuaded savior of Africa and all her people.

Having driven it twice before, Dale knew that the section of the B2 between Walvis Bay and Swakopmund was dangerous to drive at night, the reasons being sea-fog, bored young drivers and alcohol. He would drive with extreme caution and with his window down.

But they needed a break. Dale reached over and turned the engine off. Sheryl looked surprised. Then she seemed to snap out of her trance and relax. He knew what it was: it was the desert equivalent of snow-blindness. A couple of hours on a straight gravel road at night and you started driving in the center of the road, hitting the bumps a little hard, sledding on the gravel, speeding up; you needed someone to tell you to stop.

He offered her a bottle of water, their last. She drank. The water seemed to revive her.

"Let's get out of the car," he said.

As he stepped out of the car and the cold air hit him, he thought he tasted a hint of moisture, of salt. But they were still a long way from the coast. The road here was pure gravel; towards the coast it would transition into black, shiny salt.

It was a dark night, but it was still possible to see that the empty plains stretched into the distance on all sides and that there was nothing there except the finger-trace of the road itself. It was superb. There was no wind. And the world — but for the cracking of the car engine as it cooled — was silent.

Even by Namibian standards, this was not a busy road. Most traffic between Windhoek and the coast would take the B2, which looped around to the north, avoiding the mountains and the Swakop river valley. It might be a couple of hours before another vehicle came this way. They were truly alone.

Sheryl was leaning against the car, studying a map with a flashlight.

"What is it?" he said gently. "Something's changed."

"Since when?"

"Since a few days ago, I guess."

"What do you think has changed?"

"Come on, Sheryl. You didn't want to leave the house. You were spending half the day in bed. You were kind of down on everything. Down on Namibia. You seemed like you were afraid of something. You were saying things like you didn't see the point of us being here. And stuff."

She put down her map and shut off her flashlight.

"Yeah. Yeah, I guess something's changed."

"It's okay, don't get me wrong. I just want to understand."

"Yeah, I know."

"I mean, look at us here. What the heck are we doing? It's like you wanted to do this, you made a decision, and I — well, I don't know if we're doing the right thing. And — I guess this is the point — I don't know why you wanted to do it."

"Oh. I should explain, shouldn't I?"

"Maybe. If you can."

"If I can."

He leaned next to her against the car. Her skin felt cold already.

"Do you want a coat?"

"No, I'm fine."

He rubbed her forearm gently.

"I can understand some of it. You know, the city — it can be kind of a dead place. It's like it's got no character. Seems like something's missing. Kind of creepy at night. And when it's hot, you don't feel like... And I'm at the embassy, and I'm doing stuff, and I'm thinking, well, at least we're doing something — I know everything takes so long, and it doesn't seem like we're making a difference, but..."

"A dead place..."

"And the social thing, I know you're not much into that. And old Bill and Elaine, they're not party animals or anything, so..."

"Do you know exactly what happened to their daughter?"

"Huh?"

"Walter said their daughter was killed. Up in the Caprivi Strip. Elizabeth?"

"I don't know the details. Is that —"

"I guess I feel challenged. It's not right to be here and not do anything."

"Challenged?"

"Uh-huh. Don't you think this is an amazing country?"

"Yeah. I sure do. I just meant, when you're stuck in the city and the apartment and... It just wouldn't be surprising, you know. If you got a little depressed, and..."

"It's okay. I'm over it."

"Because, we can do something. If you wanted to go back home for like a month, or —"

"Dale, I'm over it. Really."

It sounded good, but he still didn't get it. He had the sense that she'd stepped out of some dull, domestic sadness into something brighter and sharper but also more scary. Something had gotten into her, and he was terrified it was something that would tear her away from him — something self-sacrificial. Or something political. Had Walter gotten to her? Why was she talking about Elizabeth Ellis?

"We're not going back to Windhoek, are we?" he said.

"Gosh, Dale, I don't know. I don't know what's going to happen. Do you?"

He thought he did. The plan, if you could call it a plan, was simple. Go find this guy George. Give him Walter's letter. Give him Callaghan's video of their bizarre little talk-show deal. Okay, so Walter wanted them to sit through it with the guy and answer questions afterward. Maybe they wouldn't do that. But they would, of course, ask George if he could help out with Bill and Elaine. Like, talk to his supposedly influential buddies. And let Walter know where Bill and Elaine were, if George actually found out.

After that, back in the car. Drive the B2 back to Windhoek. Check his messages. Avoid Jay. If Sheryl didn't want to stay, or if — kind of possible — he'd been fired, buy tickets, get on the plane, fly back to the States.

"It's a beautiful country," she said.

"No question," he said. What did she mean? "It's all beautiful down here. South Africa, Botswana. Zimbabwe's beautiful."

"We've spoilt so much of ours."

"There's enough left."

"When I first came here, I didn't see it. You know what I mean?"

No, he sure didn't.

"But now I do."

"That's good."

"Problem is, once you see it, you can't let it go. You've got to fight for it."

"Protect the landscape. The wildlife."

"The people. Let them be themselves."

"That's happening now. It's a slow thing."

"I think that's what Bill and Elaine were doing. You know, when they first came here. Fighting. Maybe they were still trying..."

He waited. She seemed to be straightening stuff out in her mind; she was smiling now. But it was hard to understand.

"And when that woman came, and they got you to talk to her —"

"Jennifer."

"Yes, Jennifer. I thought, well, I'm glad she's safe. But it's another kidnap, it's happening here now. Look at the problems the people have. And now we're going to have another War Zone."

"No, not here."

"You told me the way she talked, what she said. And you told me how they took her away. And no one knew where she was. I think she got dragged into something, and she's trying to fight back. I wanted to help. So did you — I don't think you knew why. Then there's Jay. He's CIA, you know."

"I know. Everybody knows."

"Not everybody."

Well, that was debatable.

"He's fighting something. He gave you that video, made you take it to Brian Callaghan. It wasn't just about Jennifer. He wanted to get through to Walter. He was just using Callaghan. I really don't know about Callaghan."

"No, me neither."

"But I trust Walter."

"I guess."

"He was with Elizabeth Ellis when she died. He wouldn't lie about things."

Dale wasn't so sure. Sheryl seemed to have connected everything up. She was looking at some big picture that he couldn't see. He needed to reassure her, to convince her that he shared this vision of hers, whatever it was. And he needed to pull her back, real slow and careful, from whatever cliff she was thinking of jumping off — especially if it had anything to do with Jay.

"Jay's using us too," he said.

"Yeah."

"I mean, we have no idea. No idea what he's doing."

"He's trying to stop something."

"What?"

"Walter said something's going to happen in Angola."

"Jay wants to stop it?"

"Yes. But there's something else. It's not just about stopping it there. It's about stopping it everywhere."

"Stopping what?"

"I don't know what you call it."

What *did* you call it? If you used the wrong word...

"Imperialism?" he said, cautiously.

She laughed.

"Well, good luck stopping *that*. We can't help *that*. Up to a point."

"What, then?"

She took his hand.

"What are we doing to ourselves?" she said. "Do we want to live in a world made by people like Douglas Moreland?"

"What do you know about him?"

She smiled and turned away.

Back down the road, Dale saw headlights. They came closer, slowly, and then stopped. Sheryl turned and looked. The headlights went out. Dale stepped away from the car and stared in silence.

"Maybe we should get going now," he said.

"Okay."

He got into the driver's seat and started the car.

"We're not going back to Windhoek, are we?" he said.

"No," she said.

CHAPTER 16

In a black mood and a black cab, under a blackening sky and with all image of pleasure or delicacy or sweetness or refinement blacked out in the sooty temples of his mind, Alan Vickery rode in jolting lifelessness from ragged Cricklewood to silken-cuff Chelsea in the darkening conviction that the game was rigged and that he, not being able to point the finger himself, must be the sucker. Moreover, he had the sense that he'd done something unpardonable, unspeakable — something upon which his mind refused to focus.

Leaving the Institute that morning, with the laughter of his daughter's friends, Zoë and Charlotte, ringing in his ears, and Kellerman's condescensions rankling like a refusal of credit, he'd instantly rebelled against the idea of sulking in Chelsea with the world wheeling on around him. The Vickerys didn't have a code — not yet — but if they did, such pusillanimity would be against it.

So he'd spent the afternoon touring his dominions like a demented and plotted-against emperor: the pay-day loan parlors, the foreign property pushers, the pest-control lock-ups, the mail-order junk mills. This was accomplished in the company of a bottle of Chivas Regal, purchased at a tensely-negotiated discount from Mehmet, the Turkish restaurant boss, who didn't even drink the stuff.

Tills had been checked, books scanned randomly, junior staff roughed up, managers shouted at in public. None of this was necessary — or, he knew, particularly wise — but it served to restore a sense of mastery and of self-worth. At least he had hoped it would. But the old magic had failed, and he had struggled to understand why.

It was this sense of raging bewilderment that had driven him to Cricklewood — and let's be honest, you need a bloody good reason, don't you? — to the Royal Fusilier and to the welcoming if blubbery arms of Fat Phil the accountant.

Phil was someone Vickery could trust in every way that mattered. Which is to say, financially. On other matters, he was never short of an opinion, or of advice. It was mostly rubbish, of course, but there was something soothing in his manner and his way of talking. He actually seemed to listen to what you were saying and even to understand why you were saying it. The contrast here with the belligerence of his nephew, Sean, was something at which a weary world could only shake its head.

The Royal Fusilier was a dank and dreary dump but was, thankfully, free of tapas. Last redecorated six landlords ago in the reign of Terry the Unfaithful, who had retired without his wife to Spain shortly after an unconnected post office robbery, it celebrated in images large and small the glory of the British Empire. Few of its doomed regulars, however, would have been able to explain said glories if you'd flung the collected works of Winston Churchill at their feet. And half of them, Vickery suspected, probably had reason to harbor subversive thoughts about the civilizing mission of the Englishman and his Celtic brothers.

Phil, as expected, had been perched on a stool at the less gloomy end of the bar. In his sharp but shiny light-gray suit and his famous horny glasses, he looked like an obese owl with an accountancy qualification. His briefcase, bulging with secrets, had been wedged for extra security between stool and bar. He was sipping something colorless. *Vodka*, Vickery mused — *he thinks it's low-calorie.*

Spying Vickery, Phil's demeanor had morphed from cool self-satisfaction to warm self-satisfaction.

As the cab buzzed its blurry and eager way south to more promising territory, Vickery replayed his evening with Phil, skipping over the boring bits.

"How come," he recalled himself asking Phil, "how come they're always trying to drag you back down? Irrespective, I mean."

"They do that, don't they?" Phil says. "It's the way they work, I've seen it happen."

"Just what exactly do you have to do to earn their sodding respect?" Vickery wants to know.

Phil looks grave and orders two more vodkas. "Financial matter, is it?" he asks.

"No, no," Vickery says, and bites his lip.

"One of those, then," Phil says, handing the barmaid a twenty and pre-ordering the next round.

"I've achieved a certain standing, tell me if I haven't," Vickery says.

"You certainly have," Phil says.

"You would know."

"I would."

"You would indeed."

"Is there any reason," Vickery asks, mainly of Phil but partly of the pub as a whole, "why I should be denied the opportunity to play a full and honorable role in the affairs of our great country? And, you know, foreign what's-it? What about my experience? What about my contribution? *Contributions!* And I've paid my dues."

"What about your taxes?" someone says behind him and Phil's eyes swivel cautiously.

"They can't take anything away from you, Alan," Phil says.

"Too right," Vickery says, laughing. "You wouldn't let them, would you?"

"Definitely not," Phil says. "You've got rights. Political then, is it?"

"Politics!" Vickery says, swilling the last of his vodka and beckoning the barmaid. "Politics! I've got the politics under control, don't you worry, it's the other..."

"Mariella, is it?" Phil says, shuffling his stool a little closer to Vickery and tucking his stomach under the bar with practiced ease.

"No!" Vickery says, spluttering with the absurdity of it. "No, no, no, no, no. None of that, Phil, my old love. No. Love of my life. Did I ever tell you? Yes, I did, didn't I? Not unless Switzerland..."

"Switzerland, is it, then?" Phil says, coolly, removing more cash from his wallet.

"What? No, bugger Switzerland," Vickery says, picking up another vodka.

"I should say so," Phil says.

"Your nephew," Vickery says, "your bloody nephew..."

"My bloody nephew," Phil says.

"Yes," Vickery says, triumphant, "your bloody nephew!"

But at this point the pubby tableau shattered as the cab driver skidded to avoid collision with two rocketing, unmarked police cars and the tedious compensation claims and conflicting accounts that necessarily would have followed. Vickery felt himself sawing against the seat-belt which, being a black cab regular, he'd been careful to spend five minutes fastening. The police cars screamed away into the woozy night.

"Ow!" Vickery said.

"Sorry mate," the driver said. "Another bloody bomb, I expect. It's going to happen one day, though, I reckon."

"What? What do you reckon? I thought it was already happening. What are you talking about?"

"Nah, the big one. Know what I mean? Not that we can do anything about it."

"Oh?" Vickery said, in a sneery tone intended to convey his innate contempt for defeatism. "Why not?"

"Them bloody Yanks, innit?"

"Oh it is, is it?"

"Yus."

Reminding himself of (a) the discretion necessitated by his status as a tool of British Intelligence, and (b) the futility of arguing about *anything* with taxi drivers, Vickery contented himself with a professional slur and returned to his reverie of Phil and the Royal Fusilier.

"Know the way to Chelsea, do you?"

"No need to be like that, mate."

But before Vickery could re-conjure his murky vision, the spy-phone rang. There was a snort of derision from the driver. *Nobody does it better*, Vickery mused helplessly, *Makes me feel sad...* Well, *someone* was going to feel sad. Starting with this driver when he saw his tip.

Ever since leaving the Institute, Vickery had been plagued by calls from Jason demanding to know, *a là* Mariella, when he was going to be home. Later, he'd said — not the reply he'd have given his wife, of course.

"I'm on my way," he said now. "In case you're wondering, um, Jason, I haven't got anything to report yet." He'd decided to give old Mehmet the benefit of the doubt. And he had yet to put the finishing touches to his case against Aylsham.

"Very good, Alan," Jason said. "Be here in a few minutes, will you?"

"Yes."

"Excellent. Bye!"

Wait a minute — what did he mean by *here*? But what with the wheeling and dodging of the taxi and the alcohol swarming about his ears, it was too much to worry about. Back to the Fusilier...

"Do the rounds today, did you, Alan?" Phil was saying. "Everything in order, is it?"

"Yeah," Vickery says, "everything's in order."

"That's good to hear, isn't it?" Phil says. "Credit's doing especially well, I expect you noticed."

"Yes," Vickery says.

"So no problems there, then," Phil says.

"Nope," Vickery says.

There's a pause in which Phil reorders and Vickery scans the pub. Bunch of losers, he thinks. Why does Phil like this place so much? Probably on account of it being cheap. Look at that bloke sitting under the Battle of Waterloo with a Kronenbourg; he's on the way out. Terrible skin. But never mind. Steer Phil on to the subject of... What was it?

"Sean, is it?" Phil asks, looking like an owl that knew the answer all along.

"Your bloody nephew!" Vickery says.

"My bloody nephew," Phil says.

There's another pause, in which Phil hands Vickery another drink and the barmaid gives Vickery one of those dreadful winks she reserves for Phil's better-dressed clients.

"What about him, then, Alan?" Phil says, gently.

"Who?"

"Sean."

"Your bloody —"

"It's about Sean, is it, Alan?" Phil says. "Something he did?"

"Do you know what he did?"

"Actually, Alan, I —"

"Do you know what he did?" Vickery says, suddenly roused, and giving Phil the finger-of-accusation stab in the gut.

"Yes, Alan. He's very sorry. Poor lad."

"Poor lad?"

"Yes," Phil says, rubbing the spot, "poor lad. Hopes dashed away and all that."

"Hopes dashed away?" Vickery says, softening. "But..."

"He hopes you didn't take it all amiss, Alan," Phil says.

"Amiss?"

"Yes."

"Is he..."

"Is he what, Alan?"

"The art thing. Is he still..."

"Not at the moment, Alan."

"What, nothing?"

"Not really. Got to sort himself out. You know," Phil says, looking down at his lap, or in that general direction at least.

"Phil?" Vickery says after a pause. "You ought to lose a bit of weight, you know. I mean," he says, glaring in a meaningful way at Phil's belly, "tub of lard, isn't it? No offense."

"You're absolutely right, as usual, Alan. But if there's anything Sean can do..."

"Anything Sean can do?"

"If there's anything Sean can do for you," Phil says, "I'm sure he'd be delighted."

"Delighted?"

"He's a good lad at heart, Alan."

"Delighted," Vickery says to himself. "Delighted."

"That's right. Is there anything? By any chance? Some little job? That needs doing?"

"Might be," Vickery heard himself saying.

But then the cab pulled up — not outside Vickery's house but four doors along in accordance, he had decided, with spy practice — and Vickery spilled out into the velvety Chelsea night, having flung a couple of twenties at the driver and banged the door in the fashion of the locale.

Staggering towards his front door, he was puzzled to discern that all the lights in the house were on. With Mariella still in Switzerland and Zara currently subject to a no-party order, the house should have been empty. Jason hadn't taught him how to deal with intruders so he just barged up the steps in a stupor of resentment and resignation and started rummaging for his keys.

The door swung open on its own, revealing Jason in a pale-blue cardigan and a plumply-knotted tie.

"Ah, here we are at last. Come along, Alan. I think we'll have you in the kitchen first." He seemed to be sniffing at something. "Yes, get you fixed up, I think. This way."

Convinced though he was that he knew the way to his own kitchen, Vickery stumbled meekly and wordlessly along. There was something about this Jason that made you feel there was no point resisting; it was infuriating. He heard the front door click shut behind him. Elsewhere in the house there were voices, footsteps, phones ringing. And, if he wasn't mistaken, some kind of choir was rehearsing.

What the hell was going on?

CHAPTER 17

J ason had plied Vickery with orange juice, bottled water and some strange, little blue pills. Then he'd hustled him into the staff bathroom, along the rear hall from the kitchen, and practically ordered him to shave — electric only, please Alan — plus clean his teeth and generally freshen himself up.

"Need you at your best, Alan," he'd said. "Important meeting — you'll see."

Under Jason's spell, he had complied without demur. And this, he reasoned, as the orange juice — or something — kicked in, really wasn't so surprising. For one thing, Vickery was very hot on matters of presentation and personal hygiene. It was an obsession with him and he admitted it. He rejoiced in it. Some people might say that it was all a reaction against his insalubrious upbringing — one of those psychological things. Let them say that, if it made them happy. The other thing was that Jason reminded him of Mariella. Which was odd. But there wasn't anything psychological about it.

When he came out of the bathroom, Jason was waiting for him. Rather like Mariella, in the early months of their courtship, he gave Vickery the once-over, a pursed-lip examination culminating tersely in precisely the same verdict: "You'll do".

"I've already had a lot of meetings today," Vickery complained, mentally running through his encounters with Redpath, Richard and Jason, Muller, Kellerman, Mehmet, various smelly and ungrateful employees, Fat Phil, the irksome taxi-driver and now Jason again. "Could we do it tomorrow?"

"No," Jason said, dragging Vickery back down the hall.

"I haven't got anything to report yet."

"We know that."

"Then why..."

"A very important American gentleman wishes to speak with you."

Kellerman, of course, thought of himself as important. But no one would call him a gentleman. So who could it be? Zarnoff was a gentleman: He offered his seat to women even though he could barely stand unaided; and the women always got the wrong idea on account of that gnomish leer of his, the sad result of a minor stroke. But Zarnoff wasn't important. Not these days, anyway.

"Who might that be, then?" he asked Jason as they whizzed through the kitchen on the way to the main hall.

"In due course, Alan."

In the main hall, Vickery brought their little two-man forced march to a carpet-wrenching halt by reaching across to his left and planting his right hand squarely on Jason's chest, accidentally twanging his V-neck.

"That's cashmere, Alan. Please be careful."

"The isle is full of noises," Vickery said, moodily, surprising himself with a Shakespearean quotation. It was the only one he knew and he'd picked it up from none other than Marie-Thérèse — yonks ago, when he and Mariella had swooped on her rented Santorini villa during her cats-and-Greek-islands phase. Were these pills of Jason's doing something to him?

And Vickery's house *was* full of noises — the same peculiar racket he'd heard on the way in. Whose bloody house was it, anyway? Important Americans would have to wait.

"What's all this noise in my house, Jason?"

"I really couldn't say. You find it unusual?"

"I do. This won't take a moment."

Vickery disengaged from Jason's sweater and barreled up the stairs, his first target-of-opportunity being the choir — which seemed to have mutated into a barbershop quartet.

He located it in the library. Tables had been moved. Chairs had been lined up. His satellite television magazines had been disturbed. The choir or quartet seemed to consist — quite logically, when you thought about it — of four young men. They wore short hair and blazers. Three of them had bow-ties. They stopped singing — some song about a girl called Carolina — and stared at him. He glared back. Then he saw the Bible on the table and things began to click. He had several thousand volumes in his library, and he didn't know what they were, but he'd specifically vetoed Religion. He'd been very clear about it with the suppliers: Philosophy, yes; History, yes, plenty of that; Religion, no. He was a Renaissance Man, after all.

"You lot," he said. "Liberty Club?"

They nodded.

Vickery cursed Kellerman silently.

"Well," he said, seething but unable to come up with anything more satisfying, "keep the f— , keep it down a bit, will you?"

"Sure. You got it," the tie-less one said. "Would you like to join with us for a moment?" All four of them smiled at him. He started backing away.

"Alan!" Jason shouted from the foot of the stairs.

"Just hang on a moment!" Vickery yelled back, storming out of the library and closing in on the study with its ringing phones and its snorts of laughter.

Inside, all was in disarray. His papers were on the floor, displaced by pizza boxes. Empty wine bottles from his own cellar filled the waste-paper baskets. There was a red stain on the carpet. The TV was on, tuned to some channel called FNN, and showing pictures of young women in jeans doing things with gas-masks.

Someone — *someone* — had been smoking. This was too much. The grubby, concrete "beer garden" down the side of the Royal Fusilier — well, that was one thing; poor bastards had nothing to lose anyway. But in his own house! If Mariella caught but a —

"Ah, it's our host!" someone said.

Vickery stepped inside. Lolling in Vickery's prized, red-leather, swiveling armchair and wafting his hand guiltily in front of his smirking face, was the porky git Vickery had spotted earlier at the Institute.

"I'm Nigel," this swinish creature now declared. "Nigel Weese. And that's Flint."

Flint was the mallet-headed giant. Now asleep, he had stretched himself out on Vickery's matching couch, boots on, and with Vickery's phone, still ringing, balanced on his stomach. It appeared that the two of them came as a pair, like those Watergate blokes, Woodward and What's-his-name — except that Weese and Flint were on the other side, obviously.

And although his initial instinct was to demand to know what the hell they thought they were doing, and what gave them the right, and blah-blah and so on, Vickery couldn't help but pick up on something that had been bothering him all day.

"Flint?" he said. "Flint? What kind of name is that? Flint who?"

"Flint Gunner," Weese said. "Him. Him over there. Big chap, can't miss him."

"But why —"

"Alan! Please come down here at once," someone shouted from downstairs, probably Jason.

"But why's he called that?" Vickery demanded.

"Well," Weese said, "obviously Mr. and Mrs. Gunner wanted their son to have a career in TV journalism. Plus, he's got the head."

Vickery tried to picture the scene. It didn't make any sense.

"Your friend Mr. Kellerman said we could camp out here for a few days. Much obliged to you, squire."

Squire? Vickery thought. *Squire?* Who said that any more? This porker seemed to be some kind of throwback, and was obviously drunk — at Vickery's expense.

"Alan! I must warn you —"

"I'm coming!"

"Look," he told Weese, "clear this bloody disaster up before my wife gets home. Don't mess me about. I know how to deal with journalists. And *no smoking* — or I'll have your bollocks!"

Weese made a coy pout and smoothed his greasy ringlets behind his ears.

"Oh, well, all right then. Been a bit of a day. You know. We had a small celebration. Oh, yes."

"Alan!"

Vickery retreated from the study only to catch a glimpse of a willowy, beaky-nosed figure emerging shiftily from Sara's bathroom and oozing silently into her bedroom. Aylsham! Aylsham in Sara's bedroom! But surely —

"Alan!"

"Jason, I'm... I'm..."

But what? What the hell was he going to do? His daughter and that hideous old Tory toad? It couldn't be. There had to be an explanation. There *had* to be;

no question about it. But, if that explanation had anything to do with Aylsham nabbing Sara her dream job; and Sara, grateful and vulnerable...

Well, right now he couldn't face it. His elegant four-story townhouse had transformed itself into a House of Horror and he wanted nothing more than to get out of it. Now. Even if Jason wanted to send him undercover in one of the War Zones. It couldn't be worse than this.

"I'm coming!"

He flung himself down the stairs.

"Where are we going?"

Jason looked a little bit pink in the cheeks but seemed to calm down rapidly.

"Thank you, Alan," he said, unlatching the front door. "We're going south of the river. And we do not keep Mr Moreland waiting."

"Who?" Vickery said.

*

There were two of them. One of them was large, drooping and round-shouldered, with tired eyes and gray hair thinning away to nothing. He sat slumped in his chair with his elbows on the table, his fingers entwined and his knuckles rammed up his nose. Vickery knew that look; this bloke didn't want to be here. According to Jason, this was Walsh, the embassy number-two.

The other man was quite different and, to be frank, gave Vickery the willies right from the off. He was smaller than Walsh, but infinitely more dense and energetic. His shoulders were square and somehow fierce, as if their owner had trained them in offensive combat. His face was like roughly-polished granite, semi-smooth and hard, but with that particular coarseness you acquired from half a century of kicking people around — something Vickery could recognize. You couldn't really see his eyes because of the reflections from his heavy steel glasses, but you got the impression from the lines underneath that he went about in a perpetual state of belligerent skepticism. The clenched smile that he wore much of the time, Vickery thought, was enough to freeze the soul of a lesser man than himself; it was like a dam holding back a million cubic yards of deferred rage.

In contrast to Walsh, this man was sharply turned-out — something that Vickery would have found admirable were it not in this instance so intimidating. Whereas Walsh's suit was light-gray, single-breasted, flimsy-thin, baggy and unbuttoned, this man's was dark, taut, double-breasted and made from heavy wool with very thin pinstripes. And it was buttoned up like a holding cell. The man's hair was thick and full, rather like Vickery's own. And, likewise, the gray had been dealt with. But while Vickery knew — largely thanks to Tristan, Mariella's home-visit hairdresser — how to condition and style for bounce and shine, this man had slicked his hair back with old-fashioned grease. It was extremely ominous. And this, Jason had informed him in a surprisingly sour tone, was Mr. Douglas Moreland.

Moreland was restless. He didn't sit. He paced about the room with a menacing deliberation, with Walsh's weary gaze following him everywhere. Much of the time, he clasped his hands behind his back, which made him look, to Vickery's eyes, like a cross between a British Royal and a Chicago gangster.

Jason and Vickery sat at the table opposite Walsh. Vickery had been given a paper cup of vending machine coffee, which Jason had declined. They were in the US Embassy in the sinister district of Nine Elms, Vauxhall. This was Aylsham's holy-of-holies, a kind of up-armored office block with tank traps and a moat.

Vickery didn't know how high-up in MI6 Jason was — pretty high, he'd assumed — but it had still taken them half an hour to get inside the building. Vickery had had to strip down to his underwear, a humiliation that Jason had been spared. "Don't infer anything from this," Jason had instructed him. "You have to respect their procedures. You do understand?" But, of course, Vickery already knew the routine. It was a pity, however, that he had taken the opportunity in the staff bathroom to discard his sweaty "Honor Bound to Screen Your Ass" T-shirt. It might have earned him a few points. Or at least a smile.

Moreland was in charge of southern Africa, according to Jason. Vickery knew this to be inaccurate: After being sprung from the pound in New York, he'd spent an evening listening to Muller's beery and embittered anecdotes about Mandela, Mbeki, Mugabe, Zuma, Malema and others whose names were too difficult to remember. It was evident that *no one* was in charge.

What Jason probably meant was that this bloke Moreland *wanted* to be in charge of southern Africa. Perhaps he'd caught wind of Muller and Petty's scheme and wanted a piece of the action. This might prove tricky. Vickery wasn't really empowered to negotiate — and he certainly didn't want to get on the wrong side of Harlan Petty. And what was Jason's angle? Apart from self-gratification on account of being in the loop?

They'd been in this chilly, windowless room for about twenty minutes now and Moreland still hadn't even acknowledged Vickery's presence. Jason had been given a bit of an ear-bashing though, with Moreland standing over him, spitting into his ear and pummeling the table with his fist. Poor old Jason had gone a bit pale and had loosened his tie, but his upper lip, Vickery was glad to observe, was still reasonably stiff. Thank God it wasn't Redpath in here with him.

Walsh hadn't said anything at all. Vickery considered piping up and introducing himself, but the atmospherics were all wrong. Keep it buttoned, he told himself. He was in a different league, here; even Phyllis might have quailed before Moreland — if *quail* was the word he wanted. Remember how Richard and Jason had made Redpath quail? Well, now someone was making Jason quail, big-time. This was serious stuff, in other words, and Vickery hoped he wasn't going to be next in a lengthening line of quailers.

But now Moreland turned to Vickery for the first time. He had his hands on his hips, he was squinting through his glasses and he was poking his tongue against the inside of his cheek; it was a picture of lofty disgust and really quite offensive.

"And who is this guy again?" he said, turning to Jason and jerking his thumb in Vickery's direction.

"This is Mr. Alan Vickery," Jason said, wisely not volunteering more information than the minimum required.

"Vickery?" Moreland said, as if the name simply wasn't any good. "Vickery?" Then he went into a huddle with Walsh, which lasted about a minute. Vickery gave Jason an encouraging smile, but Jason came back with a sit-tight-and-shut-up scowl.

"So he's not one of yours?" Moreland said, rearing up and aiming himself at Jason.

"Not officially."

"What do you mean?"

"He's merely a source. Low-level background."

Low-level? This was disconcerting. But perhaps Jason was being deliberately misleading.

Moreland's chest seemed to swell.

"Am I getting this all wrong somehow? Am I imagining that this relationship that we have is somehow not working according to all those many, many rules and procedures and mechanisms and agreements and protocols that we spent so many months and years building and refining and engineering? Does this sound like crazy talk to you? I'm just trying to understand. Was it all a dream? I seem to recall standing here and talking to you, or someone like you, and there being a general agreement about the parameters we adhere to in these circumstances. Did I imagine all that? I'm just asking because I want to know. Did we just blow it all off? Did we? Because, if we did, I think we are going to have to go away and sit down and get around the table and consider the consequences. Am I wrong? I don't think so. Am I? Tell me if I'm wrong."

Jason looked as though he'd been hit over the head with a rubber croquet mallet. Vickery couldn't see exactly what Moreland was driving at, but it seemed plain that Jason was getting a bollocking. Vickery wondered what might be in store for him.

"I think," Jason said — and Vickery detected a slight tremor in his voice — "that, given the urgency of the situation, there may have been an understandable misunderstanding."

Vickery had known Moreland for less than twenty minutes, but even he could have told Jason that "understandable misunderstanding" was asking for trouble.

Moreland began stalking up and down behind Walsh, but he kept his face pointed at Jason; it was as though the body moved but the head didn't and it reminded Vickery of the time he was frightened by a lion at the zoo.

"Misunderstanding," Moreland said. "Misunderstanding. My understanding is we don't do misunderstandings. We don't do misunderstandings because we have an understanding. Do you understand me? I thought it was all understood. Am I making myself clear?"

Not really, Vickery thought, but Jason was biting his lip and nodding. Moreland was stalking up a storm.

"You do not initiate," he said. "You check. You check with us. You want information, you ask. What do you do? You ask. You do not compromise ongoing operations with low-level sources. You do not compromise ongoing operations like *this*."

Vickery realized that *this* meant him.

Jason seemed about to speak, but Moreland continued.

"What is our doctrine in these matters? I think we should look at the doctrine. What does it say? It says the military is the lead actor. Do we understand the significance of that? Do we understand what it means? I understand what it means. I don't think there's any great mystery about it. I thought everyone knew. The military leads because that's what the doctrine says. The other levels operate on a down-stream basis and they delegate and they remain in-line and they do not cross-link and they do not act autonomously."

This was baffling, but Jason seemed to get it.

"And then we have the internal issue," Moreland said, coming to a stand-still at last. He seemed to go a little off the boil and his voice softened a notch. "We have to solve the internal issue," he said, making it sound as if he wanted to shove his idiot child into a home.

Jason coughed and piped up.

"We don't believe we've been affected," he said.

Moreland snorted.

"You have no evidence. You have an absence of evidence."

"But we do," Jason said, his confidence recovering, "we do have a... A source in contact with someone we suspect of harboring sympathies."

"You have a source."

"Yes. A reliable source."

"A reliable source."

"Yes."

"A source that can identify these people? We need to break this thing open, do you understand? We need to tear it out whole. It's like a cancer. That's exactly what it is. It's a cancer. It's killing us. We can pick off sympathizers until the cows come home or the ice floes melt, or whatever you will. So who is this source? Do we know? May we be told?"

Jason swallowed audibly and gave Vickery a nervous glance.

"She — I should say *the source* — is close to someone in South Africa who is a known sympathizer. If we can track this person — the sympathizer — or monitor him, or certain others close to him, then we may find a link into the Resistance."

Moreland seemed to think about this for a moment, moving his tongue behind his lips as though he were considering taking a bite out of Jason. He ambled over to Jason and brought his mouth close to Jason's right ear. Vickery flinched.

"We don't call it that," Moreland said, softly. "I won't have it called that. It's called the *internal issue.*"

Jason froze. Moreland waited a few seconds and then strode off back to the other side of the table.

"Well, let me have me your proposal," he said to Jason, resuming his former demeanor. "Let's hear it. I want to hear what you can contribute. A contribution would be appropriate, I believe. Yes, I really believe it would." Now, at last, he sat and folded his arms.

"Well," Jason said, giving Vickery another curious glance, "now that we, ah, have a better perspective on the Angola question — now that we're not, as it were, totally in the dark — we feel that Alan here, once we get him into Africa, will be able to act as a... I would say that they will come looking — they will want to make contact with him. And then, of course, at that point..."

Vickery sat up. Although, in the heat of the moment earlier, he had fantasized about being sent undercover in the War Zones he hadn't, of course, really meant it. And he had no intention of being sent to Africa. Let alone Angola. Let alone Angola with Petty in it. He was about to protest but Moreland stared him down.

"*He's* your fly-paper?" he said, with what seemed like bitter incredulity.

Jason shuffled in his seat.

"I think we would prefer to avoid these types of metaphor," he said. "But we do think Alan would be ideally placed. And there is a possibility — we're hearing this from Switzerland — that there might also be a resolution to the... The Lenehan situation."

Moreland looked like he was going to spit. But, in fact, he didn't; he simply stared at Vickery some more, as did Walsh, lifting from his torpor.

"I'm not going to say anything about that here." Moreland said.

"No," Jason said. "We just wanted to put it out there."

Vickery was beginning to feel that he didn't want to be a spy after all. He didn't speak the language and he didn't understand these people. They were beginning to frighten him. And he didn't want to go to Africa, and he didn't understand what the problem was with Ms. Lenehan — whose image had been lurking, reproachfully, in the deeps of his mind — and he couldn't follow all the stuff about this Resistance. Who or what was it? And why was he a fly-paper? And why was Jason trying to avoid metaphors?

And another thing: Why did it all keep coming back to Switzerland? What was going on in Switzerland? Switzerland and Africa. Mariella in Switzerland, Zara in Africa. Did it mean something?

"Er, Jason..." Vickery said.

"Quiet, please, Alan."

"When you say get me into Africa..."

"Alan, please."

"Okay," Moreland said, having conferred with Walsh, "we'll buy into that. What are you going to do about your fragrant Sir Richard?"

"Oh well," Jason said, trying to sound casual, "he's happy for now. He's saved the PM, as he sees it, from this awful embarrassment — you know, backing up the EU infrastructure plan then having to flip-flop into régime change. I'm sure the PM's awfully grateful. We were a bit put out to be caught on the hop, but what does that matter? In the larger scheme of things?"

"You are absolutely correct, for once. It doesn't matter at all. It doesn't matter if the PM *is* embarrassed. God knows, it would hardly be the first time. What matters is security and stability. We cannot tolerate instability."

"Especially Chinese instability," Jason said, with what sounded like a chuckle. But Moreland wasn't laughing.

"This is not a China issue."

"Er, no. I suppose not."

Moreland stopped pacing. He started inspecting his finger nails, as if he needed a manicure — which he didn't; Vickery had noticed.

"What are you doing with the Lenehan woman?" he asked Jason, in a low voice.

"Up to Richard. The word is she intends to fly home to New York, to her compact but neatly-furnished apartment — which, presumably, you've had the opportunity to visit?"

"How long have we got?"

"Pardon?"

"When is she going?"

"Tomorrow. Day after."

"Can we delay her?"

"I don't see how."

Moreland looked at Walsh. Walsh shrugged.

"All right," Moreland said. "That's it. Get out of here. Thanks for your time. And be careful in Switzerland, okay? Be very careful. Go. Go!"

Jason was on his feet, heading for the exit. Vickery started to get out of his seat.

"Not you."

Jason turned.

"But surely —"

"So long, Jason," Moreland said. "You — sit down."

Vickery sat.

Jason slunk out and closed the door behind him. Vickery could tell he wasn't happy; no doubt the spy-phone would be buzzing later.

But it was about time, Vickery felt, that he asserted himself.

"Now look here, Mr. Moreland," he said, "I'm perfectly willing to spy for my country, it's a patriotic duty and I don't begrudge for a moment the fact it's unpaid and all the expenses seem to come out of my own pocket..."

Moreland was squinting at him, his face an oddly tolerant picture of amused bafflement. Vickery felt emboldened enough to continue.

"And, as you may or may not know, I am very, highly pro-American and a very strong supporter of the New Democratic Consensus — I know you must be above politics and all that, but even so. And I am a personal friend — or acquaintance, rather — of Phyllis Ann Curtin and others in her circle — such as Paul Zarnoff and young Brad Urquist... So what I mean, basically... My point is that I'm already doing my bit. And then I've got my business affairs. Lots of them. So Africa... Not really do-able, if you see what I mean. Not really on the cards. Jason never mentioned it, and I —"

"You're the guy who works for Bryce Kellerman, aren't you?" Moreland said.

"What? No, no, no. *He* does things for *me*. And I pay him. But what I —"

"It doesn't matter. You're going to Africa, my friend."

"No, I'm not."

Moreland took a deep breath. Vickery tensed.

"You Brits," he said, "you just don't get it, do you?"

"Get what?" Vickery said.

"We are in a war," Moreland said. "A global war. An all-encompassing war. There is no place you can go where this war does not exist. You cannot hide from it. You cannot deny it. You cannot refuse to participate. Let me explain something for you."

147

Here Moreland gave some kind of secret signal to Walsh, who suddenly found the energy to kick back his chair and scamper from the room.

"Let me explain it for you," Moreland repeated. "Let me lay it all out for you, so you can understand."

Vickery knew all about the War Zones and how they represented a transitional phase between old-style tyranny and the moral, practical and financial benefits to be bestowed upon those yearning for freedom by the New Democratic Consensus, when it finally showed up in person. The moral stuff had mostly come from Zarnoff who, though he had a tendency to analyze everything in terms of what the Nazis or the Soviets did or didn't do, had sold enough books to convince most people that he knew what he was talking about.

Muller had been his source on practical benefits: If, in the process of democratization, he had pointed out, you were forced to completely smash a country up, then at some point the damage had to be repaired — and this meant jobs and, more importantly, contracts.

And Urquist had explained the enormous financial opportunities that would inevitably arise, although Vickery privately doubted that the "survivors", as Urquist called them, would take to the newly-created collateralized debt obligation market as eagerly as Urquist believed.

Two things that no one had really explained, however, were how many War Zones would prove to be required; and how long the transitional phase would last.

But, clued-in as he was, Vickery thought it best to humor Moreland.

"Fire away," he said.

Moreland poked him in the chest.

"We'll get one thing straight right here, Mr. Alan Vickery," he said. "You work for Bryce Kellerman, number one, and your fancy friend Jason, number two. You got that? You do what they say. Am I getting through to you? I hope so. Bryce Kellerman tells you to do something, you do it. Jason wants you in Africa, you get on a plane. If we ever see each other again, you and I, if we ever talk together again like this — that means you're dead meat. Do you have any problem comprehending that phrase? Is there any lack of clarity here on my part? Do you need me to clarify?"

"No, no," Vickery said. "Seems fairly clear. On the whole." Who *was* this bastard and why was he so angry?

"On the whole," Moreland repeated. "On the whole. Did you ever fight in a war, Mr. Alan Vickery?"

"Not really," Vickery said.

"You like the big boys to do your fighting for you?"

"I wouldn't say that."

"I fought the Soviets and the Cubans in Angola. And we saved Angola from the communists. What were you doing? Sitting on some campus, smoking dope and growing your hair?"

Vickery said nothing. He'd never smoked dope. His hair was now as long as it had ever been. And he'd never been on a campus — except for the Liberty Club spread in Oklahoma. This man Moreland was an idiot.

"Then I fought the Soviets again in Afghanistan. And we beat them again. We weakened them. Fatally."

Moreland seemed to be drifting off into some kind of martial day-dream.

"But, you know what?" he said.

Vickery waited.

"You kill off the big devil... And suddenly all these little devils are popping up here, and there, and everywhere."

He paused to let Vickery absorb this.

"And then there's another big devil waiting just down the pike. And, my — he's a big one. You know who I'm talking about, Mr. Alan Vickery?"

"China?"

"You got it. Not so dumb, are you?"

"No."

"You and I share the same values, don't we, Mr. Vickery? I think we do. But there are some — perhaps many — who don't. They just don't. Who can say why? They just don't. And it's because of that that they hate us. And they want to destroy our way of life. Even though they envy us, which they do. They do. And some of them even come from within our own ranks. They walk among us. Which is troubling. Very troubling. We cannot afford to wait for them to come to us. We must go to them. That is our destiny. And you must be a part of it. You're with me now, aren't you?"

"More or less," Vickery said, recalling Phil's advice that the best thing to do when confronted by a psycho was to flatter or humor them.

"We'll be allies, you and I. You will be a loyal ally for me. And I will be a powerful ally for you."

"Okay."

"And we will take the fight forward."

"Forward, yes."

"And so what do you propose to do, Mr. Alan Vickery? Do you sit in one of your charming, old-fashioned pubs and cry into your beer? Do you turn on your BBC and listen to how everything is your own fault, or the Americans' fault, and how you need to make nice with all the people who want to kill you?"

"Well, no, but you could argue —"

"We don't argue, Mr. Vickery, we act. You act. You execute your mission. We take the fight to the enemy."

"Do we?"

"We do. You are present at the inception, Mr. Vickery. You are privileged to have been chosen. Others, as we speak, are doing their part."

"Are they?"

"Yes. And now it's your turn."

CHAPTER 18

They saw him from a distance. It was a wide, unwalked street, with a desolate median and dry gutters full of sand. The houses were low and well-fenced, as in Windhoek — but without the electric wires.

As they drove slowly up the street the security lights came on one by one, reflecting off the tire-polished salt. The few dogs that weren't asleep rose to bark for the duration of the illumination and then fell silent.

This couldn't be their guy, Dale thought. He was too old, too thick and unhealthy; he looked like one of those depressed and secretly impoverished white retirees who hadn't got long to go and had already been forgotten by the trend-setting elites in Windhoek. He seemed to be watching them, standing immobile, his hands on his hips, staring down the street in their direction.

But when Dale pulled the car alongside him and stopped, he realized that the man hadn't been watching them at all. Whatever it was that had engaged this doom-struck stare of his must have vanished before he and Sheryl rolled their rented Toyota out of the gathering sea-mist and into this most unlikely street for a chalet-style hotel for the independent traveler.

"Hi," Dale said. "Excuse me. We're looking for George Fischer? The Desert Garden Hotel?"

The man turned to them and pushed his head in through Sheryl's open window, causing her to recoil.

"Excuse me?" Dale said.

The guy was checking out the car as if he were a border guard or a second-hand car-dealer.

"You are looking for a hotel?"

Dale noted a German accent, and suspicion.

"Yeah. The Desert Garden Hotel. It's supposed to be on this street. This is —"

"Yes, this is the street."

The guy ducked back out of the car and retreated to a narrow iron gate set into a high wall. Dale saw there was a small plaque fixed to the gate.

"This is it, right here!"

"That's him," Sheryl whispered.

151

Dale opened his door and stepped half out of the car.

"Okay," he said. "So are you George? Are you George Fischer?"

"Would you like to ask me if I have any rooms available?"

"Sure. I guess we need one, anyhow. How come you're standing out on the street like this? Were you expecting us?"

"You have come from South Africa?"

He had seen their license plates.

"Yes."

"I suppose you are bringing me suitcases of money."

If this really was the guy, Dale thought, Walter was going to need an update on his condition, physical and mental.

"Not really," he said. "Don't have much money at all, to tell the truth. Are you George? Is he here?"

"Then what do you want? Don't you know Arnie Muller was already here?"

"Don't know anyone by that name. How about Walter? Do you —"

"Walter Gabo," Sheryl said. "He sent us. He gave us a message for you. Look, George, we need your help. We really do. It is you, isn't it?"

There was a pause. The man stepped up to the car again.

"Yes. But you will have to prove that Walter sent you. It does not seem so probable to me. Please follow me with your car."

George led them further up the street to a heavy steel gate and an enclosed compound in which there were three other cars.

"Leave your car here," he said. "We will go in this way. Quietly, please. I have guests."

*

G eorge played the video all the way through with his fist clenched against his mouth and without saying a word. Dale sat awkwardly on George's sofa, wincing at the image of himself on the screen. He looked like a worried puppy. Walter seemed to be talking directly to George. Both Sheryls — the one on-screen and the one beside him — seemed calm and detached. But whereas on-screen Sheryl folded her hands in her lap, off-screen Sheryl put her arm around his waist.

At the end of the recording, George hit the rewind button and left the room — some kind of lounge for the residents, Dale guessed. On the coffee table were glossy travel magazines and a thin publication dedicated to What was On in Swakopmund.

"So what do you think?" Sheryl asked.

"I don't know. Doesn't look like the guy who's going to save Africa."

"No."

"Why does he think we've got suitcases of cash?"

"He thought we were someone else."

"Who?"

George returned. With him was a tall, thin, black woman with long hair, lightly braided, and a delicate oval face. It could almost have been the sister of the manageress at the Quiver Tree — a little taller, maybe. Such a striking resemblance. Or was it? Suddenly he wasn't so sure. Perhaps later he would mention it to Sheryl. Or perhaps not. Of course, one thing the manageress didn't have was a limp.

Something had happened to George. He had been taciturn and suspicious, stiff and practically hostile, a real cold-fish kind of guy; now it was like Dale and Sheryl were old friends who'd come through tough times, and not creditors come to repossess his hotel. He still seemed tense, but there was color in his face, animation in his limbs and something hot and urgent in his eyes. Well, that was how it seemed to Dale. He would have to check with Sheryl to be sure.

"This," George said, "is Roberta. Please excuse me for my earlier rudeness. There was a reason but, even so, it is not such a good thing for my business. Roberta is my manager. We have known each other for many years."

He seemed to lose his train of thought. Roberta sat next to Sheryl. George watched.

"Yes, it is so. Many years. I am afraid we must watch this video again. Then we will talk."

He started the video but then stopped it again just as Walter began to speak.

"But are you hungry? If so we will eat. After the video? Yes?"

"Sure," Dale said. As a matter of fact he was hungry, real hungry. The trouble with guys like Jay and Callaghan was they never stopped to eat. Always plotting and scheming and tricking people and never bothering to feed themselves. Starving themselves crazy. This guy George ran a hotel. He would know better.

As Dale watched the video roll for the second time it occurred to him that it looked like a kids' TV show: The three of them squished up together on the couch, with Walter the big old friendly bear; Sheryl the cool chick, flicking her hair behind her ears; and himself the token dork who wouldn't get his contract renewed. But Walter wasn't talking about movies or downloads.

Old enemies, Walter was saying; old enemies with new confidence and unlimited ambition. Everything now was out of balance; asymmetric, according to Walter. What was he talking about? Callaghan had said that the Ellises lived life like a balancing act. Walter wanted George to remember that even in the past, when they had fought with their hands and feet and guns, they had known that, one day, they would have to fight with their heads and their minds. Africa never got left alone for long. This was true; Dale had read as much in the book — a thousand-page history of Africa — that Bill Ellis dropped on his desk during his first week at the embassy. He hadn't gotten past the introduction, but the point had been made.

Walter talked about SWAPO and the People's Liberation Army of Namibia, the South African special forces and an outfit called the Koevoet, that seemed particularly to disgust him. Dale saw George nod.

"It means crowbar," Roberta said, in Sheryl's ear. "They were supposed to be a counter-insurgency force."

"Some of those gentlemen are still around," Walter said on the video, wagging his finger at the unseen George. "Do you know where they've been? Where do you think? You can guess, can't you?"

Walter was laughing, in that nervous way you laugh when someone tells you something preposterous but also hideous.

"They're fat now, like you and me, but they're fit. And they've got everything they want. All this money. More than they ever had."

Suitcases of cash, Dale thought.

"What do we have?" Walter asked sternly and then waited as if he expected George to fill in the blank. "Forget about the Russians and the Cubans. They have their own problems, God knows. China? They don't want any foreign wars. The UN? When it's too late they'll pass a resolution. George, I'll tell you what we have."

Walter went on to describe Dale and Sheryl as — unquestionably in his view — devotees of truth and justice, who had been instrumental in the essential but incomplete resolution of the case of the kidnapped American bankers. Walter was sure that George was familiar with the affair. Moreover, Dale and Sheryl were close friends of Bill and Elaine Ellis, and loyal too. This, also, was self-evident to Walter.

Close friends? Like Jay and Callaghan before him, Walter was unafraid of spin. He was a politician.

At this point George paused the video and looked at Roberta. She shrugged and smiled back.

Dale took the opportunity to ask a question. The few radio stations they'd picked up on the drive were either in Afrikaans or else seemed to play nothing but German oompah music.

"Do you know what happened?"

"Hmm?"

"After they showed the video on the BBC?"

George looked bemused.

"Yes, of course. She was in London. The Americans rescued her and the British hid her while their operation continued. She is still under their protection. There were miscommunications."

"But that isn't what happened," Sheryl said.

"Does it matter?" George asked.

It did; it mattered like hell. But Dale said nothing.

"What about Charles Barclay?" Sheryl said.

"He was not mentioned."

"Is he dead?"

George seemed to consider this a question worth thinking over.

"I think not. Not yet. It will depend on what happens now."

There was a silence. Roberta looked at George as if she knew what he was about to say. George addressed Sheryl.

"It may depend on you," he said, resuming the video.

No, Dale thought. It can't. It won't. We're out of this. No more errands, no more crazy stunts, no more crazy people. But then he felt Sheryl's hand on his shoulder.

On screen, Walter described how Dale and Sheryl had undertaken their selfless mission to his apartment. This was a story that depended implausibly on unnamed friends and contacts of Walter's who were one hundred percent reliable, and which omitted any mention of Callaghan or his hapless but luxurious assistant. Or, of course, Jay. Dale could see that George didn't buy it but didn't care either.

But George had a question.

"Dale. You appeared also in this security video with the woman?"

"Yes."

"But you were not in it when I saw it."

"No, I was in it."

"I think they edited you out."

Dale remembered Callaghan's crack about someone putting the screws on the Beeb, as he called it.

"Not so good for you, I think," George said. "But we will see."

The video ran on, but Dale stopped watching. What wasn't so good? Sheryl whispered in his ear.

"Don't you see, now?" she said.

The video ran to its conclusion — a bejeweled, female hand replacing the lens cap before turning off the camera. Callaghan had missed this and George, evidently, didn't care.

Walter wound up with a list of exhortations. George was to be prepared for unwelcome visitors; to resist all temptation (to succumb would be understandable, given the nature of the times, but nevertheless a betrayal of the gravest order); to extend his trust and hospitality to Dale and Sheryl, whose well-being was vital; to put aside any misgivings George might have concerning present leadership of the ANC or, indeed, the Economic Freedom Fighters; to remember that Walter could make available to George certain resources, should they be needed; and, most importantly, it was essential that George never try to communicate with Walter electronically — only by letter or word of mouth.

What Walter didn't say, Dale thought, was exactly what he wanted George to do. Kind of funny, that.

"There must be more." George said. Perhaps there is a letter? Perhaps Walter entrusted you with a letter for me?"

Dale remembered.

"Yes. Sure, that's right, there was a letter. It's in the car. I'll go —"

"Did you read it?"

"No. It was sealed. Shall I go get it?"

"Please. If you would."

On his way to the parking lot, Dale stopped and looked back into the lounge through the glass doors. George had taken his seat next to Sheryl. Sheryl was talking. Roberta would interrupt, as if to ask questions. He saw now that she looked nothing like the manageress at the Quiver Tree.

Outside, the air was still and cool and he felt he could feel the sea-fog crawling up over the dunes. There was silence. Moisture had begun to condense on the cars in the lot. It almost never rained here, but there was life in the dunes, sustained by the fog that came by night. Every morning this lonely, forgotten town woke up damp and waited for the sun. It was a strange — but perhaps logical — place to come to, if you wanted to escape.

George's guests were all asleep; there were no lights on. They had probably driven up from Sossusvlei today, having done the dune-walk thing in the early morning, before it got too hot. Tomorrow they would head north or east. They didn't know they were being waited on by a hero of African Independence, if that's what George was. Well, perhaps so — but somehow, Dale felt, that wasn't the sum of what George was.

He dawdled over to the car, searching his pockets for the keys. Tomorrow, they should just take off, drive a couple of hundred kilometers and stop some place. Any place — so long as no one else knew where they were. He would convince Sheryl that enough was enough. They needed to go home. Good luck to Walter and George and Africa in general and maybe even Callaghan. Good luck and we hope it all works out. Just leave us alone now, please. And Jay could take care of himself. This was a good plan. All he had to figure out was what to say to Sheryl.

He had parked carelessly to the left of the three white Toyotas belonging to George's guests. Now he saw that a large, gray pickup had blocked him in. Why? George had space enough for a dozen cars. And how had it gotten in? The gates were locked.

It was a new pickup with a double cab and tinted glass. Another Toyota. But although it was new it was already filthy. He stepped around to the front of the cab. There were dents in the fenders and dried mud and leaves in the radiator grille. Moving on around, he saw that the driver's door was scored and scratched and patched with duct tape, which was beginning to peel off.

Feeling irked and reckless, he pulled at one of the strips. Underneath was a line of ragged holes. In spite of himself he began to laugh. Who else could it be? He was about to yell out when he felt the hand on his shoulder.

"Hey, don't be doing that, Dale, my man. The sand gets in there, you know, and the electric windows, they kind of seize up."

"Jay, are those..."

"What?"

"Bullet holes?"

"Yeah."

"But who —"

"Never mind. You want this truck? I'm going to have to get me a new one."

"No. No. What are you talking about?"

"You're right. Trucks don't matter. Money doesn't matter. Letters matter. Did you give it to him yet?"

"What?"

"The letter from your old friend Walter to your new friend George."

"No. It's in the car."

"Yeah, I figured. In the car. Which, I'm ashamed to say, I could not break into. All the same, you ought to keep your important documents with you. On your person. How's Sheryl?"

"She's okay. But she's —"

"Open the car, Dale."

He was too tired to argue. But once Jay saw that the letter was sealed, he seemed to lose interest in it.

"Okay, so give him the letter. If you get a chance, take a look at it. Don't go out of your way."

"What are you doing here, Jay?"

"What do you think?"

156

"I don't know. But listen, okay? Tomorrow, we're out of this, whatever it is. We're going home. Jennifer, she's free, she's safe, and that's all I — that's all we..."

"That's all you care about? What about Bill and Elaine?"

"I want to help everyone, Jay. But I can't. Can you?"

"What makes you think she's free?"

"No, no. You're just saying that. George just told us."

"He doesn't know."

"We're going home."

"No, I don't think so."

"Are you listening? We're going home."

"Who's going to protect you?"

"Give me the letter."

Jay handed it over.

"Who do you think has been protecting you so far?"

Dale marched back to the hotel door and stopped. Jay scooted up behind him.

"Yeah. That's right. Sleep tight. See you in the morning."

Dale sighed.

"Jay?"

"What?"

"How did you get in here? It's supposed to be secure."

"I asked some English girl for the combination. Said I was a guest."

"What is that, an old CIA trick?"

"Yeah. Good night, Dale."

CHAPTER 19

Alan Vickery woke up in comfortable but unfamiliar surroundings — a luxurious bedroom of some sort, with black sheets and spot-lit artwork. Where was he? How did he get here? And was it costing him money?

He struggled to remember, winding back the fuzzy tape in his mind to the episode at the embassy in which he had tussled with the powerful and beguiling but otherwise loony Douglas Moreland, the nut who wanted to rule Africa.

That had been memorable. What had happened afterward?

He remembered tumbling from the American Embassy in a blur of conflicting emotions — pride, fear, confidence, wonder; and a queasy, gnawing emotion that he couldn't put a name to but which he had once or twice felt on the rare occasions that Mariella's mother had come to stay. It was no use trying to analyze these things; that way lay moral paralysis or, in the case of Mariella's mother, pointed questions about what he'd got to look so bloody miserable about.

But all these complex emotions had to be put on hold when he realized he'd left his spy-phone behind at the baggage check and thus had to negotiate his way back in past machine-gun-toting coppers, platoons of surly marines, committees of steel-rimmed bureaucrats and a janitor with an attitude. After all this it had been disconcerting to find that Jason hadn't attempted to contact him at all — piqued, quite possibly, that Moreland had bounced the suave MI6 man while choosing instead to fête — was that the word? — Vickery, the rough diamond. Well, fête and intimidate, to be honest.

He remembered leaning against a concrete barricade thinking what a long day it had been. Then a policewoman had instructed him that he was loitering in a designated "avenue of fire" and therefore ought to push off. He had been so tired. Power-politics, it was clear, took it out of you. He had needed a whole night of soft, restoring sleep. Doubting that he could get one at his own house, he had begun, as he dragged himself through the glistening streets of Vauxhall, to consider his options.

Option one had been the Edgware Road. But it was rest he had needed, not stimulation. He could have retraced his steps to Cricklewood — option two — and thrown cheap gravel at Phil's burglar-proof windows. But he couldn't remember everything he'd said to Phil and had felt uneasy about facing him again so soon. Or — option three — he could have set course for Paddington and the Institute and slept on the couch in his office, religious rites permitting. This, at the time, had looked like the best bet.

But it seemed that option four — the mystery option — had been selected. Black sheets: Who could it be? He flipped through his mental rolodex — the super-secure one. There was only one candidate.

Briefly, he flashed back to the scene in Vauxhall.

"Alan!" Someone had yelled. (Why were people always yelling at him?)

It was a familiar voice. Bounding up behind Vickery, his beige mackintosh flapping and cracking in the dampening air, came Kellerman, or a ghostly likeness thereof. Had he issued forth from the grim portals of the embassy itself, the belly of a black cab or merely the gates of hell? It was hard to say. But he didn't look too clever.

"Bryce!" Vickery said, as Kellerman juddered to a halt in stages — legs first, then jowls, then gut. "You don't look too clever. Everything all right? How'd you know where to find me?"

Kellerman didn't answer. Wisely, Vickery observed, he had given priority to breathing.

"Alan," he wheezed at length, "we got more problems. You gotta come back to my place."

So that explained it. This was Kellerman's crash pad or pied-à-terre. You could imagine what went on here. And it was enough to make your skin crawl. The bedroom was windowless, but at least it didn't have mirrors on the ceiling.

He needed to get himself together and plan his escape — if only he could remember what he'd done with his clothes. But Kellerman burst into the bedroom while Vickery was still hunting for them.

"Shit! Sorry, Alan. I put your stuff in the closet. Here. See?"

Kellerman activated a secret panel. It slid open to reveal a cavernous wardrobe empty but for Vickery's suit and shoes. Vickery stared at the suit.

"Oh yeah," Kellerman said. "That's right. I had them launder your other stuff. How about this? I'll have them go fetch it?"

Kellerman vanished. Vickery got back into bed. A minute or so later, a silent and suspicious maid brought Vickery his shirt, underwear and socks.

There were gaps in his memory. He blamed Jason for shoving drugs down his throat and Phil for plying him with liquor. All the same, he preferred not to remember how, or with whose help, he had disrobed the night before.

He flung open the bedroom door with the intention of muscling downstairs to the kitchen and demanding coffee as a precondition of opening any kind of negotiations with Kellerman. But he found himself disoriented, teetering on some kind of lofty mezzanine engineered out of stainless steel and brushed aluminum, with the sun in his eyes and the ocean at his feet.

It wasn't the ocean, of course — it was the Thames. Kellerman had acquired some kind of triple-height penthouse with glass walls and built-in international lifestyle. As his eyes adjusted to the brightness, Vickery took in the view. He was still in Vauxhall, he realized, and not so far from the velvety comforts of Chelsea. There had to be something potent in the soil here; it sprouted post-modern architecture (or was it post-post-modern by now?) the way Bethnal Green pushed up art galleries. Mariella and Marie-Thérèse would have hated this place. It was cold, clinical, minimalist. Which, when you thought about it, was highly ironical in Mariella's case.

Down below in the foreground and screaming for attention was the Palace of Spies, the MI6 headquarters. It reminded Vickery of the National Theatre — one of Mariella's favored venues until, she claimed, it stopped doing musicals and started pandering to text-messagers — except that it looked much more expensive and was, of course, more dramatic. Vickery pictured Jason lolling, even then, over a cappuccino and a croissant in the Secrets-n-Lies cafeteria or the Flavors of the World food court, skimming the latest hot report from some doomed dictator's boudoir.

In the background, on the northern bank of the river, was the Palace of Politicians. How strange, Vickery thought: The spies lived in a cheery, open, glassy, modern, high-tech office park; and the politicians lived in a dark, depressing, impenetrable, antique, fake-gothic rat-run. Aylsham liked to rant about the Mother of Parliaments and centuries of tradition. Let him. The world was being run — strictly under license, of course — from the other side of the river.

From below came voices, one loud and truculent, the other soft, hesitant and cautious. The former belonged to Kellerman and might even have been trademarked by him. The other was familiar; whose was it?

Vickery located and shinned down a kind of spiral stairway. In Kellerman's open-plan kitchen were two men: Kellerman himself, in a hooded tracksuit bearing some business school logo; and Fat Phil, in his customary gray suit and posture of owlish unease. They sat at a glass table loaded with pastries. It looked like a Weight Watchers' shock ad.

"Hullo, Alan," Phil said, his voice laden with a weary sadness.

"Hey, Alan! Park it here and load up. It's all-you-can-eat."

"Great. Thanks. Phil, I, er... Actually, all I want is some coffee."

"Unleaded?" Kellerman asked.

"What?"

"Decaf."

"No. No, just ordinary. Thanks. Er, Phil..."

"Oh, right," Kellerman said, "you're still having the memory problems, aren't you? You wanna get that looked at. Longer you leave it, the more it'll cost —"

"No, there's nothing wrong with me," Vickery said. "It's those bloody pills that... Never mind."

"Pills'll do it, Alan. What is it? OxyContin? I knew this guy, they had to let him go. Worked at the Supreme Court. One day it was the Constitution in Exile, next day it was building on precedent. You get what I'm saying? Extreme mood swings."

Kellerman looked like he was about to recommend a specialist.

"I'm perfectly all right," Vickery said. "As a matter of fact, I take care of myself."

Phil nodded, very slowly.

"But," he said, "you don't deny yourself an occasional evening of relaxation, do you, Alan?"

"No," Vickery said. "Why would I?" He swigged his coffee, which hit the spot immediately. "But the point is, Phil, why are you here? Why am I here?"

"We had to act, Alan. Your vital interests are at stake."

"What?"

"Is Mariella available for comment, by any chance? We know she's a busy woman. Reachable, is she?"

"Mariella?"

Why were they raving on about Mariella? And where the hell was she anyway? He couldn't remember.

"Switzerland, I think you said, Alan? Got a mobile, has she? Give her a bell, can you?"

"Tell her to fly her ass back over here," Kellerman advised — not that it was advice that anyone who knew Mariella would ever think of proffering. Phil positively blanched.

"A little word on the phone, could you, Alan?"

Vickery drank the rest of his coffee, peering over the rim of his mug, daring the two of them to start something. This nonsense had to be walked back to its origin. *Walked back* — where had he picked up that expression? Was it Jason?

"Listen," he said to Kellerman. "I want to know how I got here. And I want to know how *he* got here."

Phil bit his lip. Vickery realized he'd been rude.

"Oh Phil, you fat old bastard, I'm sorry," he said by way of apology. "Bit stressed-out, to be honest. I just feel a bit stitched-up, you know. I mean, you two don't know each other, right? And here you both are banging on about Mariella..."

Kellerman raised his paws like a bear trying to break up a fight between two other bears.

"Okay, Alan. Here it is. I found you wandering the streets in some kind of trance or stupor, call it what you will. Some issues had kind of come up, so I suggested to you, very nicely, that you accompany me back here to my humble friggin' abode. And you very graciously agreed. So we take a short walk and here we are. And you're really, really out of it by this point, but I stick with it because, like Phil says, your interests are at stake."

"What interests?"

"I'm coming to that. Jesus, Alan, I've got my own problems, you know."

There was a pause while Kellerman waited for Vickery to ask about his problems.

"Interests," Phil said, steering the agenda. "Alan's interests."

Kellerman glowered.

"We sat," Kellerman said, "at this very table. You don't remember?"

Vickery shook his head.

"I reminded you," Kellerman continued, assuming a more business-like tone, "that we had certain items of unfinished business that... That we had not addressed."

He came across now like a CEO on dress-down Friday. Phil looked like an owl who'd been appointed to the board to vote with management and make up the numbers.

"And I further advised you," Kellerman said, the new tone faltering already, "that I had a bunch of big-hitters on my ass screaming for action. And I asked you — I pleaded with you — to give me a name. Someone to call. Anyone."

Vickery's memory began to knit itself back together, in ominous and disturbing ways. Phil was toying with his napkin.

"At first you refused. I'm not going to say I wasn't hurt. Hey, have I ever denied you anything?"

Respect, Vickery thought, subversively.

"So then I gave you the news."

"What news?"

"The news about how there's a break-in at Union Bank. And a fire. And there's all this data that's missing. And suddenly your name is on everybody's lips."

"Everybody?"

"No, not everybody, you jerk. This isn't public. I'm talking about the guys who are on my ass. Did you hear what I said? I said Union Bank."

"Oh. But that's the bank that General Freaky — I mean, that woman..."

"Okay, so now you're catching on. And, as I explained to you last night, you are not going to blow this fucking deal. We are going to do this and then you are on the first plane to Amsterdam, okay?"

"Okay. Do what?"

"Nail that woman."

"Nail?"

"Nail. She's a threat to you. That's why you gave me *his* phone number."

Kellerman, it seemed, had little time for Phil's feelings.

"No, no, no," Vickery said. "How can she be a threat? I don't have any accounts there. Never dealt with them. For one thing, their charges —"

"They found your name."

"No..."

"She busts into the bank somehow. Obviously, she has help. Who? We don't know. Could be that friggin' Pennyman woman. She's political. Connected. Wants to stick it to the financial sector. But anyway, Lenehan looks in their dirty books, and *your* name is all over them. What can I tell you?"

"Wouldn't hide accounts from me, Alan, would you?" Phil said. "Course not. Mariella, I would think. Must be. Mention it at all, did she, Alan?"

"Well, no, but —"

"No one gives a shit, Alan," Kellerman said. "It's *your* name. We gotta stop her. Look."

Kellerman pushed a slew of newspapers at Vickery.

"Check it out. The Liberty guys, Flint, the others — they're all doing their bit. Now you're going to do yours. It's not like you personally have to..."

"Have to what?"

"Oh, for Christ's sake..."

"Best way, Alan, don't you think?" Phil said. "I mean, these accounts... Mariella? Who knows?"

"We know where she is." Kellerman said.

"Mariella?"

"No, friggin' Lenehan."

"We do?"

"Sure. All we're waiting for is —"

There was an urgent buzzing sound. Kellerman snatched a cordless intercom from underneath a stack of newspapers.

"Yeah?"

Kellerman seemed to concentrate for a moment.

"Okay. Send him up."

"Who is it?" Vickery asked.

"His friggin' nephew," Kellerman said, with a nod towards Phil.

"My frigging nephew," Phil said.

*

A lan Vickery never panicked, so what he gave in to couldn't have been panic. It was just something vaguely similar.

"Stop this bloody van. I'm getting out."

"What?"

"Stop the bloody van."

"We can't, Alan, we'll lose —"

"Stop!"

Sean hit the brakes — which, Vickery noticed, weren't any good because, instead of screeching to a halt as he'd expected, the van merely lumbered to the side of the street and bumped up on the pavement.

He grabbed his garment bag and leaped from his seat, a plastic crate of some sort. Stepping over coils of rope, lagoons of oil or paint and boxes of nails, he rattled the doors at the back of the van and, since they didn't immediately open, began kicking at them.

"Oh, for... Hang on, hang on."

Sean's mate — Vickery hadn't asked his name and hadn't been told — jumped out of the passenger seat, loped around to the back of the van and released him.

The van's engine revved. Vickery ran up to Sean's window.

"Sean!"

Sean said something — probably "Fuck off, Alan'.

Vickery banged on the window with his free hand. Sean wound it half-way down.

"Be careful."

"What?"

"Be careful. I mean be gentle."

"What?"

"Don't..."

"Don't what?"

"Don't..."

"Alan, are you stupid or something? Get out of the way. Fuck off."

The van lurched back on to the road and screamed away to a chorus of horns and flashing headlights. Vickery flagged a cab, flung his garment bag on the floor and collapsed on the back seat, breathing heavily even though he hadn't been exerting himself.

"Where to, sir?"

"Huh?"

"Where would you like to go, sir?"

"Heathrow."

"Very good, sir."

No, not very good, he thought; terrible, awful, bloody horrible. Really, bloody, horrible.

But not his fault.

Immediately he imagined himself back outside Sean's window, this time saying what he had meant to say: "This is not me, okay? This is Bryce Kellerman. Bryce bloody Kellerman. It's his idea. It's nothing to do with me. I wash my hands. All right?"

This seemed to cover matters. It sounded reasonable. He'd made his position clear. Sean had taken the money from Vickery's hands, true. But it was Kellerman's money. That obviously made a huge difference. And, yes, he'd been in the van. But he wasn't in it now, was he? He'd only got into the van in the first place because Kellerman had yelled and insisted. And he'd needed a lift. No harm in accepting a lift, was there? If you couldn't accept a lift just because there was a chance that...

What had he said? *Be gentle?* Some kind of hideous internal cringe formed itself in his toes and clawed its way up through his knees, stomach and throat until it sweated its way out through his forehead and he thought he was going to faint. He tipped his head back against the seat and closed his eyes. Each bump in the road and each feint of the cab jarred his skull and rippled across his brain. The straining of the engine filled his ears.

Against the insides of his eyelids and against his will, a jumpy picture show now played itself out.

Mariella: Smiling at him while her girlfriends sniggered and he tried to get his car out of a snowdrift in some French ski-hole; sweet-talking him out of his plan to buy a mansion in Chigwell; throwing out his suits from Moss Bros and Debenhams and dragging him along to her father's tailor; telling him stories about how the girls at her school had thrown away their lives and how dull and useless their husbands were; planning their first trip to America and already knowing which places to go to; proposing to him over dinner at a cacophonous restaurant in Rome while he was still fighting off the previous day's hangover.

Sara: Looking like her mother from the day she was born; questioning her father's vocabulary when she was ten; staging that never-explained tantrum when he visited her school for some art-slash-craft show; crying when she surpassed her mother's weight a week after her sixteenth birthday; calling him "Alan' to her university friends when she thought he couldn't hear.

And then Mariella again, sitting up with him all night the day his mother died, until she persuaded him to pick up the phone and call his father.

The noise of the cab seemed to fade. Feeling chilled now, he pulled his coat around him. A sensation he hadn't felt for years descended on him — a clammy, seeping loneliness. He folded his arms and yearned for the airport.

There was a fake pub inside Terminal Five. After he dismounted from his taxi and over-tipped the driver, Alan Vickery made straight for it.

Here, in a corner near the toilets and underneath a dusty display of antique agricultural tools, he whipped out his spy-phone and dialed J for Jason. For some reason his hand was trembling. He wiped a puddle of beer off the table with an abandoned newspaper, put the phone down and donned his high-tech ear-piece, making himself look like an estate agent on the verge of a stag weekend.

After about thirty seconds of computerized twittering, Jason's plump vowels came dripping across the encrypted ether.

"Good of you to check in, Alan. Everything going to plan?"

Since he didn't feel entirely in on the plan, this was impossible to say.

"Yes. I'm at —"

"Don't tell me. Mm, yes... Heathrow, isn't it?"

"Yes. I —"

"Excellent. Glad they've got that working again. And you're off to Amsterdam?"

"Yes. Jason. When you —"

"And you're going to all those meetings we discussed?"

"Yes. But —"

"Good, good. Excuse me a moment. Yes, it's working now, you can leave it. What? No, I didn't touch it. All right. Thank you. Alan?"

"Yes. Look, Jason —"

"And how did you get on with Mr. Moreland? Bit of a bruiser, isn't he? Gets results, though, we're told."

Moreland was a freak show, but if Jason couldn't see that it was his own lookout.

"Fine, fine. Listen. You just want me to..."

"To what?"

"Go with the flow, as it were."

"That's right. Just keep us informed."

"You don't want me... To do things — or not do things... To get in the way... To, you know, risk my position by acting... To change the course of history in any way, so to speak?"

"Change the course of history? Certainly not, Alan. Perish the thought. You've got enough to do. You leave that to us, ha-ha."

Ha-ha yourself, he thought, you bloody stuck-up twat.

"I mean there's no way I should be held responsible —"

"No, no, Alan. You're not responsible. What are you so het up about? Relax. Go and have a snifter of lager, or whatever you drink. So you got on with Moreland? Interesting. That's good for us, I think. A win. Well done, Alan. I'm going to put a little silver star in your file."

"What?"

"Figure of speech. It's all computerized."

Never mind the bloody computers, he thought.

"So I have immunity, then?"

"What? Oh, you're totally untouchable, Alan. Believe me. Is there anything else? We've got a lot on here. No?"

"I suppose not."

"Good. Happy hunting. Don't forget to call. Bye!"

Vickery powered off the spy-phone and ripped out his ear piece. Was there any way he could have recorded this conversation? No, forget it — it was probably futile in any case. The main point was... That he could stop worrying. At least for now. There was business to be done — exciting new business. He could be happy about that, couldn't he? And, even if Jason had seemed a little off-hand or frivolous, the fact remained that he, Vickery, was acting in best interests of the nation. And spying was a rough game. What else was there to be said?

He mused on his upcoming agenda: Offshore bank accounts, front companies, cross-ownership schemes, disguised payments, slush funds, slippery bankers, bent lawyers. With the added excitement and glamor of military hardware. Another chance to demonstrate his virtuosity. All the heavy hitters watching his progress with interest. The big time. And, when it was all over, the favors to be called in and the strings to be pulled.

After a while he remembered that he needed to go and check in.

CHAPTER 20

George Fischer stood, at nine o'clock in the morning, in the middle of the secure, gated compound by the side of his property, the modern, well-run, improbably chalet-style Desert Garden Hotel, and could not help but remark to himself how utterly different everything was today from the day before.

The sea-fog was slightly thicker than usual. It condensed on his hair and his shoulders, and the smell of the salt — never strong — was just fractionally stronger. The hummock dunes, whose historic siege against his southern retaining wall occupied him the way a small war in North Africa might have vexed Napoleon, seemed to have advanced perhaps three millimeters more than during the average night. And his electric gates did not glide quite as noiselessly as they had glided the day before.

Nevertheless, everything had changed.

Sand would regularly blow over his walls and collect in clumps and drifts — proto-dunes that, if not repulsed, would colonize the compound within weeks. On days when he felt so inclined or it became necessary he would shovel and rake, leaving a thin layer of sand on top of the compacted salt, the result being the desiccated facsimile of a Zen garden. Had he performed this rite last night he would now have been able to make sense of the tire tracks at his feet. It was almost as if there had been a ghostly, two-thousand-kilogram visitor in the night.

This visitor, if such there had been, had not interfered with the guests' cars. George felt grateful for this. There were to be no new arrivals today and, although half-affronted at himself for entertaining such thoughts, he wished his guests gone. All except for the young American couple.

As for the others — let them continue their holiday. Go and see the prehistoric rock art. Go up into Damaraland and say hello to the Himba and buy their authentic souvenirs; an indigenous culture might yet be saved. Go to Etosha. Go to the Skeleton Coast. But no — they couldn't afford that. Just go somewhere else. And then go home.

The young Americans seemed to believe that they could not return to Windhoek. This was probably so. They had driven all the way from Johannesburg, apparently taking a very bad route, simply in order to deliver a letter. And all this had been done under the influence of that wily old rogue Walter Gabo. Walter, perhaps not surprisingly, had succeeded in looking almost distinguished in his old age, although his video performance George found faintly comical. But it was probably meant as entertainment — as well as serving the function of authenticating the letter and its bearers.

The implication in the video and in the young couple's incomplete and confusing story — made explicit in the letter, of course — that George might be tempted to serve up his cherished contacts in the service of renewed military adventurism in Angola depressed him. Clearly Walter believed that Arnie Muller, or some similarly struggling expatriate diehard, had been plucked from the globalizing arms bazaars of Europe by the talent scouts of Imperialism, dusted down, sobered up, given a booster shot of ideology and dropped back into Africa to buy up — no expense too great — the only white man who could still broker deals with the ageing black revolutionary elites. Walter had a way of putting things. No wonder he became a politician.

But it was mostly rubbish. Muller wouldn't listen, of course. Perhaps he didn't care that much — except out of personal resentments harbored for decades, a special talent. His job, it appeared, was to distribute dollars by the truck-load, deducting, no doubt, a modest commission. (Were they honest dollars? Tax-payer dollars? What about the economic crisis? Did the CIA have its own printing press?) Had it occurred to Muller simply to drive his truck up to the SWAPO leadership and ask them how about it? Perhaps he foresaw that such tactlessness would fail and had decided on the subtle approach.

George had told Muller that he would cooperate. He had lied. Walter could relax about that. But Walter's other requirements — warning George's high-ranking contacts in Windhoek and Luanda; getting their active assistance; finding out where the dirty money was going; locating the imperialists' hidden bases; tracking their logistics; identifying spies and stooges — all this was too much. Couldn't Walter have figured out that many of George's former A-list comrades were now dead, retired or senile? And what was this assistance that Walter promised? Did Walter have his own private army? Did he expect George to organize, single-handed but for solid Dale and delicate Sheryl, a counter-revolution, insurgency or resistance?

And, yes, of course — did Walter even need to ask? — he would rescue Bill and Elaine Ellis from whatever non-existent, non-disclosed, black-site map reference they had been consigned to. As soon as Muller told him where it was and Walter lent him the Scorpions and the South African Air Force.

The best chance, in fact, was to do what Muller wanted. Besides, only then would he find out if Muller really knew the secret he claimed to know. Did Muller really think he knew the truth about Elizabeth Ellis? Who could have told him? Not Roberta. Had Muller ascended so high in the world that he was now on speaking terms with Douglas Moreland?

He heard the door open behind him. Roberta signaled to him. It was a familiar gesture and it meant that the guests wanted their breakfast. He picked up a strip of duct tape from the sand, deposited it in the garbage and returned to the kitchen.

Roberta was brisk and quiet. The guests ate quickly and almost in silence. A subdued atmosphere prevailed. The English couple left first; the Germans, twenty minutes later. Staff tips were disappointing. The Americans, installed in George's best room, had not appeared.

But as he shuttled between the dining room and the kitchen with the breakfast dishes he saw the young woman, Sheryl, standing outside on her own in the garden, dressed, as far as he could tell, in not much more than one of his luxurious Egyptian cotton bathrobes. Excusing himself from kitchen duties, he stepped outside.

"Two or three hours," he said, "and this will all be gone. We will see the sun."

She smiled at him — wanly, he would have said, having long been a studier of faces. With her hands thrust deep into her pockets, she glanced behind her, seemingly up at the windows of George's finest room, where the drapes were still drawn.

Why had Walter sent two of them? Not just to share the driving. Were they inseparable?

"Did you read the letter?" Sheryl asked.

She had shown no interest in the letter the night before. Her husband had done all the talking — rambling, nervous and making sense about two-thirds of the time.

"Yes, I read it."

"Walter wants your help."

He sighed.

"Walter wants many things. Walter wants too much. I am in a difficult position."

"You've already had a visit."

It wasn't a question. He wasn't sure how to respond.

"What are you going to do?" she said.

"Look for yourself. I run a hotel. I don't talk to politicians any more."

"Don't you?"

"What if they didn't listen to me?"

"If they believe you're acting for Walter they might."

This was true. But how could this woman possibly make such a subtle calculation?

"Yes, Walter has their affections, it is true. But what is it he can do, actually? Nothing."

"The South African government backs him. Unofficially."

"Exactly. It is unofficial. Nothing will happen. He expects me to do everything."

"Right. And you're already under pressure from the other side."

Again she surprised him. He took an involuntary step backwards, uncertain that he wanted to continue the conversation.

"Who came to see you?" she said.

Detached from her husband, she was almost a different woman. But the underlying sorrowfulness he thought he had detected on their arrival had not diminished; it seemed merely to have been put aside.

"Who was it?" she said.

"I don't think you know this man. But I will tell you anyway. His name is Arnie Muller."

She absorbed this without reacting.

"So Walter was right about that."

"Yes."

"When we arrived, you thought we were with this Muller guy."

"Yes."

"What did you think, exactly."

"CIA. Something. Whatever there is now."

Sheryl's eyes narrowed and the corner of her mouth turned up; was she trying to suppress a laugh? Was there some bitter humor here that he missed?

"So, George, look," she said. "You're not going to help this Muller guy, are you?"

"No."

"No?"

"No. He is a criminal. A murderer."

"Right. But..."

"But what?"

"But you're going to have to pretend to help him, George. Aren't you? Because otherwise..."

"Otherwise?"

"All this..."

She was surveying his hotel, his garden; and Roberta — standing in the lobby watching them. Again, he noticed, she glanced up at the bedroom window.

"George, we need to go talk to your friends," she said.

He stared at her: Her face was blank; her eyes, wide.

"How about Julius?" she said. "Doesn't he have a place near here? Do you think he's at home?"

Julius — former member of the SWAPO elite. How did she know about him? Walter?

"Who are you?" he said, glancing up at the window. "You are really his wife?"

"Yes. I'm really his wife."

She's telling the truth, he thought.

"I don't know what to do," he said. "You seem to know so much. You tell me."

She withdrew her right hand from her pocket. He saw that she was holding a thin book with a black and red cover.

"You should take this," she said.

"What is it?"

"Useful information."

"What kind of information?"

"We'll need it if we're working together."

He took the book and flipped the pages. Elephants, ivory — what nonsense was it?

"Let's start with Julius," she said.

Julius is past it, he thought. Yes, he knows a lot and he's clever but he's old and feeble and he slipped off the top table even before the last election.

"And I'd like to know exactly what happened to Elizabeth," she said, touching him on the shoulder and stepping carefully away across the grass towards the lobby.

No, he thought, Elaine doesn't know and you can't know either.

W hy, Dale wondered, was Sheryl standing barefoot on the grass in her bathrobe? Why was she talking to the old German guy like this when, last night, she had seemed so wary of him? Why was she giving him books? And had she seen him peeking through the drapes?

He opened the window — it was a struggle; the locks were unusual — with the intent of calling down to her. But she had gone. The coolness and dampness of the air surprised him. Really — why be out there shivering?

But almost at once he lost patience with his own questions; Sheryl did crazy things sometimes, and never seemed to want to talk about them with him. Anyhow, the plan for the day was set. Get in the car, drive around town some to make sure Jay Percival wasn't on their tail, and then head on out into the wilds and find someplace to hole up. Then, the head-to-head. Find out what was really up with her. And, whatever it was, just... Well, deal with it, somehow. Sheryl — the African adventure is over, okay? We did what we had to do, now we're going home.

So it boiled down to this: Get showered, get dressed, get in the car, hit the road. Oh, and if George could maybe lay on some munchies — German or otherwise — so much the better.

But, down in the restaurant with his hair still wet, he found Sheryl in reluctant mood. Resistant, almost, he would have said.

"Hey, c'mon, Sher," he said, trying to sound firm and encouraging but not aggressive. "Let's hit the road. You having a shower or what?"

"I just asked Roberta for coffee. You want some?"

"I guess. Let's make it quick, huh?"

"What's the hurry?"

This was difficult to answer.

"We just need to go someplace. Together. You know, so we can relax. After all this... Everything."

"It's kind of relaxing here."

"No, we need to move on, Sheryl."

She didn't answer.

"I saw you on the grass," he said. "Talking to George and stuff."

"Oh, you did."

"What are you, like... Giving him a book or something?"

"Uh-huh." She pointed at a bookshelf. "Just returning something."

She'd found time to read? But the way George had taken the book — it was the way you took a gift, or something you didn't really want. Why would he be flicking through his own book as if he'd never seen it before?

Roberta brought the coffee.

So what if, Dale thought as he spilt it into his saucer — what if Sheryl knew that Jay was following them? What if Jay had given her this book? What was this damn book, anyhow?

George came into the restaurant with a tray of food. Sheryl sat up and smiled. Dale saw the look that passed between them.

It still wasn't over, he thought. Not nearly over.

CHAPTER 21

With a dread bordering on uncharacteristic fatalism, Alan Vickery had at last steeled himself to retrieve his voicemail. He'd been sprawling in the business-class lounge waiting for his flight to Amsterdam, and the peer pressure of all those other businessmen — and businesswomen — retrieving their voicemail had forced him to the conclusion that it was crunch-time.

Mariella, it turned out, had merely wanted to berate him about some mishap that had befallen Zara in Switzerland. And also to instruct him to load up on the stock of companies connected to some American outfit called MLG.

(According to an excitable text message from Aylsham, Zara had tailed the lefty trouble-maker, Callaghan, to some tech-fest in Davos, which had promptly been trashed by rent-a-mob anti-capitalists. This same MLG had apparently been the primary object of their ire. Aylsham, of course, had seen in these meaningless events some *harbinger* of *epochal* developments to come.)

Coasting blissfully Schipol-wards — the bliss owing to the fact that he was leaving behind, at least temporarily, some very complicated and stressful affairs — he had attempted to construe or make sense of these admonitions.

Firstly, Zara was old enough — being twenty-two or possibly twenty-three by now — to decide for herself whether or not to get mixed up in anti-capitalist, anti-GM or anti-fur demos — or whichever variety this one happened to have been. It wasn't his job to explain the blindingly obvious idiocy of such a venture. Besides, she was some kind of cub reporter for the Beeb now, wasn't she? Probably just scooping up some campaigners-say-blah-blah stuff for This Week in Europe at three o'clock in the morning.

None of this meant, of course, that he didn't feel this hurt to his daughter as keenly as the next father; it was just that his sympathy had been diluted by the high spirits with which she'd encouraged Charlotte and Zoë to mock his spy-phone.

And yet the fact that she'd popped up in Europe — only to be bopped on the head and knocked down, alas — when she was supposed to be in South Africa... Well, this was a concern. And what the shrewd observer might identify as the Swiss note had been sounded yet again, like an ancient cow-bell prophesying doom.

But how was he to explain to Mariella that being floored by punks might not be the worst fate to have befallen their daughter? And would it not be humane to give the odious Aylsham a head-start?

As for buying into MLG, whatever *that* was, Mariella could forget it. She could put her own cash into it, if she wanted; let her cut down on soft furnishings and Pinot Grigio. Vickery was committing his spare resources to Ray and Marty's stealth take-over, which, he gathered from a slew of voicemails from the Caribbean, was coming along nicely. He, too, like a king of the jungle with a healthy appetite, and a delicious aroma in his nostrils, was on the hunt to grab himself a piece of Giraffe and he was loving it. For if there was anyone you could trust to make rule-bendingly outrageous windfall profits, it had to be Ray and Marty. They were an odd couple, it was true — very odd — but history showed that a marriage of delusion and aggression often prospered in the financial markets. Until the inevitable crash, that was. Vickery, of course, would jump lightly off the bus at the opportune moment.

Having danced through the fast-track facilities — so refreshingly different to Heathrow, with its tawdry shops, shuffling queues and jumpy soldiers — and having been swept into Amsterdam in an S-Class limo, Vickery began to feel the tension drain away. He almost felt like dipping his toes in the Prinsengracht, despite the autumnal chilliness in the air.

Dodging friendly trams and jolly bicyclists, he had made his way to a café near the flower market. Here, while he waited for Willem, his first appointment of the day, he sipped on a beer and gazed down from his first-floor perch on to a placid panorama of elegant gables, falling leaves, rippling canals, bike-pushing girls in boots and knitted scarves, and bright-eyed tourists with maps and take-away coffee. Funny, he thought, how you could get all wrapped up in the urgencies and imperatives of the world's power-centers and forget that, elsewhere, things moved according to a calmer, more natural rhythm.

The prospect of being parachuted into Africa remained disturbing but Vickery discounted it, regarding it as unlikely and probably just the by-product of some turf-war between Jason and Moreland. Besides, it seemed that Moreland had rather taken to him in the end. And if you absolutely had to deal with power-mad psychos, it was better to be in the tent with them, as the saying went.

Furthermore, if he stayed away from London long enough, he could avoid doing any more of Kellerman's dirty work. That Lenehan woman would get the message and go home to New York; and Kellerman would forget all about it. And Sean, after all, was not a bad lad. Despite the way he looked and the way he behaved; despite what people said about him; despite his record; despite everything, really, he was, at heart, not a bad lad. He wouldn't have done anything too... Too *disproportionate*.

It occurred to him that these were rationalizations. But then he was nothing if not rational.

As he waited for Willem, a sense of wholeness and well-being came over him and, being ever thus prone, he fell into a kind of reverie.

He saw himself on Ray's golf course, hitting his third consecutive birdie as Marty grinned and gave him the thumbs-up. And then, in the club-house with its sumptuous brunch and its champagne-waterfall ice-sculpture, he saw himself stepping up to receive the Newcomer's Cup, presented by none other than Mr. Southern Africa — Douglas Moreland himself, supported by the entire top brass of the Liberty Club stacked up in rows like a school photo and applauding. And, yes, there too were Richard and Jason, smiling at each other with understated satisfaction and clapping daintily. And there was Muller, helping himself to barbecued chicken.

But what was this? The President and the Vice President and a train of courtiers and Secret Service men; and then policemen and fire-fighters and marching bands; and then a posse of high-school cheer-leaders, with the PM and the Foreign Secretary bringing up the rear. An emissary is sent forward — it's Kellerman! Would Sir Alan be gracious enough to accept this medal? Why, yes! Why not? Even though he, Vickery, of course, had only been in it for the Giraffes, but what the hell! Everyone laughs and applauds this roguish confession. Except that wary, disheveled woman in the business suit at the back who's giving him the eye. There's always one. But here's the newly-restored King of Angola, with Mariella on his arm and a leopard-skin sash over his shoulder, offering Vickery a nation's grateful thanks and all the wildebeest he can eat. Wildebeest? The King's a little off the mark there, but never mind.

And here comes the happy couple. This day is really all about them. Flint Gunner and Nigel Weese rush forward, leading the press pack and unwittingly trampling the Foreign Secretary. You're on live TV — how does it feel? Beautiful! Twins on the way! Incredible! And they're already accepted into the Conservative Party! Wonderful! And where to for the honeymoon? Luanda! Of course! Let's gaze upon them for a moment. She's radiant; he's just sweaty: Sir Jeremy Aylsham and his lovely third wife Zara...

Oh, for God's sake, he told himself, get yourself a coffee and wake up.

Finishing his espresso, Vickery noticed a thin man in a black suit and a white, open-necked shirt loitering outside the café. Aha, he thought, this must be him: Blatant designer stubble, flimsy briefcase, shiny shoes, unnecessary sunglasses. He banged on the window. The man looked up. Vickery, still a little punchy after his day-dream, made a funny pistol-shooting mime. Willem — it was obviously him — frowned and hurried inside.

And so it began.

In Amsterdam and Rotterdam with Willem, Vickery checked invoices and inventories; handed over passwords and account numbers; laid out payment schedules in slow English and with a yellow highlighter; drew special attention to the penalty clauses, highlighting them in pink — not that he didn't have total confidence in Willem, of course; cracked open wooden crates with a screwdriver, matching up their contents with a picture-book Muller had given him; declined to visit any places of entertainment tailored especially for foreign businessmen, citing his packed schedule.

In Prague with Pavel, Vickery rewrote the entire order by hand to make sure there weren't any discrepancies; rebuffed, politely, an offer to participate in the forcible take-over of a plastics factory in Moscow; repeated his exhortations to Pavel not to try to access the payment accounts before the due date; agreed to take Pavel's word that the boxes hidden in the mortuary contained the goods as stated; succumbed to an evening in an underground disco where girls from Belarus sat on his lap and pouted at him mockingly.

In Budapest with Bela, which might not have been his real name, Vickery rode in a psychedelic Trabant to an old tram shed where he inspected rocket launchers; luxuriated a little too intimately in the famous indoor baths at the Hotel Gellert; bought a new computer when Bela's inexplicably broke down before the inventory could be printed; declined firmly to visit any business-friendly night clubs, without giving his reasons.

In Helsinki with Arno, Vickery insisted that he'd visited all of the banks in question on many occasions and had never had a problem; bought a new winter coat; conducted a line-item review during a walking tour of the Helsinki Zoo, which Arno claimed was free from surveillance and little-visited; assured Arno that the Bank of Seven Mile Beach was a perfectly fit institution for the business at hand; dined early at a vegetarian restaurant; was not offered the option of nocturnal entertainment.

In Naples with Massimo, Vickery visited the Museo Archaelogico Nazionale; drove with Massimo all the way down to Sorrento in Massimo's Alfa Romeo, stopping off at Pompeii; took a boat ride to Capri; provoked a flamboyant row about getting down to business before he had to fly out again; found a staple in his pizza; explained his concerns about overdue rifle parts from Albania; agreed to take a look at Massimo's plans for building hotels in a Turkish fishing village; fell asleep in a night club while Massimo was dancing with the owner's wife.

In Marbella with Gerald, Vickery sat on Gerald's sixty-five-foot motor yacht in the marina at Puerto Banus and brooded about the nature and potential expense of Mariella's ever-lengthening Swiss interlude; counselled Gerald on the latest techniques for evading corporate pension liabilities; encountered great pessimism regarding events in the War Zones in an Irish pub full of football fans; tried out Gerald's American-made night-vision equipment in the subtropical garden of Gerald's front-line villa; listened to Gerald's complaints about his loss of pricing power in the arms market; was disturbed in the night by Gerald's boozy wife who, it emerged, also lamented her husband's waning potential.

In Florida on his own and flaunting his "Screen Your Ass" T-shirt, Vickery arranged overlapping loans between dummy real estate development companies; set up automatic transfers between accounts designed to look like regular daily or weekly payments; thought about driving up to Fort Lauderdale and springing a surprise visit on Ray Priles, but didn't; received a text message from Marty Bazon indicating that it was nearly fucking time to start buying fucking Giraffe stock.

In George Town in the Cayman Islands on Wednesday, Vickery advised Carlos that the Bank of Seven Mile Beach should change its name; bought some jewelry for Mariella that would also do for Zara, if necessary; visited twenty-three banks, investment management companies and hedge funds in one afternoon by virtue, happily, of their all being located in the same lawyer's office above the jewelry shop.

In Kingstown on Saint Vincent on Thursday, Vickery made a mad dash from bank to bank, before they all closed at three o'clock, and successfully formed eleven new companies and trusts.

Then he island-hopped down to phone-and-TV-free Petit Saint Vincent, checked into his private hillside cottage and hauled up the red flag for a bit of well-earned rest and privacy. Shortly afterwards, he dozed off over his paperwork and slept for twelve hours straight.

It was only when, in the fresh glow of a Caribbean morning, he lowered the red flag and hauled up the yellow one that the staff brought him the urgent message from Mariella demanding his presence in Barbados.

CHAPTER 22

J ay Percival owned a farm. And he had been mighty proud to relate its history to Dale and Sheryl. It had been a regular farm with cattle and, briefly, ostriches. Its original owners — ignoring, for the purposes of this short history, the local Herero — were German immigrant farmers who had discovered a small stream and spring and named the location accordingly, only to watch the stream disappear and never return.

Subsequently, it had become a game farm, and later owners from South Africa had installed special, rigid, kudu-proof double fencing — as opposed to the flexible, game-permeable single fencing that segregated the cows — around its perimeter. You absolutely needed this because the game were very valuable. And the fences could cost millions of Namibian dollars. From game farm, the property naturally progressed to the status of hunting farm, and welcomed rifle-toting visitors from South Africa, America and Asia. A change of ownership in the 1990s brought a new ethos and Spruitfontein — that was the name of the place — had become an eco-friendly guest farm, welcoming camera-and-guide-book-toting visitors from Germany, Scandinavia and Ireland.

And now, Dale Summers reflected bitterly, it was a freaking spy-farm.

Jay really did seem to own the place. He certainly treated it as if he did. And it followed from that that the farm was not in good shape.

It had no staff. The guest bungalows were neglected. The main lodge was dusty and smelled of food. Jay had obviously forgotten to water the lawns — or perhaps he hadn't maintained the water-pumping solar panels. The forecourt was cluttered with four-wheel-drives, all of them apparently belonging to Jay.

There was nobody else about — just Jay, Dale and Sheryl. Plus, according to Jay, twenty-two kudu, about a hundred springbok, six or seven red hartebeest, both black and blue wildebeest, a dozen ostriches, plus the usual jackals, foxes and porcupines, and so on. Jay claimed he'd seen cheetah tracks. Dale doubted it.

One thing Jay hadn't neglected was provisioning the place. Banks of freezers filled the kitchen and adjacent store rooms. Boxes, crates, sacks and drums cluttered the guest bungalows and spilled out on to the rustic terrace that ran along in front. Desks, computers and telecommunications equipment occupied the sitting rooms in the lodge. Behind the generator building was a padlocked shipping container. How did *that* get there? What was in it?

The long block of guest bungalows sat at ninety degrees to the main lodge. Dale had pushed aside some heavy wooden crates, righted a picnic table and now sat gazing across the red sand of the forecourt, and the parched lawn, to the veranda in front of the lodge, where Sheryl and Jay were engaged in an animated discussion. Maybe even a fight, he thought, as he sucked on a Tafel lager (Jay was well-stocked with beer, also). Now, what could they possibly be fighting about?

Spruitfontein was remote. For that reason, at least, he felt somewhat relaxed. It would have been better without Jay there, but what were you going to do? He could have had his little talk with Sheryl here — it was a great location for it. But that idea was, well, moot.

The fact was, his wife was not his wife. No, that didn't sound right. How many beers had he had? It seemed like there were some empty bottles under the table. But no, Sheryl was still his wife. Sure she was. It was just that, as it turned out, there was this whole other thing going on with her. A whole other thing involving Jay Percival. And God knew what else. A whole other thing that... But how did they come to be in this place, anyhow? Spruitfontein. Funny name. Beautiful, though. The high plateau, the red sand, the view over the edge of the escarpment, the distant dunes to the west, the gray, brown and red mountain ranges to the east, the little rocky hills — the kopjes — the sunsets, all that crap: All beautiful.

And how many days had they been here? Four? Five? Something like that.

And how had they gotten here?

He played back the relevant events in his mind with the idea that, this time through, perhaps, and turning up his analytical powers full-blast, he might pick up on some detail that would render the whole thing comprehensible.

Sheryl had driven the Condor at top speed all the way from Swakopmund, all the way through Windhoek, stopping only for fuel and the obligatory window-wash, and then on out past the airport. At that point she'd been so tired that he'd taken over. Sheryl directed him down every gravel road that led to a farm or a lodge with an airstrip. Somehow, she knew where they all were. Had anyone seen an elderly white woman getting in a plane and flying out? No, nobody had.

They slept in the Condor. Twice they had to go back to the airport for water and fuel, which was a hassle because there wasn't a public gas station and they had to negotiate with car rental companies.

Why was Sheryl so desperate to find Elaine's tracks? But didn't Dale want to find her too? Well, yes, he did — but wasn't this hopeless? No, she had to have flown out from somewhere.

But eventually they ran out of airstrips. Then, heading north again towards the airport road, the Condor suffered a blow-out after Dale failed to avoid a sharp rock. Too tired and discouraged to change the wheel immediately, they sat in the shade of the vehicle and Dale put his arm around his wife's shoulders and asked her the question he'd been almost bursting to ask ever since they left George and Julius in Swakopmund.

"So, Sheryl. Let me ask you this. Are you a spy? You know, like Jay?"

She looked at him as if in shock, then burst out laughing. As he watched, the tears began to roll down her cheeks.

"No," she said. "Not like Jay. Not like him at all."

This had mystified him.

"Oh. But we're chasing after Elaine like we're suddenly on a secret mission. And you're telling — well, kind of telling Julius what to do. And you've got code books..."

"Yeah? So?"

"Looks like spying to me."

"Oh, Dale. You know, Jay really is a spy."

"And you're not?"

"No. What makes you think I could ever be a spy?" She started laughing again.

"Just trying to make sense of things, I guess."

"Yeah. You are, aren't you?"

"So did Jay give you that code book?"

"No."

But now she wasn't laughing. Did that mean something?

"Did you know that Jay showed up at the hotel in Swakopmund?" he said. "I think he followed us."

"No, I didn't know that. But I'm not so surprised. Did you talk to him?"

"He said he was protecting me."

"And me?"

"He didn't say."

"Well, he probably means it."

"We can't trust him."

Sheryl kicked up some red dust.

"We need to change the wheel. Come on."

And then, after they stood up and stretched, they saw the dust cloud. It was about five kilometers away and heading south towards them. A light breeze from the west blew the dust plume, intact, gently off the road to the right. It was obviously a large vehicle traveling very fast — recklessly fast — and turned out, as they knew it would, to be a gray pick-up containing Jay and his infuriating grin.

"Got a flat?" he said, springing from the cab. "They ought to put bigger tires on these things. Let me fix it for you."

"Hi, Jay," Sheryl said. "What're you doing here?"

"Oh, Sheryl — you're looking for an airstrip, I hear. Tell you what, I'll show you one. Dale, get the jack, will you?"

So then, for hundreds of kilometers on gravel roads, they'd followed Jay, who would roar ahead then stop and wait for them to catch up, until they ended up south and west of Windhoek, on the high escarpment, and Jay had announced to them that he'd been of a mind to go into the farm business.

The last twenty-five kilometers were tough on the Condor. It was Jay's private road and he clearly had no intention of filling the ruts or digging out the rocks.

Eventually, the road widened and flattened and became soft and sandy. Then it widened again and straightened and Dale realized that they were driving along the center of a huge and recently-used landing strip — a landing strip that, it appeared to Dale, was much longer than even the heftiest Cessna would require. Jay sped up and wove his truck from one side to the other, as if the airstrip were his pride and joy. It probably was, Dale had decided at the time.

So had Elaine flown out from here, after all? After a long, deceptive ride from the airport? Maybe she had, Jay said. But then he wasn't around all the time and, he claimed, airplane tracks all looked the same to him. However, he could see that Sheryl was concerned about Elaine. Now if Sheryl could just be patient, Jay might be able to ease her mind on that score. In the meantime, why didn't they both relax and enjoy themselves on the farm? Folks might be looking for Dale and Sheryl — no saying what folks might be up to — but nobody would find them here.

So for several days they'd been patient. Jay had come and gone, in one or another of his trucks, unpredictably. The trucks always looked worse on their return. Sheryl had pointed out that since they had no money, nowhere to go, no way of tracking Elaine and nothing else to do, they might as well stay put. But it seemed to Dale that she was more interested at this point in staying close to Jay. Sheryl didn't mention George or Julius. She spent her time reading — Jay had inherited a small library — and not code books, either, as far as Dale could tell. And she seemed calmer and more together. This is fine, he thought: A few days of this, then we'll borrow some money from Jay and move on.

For his part, Dale roamed the farm, looking into all the outbuildings, trying and failing to get into the shipping container, watching out for snakes and failing to locate any hidden airplanes. He also helped himself to Jay's beer stash.

So where did this analysis leave him? With an empty beer bottle, it seemed. He got up, intending to walk over to the lodge to fetch another from the kitchen. But, unsteady on his feet, he collided with one of the wooden crates and hit his knee on the edge. In pain, he took a revenge kick at the crate, crashing his boot through the side.

Embarrassed at himself for being so stupid and, possibly, just a little drunk, he tried to repair the damage but a section of the crate came away in his hands, exposing its contents. And the contents of the crate turned out to be polythene bags full of money. Each bag contained a three-inch stack of hundred dollar bills. Not Namibian dollars — American. New bills. How many bags were there? How many crates? He looked up to see Sheryl and Jay staring at him.

And then, before he knew it, Jay was at his side, gripping him by the shoulder and Sheryl was running up behind.

"Oh, now look at that," Jay said. "Dale, what have you done? Do you realize what this means?"

"What are you doing with all this money?"

"Money?" Sheryl said.

Dale tossed one of the bags to her.

"Jay?" she said. "What's this for? How much have you got?"

"What this means," Jay said, "is trouble." He let go of Dale's shoulder, dropped his customary grin and looked serious.

"You know what's going to happen?"

"What?" Sheryl said.

"Tonight? When it's dark? The porky-pines come out. And you know what? They look into everything. They're big critters. Like this."

He drew his hands apart to demonstrate.

"They see these little bags with green stuff inside? They say to themselves "Hey, look! I'm gonna get me a free salad." They make a hell of a mess. I mean, did you see the holes in the road?"

"Porky-pines?" Sheryl said.

"Yeah. We got to move this one indoors. Help me out here."

They shunted the crate into one of the bungalows.

"So what's all the money for?" Dale said when they'd finished.

"Oh Dale," Jay said. "It's for the war. What else would it be?"

"Which war?"

"There's only really one war. Hey, let me get you another beer. Come on."

He led them back to the lodge and into the kitchen.

"Oh, you know what?" he said, handing Dale a fresh Tafel. "I don't know how you-all are fixed, but if you need some money you can take a bunch. Just don't change too much at once, okay? Sheryl — beer?"

"Okay," she said.

They sat around the kitchen table. Through an open door, Dale could see red and green lights flickering furiously on a stack of ruggedized computer gear.

"So," Jay said. "Whose turn is it to cook dinner tonight?"

Sheryl made a face as she drank her beer from the bottle. Big joke, Dale thought. Sheryl had made dinner every night. After they saw how Jay had been eating, it seemed the right thing to do.

"I guess it's you again," he said.

"I guess it is. So what are you guys in the mood for?"

"Anything. Whatever you got."

"Jay, you've got everything. You could live here for months."

"Maybe a year. Run out of gas in a year."

Perhaps it was the beer; or perhaps it was the startling peacefulness of the farm; or the feeling of having stumbled into some bizarre, fully-stocked, natural sanctuary; or just the incredible concept of sitting at the kitchen table listening to Sheryl planning dinner — whatever the cause, Dale felt less scared of Jay than at any time since he'd first encountered him. Look at it this way, he reasoned: My wife's cooking dinner for the guy, let's ask him a few friendly questions.

"Jay, what's in that big old container?"

"What's in it?"

"Yeah. Kind of a weird thing to have out here, isn't it?"

"Uh-huh."

"You got it all locked up."

"That's right."

"So what's in there?"

"Nothing. There's nothing in there, Dale."

This was something new: Dale making Jay uncomfortable. He couldn't resist poking a little further.

"So how come it's locked? Keep the porky-pines out?"

"Keep everybody out."

185

"Why?"

"Forget it, Dale. I don't use it any more and I don't want anybody going in there."

All right, he thought, that's enough poking. Almost went too far there.

"Jay," Sheryl said. "If you fetch me another beer I'll make something special."

"You got it," he said, tipping his chair back and reaching for one of his huge refrigerators. "Oh. Just one moment." He got up and disappeared into the room containing the computer equipment. When he emerged there was a look on his face that Dale had never seen before — almost a look of pain.

"Have either of you two," he said, "got a cell phone?"

Sheryl shook her head.

"Yes," Dale said. "Why?"

"Is it turned on?"

"No. I don't think so."

"Where is it?"

"In my pocket."

"Give it here."

"Why? What's the —"

"Give it here. Now."

Dale gave Jay the phone. Jay swore, then ripped the back off the phone and tore out the battery.

"Dale, this phone was on. Why was it on? There's no coverage anywhere near here. Not for a hundred k's in any direction, my friend. Why was it on?"

"I don't know. Must have been like an accident. Maybe I bumped —"

"How long was it on for? Don't tell me it's since you got here."

"No. I know there's no coverage. It was off this morning."

Jay looked like he was performing some kind of mental arithmetic. Sheryl went to the fridge and got her own beer.

"Shit," Jay said. "Why didn't I check before I brought you here? Got a lot on my mind. That's what it is. A lot on my mind."

He seemed to be talking to himself.

"So what's the problem?" Dale asked aggressively, wondering if Jay had trashed his phone.

"The fucking microwave signals these things give off?" Jay said. "Do you have any idea how far they travel? Don't want to be giving off signals, Dale. No fucking tell-tale signals."

"We're in the middle of nowhere. Who's listening?"

Jay shook his head, in a bitter and condescending way.

"It's just like, well, you go to so much trouble," he said. "Do you see what I mean?"

He probably meant he didn't want anybody tracking down all that money.

"Satellites," Sheryl said.

"No," Jay said, fetching himself a beer. "Too far up. Okay, sure — they could photograph the hairs growing out of Dale's nose. But," he said, pointing at Dale with his beer bottle, "first they got to know where to look."

"I'm sorry," Dale said. "I guess."

"Got to think about these things. Ask Sheryl."

"Why? Is she a spy like you?"

Jay looked at Sheryl. Sheryl drank her beer.

"No," Jay said. "Not like me."

"Okay," Sheryl said. "Out of the kitchen. Let me work."

"Dale," Jay said. "Just let me attend to a couple of things, and then we'll go for a walk, huh? A little sundowner? And I'll try and explain a couple of things for you."

Some explanations would be nice, he thought.

"Sure. Okay."

Jay slipped into the equipment room and shut the door. Sheryl was washing her hands at the sink. Dale crept up behind her and slipped his arms around her waist.

"So this whole deal is kind of weird," he said. "How do you feel about it?"

"I'm okay about it. I could almost live out here. I mean another farm, not this one."

"Yeah. Me too. You wouldn't be lonely?"

"We'd have staff. And guests."

"Guests?"

"To make money."

"Oh, right. Though, if we need money..."

"Don't even think about it."

"Must be millions. Just sitting there. Not even locked up. Hey, that's stupid — why doesn't he put it in the container?"

"I expect he has a reason."

"Huh. Well, okay, we make money from guests. We can learn how to do that, can't we?"

"We'd have to."

"There's only one thing I'm afraid of."

She turned to look at him.

"What? What are you afraid of?"

"The porky-pines."

She looked him straight in the eyes for a moment, then laughed and pushed him away.

"Let me get to work now."

"Sheryl?"

"What?"

"Before we started out on all this, you seemed — you seemed so down about everything. I didn't know what to do. I didn't know what to say to you. It was like you were in this dark cave, or something, and you wouldn't come out, and you wouldn't let me come near? Like you were scared and just kind of, I don't know, petrified?"

"Uh-huh."

"So, what I'm saying is — what was that all about? And then what happened? Something must have happened, because you changed. You... Well, you got better. Kind of."

"Uh-huh. So you noticed."

"Yes."

"Something did happen. And it made me very unhappy."

"What?"

"And then, there was a change in the situation, a development. And I, it's true, I did feel different."

"Completely different."

"Completely different."

"What?" he said. "Tell me what."

"Dale, I can't tell you. Not right now. When the time is right."

"I don't see why you can't tell me now."

"You have to trust me. Will you do that?"

Would he? It seemed more a matter of blind faith than simple trust.

"Yes. I will. But —"

He felt Jay's hand on his shoulder again. Always grabbing you — what was it with him?

"Let's go, buddy."

"Where to, exactly?"

"There's a nice little kopje. Great view. Might see a klipspringer."

"You've got an hour and a half," Sheryl said.

"Plenty of time. Come on, Dale."

Dale noticed that Jay hadn't bothered to change his footwear; he was still wearing his stupid black dress shoes. Serve him right if the porky-pines bit his toes.

"See you later," he said, giving his wife a kiss on the back of the neck.

"Careful out there," she said. "Come back in one piece."

*

Jay's kopje was a thirty minute walk away, across flat, semi-desert scrubland, on the far side of a dry riverbed lined with camel thorn trees. Dale followed in Jay's footsteps, still on the look-out for snakes. The hill itself, of course, turned out to be much higher than it appeared from the farm, from which point of view it resembled a stack of pebbles piled up by children.

Jay led the ascent with a skill and deftness that suggested he knew the best route from experience. The pebbles were boulders, many of them loose. Dale didn't know whether to jump from boulder to boulder or risk putting his foot in the dry, grassy holes in between — perfect retreats from the impending night-time chill for sun-loving snakes. When he dared to look up all he saw was Jay vanishing over one blind summit after another.

But the view from the top, once he'd got his breath back, was, well, breath-taking. Whole mountain ranges rose up to the east; to the west the escarpment tumbled down into wastes of sand and the beginnings of the great dune sea of the Namib. There were no roads, no vehicles, no buildings save for Spruitfontein itself. The sky was empty, the stars just beginning to pierce the fading daylight. There were no planes — not even the hint of a vapor trail. Jay had chosen one of the remotest spots in one of the least populated countries in the world. And it was beautiful. But what the hell was he doing here?

Jay removed his backpack, unzipped it and offered Dale a beer. Dale accepted. Then Jay took out a pair of binoculars, hopped up on a rock and made a slow, 360-degree scan of his property.

"Down there," he said, pointing to the north and handing the binoculars to Dale. "Kudu. See the one with the sideways horns? Kind of unusual. Didn't expect him to survive so long."

Dale looked. The animals were gathered at a water-hole fed by a solar-powered pump. Maybe Jay cared more for his animals than his lawns. The kudu with the unusual horns struggled to hold its ground by the water.

"So why'd you buy this place?" Dale asked.

"Needed somewhere private."

"Who paid for it?"

"Your tax dollars at work."

The sinking sun began to color the far-off dunes orange and then red. For several minutes neither man said anything. Dale listened. The air was still and there was no sound at all. It was, he thought, the nearest thing to absolute silence he'd ever heard. Down on the farm, lights started to come on. But there was no sound from the generator — Jay explained that, thanks to the previous owners, the farm ran on battery power overnight.

"See, the thing is, Dale," Jay said, "and this may come as some kind of surprise to you — but I don't really work for the CIA."

Some kind of surprise? But everything the guy did or said was a surprise or a shock or a punch in the gut. Now what was he raving about? Why couldn't he keep it simple?

"Don't get me wrong. I am certainly employed by them. It's just that... Let me put it this way. I am not the most loyal of employees."

Okay, Dale thought, do I panic now — or wait until he tells me what crazy thing he wants me to do next?"

"What do you mean, Jay?"

"The question is, loyal to what? Right, Dale?"

Loyal to yourself, Dale thought. You've stolen millions of dollars from the CIA, run off into the desert, bought yourself a farm, of all things... And now you're running some kind of huge corruption racket and you've got us involved. Now you're going to tell us we're trapped. With you or against you. And Jennifer was laundering money — for you!

"You, for example. What are you loyal to? Your wife. Even though you now realize she's been up to stuff you know nothing about. That's very commendable. And I happen to know you're right to do it. What else? Your job. All that economic development, helping Namibia to help itself. Good stuff. Bet you could use a few more dollars, though. But you haven't got the money. I have. And the constitution — I mean the American one. Bet you're loyal to that."

"You said the money was for the war."

"It was. I just happen to think it could be better spent."

"On what?"

Jay zipped up his jacket; the air was cooling rapidly. But Dale could feel the heat building in his face.

"The agency," Jay said, "is split into factions. You're probably too young to appreciate this. It used to be different. There was a purge. A lot of the old-timers got pushed out — chiefs of station, division heads, all the way down. And in come all these kids. The Hitler Youth."

Again, Jay seemed to be talking to himself.

"What about you?" Dale said.

"Some of us were too young to retire and we didn't want to become contractors in the private sector," Jay said, emphasizing *private sector* as if it were something any right-minded spy would detest.

"The mission used to be to gather intelligence. And to fight small proxy-wars against the communists. Actually, some of them got quite big. Afghanistan. Angola. Know what the mission is now?"

"You said there was only one war."

"That's right. And our mission now is to — quote — support the administration and its policies in our work. Unquote. That's it. No more intelligence. Whole lot of war."

But you know what?"

"What?"

"The war is not under control. It grows, it changes, it spreads, it goes kind of insane and it wants to perpetuate itself. Are there people in command? Sometimes. Different people. At different times. The only real controlling influence, Dale, is the ideology. That's what we've got ourselves."

"Where are you in all this?"

"On my own. Unless..."

"Unless what?"

"Unless I see something going down that really freaks me. And then I am prepared to cooperate and assist."

"Jennifer."

"Yeah, that was one."

"Who were you cooperating with?"

Jay gave Dale one of his scariest grins.

"A bunch of very loyal folks who like to call themselves the Resistance. I think it's a silly name myself."

So Jay knew, he thought. Jay knew who they were — the two men who brought Jennifer to the embassy. This was information that Jennifer had withheld from Dale. But Bill and Elaine must have known. Or Elaine, at least.

"You're one of them."

"No. I'm not quite pure enough for them. But that's *their* problem. Also — and I hate to tell you this — they're a dying breed."

"Those two guys..."

"Oh, they're okay. For now. It's like a civil war, Dale. You ever read Paradise Lost?"

"No. But the two guys..."

"Gary and Joe. Gary's the young one."

"Who did they rescue Jennifer from? Really?"

"From us."

"Us?"

"Yeah. They thought it was a step too far. I agreed with them."

The light had all but gone and the sky was full of stars. Dale suddenly realized they were going to be late for dinner.

"Shouldn't we be going?"

"What?"

"Sheryl? Dinner?"

"Yeah. But don't you want to know what happened to Sheryl?"

"She said she would tell me when the time was right."

Jay frowned.

"Oh. Well, then I guess the time isn't right. Okay then. Let's be climbing down."

Jay jumped up and began to load his backpack. Then he froze, as if listening.

"What?" Dale said.

Jay snatched up the binoculars and scrambled on to a boulder. He pointed to the south-west.

"See anything? Hear anything?"

"Where?"

"There! In the sky. Listen!"

Jay scanned the sky. There was something frantic in the way he focused and re-focused.

"I can't hear anything," Dale said. "No, wait..."

Was that a distant hum — or just the blood drumming in his ears?

Jay turned around.

"No," he said. "I don't think there's —"

A streak of white smoke drew itself across the night sky in a cruel and unnatural diagonal, bearing down on the roof of the lodge. The roof rose and parted. Black sand flew out from the base of the building. The walls shivered and disappeared into a billowing blackness. Then came a roar like the rending of fabric and the boom and crack of the detonation itself. Two smaller explosions erupted from the rear of the building, sending a tower of flame up into the sky.

Gas cylinders, Dale thought. Gas cylinders exploding. That was the explanation. Gas. For the kitchen.

Jay was on top of him, yelling in his ear.

"Keep down. Don't move."

Dale shook him off and stood. The fire had already spread to two of Jay's trucks. Where the lodge had stood there was nothing but a furious pit of smoke and flame. He strained his eyes to focus on the fence-line at the edge of the forecourt. Sheryl would run towards them. She would climb the fence. Where was she? If he kept looking along the fence-line he would see her. She would be running towards them and waving. Where was she?

"Dale, get down. There's always two."

A second white diagonal scored its way across the first to the roof of the guest bungalows. Dale flung himself to the ground beside Jay. The flash lit up the red sand in front of their faces and the boom rolled over them. Jay seemed to be blinking something out of his eyes.

"You go to so much trouble," he said.

CHAPTER 23

By the time Alan Vickery made landfall on Barbados, Mariella had, predictably, moved her tents again. But she hadn't left him without company. In fact, there seemed to be a house party in progress, and the house itself and the garden were overflowing with elegantly-dressed people.

It was early evening, the sun was setting over the Caribbean, a balmy breeze had picked up and there was excitement in the air. The palm trees in Vickery's spot-lit tropical garden seemed to whisper secrets to each other. In his moat-like swimming pool the water lapped and gurgled with what sounded like mounting anticipation. Beneath the slim columns of his semi-circular portico, on his double-decker terrace, Vickery heard the silky, articulated chatter of expensive accents, mostly American. On his personal, six-hundred-foot-wide slice of Platinum Coast beach, a guitar strummed softly and girls in long, lacy skirts twirled languorously with the music, their supple limbs silhouetted against the deepening russets of the sky.

Taken all together you had to admit it was rather lovely, he decided, as he zipped upstairs to his dressing room to discard his "Screen Your Ass" T-shirt and slip into a favorite cream linen suit. Very nice; almost like a TV commercial for some brand-name muck with rum in it.

The pinky-white coral-stone house — or *mansion* as the local real estate crowd described it, even though it only had six bedrooms (not including staff quarters)—was recently-built and considered by some to be not in the best taste. Vickery had bought it from its original owner, an ageing rock star (one of several in the neighborhood). The rock star had fallen on hard times, having securitized his future royalty stream and then blown the proceeds on lawyers in an attempt to protect himself from the recovered memories of now-adult fans who had discovered that memories can indeed be golden. Since the rock star's own memory had long since been chemically dissolved, he put his trust in his attorneys, with the result that Vickery got the house.

The final negotiations had been acrimonious. The rock star insisted on referring to Vickery as the Rat Man. After the rock star moved out, having trashed the place as a token of good faith, Vickery modified the rock star's faked-up coat of arms over the study fireplace, replacing the electric guitar with the representation of a laughing rat.

Descending his wide, curving staircase into his marble-floored vestibule, Vickery felt confident and in command; powerful, almost. His breathless dash around Europe and his slightly more sedate jaunt around the Caribbean had gone well. He had hardly struck a wrong note; the whole thing had been like a symphony of guns and money. And he was both composer and conductor.

He paused half-way down the stairs to survey the populace. Ah yes, he thought, this looked like the NDC crowd plus hangers-on. There was Zarnoff, propped up against the study fireplace with the rat leering cheerily over his shoulder. Over there, by the pool and surrounded by female admirers, was Urquist with a loud shirt and a cigar (cigars were permitted under the circumstances, Vickery decided). Who else was here? Descending to the foot of the stairs, he spotted Ray Priles and Marty Bazon in the kitchen in tuxedos. Ray, as usual, was beaming. And Marty, if not exactly happy, looked less despondent than was customary.

But then, most gratifyingly of all, as he strode into the garden lounge, Vickery came upon Phyllis herself. Enthroned in a high-backed wicker chair — one of Mariella's purchases — she appeared to be holding court. On duty behind the chair was Phyllis's assistant or companion. Vickery couldn't swear it was the same one; he recognized the trousers but wasn't sure about the face. Phyllis was conversing on the subject of eminent domain with General Fricke, who had been obliged to perch on Mariella's matching footstool.

An *eminent domain*, Vickery thought; that was precisely what this was. Phyllis gave a him gracious wave; General Fricke, a curt nod. It was quite funny — almost as if Phyllis were Elizabeth giving Sir Walter Raleigh his orders, and Vickery were Essex just wandering by on the off-chance. With equal amusement, Vickery wondered if Kellerman — whose booming voice and aura of non-incorruptibility seemed to be absent — had been able to finesse the General's family issues. It was probably best not to bring the subject up.

So, all in all, it was quite the little get-together; almost like a summit meeting. He wondered idly who could have organized it.

Snatching a glass of punch from a passing waiter and strolling in the direction of the pool bar, he passed a number of bubbly, designer-clad groups whose members weren't familiar to him but yet seemed to know who he was. He assumed they must all be Liberty Club bigwigs, or NDC types, or associates of Ray and Marty, or possibly even some of the deep thinkers from the Weekly Consensus. Clearly, Vickery's activities on behalf of the cause had already begun to raise his status. Everything seemed to be going swimmingly. He felt he ought to take great pride in putting on such a sophisticated soirée, even though he hadn't organized it and it had come as a complete surprise to him.

But now he spied two individuals who could probably explain the whole thing. Bobbing in the water and moored-up to the pool bar were Derek and Ronnie, Vickery's two best friends on the island. And, probably, anywhere. Their presence here was a conclusive indicator of Mariella's absence.

Derek and Ronnie were generally to be found on the Sandy Lane golf course or in the drinking club they had founded together in Bridgetown. Rarely venturing off the island, they tended to confine themselves to laxly-enforced jurisdictions. This, Vickery felt, was wise. He could only hope that his own freedom of movement would never be similarly circumscribed.

Derek, potato-shaped and brush-haired, had sold pensions. Over a shortish career, he must have sold thousands of them, but had been astute enough to save the best one for himself. Ronnie, who resembled a bald pear with chest hair, had been in property, and had been one of Vickery's mentors. He had been so good at selling property, in fact, that he had inadvertently sold the same units many times over. This innocent enthusiasm had been his downfall, but — thanks to Vickery — it had not been necessary to return all the money.

"Hullo, Spud," Vickery said, employing his pet name for Derek. "What's all this about then?"

Derek looked up.

"Oh, it's the man himself. Ronnie, look — Alan's here."

Ronnie looked.

"So he is. His house, though, isn't it? Not surprising he's here."

"But he's not here that often, though, is he, Ronnie? That's the thing."

"That's beside the point, Derek. He's here now, isn't he? Standing before us. That's my point."

Vickery examined the bar. Derek and Ronnie were sharing a bottle of gin, but it wasn't by any means clear that it was their first. He took off his shoes (Mariella had bought them for him and referred to them as "loafers' but he didn't really see why), rolled up his linen trouser legs and sat on the rim of the pool with his feet in the water. For a laugh, Derek flipped the Jacuzzi jets, sending an effervescent tide in the direction of Vickery's knees. Vickery lifted them clear before the wave struck. Disappointed, Derek and Ronnie waddled over towards Vickery, drinks in hand, and leaned against the pool-edge either side of him.

"Why d'you call me "Spud"?" Derek wanted to know.

"Cause you look like one, Derek," Vickery said, confident that he had reason on his side.

"Mariella doesn't like them," Ronnie said.

"That's true," Vickery said.

"Ah, the humble spud!" Ronnie said.

"Who says I'm humble?"

"Not you. Spuds in general."

"I'm not saying I'm not humble. In the appropriate circumstances. Say if I was meeting the Queen."

"Shut up, you two," Vickery said. "For your information, Mariella is opposed to potatoes and all they stand for. Speaking of which, I could tell you a funny story about the old potato vaults in Bethnal Green — I don't know if you remember them — but what I really want to know, Derek, my spud-like old friend, is three things: Where is she, what did she want me here for, and whose party is this anyway? And am I paying for it?"

"That's four things."

"Derek, tell the man where his wife is."

"Switzerland."

"But she's just come from Switzerland!"

Derek look aggrieved.

"I can't help that, Alan. Woman makes up her own mind."

"Did she tell you that in person?"

"On the phone, Alan. She can't really stand the sight of us, as well you know."

This was true. In one of her terser moments, Mariella had described Derek and Ronnie to Vickery as "the sort of scum you should have left behind by now". Vickery had never repeated this slur to his friends; they were resigned to being persona non grata — if that was the phrase — but "scum" would have hurt them deeply.

"Just one of those things, I'm afraid," Vickery said, giving his friends what he hoped was a rueful raising of the eyebrows. "Did she say where in Switzerland?"

"Some place called Zoog," Ronnie said, as if he didn't believe there was such a place.

But, of course, there was. It was well-known to people who knew these sort of things that Zug was the most financially furtive bit of Switzerland. It was the sort of place where, so long as your political contributions were in order, your big-time fraudster could hole up and laugh at the FBI for years. What was Mariella doing there? Did she have some scheme of her own on the go?

"Ronnie," Vickery said, "did she say what she was doing there?"

"No," Ronnie said. "Except that whatever it is, it's none of my business."

"Did you both speak to her, then?"

"We had her on the speakerphone at the club," Derek said. "I'm not sure she appreciated it. Saturday night — you know what it's like..."

"There may have been some tittering," Ronnie said, judiciously. "And we know who the titterers are. But they shall remain nameless. Unless you want to know their names, that is."

Vickery snorted. Derek and Ronnie collapsed with mirth. Water slopped up against Vickery's shins. Derek emptied the pool water out of Ronnie's glass and waded off for refills.

Nice to be with friends, Vickery thought. People you could have a laugh with; people you could say anything to — well, almost anything.

"Ronnie," he said. "What's the party for?"

"Ah. Good question. Fancy crowd, isn't it, Alan? Do you actually know all these people?"

"Most of them, yes," Vickery said, exaggerating slightly.

"Very impressive. Very impressive indeed. Anyway, it's a big announcement. Someone's going to make a big announcement."

"Who?"

"Couldn't tell you."

"What about?"

"Haven't a clue. Mariella just said 'Make sure Alan's there for the big announcement. And don't let him drink too much.'"

Derek returned with three glasses. He gave one to Vickery.

"Thank you, oh spud-like one. What's this big announcement?"

"Got to be political, hasn't it? This new crowd of yours, they're all political, aren't they?"

"Everything's political, Derek."

"Is it? Not sure I agree with you there, Alan."

"That's why you're stuck on this island."

"Well. Anyway, we were mingling — before we got in the pool, that is —"

"You can't mingle if you're wet."

"No, Ronnie, it is less effective if you're wet. But while we were mingling we heard a lot of talk about a new zone."

"What kind of zone?" Vickery said.

"Couldn't really say," Derek said. "Someone is going to create one or declare one or something."

"A War Zone?"

"I don't know, Alan. Could be a no-parking zone for all I know."

"What's it got to do with me?"

"Wish I could tell you, Alan. By the way, it's you."

"What's me?"

"It's your party and you're paying for it. Drink up."

Vickery's sense of being in command had begun to erode; it almost felt as if he were in fact second-in-command — to Mariella of all people. Well, all right, that was always the case in domestic affairs, but not in business. Or politics. Why was Mariella organizing big announcements on his behalf?

But before he could pump Derek and Ronnie for more details he felt a sharp prod in the small of the back. Looking up in annoyance, he saw Aylsham grinning down at him with a glass of champagne in one hand and Zara in the other.

"Alan! Found you at last. Put your shoes on, there's a good fellow. Splendid place you've got here. Not my taste, exactly, but the location is superb. Zara, run along now and play with your little friends on the beach."

Zara gave her father a sarcastic wave and trotted off ocean-wards.

"Hang on a minute," Vickery said, struggling to get to his feet. "Sara! Zara!"

"Kids!" Derek said.

"I know," Ronnie said. "Mine were the same at that age. Wonder where they are now..."

"Ronnie," Vickery said, "just shut up a moment, will you? Jerry, I need to have a very serious word with you."

"Yes, Alan, you do indeed. For goodness' sake find yourself a towel and put your shoes on. You don't want to miss General Fricke's speech."

"I've heard his speech. It's — well, I don't need to hear it again. It's you I want to hear from. I want to know what you think you're —"

"It's a different speech. Come along, come along!"

"Listen, Jerry," Vickery said, waving his loafer in Aylsham's face, "what the hell were you playing at with my daughter in my house the other night? Don't deny it. I bloody well saw you!"

Vickery felt something buffet against the back of his head.

"Towel, Alan," Derek said.

"For God's sake, Alan. You're making a fool of yourself. Pick your towel up."

"I *will* pick that towel up, Jerry. But first I want your explanation."

Aylsham sighed, in an offensive and exaggerated way.

"Oh, very well, Alan. Not that it's really your business. I was merely debriefing her."

Vickery studied Aylsham's face for several seconds, but saw nothing except the usual petulance, disdain and aloofness. Not a spark of flippancy. Not a hint of ribaldry.

"Jerry... If you're trying to be funny..."

"Oh, this is absurd. Don't you remember? I sent her to spy on that lefty BBC chap in Johannesburg. Remember?"

"Johannesburg?"

"Yes. What's the matter with you? She was reporting back."

"Reporting back?"

"Yes, Alan. Very interesting, as it turned out."

"Interesting?"

Aylsham snatched up the towel.

"Here. Dry your feet."

Conclusions, Vickery thought as he rubbed his feet. Not to be jumped to, if you wanted to avoid looking like a prat. Somehow, any encounter with Aylsham always resulted in Vickery's humiliation. Why was that?

"Good," Aylsham said. "Now these interesting loafers."

Vickery slipped his shoes back on and unrolled his trousers.

"Alan!" Derek said. "We'll be at the pool bar, should you require our services."

"Yeah, well, you know where I keep it if you run out, don't you?"

"Certainly do!"

"Alan's putting the world to rights, is he Derek?"

"Yes, Ronnie. We can rest easy."

Aylsham led Vickery away from the pool.

"Who are those men, Alan?"

"Friends, Jerry. Just friends."

The garden lounge gave out on to a lawn. At the far edge of the lawn, Mariella had installed a rock garden. Composed of colorful boulders, expensively imported, and exotic grasses, the rock garden sloped up, steeply, to a terrace. Whether or not the terrace was Italianate, like the one in Chelsea, Vickery couldn't say, but its centerpiece was a flat, circular podium upon which stood a marble likeness of Mariella herself, in the character of some woman from Shakespeare with the unlikely name of Perdita. This eye-catching chunk of statuary, Vickery thought, had Marie-Thérèse's stamp all over it but, in practice, it looked more like Mariella's favorite super-model than Mariella herself.

And it was on this platform that General Fricke now stood, supporting himself, with unmilitary nonchalance, by leaning his elbow on Mariella's shoulder.

The lawn had filled with spectators, apparently eager for the General's performance. The General was warming up by picking out friends and supporters in the audience like a Las Vegas crooner staging a benefit show. Aylsham dragged Vickery to the back of the crowd.

Now that it was dark, everyone, the General included, seemed to appreciate the way Vickery's lighting illuminated the terrace like a natural stage. It was all intentional, of course; all part of the overall effect. A vivid and dramatic synthesis of lighting, sculpture, computer power — and plumbing. Vickery glanced at his watch and wondered idly if Mariella had remembered to deactivate the water-works. Perhaps he should nip inside and check?

But before he could make up his mind, he felt a tug at his sleeve.

"Oh my, Mr. Vickery, how delightful to find you here!"

It was the sweet and unmistakable simper of Raymond Priles, the noted golf-nut and corporate welfare queen.

"Hullo Ray, lovely to see you, too. This is Jeremy. He's been debriefing my daughter."

"Oh..."

"Like the house, do you?"

"Oh, it's delightful, Mr. Vickery. It reminds me of our cottage in the Hamptons."

"Where's Marty? I don't believe I hear his voice."

"Oh, he had to go back to the boat to fetch his medication. We're moored offshore, you see."

"Of course you are, Ray."

"I was so sorry to miss your lovely wife."

"Yeah. Actually, that's her over there. General Freaky's leaning on her."

Priles looked confused.

"Oh," he said, "you mean the statue. Yes. Oh my, she's very beautiful."

"Doesn't look like her," Vickery said. "She's gone to Zug."

Priles nodded.

"Oh, I understand. Yes, Zug. My, my."

Vickery gave Priles a nudge in order to shift him away from Aylsham — not easy because Priles was stout and well-anchored.

"Listen, Ray," Vickery said. "The Giraffe business. Not in front of Jeremy, I think."

"Oh no."

"Tell Marty, will you?"

"Oh yes."

"Ray?"

"Yes?"

"That Giraffe bloke. Lester. He was in Switzerland, wasn't he?"

"Oh yes. Marty wanted you to go there, I believe. But it's all taken care of now. Mm-hmm. But there are some dreadful rumors, dreadful. I dare say you've heard."

"No. What?"

"They say he tried to hit an elderly woman with his car. And then he assaulted this girl, after — well, who knows? The stock's down thirteen dollars and eighty-three cents. As of lunchtime."

"As much as that?"

"Yes. It's shocking."

"Look, Ray, there's nothing else funny going on is there? In Switzerland, I mean..."

"Well, it's a funny place altogether, Mr. Vickery. I think you'd better ask Marty. He's the expert."

"Right."

Vickery pondered the prospect of another one-sided swear-a-thon with Marty Bazon while, all around, the sounds of the night rippled through the perfumed tropical air: The popping of champagne corks; the steel band, which seemed to have taken over from the guitar on the beach and which was playing classical melodies; the cries of delight from the girls as they chased each other on the sand — or something; the rustling of designer gowns; the soft excuse-me's of the waiters; the sophisticated guffaws of the Weekly Consensus crew.

Then, all of a sudden, there came a hush and the General started to speak.

"Friends," he said, "we live in dark times."

This sentiment seemed to strike a chord. It was almost as if the entire crowd had chorused as one and the words had been "Oh, don't we just know it!" Aylsham nodded with particular fervor. Priles had bitten his lip and looked as if he were going to cry.

"Dark times indeed," the General said, milking the moment.

Yes, Vickery thought. Dark times — but not as dark as all that. If you lived in the War Zones, well all right. Pretty dark; you couldn't dispute it — not unless you were one of the leader-writers on the Consensus. And certain big cities in the Civilized World that he would be too prudent to name out loud had become a bit iffy. More than a bit. But history hadn't started yesterday, had it? It hadn't started a few years ago. It went back for yonks. Times might be dark but they weren't sleeping-in-a-hole-in-the-back-garden dark. Among the few unrepressed memories of Vickery's youth were the stories his Uncle Arthur told him when Vickery was a boy and still impressionable. The story he remembered most vividly, of course, was the one about the night Auntie Ethel refused to leave the comfort of her bed for the dampness of the burrow. Uncle Arthur's stories never had surprise endings.

"But we will prevail," the General said, thumping Mariella with his fist to emphasize the point.

Vickery wasn't much of a speech-maker himself, though he prided himself on his ability, held in reserve as a rule, to be eloquent. He had been a student of rhetoric, in a rough sort of way — you had to be with people like Fat Phil and practically anyone who worked in the international finance industry. And he could therefore have pointed out to General Freaky that he hadn't specified what it was that those assembled were going to prevail over. A glance at the Consensus mob told Vickery that they too had spotted this error and were trying not to let on.

"I have spoken recently with the commanders in each major theatre," the General said. "And although I cannot tell you the details of what we discussed" — and here the General gave a kind of pantomime wink, which seemed to baffle the crowd — "I can tell you this. Things are going well. Very well."

There was a short pause in which the audience waited for the General to qualify his optimism, realized he wasn't going to, and then applauded anyway. The General seemed gratified.

"Many of you," he said, "will have sons and daughters, and nieces and nephews... And other family members among our brave men and women in uniform."

Vickery wondered if the General had beaten Derek and Ronnie to the gin store. This was crazy talk, as Kellerman would say. Vickery watched for the tell-tale foot-shuffling, and, sure enough, there it was. The Consensus gang looked huffy and unimpressed, but the General didn't seem to notice.

"They are playing their part and we salute them. Yes, sir. We salute their devotion and their sacrifice. We salute those who have laid down their lives in mortal combat. We salute those who have been injured in the line of duty. We salute those who have been cut down in battle, those who have spilled their blood, those whose bodies have been torn asunder, whose limbs —"

But the General's gory catalog was cut short as a team of waiters rushed to the front of the crowd to remove a faintee — a young woman Vickery recognized as an established member of the Urquist set.

The General, it was clear, had misjudged his audience. Aylsham seemed to think so too.

"Well, this is a bit off," he said.

"I'm not sure I'm following," Priles said. "What does it all mean, Mr. Vickery?"

"I think it means this..." Vickery said, making the universally-understood *glug-glug* gesture.

"Oh..." Priles said, looking confused.

"Someone ought to tell him to get to the point," Aylsham said.

"What's that, then, Jerry?" Vickery asked, deftly taking the opportunity to pump Aylsham on Jason's behalf.

"You ought to know."

But before Vickery could challenge Aylsham on the question of why he, Vickery, was always the bloody last to find out anything, the General, perhaps having received the all-clear from Urquist, resumed.

"Ladies and gentleman, I regret the effect of my speech upon this young lady. But this is war, ladies and gentlemen. War. Let us never forget that."

This seemed to get the crowd back on his side. Encouraged, but with new-found prudence, the General proceeded.

"War requires sacrifice. And the first to be sacrificed are the proud members of our nearly-all-volunteer army. But this is a new war — a war in which the battlefield is everywhere. Yes, my friends, even here."

Vickery pictured Derek and Ronnie battling to find the key to the drinks cabinet in the study, the rat gazing down merrily all the while.

"We do not know when the enemy will come to Barbados. But wherever freedom reigns, nevertheless it is threatened," the General continued, "because the enemies of freedom will seek out any weakness, however small. They will exploit that weakness, ruthlessly, wherever they find it. We must eliminate all weakness."

This got the General a big hand and some enthusiastic cheers. Even the Consensus doubters united in grudging approval.

"This is more like it," Aylsham said.

"We cannot allow the enemy to use our own weapons against us," the General said.

"Absolutely not," Aylsham said.

"Better that we destroy those weapons before the enemy can turn them on us. Freedom must not be wasted on those who hate freedom," the General announced to popular acclaim. Even Priles, who, Vickery suspected, was still having trouble following along, seemed to think this worth a limp clap.

"War requires sacrifice," the General repeated.

"He keeps saying that but what does he mean?" Priles asked. "I wish he would tell us."

"He's coming to it. Just listen, will you?" Aylsham said, with a brusqueness that the mild-mannered Priles seemed to resent.

"All of you here have sacrificed your time and your money," the General said. "And this sacrifice will not go un-noted, you may be sure."

"Got to sacrifice to accumulate — eh, Alan?" Aylsham said.

"Thanks to you," the General said, "freedom is on the march again. And the enemies of freedom will have one place less in the world to hide out. One place less, ladies and gentlemen. And you know what? We're not going to stop. We're not going to stop, ladies and gentlemen. We're not going to stop until there is no place left to hide. And we're not going to stop until the enemies of freedom bow down before us and scream for mercy. Mercy, ladies and gentlemen. But there can be no mercy. No, there never can. And, at that point in time, my friends, freedom will have triumphed. *You* will have triumphed."

This brought the house down — or would have done, if they hadn't been in the garden. Aylsham banged his hands together so fiercely that Vickery thought it best to back off out of elbow-range. Priles, still baffled but somehow swept up in the general rapture, started calling out "bravo" as if he were at the opera. The Consensus crew, satisfied at last, were waving their arms — though one of their number, Vickery noticed, got ticked off when he accidentally slipped into a Nazi salute.

"You see?" Aylsham yelled over the din. "They're opening up a new Zone!"

"What does that mean?" Vickery shouted back.

"Opportunity. What else?"

"War Zone, is it?"

"Temporarily, Alan. Then it becomes a freedom zone. I thought you knew all this."

"Where?"

"It's your project, Alan. Southern Africa. This means they've given the go-ahead. You must be very proud."

Once again, Aylsham was making little sense. The crowd was mad with excitement and the noise made it difficult to converse. The General had snatched the opportunity to refresh his glass and the waiters had taken this as a cue to refuel the party as a whole. It was getting quite raucous.

"Pardon me, Ray," Vickery said, grabbing Aylsham by the elbow and hauling him into the relative quiet of the study.

"Alan, they're coming round with the champagne —"

"Just a minute, Jerry. I need a word."

"What, again? What is it now?"

"How do you know about my Africa thing?"

"Oh, everyone knows about that."

"No, they don't. It's a top-secret Liberty Club project. You are not a member of the Liberty Club."

"Neither are you."

"No, but they trust me. I am an *associate* member." He was making this up, but it didn't matter; it was only Aylsham.

"Oh, really?"

"Yes. But that is a side-issue. How did you acquire this information?"

"Don't be absurd, Alan. The Liberty Club is all very fine, and I'm sure their people — with your excellent assistance — will do a splendid job in Angola. But there is a larger plan. And there are higher powers."

"There are, Jerry, there are," Vickery said, thinking of Jason and Richard, and, of course, Douglas Moreland. "And you would do well to watch your step."

"So would you."

"I'm warning you, Jerry. Be careful what you say."

"Don't be ridiculous."

"We are not starting a War Zone. All we are doing is toppling the evil dictator who — no, wait, it's more complicated than that, there isn't a single... Anyway, it doesn't matter. We go in, we topple, we install, the invoices go in and we come home. Simple as that. When I say *go in*, I don't mean me personally. We have recruited professionals from the private sector. No War Zones, Jerry."

"You're such a fool, Alan," Aylsham said, backing away in the direction of the garden. "You never see the big picture, do you?" He was about to say more, but something caught his attention. He stopped and frowned. "Why is there a rat above your fireplace?"

"It's what you call poetic revenge, Jerry."

"Ha!" Aylsham said and strode off back to the party.

Vickery gazed at the laughing rat. It was easy to triumph over dope-riddled, financially-inept rock stars. You used the power of money. But with people like Aylsham it was different. They had some mysterious, special access that kept them two steps ahead of you. And in Aylsham's case, at least, there was an equally mysterious supply of funds.

So had Vickery missed the big picture? Was the Angola enterprise merely a piece of some larger plot to turn southern Africa into another War Zone? If you put General Freaky's military evangelism alongside Aylsham's more squalid variety, it looked that way. And, no doubt, the new War Zone would be just as "temporary" as all the others.

The question was, would this put him in a what's-it? A moral dilemma? For advice on such ethical posers, he normally turned to Phil. But you couldn't expect someone like Phil to rule on matters of war and peace — matters in which it was conceivable that financial considerations could be outweighed by, well, by more basic issues. Life and death; that sort of thing. Phil didn't have the depth. And suppose Vickery did help, in a small way, sort of, in starting a new War Zone in southern Africa... What view would Mariella take?

Muller had insisted that, once the toppling and installing were over, the long-suffering citizens of Angola would be vastly better off, if you considered the bloody awful time they were having now. All that Chinese investment only enriched the *elites*, apparently. And Vickery had been happy to take Muller's word for it. But if you were to ask the average Angolan bloke in the street if he fancied playing a walk-on (but not necessarily walk-off) role in the Pentagon's latest big-budget production, how would said bloke reply?

"Alan looks to that rat for inspiration, you know, Ronnie."

Vickery turned to discover Derek and Ronnie, in their baggy, dripping swim-shorts, padding across his marble.

"Alan, they're going mad out there. Mad, they are," Derek said. Ronnie looked preoccupied.

"We came to find the, er..."

"Cabinet under the window, Ronnie."

"Oh, right. Thanks."

"By the way," Derek said, "they're calling for you out there."

"Are they? What for?"

"Well, you know that woman with the funny skin?"

Derek meant Phyllis, of course.

"What about her?"

"Well, they've hauled her up on to the terrace. You know, in that big wicker chair. And there's a bunch of blokes up there in red ties..."

Probably the editors of the Consensus.

"...with this General, or whatever he is."

"Yeah, General Freaky. And?"

"And they want you to go up there and make a speech."

"Where's the key?" Ronnie called out.

"It's not locked," Vickery said. "What speech?"

"Up to you, I think. Better just nip out and say a few well-chosen, Alan. Keep them happy. You want to keep well-in with that lot."

"Thanks, Derek."

This was unwelcome. What should he say? "Thanks for coming. It's been nice having you. Now go home." How about that? The evening had begun as a dream but had turned queasy and mad.

Glancing at the rat, Vickery gave his three best friends in the world a forlorn one-fingered salute and stepped out into his roiling garden.

It was only when he reached the top of the terrace and was attempting to negotiate passage through the editorial thickets of the Consensus that he noticed the new sprinklers. They were all around the edge of the lawn. Mariella must have had them installed since he was last here. Good, he thought — keep the grass green. Then he remembered the more sophisticated waterworks that underlay the terrace. Mariella had been inspired by the magical, dancing fountains of that big hotel in Las Vegas that began with a "B". Vickery glanced at his watch. It was five minutes to midnight. Had Mariella remembered to deactivate the system? Had she — and he had urged her to do this on more than one occasion — even read the manual? Better make it a short speech, he thought.

General Fricke had ceded his spot by Mariella's side and was urging Vickery forward. Vickery hopped over Phyllis's twig-thin ankles and grasped the General's outstretched hand.

"Hullo," he said. "Remember me? Philadelphia? You made that announcement about those bankers. Funny how that turned out."

General Fricke gave Vickery a distant look, probably because he had military matters on his mind. Plus, of course, the many issues of national and international importance certain to fill his diary after his imminent, shoo-in election victory. All the same, there was a hesitancy there, a coolness. A *froideur*, Mariella would have called it, had she been describing it to Marie-Thérèse. Just the natural disdain of the soldier for the businessman — or something else? At their last meeting, Vickery had made the mistake of pointing out his status as a stalwart citizen of Ally Number One — to which the General had responded that the list was not a long one.

"So, um, what shall I talk about?" Vickery asked.

"Providing you do not reveal classified information," the General said, "it's all the same to me."

Someone at the back of the crowd had instigated a "Speech! Speech!" chant. It was almost certainly Aylsham; this kind of public-school rowdiness was alien to your American business class.

Which topic should he select? What would go down best with this mob in its present mood? A heartfelt call for the elimination of free elementary schooling? One of Phil's funny stories? Stock tips?

No, Vickery thought, given the golden surroundings, the gilded crowd, and the liquored-up emotion of the night, this was the perfect occasion for the Personal Testament.

"Ladies and gentlemen," he announced, adding "and friends' in case Derek and Ronnie were within earshot, "I trust you have enjoyed your lovely evening. It has been a great honor for me to have hosted you all here... And I only wish I'd been around to send out the invitations."

This crack got a modest laugh and he felt emboldened.

"The reason we are all here is that we share certain values — and I think that is what General Frea — General Frick-ee was trying to say. That is what he was driving at."

Vickery glanced at the General but the General showed no emotion.

"But, although we are all here together now, in this beautiful garden — which was designed entirely by my wife, who, sadly, is in Zug — we did not all start here. Not by any means. My friend Jeremy, for example, did not start here. Not at all. He started from a castle in bloody Shropshire."

Vickery felt he had the audience in his grip now. Faces were upturned towards him and the curiosity was palpable.

And then it all came out. The story of his life. He entered a heightened state of consciousness and the words flew out. Every hard knock, mishap, mischance, kick in the teeth, humiliation, setback, put-down, cock-up and wipe-out. All the shame, spite, belittlement, malice, misery, grind, back-stabbing and face-cleaning. The groveling and the scrabbling. And then the self-realization and the act of will. The determination and the blind, raging ambition. Finally, Success and then the ascension: The bloody great houses, the blue-blooded wife and that ultimate trophy, the bloody beautiful daughter.

Had he moved his audience? You only had to look at their faces.

And then it happened. As caught up in the passion of his speech as he had been, the foreknowledge of disaster had never faded entirely from his conscious-ness. Had he wanted it to happen all along? Had he wished it? And, if he had, did this mean that something psychological was going on?

The white lights in the trees went out. Up and down the garden the low-level spotlights extinguished themselves as if by hidden command. The crowd gave up a nervous gasp. All along the terrace electric motors whizzed and whirred. From the roof of the house, multicolored beams of state-of-the-art theatrical lighting bore down on and illuminated the columns and statuary. Mariella glowed a sultry purple. Red and green lasers played amongst the crowd and outlined the boulders on the slope. The audience purred and trilled and giggled. From all sides, in eleven-channel surround-sound, the roar of a Broadway-style orchestra swelled and the foliage shivered. The music rose to a climax, the tempo slowed, the drums rolled, the lasers flickered and danced, the violins squeaked to the very top of their range and the crowd wailed with pleasure.

It gave Vickery a certain illicit thrill that he, and only he, knew what was coming next. The editor of the Consensus waved at him. He waved back.

Then the computers opened the valves on Mariella's industrial-grade water jets. The shock was profound. At first it was so beautiful — you could see the awe in people's faces. The jets twisted and danced in sync with the music, and the water leaped for the sky and feathered out into mist and iridescent droplets.

But then, after a delay long enough for the shrewder to contemplate their fate, it all came back down to Earth.

Vickery — exhausted, slaked and depleted after having had his say for once and, more or less, in full — stood rooted to the spot, as if slightly outside his own body, as Mariella's soft, ecstatic rain fell.

But few around him, he noted, were able to keep their heads in the same way. Like a made-for-TV herd of wildebeest — those same unlucky animals that were much preyed upon by the former King of Angola — the crowd turned as one and beat a path to the garden lounge, discarding their black silk gloves and scarves in the tumult.

Vickery checked his watch. The show had kicked off twenty minutes after midnight and was therefore a bit off-schedule. But of course Mariella expected the help to set the clocks. Make a mental note, he thought.

Priles, probably never the most agile of the aggressive-accounting set, tripped and fell. Vickery saw Aylsham leap over him like a mountain goat.

The editors of the Consensus peeled off their jackets and turned Phyllis's wicker seat into a kind of sedan chair. All that stood between Phyllis and a dry sofa was an editorial dispute about the precise direction to take.

Urquist's girls, in a gesture of selflessness that Vickery for one would not have expected of them, had formed a kind of satiny human umbrella over him — not difficult, given Urquist's squat dimensions — and were hustling him to safety like a ladybird — or bug — with no sense of direction.

The fountains, it had to be said, were fantastic. Mariella had spent well. Close up, it was possible to observe the angling of the jets and the split-second operation of the nozzles. This, Vickery told himself, was a brilliant and legitimate application of computer power. Unlike, say, spying on people's bank accounts.

He was getting wet, but it didn't matter. For once, he'd had his say and people had listened. Had they understood? Had they taken it to heart? Or would the water and the music — some kind of instrumental take on Lloyd-Webber, he thought — wash it all away?

And then, with redundant brio, the lawn sprinklers went off. Mariella didn't think these things through. Those revelers who hadn't already made it into the garden lounge were now doomed. And Mariella, true to form, hadn't cut corners. There wasn't a square inch that wasn't getting soaked.

It was like some kind of military maneuver, Vickery mused, spotting General Fricke in the garden lounge attending to Phyllis with a tea towel. Your first explosions target the terrace. The enemy retreats in the obvious direction — towards the house. And gets cut down in the crossfire — or cross-sprinkle — of the ambush.

Now, out of the spray and mist, two figures emerged, their arms held aloft as in a kind of religious trance. If one of them hadn't been holding a bottle of gin they might have been the ghosts of Glastonbury past.

"Spud!" Vickery shouted.

"Alan! You're all wet. Nice show, though."

"Thanks. Mariella... You know."

Derek and Ronnie began their ascent up the rock garden to the terrace, where Vickery now stood alone.

"Not upset, are they? Your guests?" Derek asked.

"Oh, they'll be all right."

"Only Ronnie has something to say to you. Ronnie?"

"Yes. Well," Ronnie began. "It's just that —"

"Mariella told you to tell me something?"

"Ah. Yes. You see —"

Vickery held up an imperious hand.

"Ronnie, it doesn't matter. Everything is... All right. What's a little water between allies?"

"Glad you see it that way, Alan. Only Mariella —"

"Don't you worry about Mariella, Ronnie. Leave her to me."

"As you say, Alan."

"It's nearly finished," Vickery said. "Watch."

The music slogged to a final cadence, the jets reared up to the perpendicular at full strength and a clutch of fireworks streaked off from their special pen on the roof terrace and exploded over the beach in glittery star shapes. Then the jets cut off and the nozzles retreated to their silos. The sprinklers, left to carry the show, decided to pack it in too.

"How much do you think that cost?" Vickery asked.

Derek and Ronnie shook their heads.

"Doesn't matter, though, does it?" Vickery continued. "You spend a lot of money. So what? You go out and make a lot more. You sell pensions or houses. Or control pests. Something useful. Something people need. Or want. No mystery."

His friends were looking at him strangely.

"I'll just go and see if anyone needs anything," he said.

"Right you are, Alan. We'll be in the pool if you need us," Derek said, as if addressing a sensitive invalid.

Vickery descended to the lawn and entered the garden lounge. He found a disheveled Priles consoling himself with a Martini, but no one else. Priles gestured towards the front porch.

In the circular driveway beyond the porch, Vickery could see the limos, like lifeboats, inching past to collect their soggy survivors. It was a tale, he speculated, likely to be recounted down the ages wherever bored chauffeurs waited together.

He wandered out on to the beach with the vague intention of bonding with his daughter, or possibly her playmates. But the beach appeared empty. He removed his loafers, rolled up his trousers and padded down to the water's edge.

The warm Caribbean washed up against Vickery's ankles and teased sand between his toes. He wondered what the beaches in Angola were like. Perhaps they were just like this. Would the Atlantic be as warm as the Caribbean? Were there houses like his to be purchased? Probably not. But why not? Muller had said that Angola had a lot of oil, that it was all off-shore, and that this was a good thing. Why a good thing? Didn't it make it more expensive? And who wanted a beach-side property whose hundred-and-eighty-degree views featured oil rigs and tankers?

He turned to look at his house. It was beautiful. At one time, before he'd had the money to buy it, the vision of such a place had dazzled and enthralled him. Now, he felt — what was the word? Ambiguous? No — ambivalent. The possession of such a place comforted him. But he didn't love it. He ought to, but somehow he didn't. And he worried about the bills, even though he could easily afford them.

Vickery started back towards the house but then stopped. Out of the shadows came a thin, wiry man in a kind of straw cowboy hat. At first Vickery thought he must be a local worker — not one of the staff but a building contractor or delivery guy. But as the man came closer, Vickery recognized the slow, measured gait and the gum-chewing grin — like the smirk of a disappointed gunslinger.

Could you conjure up demons like this? He'd been thinking about Angola — an ocean away — and now here was Harlan Petty, on Vickery's own beach, probably armed to the teeth, and with no Muller or Kellerman on hand to intervene if necessary.

Petty stopped three feet away from Vickery and looked him up and down.

"Been having a party?"

"Yes," Vickery said.

"Hope you enjoyed yourself."

"Yes."

Petty was wearing tight jeans, cowboy boots and a clinging, long-sleeved shirt. Vickery didn't see where he could possibly hide a gun. Maybe a knife in the boot?

"You did a good job."

"Did I?"

"Yeah, the money. Had my doubts but it's fine."

Vickery swallowed and waited.

"Yeah, real fine job. I guess you *are* a professional."

"Yes. Thanks."

"Okay."

Petty reached inside his shirt. Vickery felt himself tense up. Petty pulled out an envelope.

"Here you go," he said, handing the envelope to Vickery.

What was it? Some kind of cash bonus? If so, it was insultingly small.

"Your plane tickets," Petty said.

"What?"

"I can use you on the other end. Now I know what you can do."

"The other end?"

"See you in Luanda."

Petty spat out his gum, turned, and trudged off, as slowly as he had arrived.

Vickery ripped open the envelope. Inside were plane tickets — one to Johannesburg, another to Luanda. Both in his name. Both one-way. He watched Petty disappear into the darkness.

Well, that was it, he thought. If Aylsham tried to send Vickery to Africa — as he had indeed sent his daughter — he would tell Aylsham exactly what he could do. He could brush off Muller. He could tell Kellerman to get lost. He could be evasive with Jason or politely decline to Richard. He would even try to resist Douglas Moreland. But Petty...

There was a bleep from Vickery's spy-phone. He removed it from his jacket pocket, relieved to find it was damp but operational. Jason had sent him a text message. "y no info yet?" it said. "pls rpt asap". There was more. Vickery scrolled down. "Honestly, Alan, we were hoping for some decent intelligence by now. Buck yr ideas up."

Vickery sighed. Then, behind him, the lapping of the waves gave way to the growl of twin diesel engines. Turning, Vickery saw a thin figure in a tuxedo jump out on to the beach from a small but super-deluxe motor launch. The bullish posture of the figure and the way the moon reflected off the top of its head suggested to Vickery a grumpy, corporate James Bond late for a dinner date.

"Hey!" the figure said, marching up the beach towards him. It was Marty Bazon, looking unwell and unhappy.

"Fucking boats," he said. "Huh? Why the fuck are you wet? Did I fucking miss something?"

CHAPTER 24

George Fischer spent the day in Windhoek, waiting in hotel lobbies, riding in Mercedes limousines with government plates and freezing in sparsely-fitted offices.

Official attitudes were calm, measured, serious, concerned. Unofficially, everyone he talked to was in a panic. Even the ones too young to have heard of Arnie Muller. George told them there was money to be had if they acquiesced in a new sphere of influence to the north, and put up with the violence that these things always seemed to bring — or they could just have the influence without the cash. When this insult brought forth, in every instance, the expected tirade — African liberation, neo-colonialist hypocrisy, the typically craven attitudes of the opposition parties and so on — he told them that he was on their side and there wasn't any lie he wouldn't tell Arnie Muller for their sake. And, since he was sure to run into Muller any time now, was there anything they'd like him to pass on?

By four o'clock he'd worked his way through retired SWAPO chief Julius's A-list and now sat scorching in the sun on the outdoor terrace of an American-style coffee house in one of the shiny new malls on Independence Avenue. There was a buzz here and the thrill of a new but still limited prosperity. Ten years ago there had been little of this. Of course, if you walked three hundred meters along the road, you found that things hadn't changed that much. But any such progress was precious.

Muller had called and told him to be here. George wouldn't pass on the threats, which were empty, or the insults, which weren't. But he would tell Muller that giving the cash away wasn't going to be easy.

He was still studying his menu — he'd never seen such a long menu in Namibia — when a shadow fell over it. But the shadow was far too narrow to be Muller, and the touch of its hand on his was much too soft.

Roberta sat down and took off her sunglasses.

"This is a nice place. Can I see?"

He handed her the menu.

"How did you know I was here? Muller is coming. Are you sure —"

"Yes. I've been following you."

This was a shock. How could she have done it? How could she ever have moved fast enough, even if her prosthetic foot were firmly secured?

"But how did you get here?"

"Julius."

"Julius?"

"I looked at the information on the Internet and then I called him."

"What information?"

"George, the book. The book that the Americans gave you."

"The woman gave it to me. Sheryl. But her husband — he didn't know anything about it."

"She told you how to use it. I overheard. You didn't seem to be listening."

"I was listening, but computers — they are not my thing."

"No. But they are mine. So I followed the instructions and I looked. They are running a *dark web*. Do you know what that is?"

"I think so."

"It's how they communicate. You need certain things from the book to get in."

"And so?"

She put the menu down.

"George, Moreland's people don't really care what you say to Julius or the Politburo or SWAPO or anyone in Namibia. They will buy as many people as they can, but they don't really care. We only have diamonds and uranium. No oil."

"Then why is Muller —"

"They want you in Luanda."

"I'm going to Luanda. Tonight."

"You mustn't."

"No, I must."

"I think Moreland wants you there."

He shuffled his chair out of the sun and sipped from his coffee.

"George, you know what he wants."

"Elizabeth."

"He's going to make you talk about her."

She was staring at him. He tried to meet her gaze but failed.

"And then he's going to kill you."

"No," he said. "You read this on the Internet?"

"He's the one running everything, George."

Of course he was. Moreland was the expert, the man with experience. Southern Africa was his unfinished business, his property. These people wrote their grudges into history.

"Muller is late," he said. "You should go before he gets here."

Roberta hauled herself to her feet.

"You can go where you want," she said. "I'm coming with you."

"I'm going to Luanda."

"All right. Luanda. Buy me a ticket."

He stood up. Then he leaned over and kissed her forehead.

"Okay, okay," he said. "We are going now."

On their way out of the restaurant, they saw Muller hunting among the tables, pushing against people and kicking their bags out of his path.

"Do you know who Thomas Lester is?" Roberta asked as they fled, stumbling, down the escalator.

"No. Who is he?"

"I don't know. But they're going to kill him, too."

"Who says so?"

"The Resistance."

"Who are they?"

"They are the CIA."

CHAPTER 25

Alan Vickery was not, to begin with, impressed by the richest country in Africa. The airport was a bloody shambles. He hadn't exactly expected a chauffeur in a hat with a square of cardboard and "Mr. A. Vickery" written on it. In a place like this, you wouldn't, would you? But some kind of welcome would have been, well, welcome.

Instead, on descending from his plane, he'd been confronted on the tarmac with a ramshackle fleet of death-trap buses and, following the crowd for once in his life, he'd picked the wrong one. It took him to an ancient propeller plane that was all-too-apparently kitted-up for its final plunge into the Heart of Darkness. He bade farewell to his many new friends and took to his heels.

Having roamed the runways sweatily for twenty minutes, being pestered and possibly mocked in what he presumed was Portuguese even though it didn't sound very Spanish, he eventually rooted out what passed for an immigration hall. Here, while batting away insistent flying insects — mosquitoes? — he discovered that the price of admission to Africa's new El Dorado was steep but negotiable. And simple prudence demanded that an offer of free, on-the-spot inoculations had to be declined with yet more cash. Fortunately, he'd stuffed his carry-on with dollars, suspecting — correctly as it turned out — that there wouldn't be an ATM on every corner.

To his immense surprise and relief, he found Kellerman waiting for him at the curb with a taxi — the only one in sight — and a disgruntled expression verging on the murderous.

"Alan. What took you? Get in the car."

"Bryce! Lovely to see you, you old bastard! Bloody brilliant! To be honest, I was a bit —"

"Get in the car."

Kellerman left Alan to load his own bags into the trunk, which, Vickery couldn't help but notice, made up for what it lacked in spare wheels by emphasizing armaments — one of those spindly rifles with the curvy ammo thing, to be precise. It wasn't in good condition. No wonder they needed new ones.

Another thing that wasn't in top form was Kellerman.

"Bryce," Vickery said, concern in his voice, as he tumbled into the back seat behind Kellerman, "what happened to your neck?" Kellerman didn't have a neck, but he did have sensitivities.

"Friggin' mosquitoes, Alan. We're all going to get friggin' malaria. Did you bring your friggin' pills?"

"Pills?"

"Never mind."

It was astonishing to find Kellerman in surroundings like these. His natural habitat comprised Washington, New York and London, the latter of which he seemed to regard as a quaint backwater or theme park and not really distinct from NY at all. There might be a recreational visit to Florida or Aspen or Las Vegas, but not to anywhere so impoverished that the shanty-towns (Vickery had just seen them from the air) covered many times the area of the capital city itself, or where — according to Aylsham, whose glee upon learning Vickery's destination had been uncontainable — to step off the fairway into the rough in search of a lost ball was to risk sudden dismemberment on account of war-legacy landmines. Someone extremely powerful must have ordered Kellerman into Angola, and Vickery could only wish he'd been there to see it.

And the only good thing to say about the ride from the airport was that it was short.

As for the city of Luanda, Vickery found it both alarming and tantalizing. There'd been a war of some sort, obviously, and, around the edges, the place was ragged and half-wrecked. Here in the center, however, things were happening. Chinese construction firms were shoving up concrete tower blocks with the same relentless dedication that Mariella devoted to the purchase of designer footwear. Talk about *animal spirits*. Was there a trickle-down, though? Why, yes! If you looked closely enough, you could see the fresh shoots of hope: A Mercedes dealership here, a posh cigar store there. That sort of thing.

But what struck him — and here was the bit that tantalized — was the potential. Especially in real estate. If only dear old Ronnie could have been there to see it. His eyes would have popped and it would have been large ones all round.

You had your elegant colonial — very marketable; and then you had your cool sixties' style for the chic set. Well, all right, there was a lot of deferred maintenance and some often-unsightly bullet-holes, but the blocks that swept up from the bay were more Rio than Peckham.

And then there was the bay itself, a fantastic horse-shoe with actual sand and palm trees. Get rid of the dogs, the rubbish and the one-legged beggars — find somewhere decent for them, naturally — and bingo. And then, to top it all off, there was a curving spit reaching up from the southern end of the bay. This already looked like the smartest spot in town and would, without a doubt, be the location of Ronnie's top, designer-style units.

"Fucking shit-hole," Kellerman said.

Vickery's day-dream of African Gold Coast property riches dissipated. He saw they were driving through a neighborhood of discreet, guarded, reflecting-glass office blocks. Those with any indication of ownership seemed to belong to oil companies. They were mostly American, but he noticed at least one famous

British name. He wondered how easy it was going to be to report back to Jason, and resolved to try out the spy-phone as soon as he could dump Kellerman.

One building, formerly occupied by a French oil company, stood abandoned. But another, boldly labelled Sonangol, oozed prosperity. This, he thought, was probably the state-owned outfit and quite possibly part of the reason for his presence here. He looked forward to finding out. After all, the former King — if such an unlikely person existed — would surely trade all the wildebeest in his realm for a seat at the pumps.

"Wildebeest," he mumbled to himself, chortling.

"Say what?" Kellerman snapped.

"Wildebeest."

"Fuck you and your wildebeest, Alan."

Clearly, there was something bothering Kellerman, and it went beyond mosquitoes or even General Fricke and his taboo-busting daughters.

This thought turned out to be clairvoyant, because the first person Vickery saw when he tailed Kellerman into the unmarked conference room was the General. He sat at a table on a podium along with a bunch of suits who, Vickery decided, were either too beefy or too seedy, or both, to be bankers and must therefore be oilmen or rough entrepreneurs from the wild fringes of the new global economy.

Unlike Kellerman, the General had doffed his suit in favor of pseudo-military fatigues, that gave no inkling of his former rank. These were set off, unhappily, by a tight T-shirt from some safari company, featuring a yawning lion, which revealed that the General had been exceeding his rations for some time. The General's trouser cuffs were stained orange-brown, as were Kellerman's. Where might they have been together? If Vickery could find out, he'd tell Jason. Wherever it was, it was fully-stocked with mosquitoes. The General looked even worse than Kellerman; clearly, Angolan insect life was no respecter of seniority.

Kellerman pushed Vickery into a seat near the back. Glancing to his left, Vickery saw Petty standing in a corner, leaning against the wall. Petty spotted him, smirked and tipped his straw cowboy hat. Then he glanced at his watch, frowned, scratched his crotch and pushed his way out of the room.

Vickery tried to make eye-contact with the General, but the General was having none of it, preferring to scribble on a pad. The suits were passing around a hand-gun, touching and admiring it in the same way that teenagers lusted after each other's mobiles. This, Vickery thought, looked like some kind of business briefing. But with a difference.

The audience was hard to make out. But for three expensively-suited gents sitting in a corner with their arms folded, it was entirely white. Tanned, wrinkled skin; sunglasses worn indoors; shoulder bags instead of briefcases; a complete lack of grooming — these didn't seem like normal businessmen. But then this wasn't a normal place. Vickery wondered if he might be in for a learning experience.

"What's all this, then?" he asked Kellerman, who at that moment was fully occupied in looking morose and scratching the back of his neck.

"Friggin' MLG presentation," he said, examining his fingertips.

MLG, Vickery thought — wasn't that the outfit that Mariella had swooned over in Switzerland? What were they doing here? Building a chocolate factory? Like hell.

"Check out the friggin' attendees, Alan," Kellerman said. "You're going to be paying most of them off."

Less commission, Vickery thought.

"Who are they?" he asked.

"Friggin' contractors. Oil guys. Diamond guys. CIA guys. Special forces. Couple of UN creeps, don't laugh. Friggin' MLG analysts. Government advisers. Ex-UNITA weirdoes. Friends of the Administration. Representatives of the friggin' leading families of Luanda. You'll be digging deep for *them*. Those three in the corner? Our pals from the MPLA. The ruling party. Answer your question?"

Someone activated a projector. A PowerPoint slide wobbled into focus. "Africa: A New Opportunity," Vickery read. Kellerman snorted in quiet derision. The next slide came up. "Military Logistics Group - CONFIDENTIAL", Vickery read, but with some difficulty. It was no good; he had to face up to it. His eyesight was worsening. He withdrew from his inner jacket pocket a pair of brand-new, gold-plated, light-reactive, super-expensive, bifocal, vision-correcting, granddad specs and slipped them on his nose. Kellerman flinched and scowled.

The presentation had moved on to a map of Africa. Angola was highlighted and chopped out from the rest of the continent like a slice of pie. How appropriate, Vickery thought. But this wasn't about chocolate. Bullet-pointed statistics popped up and had themselves parroted out by the lead suit, who hadn't introduced himself and who, to Vickery's eyes, resembled a clapped-out gentleman explorer who had decided to join a suicide cult. There was a certain mania in his pin-striped delivery, a demented energy in his tired eyes.

Barrels, blocs, concessions, platforms, pipelines, tankers, estimated reserves, geophysical surveys, inward investment, government incentives, exploration permits, refining capacity, bonus payments — Vickery realized it was all about oil. Big Oil. The slides came and went. The audience sucked it all up. Like Texans at a gusher, Vickery mused — not that he'd ever been to Texas. It wasn't on Mariella's map. Kellerman lapsed into what Vickery hoped wasn't a malarial coma.

Eventually, after a sinister and unnerving overview of the oil-dependent Chinese economy, the explorer took a bow and sat down. There was a shuffling of chairs but no applause. Then the General stood up and assumed command of the Military Logistics laptop.

His first slide was puzzling: The words "MILITARY BASES' appeared, only to be crossed out by a big, red, animated "X". A concerned murmur broke out. But the General, it appeared, was toying with his audience. He would explain, he said.

It turned out that the Pentagon had determined, from bitter experience, that having military bases in foreign countries could be unpopular. It had therefore decided that, in those countries that didn't already have bases — and, yes, there *were* some, the General informed his listeners with a knowing wink — there would instead be either (*bing!* went the slide) Forward Operating Sites or (*bing!*) Cooperative Security Locations.

This was what it must have been like, Vickery imagined, to have been present on the occasion of some great scientific revelation — such as Einstein, for example, explaining that whatever you did it was all relative and thus not necessarily your fault. The audience was, at first, baffled. Then, one by one, they got it, and a smattering of polite clapping arose.

Forward Operating Sites, the General explained, would consist of logistical facilities, weapons stockpiles, and a small permanent crew of US military technicians, but no large combat units.

"Ah...!" the audience went.

Cooperative Security Locations, on the other hand, the General declared, looking ever more pleased with himself, would be bare-bones facilities for crisis-mode operations only. They would have no permanent US presence, being maintained by military contractors and host-country personnel.

"Aha!" the audience cried to itself.

The key concept, the General insisted, was (*bing!*) "INFORMAL SECURITY ARRANGEMENTS". This concept, Vickery could easily see, was instantly a hit.

There was an important distinction to be made, the General explained. There would be no dependents, no fast-food restaurants, no supermarkets or movie theatres, only the absolute minimum of flag-flying and, most particularly, *no formal security arrangements*. And the result of this important distinction would inevitably be that local indigenous persons would no longer gain the erroneous impression that the US was seeking a permanent, colonial-like presence in their countries. And the private sector, it went without saying, was a vital partner in all this.

"Of course!" the audience told itself.

The General proceeded to work his way through a series of maps that showed the oil-producing areas of Africa and the various leftist, terrorist, separatist, anti-capitalist, ethnic, tribal, jihadi, fundamentalist, and just plain criminal groups that inhabited them.

"Gentlemen," he said — and Vickery noticed that there were indeed no women in the room — "it is imperative that we protect the oil resources and infrastructure of Africa. Yes, we have shale oil. But it's not enough. A few years from now, thirty or thirty-five percent of our oil will come from Africa. If we cannot protect that oil, our military will be crippled. And if our military is crippled, we will not be able to protect the oil."

There was much head-nodding in the stalls.

"These organizations," the General said, indicating the leftist, terrorist, separatist, anti-capitalist, ethnic, tribal, jihadi, fundamentalist and criminal groups, "are the enemy. They create and foment (*bing!*) instability. Instability is also the enemy."

He allowed his audience to think about that one for a moment. There was an outbreak of note-taking.

"Any questions?" the General said.

Vickery stuck his hand up in the air. Heads turned. The General stared. The black guys from the MPLA — whatever that was — leaned forward. Kellerman groaned. Vickery waggled his hand, not sure if the General had really seen him. The General sucked his teeth.

"Yes?" he said. "You there. Mr. Vickery, isn't it? You have a question, sir?"

"Yes," Vickery said. "I do. It seems to me that what you're saying — what you're driving at, in effect and as it were — is that protecting the oil and clobbering the tribes and the terrorists and what-have-you... Well, it's really all the same thing, isn't it?"

The General narrowed his eyes.

"Mr. Vickery, sir. Wherever there is evil, we want to go there. Wherever there is evil, we want to fight it. And we will. You got that?"

It occurred to Vickery that there was something fishy about the oil and the evil always turning up in the same place. But before he could respond there came the boom of an explosion nearby and the building shuddered briefly. Vickery, who sat nearest to the window, jumped up, hauled open the sliding doors and stepped out on to the balcony. About half a mile away on the fringe of the central zone, a column of dirty, black smoke rose up into the clearing evening sky.

A crowd gathered behind him, pushing him up against the railings. Looking down, Vickery saw a gang of children — urchins, really — jumping and shrieking like fans at a football match. He felt a sliding sensation on the bridge of his nose, but his arms were jammed against the parapet and he could not free them in time. His glasses tumbled down into the street and the urchins set upon them.

"Oi!" he shouted, knowing that it was useless.

One of the urchins emerged from the pack, brandishing the glasses aloft in a mocking salute.

"Hey!" Vickery yelled. But the urchin ran off down an alley. The smoke began to drift towards the MLG building.

"Where's Harlan?"

It was the General's voice. Vickery caught Kellerman's reply.

"He had a friggin' appointment."

"This briefing is over," the General said.

The balcony emptied, and Vickery was left on his own. What, he wondered, had blown up? And did Harlan Petty have anything to do with it? Petty — a man, if ever Vickery had known one, who was unlikely to resist the sudden urge to slip out of a meeting and cause explosions.

"Come on, Alan," Kellerman said. "Let me conduct you to your office. We got you a car and driver. Never walk anywhere, okay?"

An office and a chauffeur? More than he had expected. More, he instantly suspected, than Kellerman had been given.

"Okay. Bryce?"

"What?"

"That explosion..."

Kellerman assumed an expression of infinite sadness.

"What can I tell you, Alan? Stuff blows up." He heaved a sigh and scratched his neck.

"It just does. Come on."

CHAPTER 26

Alan Vickery looked out from the window of his fourth-floor office suite on to what he believed was Fidel Castro Avenue, or something equivalent, and noted that the smoke from the explosion was beginning to abate.

He'd asked his driver — whose name was Inácio, if he'd caught it correctly — if he knew what exactly had happened, but Inácio, a thin young man with nervous, baleful eyes, had pretended not to hear him. Then, after they'd dropped Kellerman off at his villa in a posh, hilly district, Vickery had asked again. Inácio had replied — if Vickery had understood him correctly — that there might be a situation, but Vickery was not to worry; Inácio would look after him.

Such was Inácio's apparent sincerity on this point that Vickery had felt moved to dig into the stash of kwanzas that Kellerman had given him and to fork over a cool thousand. Inácio had accepted it calmly. Vickery made a mental note to try and find out how much a thousand kwanzas was actually worth.

The office was smart, clean and expensively furnished. It comprised a conference room, a private office and a kitchenette. There were two computers, an old-fangled fax and a fancy-looking phone. Unfortunately, the power was off and there was no water in the taps. Kellerman had told him to stock up on bottled water and to save his work often.

Save his work? What work? This wasn't a place for work. No, Vickery had already seen the point of Angola. It was a place for grabbing opportunities; it was the frontier, a wild place, a place that yearned for people with spirit and vision. Such people could hardly walk down the street without tripping over unwonted riches. Kellerman's back-scratching, time-serving, palm-greasing, bureaucratic mentality would prevent him from grasping this essential reality. Kellerman was lost without his steak-houses and his fund-raising dinners.

Vickery all at once knew why he was in Angola. He was here to cast his personal magic spell upon the Angolan financial system, if they had one; to ease those capital flows, no doubt currently sclerotic, that would unleash the *animal spirits* of Angolan entrepreneurs; to empower the business-savvy emissaries of the New Democratic Consensus (they would pile in, no doubt, once it was safe for them) who would re-shape, re-invigorate, revolutionize and generally rev-up the entire economic scene — just as soon as the necessary adjustments to the ruling regime had been made, and the Chinese shoved aside.

It was a pragmatic thing, really, and not at all the idealistic and overblown crusade — if that was the word — that Aylsham fantasized about. Now that he'd actually set foot on Angolan soil, Vickery could see for himself that it was all about business. Not politics. Business. This was a place where a fairly ordinary burger could cost you forty US dollars; that fact alone spoke volumes. And yes, well, obviously, he was going to be handing out a few commissions, bonuses, consulting contracts or bribes — call them what you would — but this was an Emerging Market, after all. You went to work with the business environment you had, not the one you wanted.

He looked out again at the vanishing smoke. It wouldn't be long, he thought, before all those people up in the shanty towns were eating ready-meals and complaining about their gas bills, like everyone else in the civilized world. A brave new lifestyle awaited them — but few would ever know the name of the man who made it all possible.

Wait a minute. Was he deluding himself here? Exaggerating his importance? A little, perhaps. But there was a reason for it. It was the heady whiff of change that he had already detected in the air. Kellerman obviously didn't get it, but he, Vickery, did. It was probably all down to the momentous changes he'd brought about, through personal effort, in his own life. He had been sensitized. You didn't drag yourself up from East End street-kid to international business figure without becoming sensitized. Aylsham didn't have a clue.

Vickery identified with the Angolan people; he felt for them, felt as one with them; he shared their longing for progress and personal advancement — and freedom and democracy, too, if it came to that; he understood what they'd been through with this war-thing or whatever it was. He was here to help them. Yes. He really was. And how much was a thousand kwanzas, anyway?

The smoke was all but gone. Vickery removed the polythene wrapping from his swivel chair and sat down. What now? He wasn't sure where to start. Would *he* have to go to the movers and shakers of Luanda society, or would *they* come to him? Kellerman had talked of some *big chiefs* — the local Round Table, or Chamber of Commerce, Vickery assumed — and a *Sovereign Wealth Fund*. It all sounded very promising.

As he rotated thoughtfully, it occurred to him that he really ought to call Mariella to let her know he'd arrived safely. And to lecture her, tactfully, about the fountains. But first he would require a cup of tea. Possibly with something in it. But there was no water. He went into the kitchen and inspected the fridge. It was fully-stocked: Beer, spirits, cans of fizzy stuff, bottles of water. But he had no electricity. And no kettle.

He took out a can of orange juice and a bottle of vodka and made himself a drink. Mariella, of course, could be anywhere in the world by now. What if he called her and it was the middle of the night? Bad idea. He'd call Jason, that's what he'd do.

The spy-phone, surprisingly, worked first time.

"Alan! Where are you? We've been trying to ring you for hours. Did you turn your phone off?"

"Yes. I was on a plane, wasn't I?"

"Well, when did you get off?"

"Three hours ago. But then I was in a meeting."

"A meeting? All right. Never mind. Just keep it on at all times, if you don't mind. So you're in Luanda. Very good. Now then, what's happening?"

"Well, I've got an office. And a car. And a driver. His name is —"

"What's happening on the streets? What's the word on the street, Alan?"

Kellerman had told Vickery never to walk anywhere, so he wasn't equipped to answer this. Unless he summoned Inácio to the spy-phone and got it straight from the horse's mouth.

"I would say that there's an eerie calm," he said, extemporizing. "A tense, eerie calm." This was reasonable enough. It sounded good — the sort of stuff he could imagine Zara shoving out on the Beeb — and, looking down into Fidel Castro Avenue with its potholes, forlorn loiterers and intermittent but urgent traffic, he could almost believe it.

Jason sounded excited.

"Has the situation started to move yet, Alan?" he said. "Have you heard any reports? Have there been any incidents?"

"Well, Jason," Vickery said judiciously, "I can tell you this much."

"What?"

"There *has* been an incident."

"What sort of incident?"

"I suppose you'd call it an explosion. About half an hour ago. I was just asking General —"

"What was it? The television station? The police barracks? The Interior Ministry?"

"No, I don't think so. No. It was up in the shanty-towns. It's all over now."

"Oh." Jason seemed disappointed. "Just the one explosion, was it?"

"Yes."

"Someone left the gas on, did they? Right. Look, Alan, we're sending some chaps around to see you. Help them anyway you can. We need the bloody oil as well, you know. One of them is a kind of special-forces type bod. Watch yourself. Don't upset him. You might need him. What's your address?"

Vickery told him, relishing Jason's distaste at the name Castro.

"And don't say anything to your chum Kellerman, hmm?"

"No, all right. Actually, he's in a funny mood. Something's got to him. Don't know what."

There was a cackle at the other end of the line.

"Don't you? Ha-ha. Never mind. Ask him about the General's daughters."

No, it wasn't that, Vickery thought, you're barking up the wrong drainpipe there, Jason, old lad. It was something much more serious.

"Don't you want to know about my meeting?" he asked.

"What about it? Suborning more bank-managers, were you?"

"I attended a high-level strategy presentation. Military Logistics Group. Heard of 'em?"

"MLG? Really? Well done, Alan. Good work."

Here there was some off-stage conferring.

"And what *is* their strategy?" Jason asked.

"Well, I'll summarize it for you. Basically, if you've got oil, they're going to dominate you militarily. But they're going to do it in such a way as you don't notice."

"Really? Really? Very interesting..."

There was some excited back-chat at the other end.

"We want you to keep a very sharp eye on them, Alan. Get as close as you can."

"Right-ho."

"Oh, one more thing," Jason said. "If you come across a Yank called Lester, let us know, will you? Bloody trouble-maker. First name Thomas."

"No problem. Shall I ask around? Bryce might know."

"Don't say anything to Kellerman."

"What about Harlan?"

There was a pause at the far end of the line.

"What about who, Alan?"

"Harlan. Harlan Petty. He's here. I would've mentioned it but I assumed you knew."

The pause continued.

"Jason?"

"Alan. Am I correct in inferring from your tone that you're familiar with this man?"

"Wouldn't say familiar. Find him a bit creepy, to be honest. Met him in New York. Why, what's the matter?"

It sounded as though Jason were arguing with someone — arguing quite bitterly, in fact.

"Jason?"

No answer.

"Jason?"

"Just shut up a moment, Alan."

It was funny, he thought. There were certain individuals whose names, when dropped casually into a conversation—

"Alan!"

"Yes?"

"We want you to stay away from this man. And why, for Christ's sake, didn't you mention him before? Oh, don't bother answering. All right, that's it for now. Just get on with it. And call us at least once a day. Got it? Right. And be careful. Got that?"

"Yes. I hear you."

Jason's voice seemed to soften a notch.

"Seriously, Alan. Be careful. Do. Really."

Jason seemed reluctant to hang up. Vickery wondered if he should mention his suspicions concerning Petty and the explosion. Perhaps next time.

"Bye," he said.

"Bye," Jason replied, weakly.

Vickery performed a ruminative spin in his chair and sipped the last of his vodka and orange. Jason, although from time to time an irritating prat, was basically a decent enough bloke. But Vickery couldn't help but feel that Jason did not have, to be blunt, an adequate appreciation of the situation on the ground in Luanda. Distance precluded it. This made it all the more essential that Vickery take the initiative and trust his instincts. The first thing to be done was to find out what had got up Kellerman's nose to such morbid effect.

But before Vickery could act, there was a knock at the door. Inácio, whose duties Vickery, began to suspect, extended well beyond tending his Mercedes, introduced a tall, elegant, fashionably-dressed woman of about fifty-five, whose skin color was curiously paler than Inácio's. Inácio gave Vickery a cool, encouraging look and vanished.

And this was how it went for the next three hours or so.

Isabela wanted her accounts set up in Panama, for some reason, and she wanted statements every week, not every month, and the statements had to be sent to an address in Lisbon, which Vickery would be given later. Vickery, unclear as to Isabela's rôle in the régime-to-be, said little but noted it all down. Isabela predicted that Luanda would once again be the beautiful, refined city it was when she was a girl, but this time without the horrible leftists, and without the greedy Chinese, and with the Americans to keep everyone in line — especially the *Bailundos*, whoever they were. Vickery nodded sympathetically.

Raimundo wanted to know who to talk to about taking over Chinese construction contracts and, indeed, contracts on other construction bosses — the Americans would turn a blind eye, wouldn't they? Well, they can't be everywhere, Vickery said, thinking to himself that Ronnie, after all, was probably better off where he was. Raimondo wondered if Vickery knew that his brother held a senior position in Sonangol. Vickery said he did now.

Luis complained that all the highly-relevant information he had supplied to the Americans had not resulted in the timely compensation he had expected and wanted to know if he could have a few thousand on account. Kwanzas or dollars, Vickery asked. Dollars, of course, Luis said, grumpily. Or, better still, euros, he added in a low voice. Vickery said he'd see what he could do.

Duarte told Vickery that he could undercut Vickery's European suppliers, no matter what kind of armaments Vickery required. Vickery said that the Americans were quite up to supplying their own guns, thanks, and as for Military Logistics — well, their name spoke for itself, didn't it? No, Duarte said, grimly, for the irregulars. The squads. The *special* squads. Vickery said he was doubtful but he'd look into it.

The names of subsequent visitors blurred in his ears, but he noted down their various requirements. And then, suddenly, there came a name that stuck out from the rest.

"Colin?"

"That's right, mate. You Vickery?"

"Yes."

"Fucker Jason sent us. Got any tea?"

"No, sorry. There's a fridge. Help yourselves."

There were two of them: These had to be the *chaps* that Jason, during Vickery's recent spy-phone debriefing, had promised to *send round*. The ones who were interested in oil.

Colin was obviously Jason's *bod* — the special-forces one. But, whatever the forces in question were, they couldn't have been that special. Colin looked like a lorry driver who'd been spicing up his burgers with steroids. His companion, on the other hand, was a seedy bean-pole with thin, lifeless hair (didn't these people know the meaning of conditioner?) and a dirty, over-stuffed safari jacket. Oil-man, Vickery thought. No cowboy hat, therefore British oil-man.

While Colin assaulted the fridge, the bean-pole introduced himself.

"Alan, isn't it? Geoffrey Johnson-Jones. Bit of a mouthful, I'm afraid. Call me Jo-Jo. Everyone else does."

Jo-Jo, Vickery thought. It sounded about right.

"Are you an oil-man?" he asked.

"How could you tell?"

"You work for Jason?"

"Yes. On a contract basis, of course."

"Ah — private sector?"

"Yes. Very private, ha-ha."

Colin returned from the kitchenette with Vickery's vodka. He slurped from the bottle and then offered it to Jo-Jo, who declined.

"Like MLG," Vickery said, flaunting his affiliations.

"Yeah, right," Colin said. "MLG, right? They're like fucking Wal-Mart, okay? And we're the shop on the corner."

"We're a boutique," Jo-Jo said.

"What're you called?" Vickery asked.

"Global Executive Management Solutions."

"Good name. Have a seat."

But there was only one other chair, Vickery realized. He'd have to mention it to Inácio. Colin and Jo-Jo looked at each other, then Jo-Jo sat on the floor.

"What can I do for you?" Vickery asked.

"We need to know what our American friends are offering the Angolans. You know, so the Yanks can take over the Chinese oil concessions," Jo-Jo said. "After the Chinese are kicked out, that is."

"I see," Vickery said. "Why?"

Colin and Jo-Jo exchanged glances. It was happening again, Vickery thought. Was his direct approach simply too much for some people?

"So we can outbid 'em," Colin said, as if addressing an idiot. "Jason says you're our bloke on the inside."

"That's right, I am. Course I am," Vickery said, feeling his aura of omniscience beginning to wobble.

"Well, we need to know, don't we? You need to get your mitts on the papers."

"What papers?"

There was another infuriating glance-exchange.

"The papers that your bosom buddy, that fat git Kellerman, carries around. He's in on the negotiations, isn't he? What with him having all them energy industry contacts and what-not."

Kellerman might have been a fat git, but at least he was a well-dressed, finely-groomed fat git — unlike some of those present.

"Why can't *you* get *your* mitts on them?"

"We don't know where he lives, do we?"

Vickery permitted himself a quiet sniff of satisfaction.

"Oh, really? Well, follow me, gentlemen."

*

By night, Kellerman's villa looked serene but unlived-in. There were no lights on, except for a security lamp. But, as Inácio explained, this was only because there was another power-cut. Kellerman, Inácio had established by talking to the security guards in their Toyota pick-up, wasn't in.

"Shall we?" Jo-Jo asked in a suggestive manner.

"I think we bloody well shall," Colin said. "Alan, give them security blokes some dosh and tell them they never saw us."

Breaking and entering, Vickery thought with some bitterness. It might be Sean's style but it wasn't his. Was it really necessary?

"Why can't I just ask him about the concessions?"

"Because then he'll know you know, won't he?"

Vickery hauled out his wad and offered a thousand kwanzas to Inácio.

"Um, Inácio —"

Inácio held up a hand. Then he took the thousand, and the entire wad, and slipped out of the car.

Vickery turned to Jo-Jo.

"How much is a thousand kwanzas? In real money?"

"Thousand kwanzas? Col?"

"About six quid," Colin said.

Vickery cursed silently. He was supposed to be a master of international finance, after all.

A moment later, Inácio was back.

"Okay. You go now," he said. "Try the back."

Kellerman's back door proved reinforced and highly resistant to Colin's approaches. Happily, Kellerman had left a window open.

As they roamed the residence, it struck Vickery that there were few signs of committed habitation. Kellerman was neat in person and kept his various abodes — with the aid of the informal economy, of course — spick and span. Hotels and rented accommodation were another matter; in these he tended to the slobbish. But here, in what must have been one of the swankiest pads in Luanda, he had left hardly a trace. In the bedroom, which Vickery entered with trepidation, they discovered that Kellerman was living out of a suitcase. It was almost as if he couldn't bear to be in the place.

As for papers, there were none. Colin wasn't happy. Vickery pictured Jason refusing to sign the latest, red-ink invoice from Global Executive Management Solutions until presented with something juicy in the way of Chinese concessions. Well, business was tough. First thing you learned.

"Bugger," Colin said.

227

"Yes..." Jo-Jo said, shrewdly, as if subjecting Colin's remarks to careful chemical analysis. "It is a bit of a bugger, isn't it?"

"Don't worry. Leave it to me," Vickery said. "I know how to handle Bryce. I'll get your Chinese what's-its."

"How?"

"Never mind how. Just tell me how to contact you."

"We'll contact you, mate. All right?"

"If you say so. See you later, then."

"What? Aren't you coming?"

"No. Think I'll stay here and wait for Bryce."

"But how do you explain —"

"He left the window open, didn't he?"

"Yeah. Right. Okay. See you around, then. Um... Can we borrow your driver?"

"Yes, yes. Just send him back when you're finished. Bye!"

Colin and Jo-Jo squeezed back out of the window. A moment later, Vickery heard Inácio's Mercedes speed off down towards the bay.

He thought back to his first encounters with the British secret services. How naïve he had been. Spies were like everything else in the real world — mostly crap.

Sighing to himself, he wandered about the house hoping to spot something of interest that had eluded Global Executive Management Solutions' finest.

What he found, obscured behind a tapestry depicting — of all things — herds of wildebeest sweeping across the savannah, under the baleful gaze of a mangy lion on an outcrop, was the door to the basement. He rattled the handle and found the door to be locked. He was about to step away when he heard a strange sound. It was a human voice, coming from the basement. And its tone was unmistakably distressed.

He ransacked the kitchen and returned with a heavy, cast-iron frying-pan. There was a sufficient gap between the door and the frame for him to insert the handle. After six or seven heaves the door-frame splintered and Vickery ventured half-way down the steps.

It was very dark. Feeling his way, he continued his descent, one step at a time.

"Hullo?" he said. "Hullo? Anybody down here?"

No reply.

"Hullo?" he said again. "Bryce? Is that you?"

There was a rustling-and-clinking sound.

"Bryce?"

And it must have been just then that the Angolan power grid decided to pull itself together because the lights came on.

Vickery found himself staring at a large, strong-chinned, craggy-faced man dressed in some sort of grubby tracksuit. He was sitting on a mattress on the floor.

"Oh. Hullo. Who are you?" Vickery said, only then noticing that the man's feet were chained together and his left wrist was manacled to what might have been the water main.

"Charles Barclay of Paterson, New Jersey," he said, in a tone that Vickery took for defiance. "Who the hell are you?"

CHAPTER 27

Dale Summers didn't know how he'd covered the distance between the kopje and the farm. He didn't know if his legs ached, or if his eyes burned, or if he was still breathing. His mind turned too fast for anything to make any sense. So he just floated on the spot, and he looked.

He stood at the entrance to what had once been the Spruitfontein Guest Farm. The gates had been blown open by the explosions and one now dangled by a solitary hinge. Away to his left he was aware of a group of springbok moving slowly past, as if nothing had happened. When he turned to look, one animal stopped and returned his gaze for a moment before moving on with its fellows. It could smell a cheetah or a leopard, he thought. But it couldn't smell evil.

At his feet were fragments of metal. He picked one up. It was still warm. The quality of its high-tech manufacture was evident; its function, obscure to him. It had a bar-coded sticker on it.

The main house, even though built of stone and cement, was rubble, the outer walls reduced to a height of about a foot. Jay's vehicles were burnt-out hulks. The roof of the guest bungalow building had collapsed and there was a forty-foot hole in the front wall. Only the Condor, parked behind the bungalows, seemed to have escaped.

She wasn't in it. Dale knew that, didn't he? He must have checked already.

Smoke billowed from the rear of the main house, where the kitchen and the gas bottles had been located. Dale took a step forward, his mind absorbed by and fixated on this point, but immediately he felt Jay's hand on his shoulder, restraining him. For once, he wasn't annoyed.

"No. Wait here," Jay said.

Dale kicked away the shrapnel and sat down in the dirt. A hollowness seemed to rise up from his stomach and choke him, and the world started to spin. He dug his fingernails into the dirt and watched Jay approach the house

Jay moved with uncharacteristic caution, ignoring his smoldering trucks. First he stepped up on to the veranda and peered into the front of the house. Then he made a wide circle around the back. For a minute or so he disappeared. Dale lay flat on the ground and stared up at the night sky. The white arcs of the missiles redrew themselves in front of his eyes, over and over.

Jay came running back from the house.

"She's gone. She's gone, Dale. I am truly..."

He turned his back on Dale for a moment. Dale waited.

"There's nothing to see. So..."

"Nothing?"

Jay turned around again. He shook his head.

"There's nothing for me to see," Dale said.

"No. No point, Dale. So... *Don't*, okay?"

"All gone. Nothing left."

"Yeah. That's how it looks. That's how it is. Otherwise, it's..."

Dale sat up. Look at me, he thought, *look at me*. But Jay didn't want to.

"What?"

"Yeah, what I mean," Jay said, "is it's just the regular, you know... Boom. None of that nasty stuff."

Nasty stuff?

"Hey, don't ask. Doesn't matter. Doesn't matter now."

Doesn't matter now. What should he say?

"No."

Jay sat down beside him and began brushing the dust from his shoes.

"I can honestly say," he said, "that I did not see that coming." He took his left shoe off and emptied the dust from it.

"Total surprise. You know? Because I've always made a big deal about..."

He seemed to freeze for a moment. Then he smacked his shoe twice on the ground and slipped it back on his foot.

About microwaves, Dale thought. He couldn't decide whether he wanted to put his arms around Jay and cry his eyes out or punch Jay in the face and watch him bleed. He would, of course, do neither.

"I know what you think of me," Jay said. "So I don't know what to say that isn't going to sound stupid."

Everything I ever said sounded stupid, Dale thought. Especially to her.

"So let me try this," Jay said. "I..."

Dale waited. Jay was on the edge; let him step off, he thought. Let him step off, and then I'll catch him. Maybe.

"I... This is exactly what... Exactly what she was fighting against and... And I knew her better than you think, and... And she knew, and we all knew, that... What am I saying? What am I saying? This is so fucked-up Dale, this is just so..."

"I know what it was."

Now, finally, Jay dared to look at him.

"It was a Predator. That right?"

"Yeah. That's right."

"Two missiles. What are they called?"

"Hellfire."

"Right. So what's in them? How do they work? Is it laser? Satellite?"

Jay hesitated. He doesn't know what I'm doing, Dale thought.

"Satellite," Jay said. "In this case."

230

"And who has them?"

"What?"

"You do, don't you?"

Jay kicked at the dirt.

"Yes, Dale. We do."

"I have to look," Dale said, getting to his feet.

"No, you don't."

"I have to."

"Don't. There's nothing to see."

"There must be something."

"Nothing. You won't see anything. There's almost nothing."

"I should listen to you, shouldn't I? I've got nobody else."

"That's right. You listen. Come with me. It's going to get cold."

"In the bungalows?"

"No. Not safe."

"They might come back?"

"Right."

Jay pointed to the dry river bed.

"We get in your car, we drive out over there, we park under the trees. Okay?"

"Okay."

"We'll need to talk about some stuff."

"Will we?"

"Yeah. You bet. It's different now, isn't it?"

"Yes. It's different."

Different, he thought. I'm different. I'm dead. What do I do now? There was only one thing he could think of.

CHAPTER 28

"**I** said, who the hell are you?" This demand was issued with such force and determination that Alan Vickery's ordinarily robust defenses crumbled into meekness. The bloke seemed to mean it.

"Alan Vickery."

"Who?"

"Alan Vickery."

There was a moment of silence — not stunned so much as baffled or frustrated — which gave Vickery enough time to wonder why Kellerman was running a private dungeon in his basement, and what this bloke could possibly have done to upset him. Kellerman, when crossed, could be spiteful and vindictive, but tended to limit his retribution to sexual smears and planted evidence. Actually imprisoning someone was a step into new territory — and a disturbing and delusional one at that — possibly brought about, Vickery speculated, by a deadly combination of cable TV and prescription drugs.

"British?"

"Yes."

The captive seemed to find this hard to take, as if he'd requested a different sort of visitor altogether.

"Well, okay, I don't care. Just get me out of this. Come on. Don't just stand there."

"Get you out?"

"No, let's have tea first. Yes, for cryin' out loud. Get me out!"

Vickery hesitated. If Kellerman was capable of this, what other horrors might he see fit to wreak, given his current condition?

"What are you waiting for? Come on, for God's sake. What happened to Jennifer? You got her, too? She's okay, right?"

Jennifer?

Vickery's brain performed another flashback — this time to Philadelphia and General Fricke's somber — but mistaken — announcement at the Liberty Club bash. Union Bank of New York. Jennifer Lenehan and Charles Barclay. This creature before him, surely, was the latter.

"So you're Charles Barclay," he said.

"Of course I am. I told you I was. Throw me the keys."

"Well, that's an incredible coincidence."

"The hell it is."

"Isn't it?"

"No, it isn't. You've found me, now get me out."

"No, what I mean is, I know your friend. Jennifer. Sort of. Not to speak to."

"Is she okay?"

"Oh, yes. Absolutely fine." Vickery thought for a moment, then added, "You know, except for the usual wear and tear. Accidents and so on."

"*Wear and tear?*"

"Yes. You said something about keys?"

"Throw 'em over."

Vickery decided to put aside his personal feelings about bankers and do the right thing. Kellerman would have to be confronted with his actions sooner or later, and who knew when the mood might take him to descend into the basement with the crocodile clips or red-hot poker or whatever else his perverted fantasies dwelled upon.

"Well, all right. Um, do you happen to know where he keeps them?"

"Who?"

"Bryce."

"Who the hell is Bruce?"

"Bryce."

"Whatever."

"You don't know him? Big fat bloke, greasy hair, smart suits, bit of a loud-mouth?"

"Are you saying you don't have the keys?"

"Basically."

Charlie, as Vickery had already decided to call him, held his free hand to his forehead and rubbed it. Only chained by one hand, Vickery noted; Kellerman wasn't all brute.

"Well, there is some heavy guy upstairs who kind of stomps around from time to... But it doesn't matter. Get the keys!"

"Wait a minute," Vickery said, his brain whirring. "You and Jennifer were kidnapped in Johannesburg. But then she was grabbed, bang off the mark as it were, by the special forces or what-have-you. And they hid her in London. But you —"

"No, no, no. That's total garbage. Look, I'll tell you what happened, but get me out of here first."

"But I don't understand why you're in Bryce's basement. *He* couldn't have kidnapped you. He was with me at the time."

Charlie rubbed his head again. He seemed to have acquired a headache, somehow. It was probably the stuffy air in the basement.

"So what are you? Some kind of secret agent? You don't look like the military. Not even the British military."

"I am, actually. Don't know how you guessed."

"Go look for the keys, okay? Just go look, will you?"

Vickery, ever resourceful, pulled out his spy-phone.

"All right. Tell you what, I'll put a call in to Jason, in case we need reinforcements or something. Although the only two —"

"Jason? Jason who?"

"Don't know his last name."

"Put the phone away."

"But —"

"Listen, Mr...."

"Alan."

"Listen, Alan. Maybe it's not the same one. Maybe it's a common name. I don't know. But I don't want you talking to anybody called Jason. No Jasons."

Vickery pondered. Jason? Kellerman? Charlie? Total garbage? He had the feeling, once again, that he wasn't getting the whole story.

"I'll go and look for the keys, then."

"If you can't find them, get a bolt-cutter or a saw."

Yes, thanks, Vickery thought. I could have worked that out for myself.

He was half-way up the stairs when he heard the sound of a large vehicle pulling up in the driveway.

"There's someone coming," he said. "It's probably Bryce. Let me deal with him. You stay there."

"You want me to stay here, is that it?"

"Yes."

"Okay. That's what I'll do. Jesus!"

"Sshh!"

"Oh, for..."

"Sshh!"

Vickery raced to the top of the stairs, jammed the broken door closed, dragged the wildebeest-and-sad-lion tableau back into position, flung himself into Kellerman's leather armchair, crossed his legs and folded his hands jauntily behind his head.

But it wasn't Kellerman who came through the door. It was Muller, in a bulging safari vest and military-style bush headgear. And he was accompanied by Petty, in his most insidious straw cowboy hat.

Arnie Muller gave Harlan Petty a poke in the ribs and a triumphant leer.

"There you are, Harlan. What did I say? Here he is in person."

Petty, whose visage had looked a bit on the severe side, must have been mollified by this, because he slapped Muller on the back and resumed his habitual chewing. Whether he had brought his own supply of gum, or was sampling the psychedelic crud the locals seemed to favor, Vickery couldn't say. But he hoped it was the former.

"Harlan thought you'd skipped town on us, Alan," Muller said, laughing nervously. The warthog seemed mightily relieved. But why?

"Not at all," Vickery said. "I find there's much here that requires my attention."

There was a short pause. Neither Muller nor Petty spoke. And, more surprisingly, there was no satirical exchange of glances.

"I've been very busy," Vickery said, trying to break the tension.

"Good, Alan. Very good. That's what we want to hear."

There was another pause.

"What about money, Alan?" Muller said. "How are you for cash?"

"I'm glad you mentioned that, Arnie. I'm all out of kwanzas. Stuff's been flying out of my hands. You know how it is. When you're new in town, the expenses are —"

"No, Alan. I'm not talking about expenses. I mean dollars. For rebuilding Angolan democracy and establishing new institutions."

"Oh, that. Well, I've made a start, but —"

"I've got a couple of million in the car, Alan. That will keep you going for a few days. Then I will get you some more."

"Right ho."

Vickery had the sense that all this stuff about institutions and building democracy was just small-talk, and that there was some larger issue looming. Petty, for example, had remained ominously quiet, even by his standards.

"I was just waiting here for Bryce. He left the window open," Vickery said, in case they were wondering. "Only been here a couple of minutes."

"He's probably at the Explorers' Club," Muller said, and this time he and Petty did exchange glances.

"Ah," Vickery said. "Well, as soon as my driver comes back — Inácio, helpful chap — I'll pop over. Need a quiet word. Don't know if you've noticed, but he's a bit... A bit off, you might say."

"He's under a lot of pressure, Alan," Muller said, and a smile flashed across Petty's face.

"Man's drinkin' his sorrows away," Petty added, sounding like an actor in a Southern melodrama.

There was another pause. Muller and Petty held their ground, making Vickery feel ever more uncomfortable in his armchair. He removed his hands from behind his head and drummed his fingers on the arms of the chair. He imagined Charlie crouching downstairs with his ears cocked.

"Well, don't let me keep you," he said in a loud voice.

"Oh, you're not keeping us, Alan," Muller said. "But Harlan here — you see, his schedule is very full."

Yes, Vickery thought, but full of what? More mysterious explosions? And did Petty — who had tucked his thumbs in his belt and was grinding the heel of his boot into the floor — know about old Charlie in the basement?

At that moment, Vickery's spy-phone rang. Petty looked up.

"Fuck was that?"

"Oh, just my phone," Vickery said, taking a surreptitious peek at the display and seeing Jason's name blinking. Petty took a step forward.

"Network's been down for two days."

"Has it?"

"You got your own private network, Mr. Vickery?"

"What? No, no. Nothing like that. What it is, is — it's a reminder, that's what it is."

"What do you need reminding about?"

"Oh, everything. You know. Appointments, shopping lists, wife's birthday. Forget my own name, sometimes."

Petty held out his hand.

"Show me."

"Yes," Vickery said. "Of course. Perfectly ordinary phone, ha-ha. It's just that..."

Muller reached out and touched Petty cautiously on the elbow.

"Harlan, trust me, it's perfectly okay. Alan has been thoroughly checked out. I saw to it personally."

Petty lowered his arm.

"Yeah. Sure. Okay, Arnie, my man, tell him what's happening."

Yes, Vickery thought, please do. And why couldn't that idiot Jason have given him a phone that vibrated — had the stupid prat never been in a business meeting?

Then, recovering from his fright, Vickery began to wonder why Muller, normally so deferential in Petty's presence, had intervened so crucially. And did either Muller or Petty know there were bankers chained up in the basement? Did they know anything about some Yank called Lester, as Jason had put it? And was this the same Lester whose exploits in Switzerland had so enraged Marty back at the Glue Factory?

And was there a Swiss-Angolan connection? And did it have to do with MLG? And who put Mariella on to MLG? And what was she really up to in Switzerland? And how was he going to release poor old Charlie, blinking, into the sunlight — well, all right, it was dark now, but the principle applied — if these two thugs didn't bugger off and leave him alone?

"Yes, Arnie," he said. "Please do. Please do tell me what's bloody well happening."

"All right, Alan. Please do not get excited. We don't want you ending up like your friend Mr. Kellerman, do we? It is necessary at this point to take a little trip into the bush."

Muller looked down at Vickery's feet and frowned.

"Have you got any other shoes, Alan?"

"No."

"Well, never mind. Perhaps you can borrow some at the camp."

Camp?

"I trust you have your pills?"

Pills?

"Gonna be a nice little outing for you, my friend," Petty said. "Get you all trained up and shit. Let's go."

Petty hauled Vickery out of his chair and marched him to the door. Muller brought up the rear. Outside, Vickery saw Inácio draw up at the curb — or, at least, where the curb would have been if the curb stones hadn't been stolen — in his Mercedes. Muller stalked over to Inácio's window. Vickery heard him tell Inácio that Mr. Vickery would be back in two days. Or so. Inácio had time to give Vickery a forlorn stare before Petty shoved him into the back of an olive-green Land Cruiser.

"Okay," Petty said, jumping into the driver's seat. "Now we're going to have some fun. Some real good fun. Are you excited?"

CHAPTER 29

"So what's the story with the container, Jay?" It was their second night sleeping under the cold sky beside the Condor, wrapped in blankets salvaged from the guest bungalows.

Jay had insisted at first that they sleep in the car because some of the drones had incredible infra-red sensors, but this hadn't worked out well in practice. And since the attack the skies had been empty, the ruins of the lodge had grown cold and Dale had begun to question how much either of them cared about what happened next. When he asked Jay why they didn't just get in the Condor and drive, Jay said it was better that they just wait. The Condor was such an easy target.

And so Dale felt that, sitting there, between two lives — the first full of positive purpose, or at least the illusion of it, and the second a threatening void — there was no reason not to beat up on Jay about his stupid, secret, mad, destructive life.

"Aw, come on, Dale. You know what that is. Don't make me say it. I told you I — we stopped using it."

"What do you do to people in there?"

"Not any more."

Sure, he thought. Now you're a nice guy, or kind of. You used us. But in a good cause. You tried to protect us. But you failed. And before you were a nice guy, you were in the container, doing what people like you do these days. A little pre-emptive torture, maybe? So what? But when did the change begin? What kicked it off? What's the matter with you, Jay?

"So there must have been a moment when you, like, said to yourself, 'Why are we doing this? This can't be right.'"

"No," Jay said. "There wasn't a moment or a particular time or an incident. It was a gradual thing."

"Oh, I get it. So you didn't just have a fight with your boss, or something. The doubts kind of grew. You had doubts and they just got worse and worse and —"

"Let it go, Dale."

"— and worse. And eventually you couldn't live with yourself. And you're thinking, 'I don't care how many memos these lawyers write, why don't *they* try it and see what it does to *them?*'"

Jay pulled a blanket up over his face.

"You know how people think about you, don't you? Like all the civilian folk at the embassy? They see you coming, or some other CIA guy, and they think 'Yeah, I wonder what he's been doing.' I mean, that's got to bug you, right?"

Jay grunted under his blanket.

"Bugs me a lot, Dale. It's bugging me now."

"But now you're one of these — I guess you call yourselves dissidents or something. What do you call it?"

"It's called the Resistance."

"Yeah, that's a cool name. Are you kidding?"

"No, it's serious."

"Really? Like the French Resistance?"

"Yeah. The French Resistance."

"So who are the Nazis?"

Jay grunted and rolled over, turning his back on Dale.

"Well, it's just a name."

But names were powerful things, Dale thought. Full of meaning. But delicate, too. And then again, sometimes, like little bombs waiting to be dropped.

"Jay," he said. "What happened with you and Sheryl?"

It was the first time he had spoken her name out loud since he saw the white streaks ripping up the ancient Namibian sky.

Jay sat up.

"There could be a better time for this, you know."

"You were all set to tell me before. When — when we were up on the hill."

"Yeah. But now I have to tell you all of it, because..."

"Because Sheryl's dead."

"Yes."

"Sure you want to tell me?"

"Yeah, why not?"

Dale felt a tremor start up in his chest. He'd given Jay permission to rewrite the story of his life with who knew what kinds of ugliness, and this guy — well, he might just go ahead and do it. And then it would never be possible to repair anything that got broken in the process. Even the image of Sheryl in his mind, an image that refused to settle and be at peace — because Jay had become part of it.

"Okay," Jay said. "Let me ask you this. Why'd you come to Africa?"

"Because of this."

Dale nodded towards the escarpment edge and the dune sea.

"Exactly what do you mean by that?"

"I mean there's space here. We haven't filled this place up yet. You can breathe."

"Breathe, huh?"

"It's still natural. Okay, not everywhere. But it's so huge. Look at Europe. Or America."

"It's poor, Dale. That's why. Dirt poor. And it's going to stay that way."

"Not if things are done right."

"And you came here to do things right."

"Yeah. What's wrong with that?"

"And what's your budget?"

"It's about making a difference."

"Dale, you talk some shit sometimes. The only time you made a difference was when I sent you to Johannesburg, and that wasn't even my idea. Do you know how much those missiles cost? The missiles that killed Sheryl?"

Not his idea? What did he mean?

"Hundred and thirty thousand dollars each. Course, that's just a fraction of the total mission cost."

Dale couldn't help himself — two hundred and sixty thousand dollars plus. What about a million, all in? What would he have done with a million dollars in his budget?

"You and Sheryl..." he said.

"That's right," Jay said. "Me and Sheryl. Now you see, don't you?"

"She wanted us to go to Johannesburg. From the beginning. She told you."

"I thought you'd screw up. But she persuaded me."

"But you... Why would Sheryl..."

"Because I recruited her, Dale. And then she recruited me. Listen. All this shit about being able to breathe in Africa? All this semi-socialist development bullshit of yours? You go round talking about liberation and freedom — the wrong kind of freedom I mean — and you're going to attract some attention, Dale. So one day you're in my in-box. Oh great, I think. What a waste of my valuable time. So I talk to old Bill, thinking he'll say "Forget it, Dale's a harmless dope" but he gets the wrong end of the stick and thinks I'm talking about Sheryl. So then I have to go check her out. And that's how it starts."

Dale said nothing.

"Are you really that innocent? Why d'you think she was so unhappy? Until she flips me over and she's off on her fucking mission of a lifetime."

"This really happened?"

"I'm sorry, Dale. Yes, it really happened. You're such a dope. If the world was full of people like you, then fine. But it's not. As you're starting to find out."

"People like you..."

"What, Dale?"

"Do *that*."

He expected Jay to look back at the blackened ruins of the lodge, but he looked up instead.

"Hear anything?"

"You got her into this. You let them kill her."

"Elaine got her into this. Listen, will you?"

"Elaine?"

"Yeah. She's one of them. The Resistance. Not so surprising if you know her history. After Bill tells her I'm on Sheryl's case, she naturally wants to put the girl straight."

"You're fighting over her?"

"Uh-huh. And Elaine wins, of course. And then Sheryl — she turns me right around. Who would have thought. So now Elaine says we have to take care of this woman the Resistance is bringing down from the Caprivi. And not a word to Bill and so on."

"Bill's one of them? Like Elaine?"

"No."

"But you are."

"Not really. They won't let me in. I'm like an honorary member."

"So you can't contact them."

"No."

"That's why we're waiting."

"Yes."

"Why wouldn't they let you in?"

"Oh, these people. They want to see your résumé, you know?"

"And yours —"

"Well, exactly."

"And Bill doesn't know?"

"Doesn't want to. Can't. He's Elaine's protection. Or was. Up to a point."

"Where are they now?"

"I really thought I heard something. Listen. Yeah, there it is."

Dale heard it too — the sound of a plane, coming from the east. The Predator had come from the west, he thought — though not from the dunes, surely? Perhaps from the sea?

"Okay," Jay said. "It must be our friends from the Resistance. Maybe Gary and Joe. They haven't been able to contact me and they're coming to check things out. That's the good news."

Dale waited.

"Bad news is they're coming in a fucking jet, for some reason, and the strip — well, as you know, I've been busy."

"Can they land?"

"Maybe. We better put out some lights."

"Like what?"

"Yeah. Okay, get in the car."

Jay drove the Condor out of the river bed and up on to the landing strip. Then he raced to the far end, cursing at each bump and rut. He pulled up behind the lodge, about fifteen yards from the container.

"Stay here."

He jumped out, ran over to the container, unlocked it and opened the door. Dale watched until Jay disappeared inside, then clicked his door open and slipped out.

Half-way to the lodge he stopped. He could see where the gas bottles had once stood. The kitchen window had been just to the right. And the window had been in front of the sink. That was probably where she had been standing. He took another step forward. There was enough moonlight to cast shadows but not enough to see clearly. He advanced another step. The door to the container slammed and he spun around.

"Don't do it. Get back in the car."

Jay was holding a battery and a lamp.

"Come on, Dale. These guys need to land. They can't see the strip."

Dale climbed back in to the Condor. Jay roared off down the landing strip. He positioned the battery lamp at one end, sped back to the other, then turned the Condor around so that its headlights shone down the strip.

"Which way are they coming in?" Dale asked.

"That's up to them."

They waited. The sound of the plane grew stronger.

"Why don't you want me to look?"

Jay tapped the steering wheel.

"Because I care what happens to you."

CHAPTER 30

George Fischer had to admit he was impressed. Before him were rows of precision-guided, all-weather tents and pre-fabricated huts, surrounded by a floodlit razor-wire fence. This was almost a little town, part military base and part corporate campus. There were men in suits as well as men in uniform. Women, too. And it was clear to him that the whole thing belonged to Military Logistics Group, even if they hadn't hauled up their flag or stenciled their logo on the tents.

The location was a good distance to the south of Luanda, he thought, possibly even quite close to the Namibian border. Muller, tempted by George's imaginary list of eager collaborators, had arranged a helicopter — and also a blindfold. The air was sticky here, and the heat oppressive. The lights illuminated columns of mosquitoes.

Despite its well-equipped and business-like appearance, this seemed a place unlikely to harbor Douglas Moreland, much as a branch office would rarely attract the average self-adoring CEO.

Arnie Muller was another matter. He came loping towards George, his face flushed and his moustache drooping in the humidity. His customary belligerence came modulated, unusually, with embarrassment.

"George — now you are here, what do you want? You could have emailed the list."

"I want to see Douglas Moreland."

Muller seemed taken aback.

"What do you want to see *him* for? I would have thought the last..."

"Nevertheless."

"He's not here. This camp belongs to a private corporation."

"Of course."

Muller swatted a mosquito away from his neck.

Muller led the way to a tented cabin with mosquito-proof mesh over the windows. Inside, he pulled a string to operate an electric light. Somewhere in the distance George could hear the rumble of a generator. Muller pulled another string and cool air began to flow. Air-conditioning, George thought. Here?

"I don't know why they had to put it in this bloody swamp," Muller said. "These bloody mosquitoes are a menace."

Well-hidden, George thought. Out of the way. Few local settlements. Easily re-supplied by sea. Close to the potentially-useful port of Lobito. Within striking distance of Luanda. Handy for policing the Namibian border.

The cabin seemed to be Muller's home. It was a mess. Clothes, papers, boxes of ammunition, plastic bottles, military magazines and pharmaceutical detritus were strewn randomly. George sat on the end of a canvas cot.

"You're living the high life here, I see," he said.

"I've got everything I need. These people know how to run things."

"Do they? Tell me again how they are going to run Angola."

"It's none of your business. You should be in Luanda. And where were you in Windhoek? I was looking for you."

"We must have just missed each other."

Muller drew his hand across his brow and wiped it on his shirt. Then he pulled up a folding stool and sat, leaning back against the side of the cabin and causing it to rock gently.

"Sure. You want a beer? This camp is dry, but —"

"No, thank you."

"You run a bar in that place of yours but you never drink?"

"Not so much."

Muller took a beer from a cooler and began to drink.

"American beer," he said. "That's all we get. Smuggled in."

"Arnie," George said. "Where's Moreland?"

"Not here. You should have stayed in Luanda. Have you talked to your MPLA chums, by the way?"

"Some of them."

"Or are you letting your girl do it all for you?"

George said nothing. Bringing Roberta to Angola had been a risk. But he couldn't bear to leave her behind, and he had felt — in a moment of self-deluding madness, no doubt — that, were he to contemplate something really stupid, she would stop him. And, besides, she was a native Angolan and understood the land, its ethnic complexities and political pathologies better than anyone could hope to whose main experience of the country was watching it explode from the air.

He should have expected that Muller would find out. But were Muller ever to touch her, then the George Fischer who ran the Desert Garden Hotel in Swakopmund would at once be revoked, abolished. And his younger, baser self — Muller's buddy-in-arms, Elaine Ellis's reformed terrorist — would surely re-inherit.

"Taking a bit of a chance, aren't you?" Muller said. "Bringing her back here?"

"If you touch her..."

"What do I care now?" Muller said, finishing his beer and flinging the empty can into a corner of the tent. "No one's touching her. If you want her, you have her."

"What about Moreland?"

"You have that man all wrong. It's not personal."

"Then what is he doing with Bill and Elaine Ellis?"

"George, they're just a minor annoyance. That's how he sees it."

"Why doesn't he let them go?"

"Perhaps he will. When the operation is complete. Perhaps it depends on you."

"Are they here?"

"If I knew, I couldn't tell you."

Muller opened another beer.

"Tell me about your MPLA chums."

George sighed.

"So far, I would say they are fatalistic."

"That's excellent news, George! Why didn't you say?"

"They say they would rather have the Chinese steal their oil, but the Chinese can't provide security."

"Excellent. Listen. We have this chap. We've set him up in an office. He's English. He's a bit peculiar, but apparently he's very good with the financial arrangements and all that crap. I'll give you his details. Send your people to see him. But not for the next couple of days, okay?"

"Yes."

"Here it is. Take this."

Muller offered George a business card. *Alan Vickery — International Financial Consultant*, he read.

"And what about your SWAPO people?" Muller demanded. "We know you talked to Julius."

"I talked to all of them. They are not very happy."

"Well, screw them. No money for them. Fucking Namibia, who needs them? They'll regret it."

"I am sure they will."

"All right, George," Muller said, flinging his beer can with a casual and brutal enthusiasm and cracking open a third. "This is progress. We will overlook your pointless visit. I will tell Douglas Moreland everything is okay. Tomorrow, you can go back to Luanda. So good night and get out."

George stood.

"Is there somewhere I can sleep?"

"Try down the end of the next row. There might be somewhere."

George left Muller's tent and began to wander. Activity around the camp had dwindled and some of the lights had been shut off. The air was soupy and still. From all directions came the whirr of air-conditioners, mingling with the sounds of truck engines and TV sports shows.

Few people wanted to leave their tents. Mosquitoes, George thought. Sometimes, if you were lucky — a very special person indeed — the mosquitoes left you alone. He gave thanks for his luck and began to explore.

CHAPTER 31

Alan Vickery sat in his tent and sulked. From the moment he'd clambered down from the helicopter with Muller and Petty, mosquitoes had feasted merrily upon his face, neck and wrists. This hell-hole — whatever it might turn out to be — was surely where Kellerman and the General had obtained their battle scars. No wonder Kellerman was in such a foul mood — though it still wasn't enough to explain his new-found attachment to the dungeon trade.

And yet... No, bugger Kellerman, he thought. Bugger the lot of them.

In his distress, he'd attempted to rouse his neighbors, hoping to cadge a spray or a dab of ointment or something. But one tent turned out to be empty; the other, occupied by a Bible-reading youth — shades of the Liberty Club kindergarten there — who couldn't understand his accent and offered him a Diet Coke. And so, abandoned and misunderstood, he suffered alone.

But not for long. The door to the tent twitched and a face appeared — a small, roundish face with heavy, sad eyes and not the slightest trace of mosquito-related activity.

"Excuse me, please. The tent next to this one — is it available?"

The accent was strange — a bit stilted and formal, like Muller, but not South African.

"Could be," Vickery said. "Don't really know, to tell the truth."

The tent-seeker ventured into Vickery's private space and looked at him, strangely.

"Why don't you move in," Vickery said, prudence dictating a helpful and constructive attitude towards this potential psycho and his secret sorrow. "Then if someone else comes along, and says... What? What's the matter?"

"Are you English?"

There was no pretending, Vickery thought.

"Yes," he said.

"Is your name Vickery?"

"Yes."

"And are you an International Financial Consultant?"

What did he want — an off-shore savings account?

"No."

"You're *not*?"

"No, I am a businessman. Pure and simple. And entrepreneur. Wish people would get it right."

The stranger looked doubtful.

"Look, no offense," Vickery said, tersely, "but who are you?"

The sad-faced intruder gave Vickery another penetrating stare then sat on the floor. Vickery edged away.

"My name is George Fischer. I run a hotel in Swakopmund, Namibia. I used to be a mercenary here in Angola. I fought on both sides. I killed too many people. Far too many. I was given another chance and I took it. But now I have come back to help you destroy this country again."

"Destroy it?"

"Yes."

"Me?"

"Yes, you."

Despite this unpromising introduction, and relying on nothing more than native smarts and a subtle line of questioning that would surely have impressed Jason — a conversation that was really an interrogation, spy-style — Vickery quickly succeeded in establishing a few basic facts about George Fischer from Swakopmund.

He was German. This didn't bother Vickery in the slightest, Vickery being of a highly international mind-set — unlike the Europhobic Aylsham. And, despite appearances, George wasn't a psycho; he'd just been having a bad day. A chum had been injured in an accident and someone had shouted at him.

But the most interesting fact of all was that George had been tasked by Muller, no less, with sounding out the powers-that-be in Luanda with a view to purchasing compliance with the upcoming régime re-jig. And the person doling out the sweeteners was, of course, Vickery himself.

This was, on the face of it, a happy arrangement and a fortuitous meeting. But George — and this was the second most interesting fact — wasn't happy. Not happy at all.

"Alan, may I ask if you are aware of the history of this country?"

"Just the basics, I suppose. They used to have a war, and now they've got oil. And a bad régime, of course."

"Oil *is* the régime."

"Don't quite follow you."

"You can put *this* group in charge. You can put *that* group in charge. It will remain the same. But you are doing something worse."

"Worse?"

"You are putting the Americans in charge."

"Shh. Keep your voice down."

"Not just of the oil. Not just of Angola. Of the whole of southern Africa."

This sounded like one of Aylsham's fantasies — with a negative spin, of course. But could it be, perhaps, a bit less of a fantasy than Vickery had supposed?

"Muller says we're just toppling and installing," he protested, weakly.

"Muller says you're an idiot."

Muller thought *Vickery* was an idiot?

"Does he?"

"He speaks of you with contempt."

This — if true — was outrageous.

"But he needs me! He's lost without me! All the accounts, the off-shore corporations, the layered transactions, the paperwork —"

"The paperwork?"

"Stacks. You wouldn't believe it."

"Even so. You must ask yourself this. Why are you really necessary? Look around you. Did you finance all this? Does MLG need *you?*"

"MLG?"

"Does Muller really need *me?* He doesn't care about the Namibians and probably the Angolans are already queuing up outside your office."

"You're not far off there."

"So why are we here, the two of us?"

"What — some other reason, you think?"

"It must be so."

Vickery brooded. Was it possible that Muller and Kellerman had been manipulating him? Well, obviously, that was what Kellerman did for a living, and it was brutally apparent. But was there something going on below the surface, as it were? He reached for a thingy — a metaphor.

"Icebergs," he said.

"I don't understand you."

"There's a lot going on that doesn't make sense. At least, it didn't until now." He pondered. "Well, no, it still doesn't make sense — but at least I know now that it really doesn't."

"You are losing me again."

"For example. Why does Kellerman have bankers chained up in his basement?"

"What did you say? Who is Kellerman?"

"Big fat bloke, greasy hair —"

"Okay, yes — but you said bankers. In the basement."

"Chap called Charlie Barclay. He was in the news, everyone thought he was a goner."

"You know where he is? You've seen him?"

"Yes. There he was, large as life. In the basement. Bit moody, but what would you expect? I was all set to release him when Muller and Petty barged in and dragged me down here."

"Harlan Petty? I have heard of this man. Alan, my friend, we are in big trouble. You are lucky I found you in time."

"Harlan? I know he looks a bit alarming, with that hat and everything. But I've been getting along with him quite well. Different background, that's all."

"You don't know how truly you speak. Why did they bring you here? This is MLG. They don't need your money."

"No. But there's another camp — I don't know if I should be telling you this — and they need me there."

"Don't worry, I've already heard about it. But I don't know why they need you."

"Good financial advice is often hard to find."

"Alan, my friend, you have the best sense of humor. Very English. Very dangerous."

Vickery bit his lip. This note of doom was becoming irksome. Petty had told him he could have four hours of sleep. This weird desperado-cum-hotelier was eating into it. He had to go. But, first, Vickery had a request.

"Look, George, d'you mind if I ask you something?"

"Not at all."

"These blasted mosquitoes — have you got anything?"

"Let me see."

George removed his backpack and began to empty it.

"You are taking your pills, of course?"

"What pills? Everyone keeps on about pills."

George stopped unpacking and looked up.

"Malaria pills, what else?"

"If I get it, I'll take some."

"No, no. You must take them every day. Muller didn't tell you? Perhaps he doesn't need you much longer."

"All right, all right. Have you got any?"

"You can have these."

George tossed Vickery a small, white box.

"And you can have this spray, also. Good. Now perhaps you will survive."

Vickery surveyed George's choice of travel accessories.

"Thanks. Why have you got two books the same?"

"This is a very special book. But I don't think it is much use to you. It gives you access to a secret world."

Here we go again, Vickery thought.

"But why two?"

"This one," George said, "was given to me by a young woman. She was very brave."

"Don't see what's brave about that."

"She thought she could protect her husband, but I am not so sure."

Figures, Vickery thought.

"And that one," George said, "I found it on the ground in Luanda."

"How come it's burnt around the edges?"

"It was in an explosion."

"An explosion? In Luanda?"

"Yes, just a day or so ago. Perhaps you heard it?"

"Yes. Lost my glasses because of it. What happened?"

"A bomb. Three people and some children were killed. I am sorry about your glasses."

Three people and some children. He said this as if he were reading the weather forecast and predicting scattered showers and sunny intervals. *Some children*. This bloke had a kind of sang-froid — if that was the word — that put Phil to shame.

"But..." Vickery said. "Why? Who would do that? Who were they?"

"The children, nobody knows. They were probably orphans. There was an EU lady from the Netherlands, a friend of a friend of mine, and an American businessman. I think this was his book."

Vickery's brain was tired, but it still managed to whirr.

"This American businessman. Not called Lester, by any chance?"

George made a face — half disapproving, half impressed, Vickery thought.

"Yes. How did you know? Are you a spy for your MI6?"

Vickery laughed.

"Perish the thought. Know him through business, sort of."

"But what made you think he was in Luanda?"

Vickery laughed again — but mainly to give himself time to think of an answer. George leafed through the book with the blackened edges.

"I expect you know of his charity work."

"That's it."

Vickery's mind travelled back in time to his first meeting with Ray and Marty. *Kill the fucking aid program*, he heard Marty say. *Change the fucking name.*

"Giraffe something," he said.

"Foundation. But without Mr. Lester..."

"No Giraffe."

"No."

Despite the heat and the humidity, an ice-cold shiver took a leisurely stroll all the way down Vickery's spine. Businessmen and children — murdered. Orphans. Marty didn't go in for murder, unless you counted the so-called corporate kind, which Vickery didn't. There was no need — the take-over scheme had been bubbling along nicely. But what about Petty?

"Who did it?" he asked, adding, pointedly, "And why?"

"Why?" George asked, rhetorically. "Why? Maybe this."

He dropped the book in Vickery's lap.

"All right," Vickery said. "We'll come back to that. Let's try who."

"Well, if you want to ask me whom I suspect, I suspect your friend Mr. Petty. But I have no proof."

"He left the meeting just before it happened!"

"What meeting is this, please?"

"Oh, MLG. Lot of stuff about bases not being bases. Rubbish, really — look at this place! General Freaky, ha-ha. Likes to make speeches. Doesn't mean anything."

"I think it does."

"Did you hear about his daughters?"

"I don't care about his daughters."

"No. Never mind. Look, why would Harlan want to kill Tom Lester because of this? It's crazy." Vickery brandished the book.

"Alan, please. Let me put a question to you. Have you heard anyone speak of some kind of a secret organization, an underground, or an enemy within, perhaps?"

Vickery considered. This sounded like conspiracy-nut stuff, but he was beginning to feel he ought to take George a bit more seriously.

"The only thing I can think of," he said, judiciously, "is a high-level meeting I had with Douglas Moreland and..." He was going to say "Jason', but stopped himself in time. "...And someone else."

"Douglas Moreland?"

"Yes. Do you know him?"

"I know him. Where did you meet him?"

"Embassy in London. Seemed to be more or less in charge of the place."

George made a groaning sound — almost as though he were in pain.

"You know, Alan, there was a time when this man would not have been permitted in the embassy. Any embassy. But we move on. What did he say?"

"He said there was resistance and he was going to crush it. Words to that effect."

"What else did he say?"

"Well, there was an argument about whether MI — whether the UK was affected."

"Is it?"

"Don't know. Don't really know what they were talking about."

"No. But I do, thanks to you. I am very grateful. Please let me give you some advice."

"If you must."

"You have been very generous in talking to me. But you must not talk like this with anyone else. You must be careful with Mr. Petty."

Tell me something I don't know, Vickery thought.

"You must be careful tomorrow — but also observant. I will need to know what you see."

Great, Vickery thought. Now he was spying for George as well as Jason.

"And, if you return from this trip, I will visit you in your office."

"Fine. No problem."

"One more question, since you are so accomplished at finding missing persons. I am looking for a couple called Ellis. A man and a woman. They are quite old."

"Never heard of them."

"You will look and listen, yes?"

"Look and listen. Absolutely. Ellis."

"Good. Now, I need to know where Mr. Barclay is, please."

"Should I be telling you all this?"

"Yes, if you would like me to get you out of the mess you're in. Or perhaps you would like to die in Angola? Many people have."

The shiver made a return journey up Vickery's spine.

"All right, all right. Whatever you say. It's a big pink house. Miramar. Road's called Vista del something."

"Good. I can find it."

"Look, you haven't told me why Harlan's blowing people up. There has to be a reason."

"You're holding it in your hands."

"This book?"

"But you cannot keep it. I must take it back."

Vickery let George have the book. George reloaded his pack.

"Now I go next door to sleep. Don't worry — I don't snore."

"Yes, but..."

But George was gone. Vickery considered following but he, too, was tired. And he only had three hours to go before Petty's early-morning wake-up call.

CHAPTER 32

Alan Vickery had eaten too many pancakes and too much maple syrup — too much, that is, for an international businessman habituated to Club Class comforts who now found himself dipping, swooping and zigzagging at tree-top level in a thundering military helicopter with some death-wish speed-freak at the controls and only Harlan Petty for company.

Petty sat at the open door with his legs dangling over the edge. He reminded Vickery of the sort of dog that likes to ride in the car with its head out of the window. The helicopter carried a cargo of wooden crates and canvas sacks. Petty hadn't said what was in them. Or where they were going.

The day had started well enough. Vickery had discovered that his tent was air-conditioned; this had made a soft, restorative sleep — albeit a short one — possible. George's mosquito spray seemed to work; the little wingèd furies recoiled from him as Mariella would from a Bulgarian rosé.

Vickery got up at dawn, peeked in the tent next door to discover that his eccentric German neighbor had already packed his towel and set off for the beach, then roamed the complex of tents and huts until he found a zone of larger structures including, as he had hoped, a showering facility. Here he found everything he required for a decent facsimile of his morning ritual, save for the exfoliants and the moisturizer. They must have run out. But you had to give these MLG people high marks for effort in what must have been a challenging location.

The humidity made it hard to get dry, but simply feeling clean had raised his spirits no end. Whatever Petty had in store for him, he was ready for it — almost. Arriving back at his tent, Vickery found Muller waiting for him, tapping his oversized watch in a blatant show of impatience. Muller looked sweaty, limp and rumpled, like a warthog who'd been in the shower too long.

"Where have you been?" he said. "Harlan wants you ready in ten minutes."

"Uh-uh-uh," Vickery said. "Haven't had my breakfast yet."

"What do you think this is — a bloody holiday camp?"

Vickery reflected to himself that he'd been in one or two that were a damn sight worse than this.

"I'm not going to be any use to Harlan if I haven't had my breakfast, am I?"

Muller didn't seem to appreciate this breezy tone; he was a man who never took the time to smell the what's-it. What was it, now? The coffee? The roses? The scent of the heather rolling down off the Angolan moors?

"There isn't any," Muller said.

"Don't be like that," Vickery said. "I can smell it. These Yanks always do a fabulous breakfast. Point me to it."

Muller flung his arm out.

"That way. Hurry up," he said, before marching off with his fists clenched.

The warthog, Vickery mused, was, by and large, a care-free, light-hearted animal. Not really like Muller at all.

The cafeteria turned out to be spectacular. It was also where the action was. If half of its many dozens of enthusiastic patrons hadn't been in uniform, it could have been the casual-class buffet on a cruise ship. If the régime-toppling business didn't work out, Vickery thought, MLG could go into catering, and do well.

Getting up close to his fellow diners at the fresh fruit table, Vickery noticed that the decorations and insignia worn by those in military dress were charmingly non-specific. In his business suit, he merged in well with the non-uniformed crowd. The atmosphere was very much corporate, he felt; there was little *ésprit de corps* that he could detect, no regimental pride or fervor. These did not seem like men and women, drenched in the stew of combat, who would be leaping back into the trenches as soon as they'd finished their smoothies. They did not look about to fight a war with their bare hands; rather, they might control one remotely, or sub-contract one.

Vickery didn't normally eat pancakes, but he had found them irresistible. Now he was regretting his weakness.

Petty must have grown bored with swinging his legs out of the side of the helicopter. He flung himself on to the bench where Vickery sat. Vickery, strapped-in with belts, buckles and a rising sense of nausea, was unable to move. He felt Petty's hot breath in his ear.

"Enjoying the ride," Mr. Vickery?

"Breakfast," Vickery said. "Had a bit too much."

"Door's open if you want to puke."

"I'll be all right."

The tree-tops flashed past, the helicopter ducked and rolled and the wind ruffled Vickery's hair.

"Ate too much, huh? Door's right there. Hold your legs for you, if you like."

"Thanks. Okay for now, I think."

"I'm saving myself."

"Are you? What for?"

"You know what tonight is?"

"No — what?"

"Barbecue night. That's why I'm saving myself."

Barbecue night?

"They do a theme night couple of times a week. Tex-Mex. Italian. Cajun. Don't do no English night, as I recall. Bet you're a curry man, ain't you?"

Please, Vickery pleaded silently, shut up about food. Was the man doing it deliberately?

"We're more your modern continental," he said.

Petty looked skeptical.

"Hell is that?"

"Fish," Vickery said. "Vegetables. That sort of thing." It was true. Kebabs were a solitary treat.

"Sounds like what your wife eats."

"Yes, that's what she eats. When she eats."

"What's her name?"

"Mariella."

"Mariella?"

"Yes."

"That's a nice name."

"Yes."

"She a thin lady?"

"Yes. Yes, she is."

"Real thin, real pale? Looks like she ain't never been out in the sun?"

"She is a bit pale, yes. It's just a look. Why? How do you —"

"Think maybe I seen her somewhere."

The idea that Petty had been observing Mariella did little to settle Vickery's stomach. And where, exactly, had Petty been mounting his unauthorized surveillance? Chelsea? Barbados? Harvey Nicks? Or was it Switzerland?

"You want to bring her to barbecue night. Put some meat on her."

"Ah, well, she's not here, you see."

Did Petty really think he'd bring Mariella to Angola? And, if he did, how was Mariella supposed to nip down from Luanda for barbecue night?

"Well, where is she?"

"I don't know."

"You don't know where your lady is?"

"Not as of this precise moment. She does tend to get around."

"That right?"

"She has a lot of interests."

Petty smirked.

"You're something else, ain't you, Mr. Vickery?"

Vickery smiled and nodded. When you were in a speeding helicopter with the door open and a psycho by your side, what you did was smile and nod.

Petty seemed satisfied. For some time he said nothing, contenting himself by leaning against the side of the helicopter and pulling his hat down over his eyes. Vickery noted, however, that his toes continued to twitch inside his cowboy boots. Eventually, though, the spirit animated him once again.

"Goin' to be a long, long war. It's the policy."

Vickery smiled and nodded.

"It's been decided. You know that, don't you, Mr. Vickery?"

Vickery nodded. Then he said, "No, wait. I thought it was all supposed to be over by Christmas? I've got commitments."

"I'm not talkin' about Angola. That's just a battle in the long war."

"If you say so. Had me worried."

"You ought to be worried, Mr. Vickery."

Well, obviously, he was. He was worried about the nut sitting next to him. A nut, moreover, allegedly responsible for the blowing up of businessmen and children.

"Why?" he asked, tentatively.

"The enemy is powerful. His power is growing. Studies prove it."

Studies?

"What enemy is that then, Harlan?"

"He's always there, the enemy. He takes on different forms. Sometimes he disguises himself. Sometimes he tries to hide. He'll make like he don't exist. But he's always there. Our job is to seek him out. And confront him."

Vickery gave the smile-and-nod routine another try.

"I see you agree with me."

"Absolutely. All the way."

"History proves it. Don't you agree?"

Well, Vickery thought, history was like the Bible, or opinion polls. You could use it to prove anything you wanted.

"I expect it does," he said.

"Sometimes it was you guys."

"What was?"

"The enemy. I'm talking about history now. You guys got the message in the end."

"Did we?"

"Then you got the Mexicans, the Spanish. Before you know it, the Japs. The Nazis, they wanted to be powerful."

Petty shook his head, apparently in disbelief at the hubris of the Nazis.

"Then you got the communists. That's the big one. But we won that, too."

"Good one, yes."

Petty gave Vickery a piercing look.

"You would have thought that was enough, wouldn't you?"

"You would, yes."

"But here we are."

"Here we are."

"Turns out, the job's not done."

"No."

"I know what you're thinking..."

No, you don't, Vickery thought.

"...But it's not just Africa. It's not just the moolahs and the jihadis. It's bigger than that."

"China?"

"Bigger."

"Bigger?"

What could be bigger than China, Vickery wondered. Did Petty want to confront Mars?

"Why d'you think it's called the long war, Mr. Vickery?"

"I — I don't know."

"Who's the enemy now, Mr. Vickery?"

"Is he hiding?"

Petty shook his head.

"The enemy," he said slowly, fixing Vickery with another unnerving stare, "is people..."

"People?"

"...Who don't like us."

This was said with a rising inflection so that it sounded almost like a question. Vickery realized that this assertion was based on something very deep and very inchoate, and was not to be challenged.

"Right," he said. "Right."

"They ain't gonna start likin' us anytime soon. Leaves us no choice."

"The long war."

"You got it."

Well, Vickery thought, here was a revelation that explained much. Whenever Aylsham or Kellerman (in certain moods) or Zarnoff or any of the big-wigs at the Liberty Club got hot under the collar and started ranting that of course it wasn't about oil, they were being sincere. It was all about some sense of personal slight, writ large — very large. Then again, when you listened to General Fricke or Kellerman (in certain other moods) or Jason or Global Executive Management Solutions, you knew that oil was topic A on the practical agenda. There was a phrase for all this — cognitive something.

"Still," he said, "it's a good idea to get on with people. You know, if you can."

Petty stared.

"What are you saying?"

"Just that we don't absolutely have to dominate everyone. Do we?"

Petty's face went blank and the corners of his mouth fell.

"Well, just what do you think we should do, Mr. Vickery? Huh? Just let people alone? Just let them do what they goddamn please? How d'you think that's going to work out?"

"No. No, I see what you mean. Right you are, then."

Petty seemed to fall into a state of sour rumination, his brows knotted. Vickery wondered if he'd said too much.

Outside, the landscape wound by, mile after mile. It looked verdant and fertile, Vickery thought. But where were the people? Where were the animals? Where were the farms and the roads?

As he brooded, his mind turned febrile. Where were the wildebeest and the lions? Where were the happy farmers? Why was Charlie Barclay chained up in Kellerman's basement? Why did German George need two copies of the book to get himself into the secret world? Why couldn't he spare one for Vickery? Why was Petty stalking Mariella? Why was Mariella so pale?

Meanwhile, Petty dozed or perhaps sulked; it was hard to tell. And Vickery meditated on the paradoxical condition of the richest country in Africa. This state of affairs persisted for some considerable time — until the helicopter touched down in a boggy clearing, in fact.

And it was as he jumped down from the helicopter that Vickery saw one of the most incongruous — and alarming — sights he'd ever seen.

It was Kellerman. He was dressed as usual, except that he'd lost his jacket and tie and had rolled up his shirtsleeves. But he looked like he'd slept in the jungle, possibly molested by beasts of the night; he was dirty and disheveled and he didn't look well. Sweat dripped from his shiny brow. But the most striking thing about him was that he now came equipped with a mean-looking automatic rifle and was brandishing it like it was the most natural thing in the world.

"Bryce!" Vickery said. "What on earth..."

"Bandits," Kellerman said. "Friggin' bandits. They'll steal anything, Alan."

"Hey!" Petty said. "You gentlemen follow me. You put your feet where I put mine. That clear?"

"Better do what he says, Alan," Kellerman said.

"Why?"

"Landmines. They're everywhere."

"What — left over from the war?"

"Yeah. Plus the ones you shipped."

"Me?"

"Yeah. Some of the fuckers are plastic. You can't detect them."

Vickery flashed back to Amsterdam, then to Budapest and Naples. Landmines? Kellerman was right — but Vickery couldn't remember who he'd bought them from. As for metal or plastic — had he even asked?

"You better take this," Petty said, poking Vickery from behind with something pointy.

When Vickery turned he saw that the helicopter pilots had dismounted and were preparing to defend their craft with a machine gun on a tripod. Petty thrust a rifle into his hands.

"But I — what do I do?" Vickery asked, suppressing the urge to panic. "How does it work?"

"You pull the trigger to start," Petty said, "and you let it go to stop. That's after you aim it, okay?"

"Alan, you be real careful where you point that," Kellerman said, in a sincere tone that seemed alien to him.

"Follow me," Petty said.

They wound their way through tall grass and trees, with Kellerman — as the more experienced marksman, Vickery assumed — bringing up the rear. Vickery took great care to put his feet into Petty's footprints. After about twenty minutes of this tip-toe stuff, Petty stopped short. He made a flapping gesture with his arm and ducked down.

"Get down, Alan," Kellerman said in a loud whisper.

Vickery ducked. Petty shuffled up alongside him.

"See over there?" he said.

Vickery looked. A lithe, black-skinned figure in a T-shirt and jeans moved cautiously between the trees. It was carrying an object the bulk and shape of which reminded Vickery of a catering-size tin of instant coffee, although he couldn't see exactly what it was.

Petty took hold of the barrel of Vickery's rifle and raised it gently to the horizontal.

"Just squeeze one off, if you wouldn't mind, Mr. Vickery."

"What?"

"Pull the trigger."

"But... But he's not doing anything. He hasn't even got a gun!"

"You're not gonna hit him. You're gonna make him run. Pull the trigger."

"But I —"

"Pull it."

Vickery squeezed. The rifle fired — not with a bang, to his surprise, but merely a short, intense crack. The figure froze for a moment, looked in the direction of the shot, and then ran to the left. Vickery expected him to vanish into the trees, but he came to an abrupt halt, seemingly unable to decide which direction to take.

Petty swung Vickery's barrel to the left.

"One more," he said.

Vickery closed his eyes and squeezed. Another crack rang out. When he opened his eyes, he saw the figure running again, this time at full pelt. And then, moments later, there came a deafening thud, and a flash of red and green. Red-brown earth showered down through the leaves of the trees on to the grass. It was all over in about five seconds.

Petty stood up.

"See this?" he said, tapping Vickery's rifle. "That's one of yours. And that? That was yours, also. What a guy. Onward."

Petty started to walk. Vickery stood but found himself unable to move his legs. Kellerman came up behind him.

"Bryce..." Vickery said. "Bryce? Did you... Bryce?"

"I know, Alan. I know. Better get going. We'll talk later."

Vickery shuffled forward, but his world was spinning.

What was he doing in this awful place?

And what had he become?

*

"Alan! Look at me. Are you okay? You look like shit. Tell me you're okay." Vickery focused his eyes on Kellerman's face. It was a round, shiny face; it had those little piggy eyes that he knew so well; and its expression betokened warmth, concern, fellow-feeling and, to be brutally honest about it, a touch of panic. In short, it was a friendly face, the face of a companion in adversity, a face he could trust — couldn't he?

"What's going on, Bryce? What's happening? Please tell me."

"This is a friggin' nightmare, Alan. Harlan's running some kind of guerrilla training camp. You should see these guys, they're fucking wild."

Vickery sat up and looked around. He and Kellerman were alone in a small thatched hut with a mud floor and a pile of dirty blankets in the corner.

"Where are we?"

"I told you. Harlan's training these guys. They think they're going to Luanda and they're going to take over the friggin' government. They're all going to be fucking millionaires and they can't even tie their shoelaces. I'm telling you, Alan, you would not believe how crazy they are. Half the time they're drugged up to *here*."

"But Bryce — Harlan made me... He pointed the gun, and then he made me —"

"You've got to get over it, Alan. It wasn't your fault. You had no way of knowing."

"He said it was my rifle, and it was my —"

"This is a crazy, crazy place, my friend. We got to get out."

"How?"

"I don't know."

Vickery closed his eyes and made an effort to breathe rhythmically. Slowly, he felt his heartbeat moderate.

"Harlan has an army?"

"I wouldn't call it that."

"And they're all crazy?"

"Homicidal."

"And there's no way they're going to — to topple..."

"Not a hope. It's ridiculous."

"And this is where all the — the equipment that I organized... This is where it came?"

"Yup. I believe you just flew in with the latest consignment."

"But I don't understand."

"Alan. You flew here from the MLG compound, correct?"

"Did I? Yes. Yes, I had the pancakes..."

"Never mind the pancakes. Did you see all the shit they have there? All those fucking warehouses? The helicopters? The vehicles?"

"Um, some of it, I suppose."

"Did it look to you as if they lacked anything — anything at all — that they could possibly need?"

"Not really."

"Come here."

Kellerman beckoned Vickery towards the doorway of the hut.

"Come on. Look. What do you see?"

To his left, Vickery saw a patch of dirt and some shirtless youths in camouflage trousers playing football. He saw a broken-down pickup truck. He saw cooking pots bubbling on open fires.

Directly opposite, in the shade under a tree, he saw a rusty metal cage. Inside the cage, a ragged, bony lion paced to and fro without pause. The cage was small: Four demented, compulsive strides, and the beast had to turn around. It was beating a trench into the red dirt.

"It's going mad," Kellerman said. "Harlan threatens to feed the kids to it if they rile him. What else do you see?"

To his right, Vickery saw other youths drinking beer and throwing the empty cans up in the air so that their comrades could take pot-shots at them. He saw a lone youth sitting in another doorway, smoking a home-made cigarette and counting dollar bills.

"Do these look like freedom-fighters to you, Alan?"

Vickery squinted in the light.

"On the face of it," he said, "no."

"No. Do they look like pragmatic free-marketeers?"

"Not really."

"Democracy-lovers?"

"Possibly not."

"Compassionate friggin' conservatives?"

"Hard to say."

"See him over there, with the hundred-dollar bills? Are we looking at the face of the Thomas Jefferson of Angola? Huh?"

"Probably not."

Kellerman coaxed Vickery back into the dusky interior of the hut.

"Alan, old pal," he said, "we've been friggin' had."

The hut darkened as a shape filled the doorway.

"Gentlemen," Petty said. "Your assistance is required."

CHAPTER 33

Díaz claimed to be Deputy Minister for Internal Security. Whether this post actually existed, George decided, didn't matter. And George's main contact in Luanda, his old friend and comrade Fernando, had agreed. Fernando was a veteran of most of the UN missions to Angola in the old days. He was a pilot: a good one, invaluable to the UN, but reckless. When the UN finally departed, Fernando had purchased a number of their planes and vehicles at knock-down prices. But few of them, George believed, were still operable. These days, Fernando retained a critical interest in public affairs, and, having no influence, was tolerated.

So Fernando had pointed George in Díaz's direction with the advice that Díaz was one the few members of the government likely to be inclined to take time out from counting his cut of the oil money to listen to an old-timer like George. Fernando had insisted that Díaz was powerful, and indeed it appeared that he was powerful enough to command a magnificent residence in Miramar.

George and Roberta had driven Fernando's old, UN-liveried Land Cruiser past Díaz's guards and up his drive, causing some commotion. Díaz had refused to meet them until, a curtain-twitching ten minutes later, Roberta had succeeded in persuading the guards that she and George represented neither international law nor humanitarian interference, but only the best interests of the Deputy Minister himself.

On the way to Díaz's house, they had passed by the villa that, according to the deluded Englishman called Vickery, contained the missing American banker. The villa was guarded and unapproachable. In the city center, the streets had seemed quieter than before. Rumors, Roberta had said. Luanda had always been a city of rumors.

Díaz was tall, gaunt and pale-skinned, a mestiço. His posture was stiff and slow, as if he wanted to conserve every last drop of energy. A survivor, George thought; a man who might trade a little, if the risk profile seemed amenable.

Díaz showed them into an ornate drawing room filled with modern furniture.

"So how is your friend Fernando?" he asked in smooth English.

"Fine."

"Good. He is a nuisance, but I would miss him."

"He asked me to give you some information."

"I think I have more information than I can use. There is so much happening now in Angola. Because of the oil price. We are seeing a great deal of activity. We have become interesting to the rest of the world again. This is what we need, don't you think? But this time we will benefit. And not the foreign powers and the mercenaries. We don't need the UN or the IMF. We are about to become rich. But thank you for thinking of us."

Translation, George thought: I've got my deal in place so why are you wasting my time?

"There's a rebel base north of Kuito," he said.

Díaz smiled.

"I don't think so. There are no rebels. What is there to rebel against? We are having elections."

The elections, already overdue, could be delayed long enough for their outcome to be arranged under new management, George thought. And, of course, there weren't any rebels. But what did Díaz think was really going on?

"What about all these assassinations?"

"I only know of three. There were different circumstances in each case."

"But what would you do if you were wrong? If there were rebels? If they attempted a coup?"

"We are strong enough to repel them. If they existed."

"What if they attacked the oil installations?"

Díaz laughed.

"The oil is in the sea. The land installations are defended. Even in Cabinda there is no problem."

"What about the oil companies here in Luanda?"

"No one is going to attack the oil companies."

George glanced at Roberta. Her face was blank, but he felt he knew what she was thinking. The ruling families — the *owners*, as they were known — would never change. They would accommodate themselves to any kind of capitalism that the post-multilateral world chose to impose on them, so long as it wasn't the open, competitive sort. As for the people, they would get privatization and cut-price sham democracy, and a lecture on rejoicing in their new freedoms. And if Roberta wasn't thinking this, well, it was true anyway.

Díaz looked bored. At any moment he would declare the meeting closed and instruct George to convey his regards to Fernando. Roberta raised her eyebrows; get on with it was what she meant.

"I am working with the Americans," George said.

Díaz sat up with a start.

"You?"

"Yes. Even I must have a job now."

"Did you tell Fernando?"

"No. Of course not."

"But why send you..."

"You are accustomed to someone else."

Díaz said nothing.

"You need to know," George said, "that there are two factions."

Díaz groaned.

"You see?" he said. "With the Chinese there are no factions. This is what I have always said. But what are these factions? Please don't tell me it's complicated."

George shrugged.

"Do you want to know or not?"

"Yes. Very well. Please. Tell me."

"And we will have an understanding?"

"I suppose so. If I believe what you tell me. What do you want?"

"Money. And some information."

"Don't they pay you enough?"

"I am just an employee. Not an *owner*."

"So, what are you doing for them?"

"My job is to find out who is with them and who is against them. They are very keen to know this. You know how they are. It means a lot to them."

"I am with them. They know that."

"Yes, but which faction?"

Díaz seemed about to lose his cool demeanor.

"One side backs the rebels," George said.

"But the rebels are only..."

George let the question hang for a moment.

"Imaginary?"

Díaz gave a sour grin.

"That would be very foolish. So unnecessary. There is a perfectly good government here already. Waiting to be used — with the few exceptions that you mentioned. So why —"

"Perhaps they think they will have less trouble with puppets from the countryside."

Díaz scowled.

"They won't."

"You may be in a position to tip things one way or the other."

Díaz grunted and looked thoughtful.

Roberta got it right, George thought. The rebels attack Luanda, without actually destroying anything valuable — such as the oil ministry, for example. They make a lot of noise, kill some people, frighten everyone else. The government screams for help. Save our fledgling democracy! Save our free-market ethos! In come the Americans, out go the Chinese, and everyone settles down to fifty or sixty years of oil-drilling, regional security, cronyism and managed poverty.

"Which faction," Díaz asked, "is winning?"

"It is close. But I would say the rebel faction. Would you like me to find out?"

Díaz shifted in his seat and rubbed his knuckles against his forehead.

"Yes, yes. Find out. I can't believe this. No, what am I saying? I do believe it. But it is frustrating. A deal should be a deal, should it not? How can you do business without trust, without rules?"

"I feel sorry for you," George said. "It must be difficult. What about my money?"

"Oh, your money. They all want their money. Just one moment."

Díaz left the room, returning briskly with a business card that he handed to George.

"See this man. Tell him I sent you. He'll remember me. Ask for whatever you want."

George looked at the card. Alan Vickery, he read. International Financial Consultant. Avenida Castro. The entrepreneurial Englishman was evidently good at making friends.

"One more thing," he said. "Two Americans called Ellis. Have you heard of them?"

Díaz lowered his voice.

"Now you are asking too much. I think you should go."

CHAPTER 34

Vickery and Kellerman rode in the second of five pickup trucks that bumped and lurched their way along rutted forest tracks. The heat was heavy and sticky.

Vickery had left his jacket in the camp and had rolled up his sleeves, like Kellerman. He had, of course, removed his wallet from the jacket and stowed it in his right front trouser pocket — even though this seemed, in the circumstances, a little ridiculous. Petty had forced him to tour the camp handing out cash — *you gotta pay your troops, Mr. Vickery!* — and, even now, as he sat with his back to the cab and Kellerman's elbow in his ribs, there was a dollar-stuffed canvas tote bag between his knees.

Also between his knees were the legs of the soldier manning the machine-gun mounted above his head. Whenever the truck hit a particularly large bump the gun tilted and cracked Vickery on the skull. Kellerman, despite Vickery's generosity in the bug-spray department, remained mosquito-bait.

The first three trucks were packed with shirtless, rifle-wielding fighters who, having just been paid, looked pumped-up and enthusiastic, if otherwise clueless. Petty rode in the first truck. In the fourth truck were three grim-faced, white soldiers-of-fortune, all of whom had been careful to keep well away from Vickery and Kellerman.

The mission, Petty had said, was a recruitment drive. The fifth truck was empty.

As they rolled into the village — it must have been a small town once; its colonial and modern buildings had been destroyed and half-patched-up; huts and shanties filled all the gaps — the inhabitants dropped what they were doing and fled. Petty didn't need to order his troops into action. They knew what to do. They jumped from the trucks, yelling and screaming, and ran into the warrens of dwellings, the white mercenaries swaggering along behind as if this were just another day in the plantation.

"All they got left here are kids," Kellerman said. "The men all ran away. Jesus, I don't blame them."

"What about the money?" Vickery said.

"Money? They're all going to get killed, Alan. They're going to Luanda and they're going to get killed."

"Luanda?"

"It's a scam, Alan. These kids attack the capital. It's totally hopeless. They get wiped out. But the government claims it's under siege. Their free-market reforms are under attack and all that crap. *They* send out a plea for help to the international community. *We* tell the international community to get lost, and in we come. And MLG takes over the economy, the Chinese get cut out of the oil — don't let anyone tell you there's a world market and it doesn't matter — southern Africa becomes another friggin' War Zone, and those strategic master-brains in the Pentagon have another country to screw up."

Vickery felt stunned. Kellerman seemed to have undergone a transformation, from lazy, corrupt, cynical realist to bleeding-heart liberal in less than a fortnight. Was it the mosquito bites?

"And you think it's all a bad idea?"

"Yes! Don't you?"

Vickery pondered. From the far side of the village came the sounds of gunfire and screaming.

"I see your point. But you sound..." He sounded like Christine Sharp, of all people. "Well, you sound like some bloody awful lefty, to be honest."

"Alan. Open your eyes. I am not a friggin' lefty. This sucks! It's wrong!"

A thought hit Vickery like a brick falling from a factory chimney.

"Then why have you got bankers chained up in your basement?"

"*I* didn't do that, you idiot."

"No? Well, why didn't you let him go?"

"Because —"

"Gentlemen!"

It was Petty's voice.

"Would you mind standing up for one moment?"

They stood, Kellerman steadying himself on the machine-gun.

"Thank you, gentlemen."

Petty laid his rifle on the ground and put a hand inside his jacket. The sound in Vickery's ears faded to nothing. Kellerman put his hand on Vickery's shoulder.

Slowly, Petty withdrew a tiny, digital camera from his jacket. He took two steps back, crouched and snapped.

"Should print out real good," he said. "Thank y'all for that."

Vickery and Kellerman sank back into the truck.

"Oh, Mr. Vickery," Petty said, "I believe we found us some new recruits. You want to give them their signing-on bonus?"

Vickery looked at Kellerman.

"Just do it, Alan."

Vickery clambered down from the truck.

Dispensing a single hundred-dollar bill to each of a half-dozen frightened teenagers — he told himself they were teenagers, even though they looked younger — as Petty's overseers bundled them into the fifth truck, Vickery began to feel a tug. It was a strange tug — an emotional tug, a visceral tug, a knot in the stomach that seemed to reach up into the brain, almost a physical thing. It seemed like the dawning or the birth of something. He didn't know what it was, but it frightened him.

There was a flash. Petty had taken another snap.

"Pick it up, there, Mr. Vickery," he said. "We got to get you back in time for barbecue night."

"Barbecue night. Yes, right," Vickery said. But his heart wasn't in it.

The final recruit was a smooth-cheeked, wide-eyed youngster of five feet and not much more. Vickery stared down at him. He was wearing a blue, silky, V-necked T-shirt that reached down to his knees. There was a large number woven into it, and a name. It looked awfully familiar. Vickery, not meaning to be rude but taken up in the shock of the moment, pointed his finger at the kid.

"Chelsea!" he said. "Chelsea!"

The kid stared back at him.

"Chelsea Football Club!" Vickery said. "Bloody hell. Didn't know they had fans out here. No offence, son, but how can you afford a shirt like that?"

He wasn't going to mention it, at this point, in case the kid got upset, but he was pretty sure that the player memorialized before him had long ago tired of the Chelsea glitz and had made a career move or two since the shirt was manufactured. To Barcelona, or Milan, or somewhere like that.

"Chelsea Football Club!" he repeated.

The kid began to smile.

"Not really a fan myself. Just live there. All the same..." He turned his pointing finger on himself. "Me! Me from Chelsea!"

"You?" the kid said, dubiously.

"Yes! Chelsea! What's your name? You! Who — are — you?"

The kid thought for a moment then got the idea.

"Aurelio," he said, pointing at himself.

"Aurelio? Good name. Sounds like a footballer. Got a head start there, anyway. Look..."

Vickery mimed kicking a football.

"You! *You* play for Chelsea! Yes? One day? Maybe?"

The kid laughed. It was true after all, Vickery thought. Those twerps on TV who said that sport was the international language. True after all.

"Me live in Chelsea!"

"Mr. Chelsea!"

"You come to Chelsea!"

"Mr. Chelsea!"

"You come —"

"You get on the truck, Mr. Vickery," Petty said quietly and from a very short distance behind Vickery's head. "You get on the truck now, y'hear?"

The kid ran to join his fellow recruits. Vickery felt off-balance. He turned to address Petty, the vague idea of questioning Petty's recruitment policies somewhere at the back of his mind, but Petty was already walking away.

As the convoy reversed itself and hauled away out of the village Vickery saw women and small children emerge from the shadows. He raised a hand in a half-hearted farewell, but there was no reciprocation.

By the time they reached the camp, the sun was low and the mosquitoes were assembling for the night shift. Kellerman's mood seemed to sink even further.

"Alan," he said, as they dismounted wearily from the truck, "if I don't make it out of here, I want you to do something for me."

Vickery stared.

"You're supposed to ask what."

"What?"

"Go see my wife. Tell her she can take it all. She can have the Bentley. Tell her..."

"You still love her?" Vickery suggested.

"No, tell her to fire the lawyers."

"Right. Look, Bryce, don't be like that. We'll get out of here together. We'll go to barbecue night — together. The two of us."

"Screw barbecue night."

This was a new Bryce Kellerman talking — well, almost new.

"I'll tell Harlan you're coming back with us."

"You'll tell him, will you?"

"Yes. Unless... Look, Bryce, I'm sorry to keep banging on about it but why have you got old Charlie —"

"Mr. Vickery!"

It was Petty's voice again.

"You ready Mr. Vickery? We're all waitin' on you."

"Um, yes. Bryce is coming with us. The barbecue —"

"Mr. Kellerman can't leave right now."

"No?"

"His place is here."

"Is it?"

Petty nodded.

"He oughta be getting back to his hut."

Vickery didn't think he'd ever seen a pleading look in Kellerman's eyes before. But he was seeing one now.

"I'll be with you in two minutes, Harlan."

"Two minutes, huh?"

"Yes."

Petty made a skeptical face while he considered this.

"I guess you want to say your goodbyes. Okay, Mr Vickery. But don't make me come back for you, y'hear?"

"No. I won't."

Petty sidled off into the gloom.

Vickery waited for him to vanish.

"Go back to the hut," he told Kellerman.

Then he ran to the lion's cage. The animal ceased pacing and retreated to a far corner. Vickery stared at the beast. The lion gave out a low moan. Vickery slid back the bolt that secured the cage door. He heard Kellerman call out to him from the hut.

Then, without consciously making the decision at all, Vickery flung open the door. For perhaps fifteen or twenty seconds, the lion didn't move. Then it turned its head towards Vickery, and Vickery found himself staring into its eyes.

An explosion of red dust, and it was gone.

CHAPTER 35

Dale Summers shuffled along amid the crush of passengers in the overcrowded basement section of Johannesburg's International Terminal. He felt a hand on his shoulder — not Jay's this time but Callaghan's. Callaghan drew him into a corner where the eddies of the crowd could pass them by and a wall of babble protected them from being overheard. Zara, Dale saw, stood at the top of the escalator bank waiting for Callaghan to return.

"This is it, then," Callaghan said. "One of those moments. Will we see each other again or won't we?"

"Kind of hard to say," Dale said. But easy enough to know, he thought. "What are you going to do?"

"Zara and myself — we're going to make ourselves scarce. Very scarce. Follow up on an important story somewhere very remote, if I can think of one."

"So you still have a job?"

"It's a funny thing, Dale. Poor Zara was sent over to expose me as some dreadful old leftist. Which, of course, she did, bless her. And so there I was, all set up to be fired — because the Beeb's very hot on balance, these days. You know, if people have been abused or abducted or blown up, you can't just assume there isn't a good reason for it. Unless, of course, it was all down to pure evil."

"Right. I know. So..."

"So then they must have said to themselves, hang on — how can we fire him when Zara's coming up with all this marvelous intelligence?"

"Intelligence?"

"Poor girl's working overtime coming up with good material."

"Well, good luck to her. And you."

"Thanks."

"Zara's a smart girl. I hope you take care of her."

"Yes. I will. I will indeed. Um, Dale..."

"Mm?"

"Are you sure it's the best idea? Going back to the States?"

"It's where I have to be, Brian."

Callaghan glanced back at Zara and made a *five-minutes* gesture.

"You mean... Sheryl's family?"

"There's that."

"Dale, you do know that — that nobody, that none of us thought..."

"Took me by surprise, too."

"I could come over all balanced about it but... It doesn't work does it?"

"No, you're right. It doesn't."

"That's the problem, though, isn't it? If there aren't any rules, you can't play by them, can you? You can't predict. You don't know the risks. Look at poor Jennifer..."

Well, he had to mention her, Dale thought. It was reasonable; it was right. Callaghan was full of the right arguments, even if he didn't dare, right here and now, to make them. It didn't matter. They understood each other.

"Not planning anything risky yourself, are you?" Callaghan asked.

"No risks," Dale said, "no calculation required."

Callaghan rubbed his hands and then tapped his fingers together.

"Good," he said. "Good. Young chap like you. Fresh start. Never forget Sheryl, of course. Nor me. Never. Impossible. Dare say nor Zara."

Was he about to crack up, Dale wondered? If so, it was time to go. For a moment he remembered Bill Ellis standing chest-deep in his pool on Hilltop Drive, drops in his eyes, the day that Dale had first heard the name George Fischer and the day before Bill and Elaine had vanished into the shadow moving in across sunny southern Africa from the cold Atlantic.

"Got to go, Brian. Be safe."

"Yes. Thank you, Dale. Thank you. For everything."

"Sure. Bye then."

"Yes. Good journey."

"It will be."

He picked up his bag and joined the last few passengers heading out to the bus. As he offered up his boarding card he turned to look back at Zara one last time.

But she had gone.

CHAPTER 36

Alan Vickery hadn't known how many different types of barbecue there were, or how many ways there were to smoke it, or dress it up, or how many different sauces it was possible to slop over it. It was a world all on its own. MLG's culinary expertise, once again, took his breath away — as did the mere smell of one or two of the sauces.

The focus of Barbecue Night was an open, floodlit rectangle, at the opposite end of the compound to Vickery's tent, whose normal, everyday usage appeared to be basketball and target practice. Trestle tables, covered with red, white and blue checked tablecloths, had been arranged around the perimeter. Each table had a flag — what these represented was obscure to Vickery — and a pair of chefs in tall, white hats. The barbecue itself was arrayed, garnished and decorated as if it were auditioning for a part in the Harrods Food Hall end-of-term show.

A crowd was gathering apace, and the mood was one of responsible good humor verging on corporate jollity. On a low platform just in front of the perimeter fence, a fresh-faced band in jeans and boots played lilting country rock. The temperature had dropped and a light breeze seemed to soak up the humidity. Even the mosquitoes seemed reluctant to intrude on the occasion. It was, in other words, quite the pleasantest possible evening and it jarred on Vickery's sensibility no end.

What, he asked himself, was Kellerman having for dinner? What about those poor kids who'd been press-ganged into Petty's doomed regiment? What about old Charlie, chained to a drainpipe? Had anyone remembered to feed him? It was obvious now that Kellerman was not to blame. But who was? And what about George the loony German? He seemed to be giving Barbecue Night a miss; was he springing Charlie even now? And where was Petty? How could he skip Barbecue Night after the build-up he'd given it?

Vickery grabbed a salad, picked up a plastic fork, sauntered close to the stage and gazed up at the girl singers. One of them smiled at him. He waved his plastic fork in reply.

Meanwhile, the spy-phone was burning a hole in his pocket. He knew he ought to check in with Jason, but he was going off Jason and was feeling rebellious. It was a common syndrome — you saw it in all spy films — in which the abused and embittered field operative, forced to face up to gritty reality, comes into conflict with his comfortable, cynical, amoral, upper-class superiors. What a joke — but it was true. He was the *Spy Who Wanted To Come In From The Heat*, but he was stuck.

And would the spy-phone even work here? He pulled it out of his pocket. Presumably, it was top-secret, highly-advanced British Technology, designed especially for tough assignments — like Land Rovers and Kendal Mint Cake. He turned it over in his palm. Made in China. Yes, okay, he thought, but designed... Well, never mind. He called up Jason's number.

A strange symbol appeared in the display, one he'd never seen before. *Satellite*, he thought. That was what it meant. How clever. For a moment he wondered if his illicit signals might be detected by ever-vigilant MLG technicians. But then, taking in the swelling size of the barbecue crowd, he decided not to worry.

But Jason, in a bored and brisk tone, declared himself to be in a meeting. Vickery was commanded to leave a message after the beep. *Fine*, he thought, *I'll leave you a bloody message, Jason, you smarmy git.*

"Jason," he said. "Alan. Well. Don't know where to start, really. We're having Barbecue Night, would you believe it? I'm at this secret MLG place. Pretty impressive. I expect you want to know the location. It's sort of in the middle, bit to the south. Hope that helps. Erm, that music you can hear? That's country music. I'm right by the stage. Anyway, it's really big, lots of people, helicopters, all kinds of equipment. Arnie Muller's here. Petty. Fantastic food. Can't answer for the barbecue — it's not really my thing. Great, great breakfast though. What else? Oh, there's some rebels. They're going to attack but it's some kind of set-up. Bryce is with them. I don't think he wants to be. Not looking very well. I'm sure there was something else..."

There was: Charlie. But what had Charlie said? *I don't want you talking to any Jasons.* It was almost as if Charlie were implying... Well, whatever. Charlie got the benefit of the doubt. He was manacled to a sewer; it was the least Vickery could do.

"...Oh, right. That Lester bloke you mentioned. Got blown up — I believe I mentioned a small explosion in my last report? Plus I have acquired a high-level source and he says... Well, he blames Harlan. I suspected Harlan from the beginning. Did I mention that? Anyway, let me know if you need proof."

Was there anything else? Yes, there was.

"One last thing, Jason. Global Executive Management Solutions. Colin and Jo-Jo. Complete wasters. The talent's out there, Jason. It's your job to find it. Bloody lucky you found me. I'll get your Chinese concessions, if it's so important to you. All right, that's all for now. I have to follow up some leads. Bye."

But this wasn't true. He didn't have any leads. He didn't really have anything at all. As the band started into a slow number on the subject of girls pining for their loved ones in the War Zones — the boys didn't pine so much, it seemed — Vickery wandered to the back of the stage and tapped Mariella's number into the phone. The phone demanded a PIN code. Bloody Jason, Vickery thought. He tapped in 0070. The call went through.

"Yes?"

"Mariella? Darling? It's Alan."

"Alan? What do you want? Look, I'm in the middle —"

But Vickery didn't get to hear what Mariella was in the middle of because he had dropped the spy-phone. And the reason he had dropped the spy-phone was that, emerging from the palm trees and long grass on the far side of the perimeter fence; with ruffled hair and a dirty face; in crumpled hiking clothes and dark-green T-shirt; with the most intense expression on her face and the most inappropriate shoes on her feet — floating up like a ghost from the gloom of the depopulated Angolan hinterland was *that woman*, her hand extended in solicitation or accusation or possibly both.

And Vickery, embittered old spy though he was, with a sickly ballad of patriotic loss still ringing in his ears, fairly melted on the spot.

Moments — or was it minutes? — later, he came back to life. He picked up the spy-phone, switched it off, and returned it to his pocket. He had made his decision.

Now he began to walk to his right, along the line of the fence, a twelve-foot-high double-chain-link affair topped with coiled razor wire. To make sure he was making himself plain, he held his left hand close to his stomach and made a pointing-finger gesture. As he walked, Jennifer made her way between the trees and through the long grass, keeping almost parallel with him. Others, in the shadows, tracked her at a distance.

After about a hundred yards the noise from the party had faded, but the fence seemed to go on forever. What was he looking for? A burnt-out light that would allow her to approach the fence. He had the feeling that MLG would replace a dead bulb in about a minute and a half. But at least there were no cameras that he could see. If MLG felt secure enough to throw parties, perhaps they thought they didn't need them.

Rows of tents gave way to larger, more solid structures. Alongside one of these was an enclosed truck about the size of a small delivery van. Pizza, he thought. Pizza was the answer. Next to the truck was the pizza joint itself. Inside he found the implement he required — a long, wooden pizza paddle. It was the work of a moment to climb on the roof of the truck and smash the nearest overhead light.

She ran up to the fence and waited for him to descend. He approached the fence slowly and leaned into it, raising his arms and gripping the wire with his fingers. What did he most resemble, he wondered — a caged gorilla or a prisoner-of-war? Without speaking, he looked her up and down, his face, he was sure, a picture of bafflement, relief and fear.

She brushed her hair out of her face and cleared her throat. He looked at her and bit his lip, expectant. She cleared her throat again.

"See, here's the thing," she said. "We've never been properly introduced. We've been very close — at least once that I know of. In London. But... The circumstances, I guess..."

He nodded, his manner a kind of guilty commiseration.

"And these circumstances are pretty strange, too, huh?"

Again, he nodded.

"But you don't want to hurt me this time, do you?"

He shook his head.

"Alan," he said, his voice sounding tight and half-strangled. "I'm Alan."

"I know all about you. Guy called Richard told me."

Great, he thought.

"I'm Jennifer."

"I know."

A pause.

"But how..." he said.

"How what?"

"How... Did you get here?"

"Came looking for you. With Walter. And Gary and Joe. Do you know them? They're from the Resistance?"

He let go of the fence and stepped back.

"Hey, it's okay," she said. "Don't be afraid. I just want to talk to you. I don't care about your money or your guns."

Neither did he, now.

"Can we talk?" she said.

"It's a bloody trap," he said, stepping forward again and shaking the fence. "A bloody trap. And I'm bloody well in it, aren't I?"

"Are you? Maybe we can get you out."

"Too bloody late, isn't it?"

"I don't know. Maybe not."

She pointed at the compound behind him.

"Do you know what this is all about?"

"More or less."

"Not what you thought, right?"

"Not quite."

"And neither am I."

"Probably not."

"And maybe you're not what I thought."

"All depends. I expect."

"We'll help you. Will you help us?"

"I don't know what I can do. Anyway, how did you know?"

"Know what?"

"Well, I'm supposed to be on the other side, aren't I?"

"What side is that?"

"Arnie Muller, Harlan Petty, bloody MLG. Liberty Club. Douglas bloody Moreland."

She ran her fingers along the fence.

"*Are* you on their side?"

"Bloody well looks like it, doesn't it?" Vickery said, rattling the fence with deliberate vehemence.

"So, you're going to see the whole thing through?"

"What else can I do?"

"But you're making a lot of money. That's the upside, right?"

The vehemence faded. Vickery leaned his shoulder against the fence.

"I don't know. Well, I suppose so, yes. Haven't been thinking about it much lately, to be honest. It's hard to keep things... I mean, look at all *this*..."

He made a sweeping gesture intended to take in the entire MLG compound and perhaps something else beside.

"How much did all *this* cost?" he asked, adopting the tone of an outraged taxpayer.

"Alan —"

"I've been handing out cash like you wouldn't believe. It doesn't mean anything here. But then it also means everything, if you can follow what I'm saying. Those poor bastards out in the jungle —"

"Alan —"

"You give them a hundred dollars and it's like you own them. This one poor kid —"

"Alan —"

"I said to Bryce, when we were going back to the camp —"

"Alan, listen —"

"He's going to Luanda, he's not even going to have a chance to spend —"

"Alan!"

"What?"

"You need to help us. We need to get through this fence."

"Can't you climb over?"

"Look at it, Alan."

He looked.

"No. All right. Wait a minute."

He trotted over to the delivery van and peered through the window. Then he gave her a thumbs-up sign and opened the door.

"No!" she said. "Too much noise!"

Vickery came trotting back.

"It's all right," he said. "They won't hear. It's Barbecue Night."

"Barbecue Night?"

"That's right," Vickery said. "Lucky it's not Italian Night, 'cause sometimes it is, apparently."

He jumped into the van and started the engine. Then he spun the vehicle around, pulled it forward as far as he could go, and threw it into reverse. He put his foot on the accelerator but the van didn't move — he had the parking brake on. When he let it off, the van shot backwards. Jennifer ran out of the way. He brought down the inner fence on the first attempt. Two further assaults left a twenty-foot section of the fence flat on the ground, and the razor wire draped over the top of the van like a victory garland.

"There you are," he said. "Now what? Bloody hell, who's this?"

"I told you. Walter, Walter's guys. Gary and Joe."

"They can't all bloody well come!"

"Just me, then."

"All right" Vickery said. "Do you want to come to my tent?"

"You've got a tent?"

"It's air-conditioned. It's just over there."

T he tent was cool, comfortable and well-lit. He could see her face clearly for the first time. It made him want to cry.

"No chairs," he said, flustered. "Sorry. Have to sit on the bed."

"Ow," she said as she sat. "Ouch!"

"Are you all right?"

"I'm still a little bruised, Alan. You know? Your friend Sean?"

"Sean. Ah."

"He mentioned your name. Last thing I heard before I passed out."

She waited a moment.

"Was there anything you wanted to say about that?"

"Yes," he said. "There is. There's bloody loads. I just don't know... I can't see..."

"Kind of difficult to talk about, I guess. Like with me sitting here right next to you."

"I've had such a struggle," he said. "My whole life."

"I know. So have I."

"And I've always tried to do the right thing. Course I have."

"Of course you have."

"But I don't make the rules, do I? It's always someone else. And it's never fair. And it's always changing."

"No, it's never fair."

"So you say to yourself, am I just going to lie here and take it? Or what?"

"You have to make your own rules. Otherwise..."

"Otherwise you never get anywhere. They'll just walk all over you. But, obviously, the problem is — if you're coming in from the outside and you do that..."

"There's a problem?"

"You can't go back. Ever. You're stuck with it."

"What's 'it'?"

"Bloody politics!"

She sighed.

"You know, I was really hurt quite bad," she said, softly.

"I must be worse than Sean," he said. "He didn't even think about it. But I did, didn't I? You know what Bryce said? When we were up in the jungle and they were rounding up those poor bloody kids? He said — and I swear to you I've never heard him talk like this before — he said "This sucks. It's wrong!" And I said something like "Oh, is it?" But he was right, wasn't he? He put his finger on it."

"I guess he did," she said. "Whoever he is."

"And then there's poor old Charlie."

"Charlie? Charlie who? Are you talking about —"

The tent shuddered and snapped at its moorings as two helicopters flew directly overhead and then seemed to hover a short distance away.

"What's happening?" she said.

"I don't know. They normally land right in the middle. let's have a look."

"Wait, wait. You said Charlie?"

"Old Charlie Barclay. They hitched him to a drainpipe. Wait a moment. That's right! You know him!"

"Where is he, Alan?"

"Bryce's basement."

"Where's that?"

"Luanda."

"Where in Luanda?"

"Avenida — no, Vista something —"

"You can find it?"

"Yes."

"Alan, we've got to go there. You've got to get me to Luanda. I need to find Joe. Come on."

She pulled Vickery out of the tent. Outside, the gangways between the rows of tents, hitherto empty, had filled with people. They were all moving in the same direction, towards the area where the two helicopters had landed.

"Know what I think?" Vickery said. "Some bigwigs flew in for Barbecue Night. Shall we take a peek?"

The two helicopters — one black and shiny, the other white and dirty — were small enough to have landed either side of the stage beside which Vickery had paced and shuffled with his lonely salad. From the rear of the crowd, he saw the passenger door on the white helicopter open. First out was a mallet-headed giant dressed in a voluminous, silky bomber jacket with the letters "FNN' stitched to the back. A roar went up from the crowd. Following him and waving — in an exaggerated effort to keep the adulation going — what appeared to be a beer can, was a dumpy, frizzy-haired figure in a bulging safari vest and stained white T-shirt.

"Shit," Vickery said.

From the black helicopter came a broad-shouldered man in a dark-gray business suit. When he turned to face the crowd, Vickery saw that he wore steel-framed glasses and a white dress shirt with no tie. He stood upright, almost to attention, and raised his right hand in a high salute. The hooting and hollering of the crowd mutated into the straight-backed, wide-smiling, high-handed applause of a political rally.

Vickery emitted a soft moan.

"Is that..."

"Yes, it's him," she said. "Moreland."

"Shit."

CHAPTER 37

That Douglas Moreland had come all the way into the mosquito-ridden Angolan bush just to make a speech did not surprise Alan Vickery one bit. The bloke simply loved to mouth off, didn't he?

As Moreland ascended to the stage, the musicians, unbidden, abandoned their instruments and slipped away in the opposite direction. Moreland made a show of adjusting the singer's microphone. Then he stood with his fists on his hips, surveying his audience with the confidence and bravado of a minor but successfully belligerent god.

Flint Gunner and Nigel Weese, meanwhile, began a procession through the crowd. Gunner, hand aloft, collected high-fives as he went. Weese, a foot or more shorter than Gunner and following in Gunner's wake like a dinghy behind a yacht, brandished his beer can like some blue-collar torch of liberty.

The two Resistance blokes — Gary and Joe — had, contrary to Vickery's orders, crept up behind him.

"Jennifer, they're not here," Joe said. "This is all command and logistics. Moreland wouldn't let Gunner anywhere near —"

"Charlie's in Luanda," she said. "Alan's seen him. Alan knows where he is."

Joe turned to Vickery.

"What about the others, Alan? Bill and Elaine Ellis?"

"Never heard of them. No, hang on — George was on about them. Who are they?"

"Who's George?"

"Funny German bloke. Came into my tent —"

"Walter knows him," she said. "Where is he, Alan?"

"Don't know. Probably gone back to Luanda. Said he was going to come to my office."

"You've got an office?"

"Yes. Why not?"

"Joe," she said, "we have to get to Luanda."

"Sure, but how? Walter's guys can't fly us any further north. We can't go all the way back to Windhoek. There isn't time. We can't take a commercial flight, they'll pick us up. Moreland's here, Gunner's here — so it's going to start soon. If Charlie's in Luanda, it's because that's where he's supposed to wind up. That's where they want him to be found. And maybe the others. There's no time."

"What about Bryce?" Vickery said. "What happens to him?"

"We need to get out of here," Joe said. "Unless you want to hear Moreland's speech. Gary, tell Walter —"

"We can't just leave it to George," she said.

Vickery shook his head.

"I wouldn't. And what about me? I don't want to stay here. I've met this bloke Moreland. He's got some very funny —"

"Joe," she said. "There's got to be a way."

"No. There's no way. Gary, tell Walter we're getting out. Jennifer — come on..."

"No. Listen, Joe. Can you fly a helicopter?"

"Yes. But —"

"Take Moreland's."

"That's crazy."

"Fly fast, they won't catch us."

"You know what happened to Jay's house. They just click on a screen."

This remark— whatever it meant — seemed to shut them all up, Vickery noted.

Meanwhile, the sound of Douglas Moreland's amplified voice echoed around the camp. He laughed, he breathed enthusiasm, he told anecdotes of his journey down here today. Nervous laughter and applause rippled through the crowd. He congratulated the men and women of MLG on their professionalism and the pride they took in their work. They'd done a superlative job, he said and, gosh, it was hard to imagine how we'd all be doing without them.

Had people — the doubters, the nay-sayers, the negativists, and the defeatists — told him it couldn't be done? Why, of course they had. Did the old, fuddy-duddy, so-called realists complain and whine and criticize and nit-pick? Sure they did — that was their default mode, you had to expect that. But no one listened to them any more, and the plain fact was that, whatever the minor problems at home, the people trusted the President on foreign policy and they shared his idealism. He, Douglas Moreland, in his humble capacity as director of this little operation, had brought them a message. And the message was: *We will prevail.*

"Okay," Jennifer said. "Alan, it was an interesting meeting. You're an interesting guy. I hope things work out for you. Take care."

She turned to follow Joe, but Vickery had taken hold of her wrist with both hands.

"No, no, no," he said. "Listen. I can do it. I think I can do it."

"What?"

"Get you a helicopter."

"How?"

"Have you got any alcohol?"

"What?" Joe said.

"Anything'll do."

"What are you talking about?"

288

Vickery gestured at the white helicopter.

"Flint and Nigel. I know them. Stayed in my house. Buggered up my study, the bastards. We can borrow their bloody helicopter. I'll talk them into it."

"How are you going to do that?"

"Make them an offer they can't refuse."

"What's the alcohol for?"

"That's for Nigel. This camp"s dry as a bone. He doesn't know that yet."

"Jesus. Gary — ask Walter if his guys have got anything."

Gary grimaced and ran off.

"Alan," Jennifer said, "do you really think you can do this?"

"I can be very persuasive. Plus I'm still pissed off about the study. Go and hide in my tent. Go on."

She looked at Joe. His face seemed set like marble. But then the corner of his mouth twitched and he closed his eyes.

"Okay."

Gary returned.

"Is this okay?"

It was a half-liter bottle of some murky, brown liquid. There was no label.

"What is it?" Vickery asked.

"He says it's home-made brandy."

"Perfect."

*

As Vickery bore down on Gunner and Weese, he saw that they had erected a video camera and were instructing an MLG technician in basic camera techniques.

"Oi! Nigel!" Vickery yelled over the laughter of the crowd as Moreland told another anecdote of what he'd said to the President and what the President had said to him.

Weese looked up like a startled ferret. Seeing Vickery loom above him, a grin of pleasure spread across his face.

"Bloody hell, old Alan's here. Flint! Look!"

"This the guy with the crappy institute?"

"That's right. We stayed at his tasteful Chelsea residence. One of our leading public intellectuals, isn't he?"

"Is he?"

"Bit surprised to find him here, though. Getting his hands dirty. What are you doing here, Alan?"

"Deals, mainly," Vickery said. "Big money. Oil money."

"Really? Fancy that."

"Nigel?"

"What?"

"I need a word."

"In a minute, Alan. We've got to get some pics of old Duggie. The light's not very good, that's the trouble."

"Douglas Moreland?"

"Old Duggie. He likes to record all his speeches. Vanity, of course. But they all say he's a great visionary."

"You're not going to put this out over the Effing News Network, or whatever it is?"

"Freedom," Gunner said, severely. "Freedom."

"Freedom," Vickery said. "Are you?"

Weese grinned.

"Don't suppose so. Tends to get a bit X-rated, he does, if he goes on long enough. Politically speaking. Private viewing only. Parental advisory."

"You've come here just to video — to video Duggie?" Vickery said.

"Don't be daft. This is just a sidebar. We're here for the main event. And the Wyoming special, of course."

"What?"

"Your old pal Jeremy is going to be there. Did you get your invite yet, or is your valuable presence required here?"

"I don't know what you're talking about."

"Wyoming. You know, the big —"

"Never mind about Wyoming. Listen, Nigel. I've got a proposal for you."

"Have you now? If it's the story about General Fricke, we won't touch it. Will we, Flint?"

"Fucking liberal propaganda. Fucking sick minds."

"Not in the public interest," Weese said. "Could do something small in the UK, if you've got pictures."

"No, no, no," Vickery said. "Look. Do you want to make some money?"

"Money? Why didn't you say so? Thought you business types always got straight to the point. Come on, then. Let's adjourn to the bar and have a chat."

"We can't."

"Why not?"

"There isn't one."

Weese seemed to reel. Gunner gripped Vickery's lapel.

"You better know what you're talking about, big fella."

"They don't allow alcohol in the camp," Vickery said, spelling it out for them. "Where do you think you are?"

"Nigel?" Gunner said. "Nigel!"

"What?"

"Can you hold out, big guy?"

Weese moaned something inaudible.

"I want your helicopter," Vickery said.

"Well you can't bloody well have it."

"I only want to borrow it."

"Why can't you wait for the next supply chopper? Not posh enough for you?"

"I've got an urgent meeting at the oil ministry."

"Oil?"

"Yes. I told you. I'm handling oil contracts. That's why I'm here."

"Oil contracts?"

"Yes."

"Must be a lot of cash involved."

"Tons. Want some?"

"Possibly. Although..."

"Although what?"

"Erm, well, technically, the helicopter belongs to FNN. Well, they rented it, anyway. Um, Flint..."

"I don't trust this guy, Nige."

"Yes, I know. I know. But..."

"Fucker's slimy as all hell."

"Yes, yes, I know he is. But..."

"You wanna know, you ask General Fricke. He'd tell you."

"I dare say he would. And yet..."

"Nige. Let me just say this. I know you don't make the big bucks. You operate in a small market. It's got to be tough. Maybe you're a little hard up. But you got to stick by your principles, man."

"Do I?"

"Sure you do."

Vickery pulled out the brandy bottle and flourished it. Weese's eyes bulged. Gunner's eyes swiveled and focused on Weese.

"Name your price," Vickery said.

"A hundred thousand," Weese said, gasping.

"No," Gunner said. "No way."

"No way?" Vickery said, his confidence wavering.

"Two hundred thousand."

"Make it a round quarter mil," Weese said.

Vickery scowled — faking it, of course.

"Done," he said. "Leave the keys in the ignition. Get rid of the pilot. We — I mean, I don't need him."

"No problem, Alan," Weese said. "Where's the cash?"

"Cash? Who said anything about cash?"

"But..."

"Oil, Nigel. Barrels of oil. Where do you want it?"

Weese and Gunner looked at each other. Here we go, Vickery thought.

"Well, how many barrels are we talking about?" Weese asked, plaintively.

"Quite a few. Obviously."

Weese and Gunner were silent for a moment. Moreland's voice boomed out across the compound. Vickery caught the words "revolution' and "enterprise".

"Would you like me to sell it for you?"

They considered this.

"Could you?" Gunner asked, cautiously.

"If that's what you want."

Weese nodded.

"Yes. Yes, I think that works for us, doesn't it, Flint?"

"I guess so."

"All right, Alan. Deal it is. Can I, er..."

Vickery handed over the bottle.

"Thanks. Flint, tell what's-his-name to hop out of the driver's seat, will you?"

"Sure, you got it. I just want to say one thing to Mr. Vickery here."

"Certainly, Flint. You have my permission."

Gunner gripped Vickery again — this time by both lapels.

"You don't bring that chopper back, I'm gonna jump ugly all over your prissy little face. Understand?"

Yeah, right, Vickery thought. *My* prissy little face? At least I don't wear makeup.

"Yup," he said. "Understand."

Gunner released him.

"Wait 'til we're out of sight," he said, "then you can take it."

"Fair enough. Thanks."

Vickery ran back to his tent, glancing once over his shoulder to see Weese remove the top from the bottle and sniff suspiciously.

Inside the tent he found Jennifer's two super-protective friends — renegade spies, or suchlike, presumably — sitting on the floor looking anxious. Jennifer had stretched herself out on his narrow, military-style cot. She looked exhausted. Her clothes were creased and dirty; her hands, roughened; her face, still bruised — in the filtered light of the tent he could see it clearly and it made him tremble. There were white spots in her nails, a bad sign. She didn't open her eyes when he came in.

"I've got it," he said.

Jennifer opened her eyes and sat up.

"Oil concessions," he said. "Everyone's mad for oil. They couldn't resist it. We can go."

"We?" Joe said. Vickery's heart fell.

"Alan's got to come," Jennifer said. "He knows where Charlie is."

Joe shrugged.

"Okay."

"What about Walter?" Vickery asked. "Don't want to leave him and his chaps in the lurch."

"They're out of here," Joe said. "Had to go. Any time now these guys are going to notice somebody drove a pizza van over their fence."

"Besides, we trusted you," Gary said. "You look like a man who knows how to borrow a helicopter."

"Ha-ha, yes. Thanks."

"We wait 'til Moreland finishes his speech," Joe said. "Take a seat, Alan. Listen to the great man."

Vickery sat on the ground. Jennifer gave him a congratulatory slap on the back. He flinched.

For some minutes they sat in silence. Vickery felt too distracted to absorb Moreland's megaphone oratory — he wondered whether Weese had seen him return to the tent and whether at any moment he and his revolting ringlets might thrust themselves through the door-flap to demand a refill — but an occasional phrase or two wafted across his consciousness.

Forward-leaning, Moreland said, and Vickery imagined Weese tripping over a tent peg and plunging into their midst. *Aggressive posture*, Moreland said, and Vickery thought of Gunner's face when the realization dawned — as it would — that Vickery was not going to return the helicopter. *Total spectrum dominance*, Moreland said, and Vickery flashed back to the embarrassing moment in Barbados when he had all but accused Aylsham of seducing his daughter. *Helping the enemy*, Moreland said, and Vickery looked at Jennifer only to feel his face flush when she returned his stare.

But then a great roar went up and continued for perhaps a minute. As it faded, Vickery heard music playing again.

"Time to go," Joe said. "Stick together. Follow me."

Joe left first, followed by Jennifer then Gary. Vickery, in a sudden panic, realized that his spy-phone had fallen out of his jacket pocket. Cursing frantically, he cast around the tent for it. How could something so bloody pink be so bloody easy to lose? And why did he have to lose it now, just when he had so much really good material for Jason? In desperation, he flung the cot on its side — and there it was, pink and beautiful as ever. He snatched it up, stuffed a wad of kwanzas — which had evidently decided to keep it company — in his pocket and raced out of the tent.

Which way had the others gone? He looked right: No sign of them. He looked left: Gunner and Weese were signing autographs — or, rather, Gunner was while Weese tried to chat up Gunner's female admirers. His heart in his mouth, Vickery ran straight ahead — and immediately collided with a solid object.

"What the..." Moreland said. "Who the hell..."

"Shit!" Vickery said.

"You! I know you!"

Moreland seemed delighted rather than angry, possibly because he was still basking in the rosy afterglow of his speech. But the last thing Vickery wanted now was a chummy chin-wag about old times in London and dreams of world domination.

"Hullo," he said. "Got to run. Sorry."

"Hey, hey, hey. Hold up there. Mr. Vickery, isn't it? And here you are, out on the front line. Gosh, how about that? I told that old fool Walsh at the embassy, I told him. He said you were a deadbeat. I said, hey — we go with the guy we've got. Trust me. It'll work out. He thinks the right way. He thinks like us. He understands what we're about. So. The plan is working, isn't it? You can tell me it's working."

"Oh, brilliant," Vickery said. "Fantastic. Rushed off my feet. In fact —"

"You know, we're about to have dinner. How would you like to be my guest? There's no alcohol here, as a rule, but since we just got the final go-ahead we're of a mind to celebrate and we brought a little something."

"Love to, honestly. Love to. Only —"

"And they say we don't have allies. Is this an ally or what? Am I not seeing this? Am I deluded?"

You said it, Vickery thought, wondering if that noise he could hear was the sound of Joe revving up the helicopter.

"Not at all," he said. "The thing is this..." His mind scrambled; what was the thing? There had to be a thing.

"Old George," he said. "George Fischer. Something's come up. Needs my help."

Moreland's smile all but collapsed, remaining just that little bit twisted on one side. He formed his right hand into a fist and gave Vickery a gentle but decisive tap on the breastbone. Then, without a word, he turned and walked off, pursued by an attentive and well-behaved entourage.

Vickery ran. The FNN helicopter, he reasoned, had parked to the left of the stage. If he ran against the tide of people, he would locate the barbecue zone and thus the stage and the helicopter. But the tide was so great that he was forced to loop around to the right, finding himself, eventually, at the very spot where Jennifer had first emerged, so stunningly, from the bushes.

The stage stood between Vickery and the helicopter. He could see its blades whirring, hear its engine pumping. Was it actually lifting off the ground? He did what Muller would have done. He charged across the stage like a wild animal, elbowing the singer out of the way, tripping over the bass player's lead and dislodging an undisclosed number of cymbals.

The helicopter was off the ground — but Jennifer was holding the door open for him. He made a leap for it. She caught him by the collar and hauled him in — a maneuver which, in the strange heat of the moment, reminded him of his first serious encounter with the forces of law and order.

As the helicopter rose and banked and he scrambled for his seat, he found his face pressed against the glass of the window. Down below, he saw a thin figure standing all alone and looking up. He felt Jennifer's hands around his waist fastening a belt, or something. But he couldn't detach his gaze from the dwindling figure below. As he watched, it removed its straw cowboy hat and held it high in a gesture of broad and theatrical valediction.

CHAPTER 38

Vickery didn't know which made him feel more nauseous — Joe's helicopter flying or Inácio's driving, or the thought of what Petty was planning for him. They were back in Luanda, and their mission — everyone had agreed without consulting him — was the liberation of captive bankers.

Inácio took a back-street route, avoiding the main avenues. The business district was almost empty of people; here and there Vickery saw thin shapes huddled in doorways or flitting down alleys. Gunshots rang out but there were no sirens and no police. The city was hiding from itself.

They drove up into Miramar. Here Vickery saw activity — uniformed guards, four-wheel-drives, white faces, children at upstairs windows. Outside Kellerman's grandiose villa, they slowed cautiously to a stop.

"Inácio," Vickery said. "Work your magic, would you? Need any cash?"

"Cash?"

"For the guards."

"I see no guards, Mr. Vickery."

"There's no one here," Jennifer said. "The place is all shuttered up."

She ran around to the back of the house. Gary and Joe followed. Vickery brought up the rear.

"But there *is* someone here," she said.

"It's Bryce — he's back," Vickery said. "Let me go first and talk to him. No telling what state he's in."

"Hold up, Alan," Joe said. "Something's not right here."

"I'll just take a peek." Vickery tried the door. "See — it's open. Bryce! It's Alan! I'm coming in."

Vickery stepped inside. He heard Jennifer follow behind, with Joe, muttering, on her heels. Gary waited outside. They were in a darkened kitchen. The window shutters blocked most of the light, but it was possible to see the remains of a large meal on the table. The air was full of sweat and cooking smells — and an oily, metallic odor.

"There's a hallway over there," Vickery said. "You've got the main stairs, and there's a door underneath — it's hidden behind the wildebeest. It goes down into the basement. That's where he is."

There was a sound of coughing — but it didn't come from the basement.

"Bryce?" Vickery said, softly. "Where are you? This is Alan. Everything's going to be all right."

He edged towards the hallway.

"No need to panic, or anything, Bryce — okay?" Vickery said. "We've just come to collect old Charlie. You can come too, if you want. I've brought some friends..."

Once again, the coughing came. Vickery entered the hallway and peered into an open doorway. Jennifer ran to his side, and froze.

It took a moment for his eyes to adjust to the dimness, but then he saw what she'd seen — twenty or thirty pairs of eyes staring back. And about the same number of shiny, new rifle barrels.

"Ah," Vickery said.

Nobody moved. Out of the corner of his eye he could see that Joe, too, had frozen, his hand reaching inside his jacket.

"Ah," Vickery repeated.

There was a shuffling and a clinking of gun barrels, but no response. They were all kids, he realized. No more than teenagers at best. And they had no idea what to do; armed as they were, they were cowering in the dark.

"Don't suppose anyone here's seen Bryce, have they?" Vickery said, slowly. "Bryce? Big fat bloke? Mosquito bites?" Vickery mimed a vicious mosquito attack. "No?"

Again, no response.

"Charlie?" Jennifer said. "Anybody know Charlie? Is he here?"

There was another outbreak of shuffling. Then one of the kids stood.

"Hey! Mr. Chelsea!"

The kid stepped forward, dragging his rifle behind him, like a toddler with a wheeled toy.

"Mr. Chelsea!"

He was wearing a blue shirt with a number and a name on it — a football shirt. The kid was barely five feet tall. The shirt hung down to his knees.

"Well, blow me!" Vickery said. "It's little Aurelio, isn't it! Recognize that bloody shirt anywhere. Can't be many of those in Angola, can there?"

"You know him?" she said.

"Met him up in the jungle. Aurelio! What are you doing here, you little... You little..."

What was the right word, he wondered. Was there a right word?

"So what were you doing up there?" she said.

"Not much. It was Harlan's idea."

Aurelio slapped playfully at Vickery's pockets.

"Mr. Chelsea! Dollar!"

"Oh, I get it," she said.

He flashed her a look which wasn't meant to be guilt, but probably was.

"Aurelio!" he said. "No dollar. Kwanza!"

"No kwanza! No kwanza! Dollar!"

"Alan," she said. "Where's Charlie?"

Vickery pointed.

"Behind the thing with the wildebeest and the lion. Down the stairs."

She pulled the tapestry aside. It fell to the floor. The door to the basement was open. The light was on. She put her foot on the first step.

"Charlie?"

There was no reply.

"He's not here," she said.

"He *was* here," Vickery said. "But he's been taken somewhere else."

"Why?"

"I don't know. Maybe because of the kids."

"Why are *they* here?"

"The rebellion is a fake," Joe said. "It's a pretext for a take-over. A way of pushing the Chinese out."

"But these kids..."

"And other kids, in other houses, all across the city. They're here to provide a target-rich environment. That's what they're doing here. Don't even need to leave the house."

"They've got to get out," Vickery said. "We've got to get them out. Inácio! Translate for me."

Vickery addressed himself to the kids.

"This is a total wind-up, Aurelio," Vickery said. Inácio flashed him a look of irritation.

"They're taking the mickey. You're all going to get killed!"

Inácio translated frantically, and at much greater length than seemed necessary. Aurelio made a short, dismissive reply.

"He says he trusts you," Inácio said, "because you give him money. And he says they will all be rich after they bring down the government, which has stolen everything from them. He says he didn't really believe in the plan until he met you."

"No, no, no," Vickery said. "Tell him he can't believe anything I say. But I didn't say anything anyway. What's he talking about?"

Inácio began another animated exchange with Aurelio.

"He says you told him he could — I don't know if this is right — he could play at Chelsea? He says if he doesn't come to Luanda to fight the government he doesn't have any money to go to England."

"Tell him he's got to go home. They've all got to go home. If he wants to come to England, I'll buy his ticket. But he's got to get out of Luanda."

"Alan," Joe said, "Charlie's not here. We have to move on."

"He says thank you for the ticket," Inácio said, "but he must stay to help his friends fight the government. They have been sent weapons from America, so they cannot lose."

"No!" Vickery yelled. "That was me! I did that! I know I shouldn't have but..."

He put his hands on Aurelio's shoulders and shook him.

"It's a set-up! You're all going to get killed! Listen to me! Do you understand? They're lying to you!"

Aurelio pulled free and backed away, dropping his rifle.

"Mr. Chelsea! Crazy man!"

The other kids began to laugh and shout. Joe grabbed Vickery by the arm and dragged him back through the kitchen. Jennifer looked at Inácio.

"Can't you —"

"No, they won't listen. They believe the only way to be rich is to fight and take it. They are Savimbi's babies."

In the car, Vickery was silent. When Inácio asked for instructions he didn't reply.

"Back to the office," Joe said.

Inácio put the Mercedes in drive and took his foot off the brake.

"Stop!" Vickery shouted. He flung open his door and ran back up the driveway.

When he returned, Aurelio was with him, minus his rifle.

"Make room," Vickery said. "Make room. He's changed his mind. Bloody kids. And not the office, Joe. There's somewhere else."

"You have a plan?"

"I do."

"Well, I hope so, Alan. Because I sure as hell don't."

Aurelio looked up at Vickery and grinned.

"Mr. Chelsea," he said. "You bad. I like you."

CHAPTER 39

I nside the Explorers' Club the air was heavy with sweat, alcohol, cigar smoke and anticipation. The room was crowded, the noise intense, and the excitement tangible. Some kind of hard rock played over the speakers. In recognition of all this, there was a lot of drinking going on. To Vickery, it felt like the squalid antechamber to some twenty-first-century boys' adventure in plunder — a guns-and-money video game about to step up to the next level.

He had made quite an entrance.

Inácio, primed with dollars from Vickery's safe, his AK slung over his shoulder, had led the way. Vickery had swaggered into the bar and slammed down a stack of his business cards on the counter. This had caused a stir, and some nervous laughter. Then, with Inácio again easing his path, he had commandeered the best table and, effectively, declared himself at home. Inácio had fetched drinks — beer for Vickery, water for Jennifer, and an orange juice for Aurelio, who, it was plain, had never been anywhere like the Explorers' Club before. Colin and Jo-Jo, tempted by Vickery's confident promise of oil concessions, snuck in behind and, with all the discretion at their command — not much — positioned themselves at the bar.

And so there they sat, implausibly, like some weird English family on a weekend trip to the village pub. The crush was formidable, but Inácio managed to enforce a minimal exclusion zone around the table.

Vickery spoke in Jennifer's ear.

"This lot," he said. "Recognize most of them from the MLG briefing. Already had some of them round the office with their begging bowls. See what happens."

It would have been an intimidating experience, but for Inácio's presence. But his rifle didn't seem to cause alarm; it was accorded the kind of respect with which you avoided treading on someone else's small dog. Vickery sipped his beer and sat back. From time to time he would make eye-contact with Colin or Jo-Jo. For some reason, Jo-Jo winked back.

The business cards proved popular. Though the stack dwindled, he never spotted anyone in the act of taking one. Vickery quickly became the target of glances — furtive but respectful. Aurelio, too, attracted attention, but this seemed like bafflement tinged with suspicion. As for Jennifer — she was one of only a handful of women in the bar — the only white one, Vickery noticed, with a sinking feeling — but no one seemed much interested in her. Wasn't her face well-known by now? Did the Explorers' Club crowd not care for the TV news? Were they too busy manufacturing their own new realities?

Vickery signaled to Colin. Colin fought his way across the room.

"That one in the cream suit," Vickery said. "He's been giving me the eye. Send him over. Bottle of whatever he's drinking."

"Gotcha."

"And another beer for me."

Colin set off towards the bar.

"These people aren't going to talk," she said. "Even if they know. Look at them."

"We'll see."

"How?"

"In business you have to schmooze. You should know that."

"I've never been in your business, Alan."

"Well, there you are then. Watch me."

The cream suit approached, shepherded by Colin with a bottle in one hand and Vickery's beer in the other. Inácio tilted his rifle against the floor, as if granting symbolic entry or operating an imaginary portcullis.

"Oh, hello — so you're Vickery?" the cream suit said. "Fantastic."

"Have a seat," Vickery said.

At that moment there came an explosion loud enough to rattle the glasses hanging above the bar.

"Bloody hell," the cream suit said. "Bit close, that one, wasn't it?"

"I'll tell you what's close," Vickery said.

"What?"

"For the right information," Vickery said, "a million dollars. Right now. You know I've got it."

And so it went for a while. The cream suit hadn't anything to offer concerning stray bankers — American or not, captive or otherwise — except that he'd heard a rumor that the entire economy was about to be dollarized and that Vickery, if he wanted to know what was good for him, would dump his kwanzas pronto. Vickery, distracted for a moment, had wanted to know what the rate was going to be. Not super, cream suit had insisted mournfully. Vickery had thanked him for the tip and promised him a slice of reconstruction pie.

There followed a succession of wary but lip-smacking supplicants. Vickery relaxed into his technique — easy, louche, co-conspiratorial. This really was his line of work, wasn't it? It was what he did. But to no avail.

"Do you think a million's enough?" she asked him.

He made a face.

"Not enough? For this lot? Plenty I would have thought. Some of them look a bit desperate."

"Not that much to you, though, is it?"

Was she trying to be hurtful?

"How can you say that? Jennifer, come on, now — how can you say that? To me?"

"I thought you were rich."

He swallowed and sniffed.

"It's not the same thing. It *is* a lot to me. It still feels like a lot. It *is* a lot."

"Oh, please, Alan. I know a lot more about you than you probably think."

"Oh, right. Bloody Richard. Richard and Jason. Bastards. Look!"

He pulled his spy-phone from his jacket pocket and thrust it in front of her face.

"Pink?" she said.

"Get the idea? Do you see what I have to deal with? These are the people looking out for my bloody freedom and liberty?"

"This guy Jason —"

"You've got to look out for your bloody self these days. Look what's happened to Bryce."

"And Charlie."

"Yeah, him and all."

"Alan," she said, "who's this Jason?"

Vickery thought for a moment.

"You know what's funny? Charlie. He said 'Don't talk to me about Jasons.' He said 'I don't know if it's the same one.'"

"The same one that..."

"He didn't say. We were interrupted."

"Alan. Do you know what the Resistance is?"

"Sort of."

"It's the only hope you've got left, if you really care for your freedom and liberty."

"Course I bloody do."

"I think you should give me that phone, Alan."

"Why?"

"Because I think your friend Jason works for the people who want to kill Charlie."

"Does he? Well, what are they waiting for? Why delay?"

"Because he's meant to get blown up along with the rebels. And because they want to catch Gary and Joe. And I guess me too, again. They'll want the names. Of all the people in the Resistance."

"Gary and Joe. And you?"

"And others."

Vickery took the phone out again.

"I didn't tell him. Jason. About finding Charlie. Same name — it seemed a bit iffy. So it wasn't because of me —"

"— that they moved him. No. I know."

Vickery switched his phone off. Then he smashed its base against the table until the rear cover broke away. He removed the battery, brushed the debris off the table into the palm of his hand and put it all in his pocket. Jennifer glanced at the bar, hoping that Colin and Jo-Jo hadn't seen anything.

"What about them?" she said.

301

Vickery shook his head.

"Jason's pets. Probably harmless. No one could act that stupid."

"What are we going to do about them?"

"I don't know. Nothing yet. We might need them. Just be careful."

Outside, a clattering fusillade of rifle fire echoed down the avenue behind the Explorers' Club. A drunken cheer went up from the bar.

"All right, Jennifer," Vickery said, "it's your turn. Got any ideas?"

A smug look came over her face, as if she'd been waiting for this cue.

"See those ladies over there?"

"Uh-huh."

"I'm going to talk to them. Aurelio?"

Aurelio looked up. She held out her hand.

"Come with me, sweetie. I need your help."

Towing Aurelio behind her, she began to push her way through the crowd.

"Good luck," Vickery shouted. "Get me another bloody beer."

CHAPTER 40

D iane Pennyman was, Dale learned, a plutocrat of the better sort; an investor, a bailer-out of bad banks; a philanthropist, like her personal friend, the late Tom Lester; and a close ally of the former Chairman of the Senate Banking Committee.

It was the former Chairman who had heard, from *intelligence sources* — and Dale could easily guess who *they* were — of the river of dirty cash flowing from New York to southern Africa. And it was Diane who, as a favor to the former Chairman, had tasked Jennifer and Charles with *following the money* to Johannesburg.

So Dale could understand that Diane felt a certain responsibility, couldn't he?

But Diane had also been a target. Of take-over artists and green-mailers; of the Freedom News Network; of right-to-lifers and gun-nuts — sometimes, she told Dale, simultaneously; of every government agency except maybe the National Endowment for the Arts (did that still exist, by the way?); of ayatollahs, both foreign and domestic; of narrowly-focused financial regulation; of presidential disdain and congressional ire; and, lately, of a willfully mishandled Mercedes in Davos, Switzerland.

From all this, she told Dale, as they sat together in a West Village coffee shop just down the block from Diane's apartment, she was tired. But not so tired as to fail to rise to one final challenge. Low down on her list of afflictions were two petty swindlers who went by the names Raymond Priles and Martin Bazon. Had Dale ever heard of them?

"No. Who are they?"

"They used to be sweethearts of Union Bank until I cleaned house and tossed them out with the garbage. They were padding their revenues with the bank's money. You remember a company called TechStar?"

"Maybe. Were they on some magazine?"

"Oh, my God, yes. They were Shareholder Value Heroes of the Month, or Most Admired Balance Sheet Riggers, all that nonsense. But, as I say, they were petty swindlers. When I say petty, I mean eight figures not nine, just to be clear about it."

Dale worked it out on the table with his fingers.

"Uh-huh. What happened to them?"

"Well, TechStar went bust. Everybody was totally shocked, just as you'd expect. But, by that time, the money had all gone overseas and nobody could find it. Except maybe Tom Lester at Giraffe. He would have looked for it, except he was helping Charlie Barclay with something much more important. Anyway, it turns out that Raymond and Martin have much bigger friends than we knew at the time. And they wanted Tom's stuff. So they came after Tom, and me too. I don't know how they did it. And there's *no evidence*, as everybody likes to say these days. But look what's happened. Tom's dead, I'm in this mess, and MLG got Tom's software and handed it over, with the appropriate mark-up, I'm sure, to the Pentagon. I don't know exactly how well Ray and Marty did out of it, but they must be pretty pleased with themselves."

"Must they?"

"Sure. That's why they've invited me to Wyoming."

"It's a party, right?"

"How did you know?"

"There's a weird guy in Johannesburg. He's going. Some Brit called Aylsham. He's like a lord or something."

"Really? What would they want him for?"

"Brian Callaghan thinks he's dangerous."

"Okay, you know Brian. Good. He seems to know what he's doing. Tried to talk Tom out of going to Angola. But, well... How about that assistant of his? Has he got rid of her yet?"

"Zara. No, it's really weird. He's, like, converted her or something. They're sticking together. They're like a..."

"Couple?"

"No. I don't think so. More like partners."

"How old is she?"

"Twenty-three, maybe."

"Ah, well."

Diane seemed to be drifting away. Dale wondered if she was going to ask *his* age next.

"So what about this party in Wyoming?" he asked.

"I presume they want to gloat over me. But I'm going anyway. How would you like to accompany me?"

Thanks, he thought, I figured you were never going to ask.

"Okay," he said. "Sure. So these guys — Ray and Marty — they live up there?"

"God, no. Florida, Bahamas, Barbados — that's more their style. No, Wyoming is where Phyllis has her ranch."

"Phyllis?"

"Phyllis Ann Curtin? Haven't you heard of her?"

"Not really."

"Have you heard of the Liberty Club?"

"Is that like a think tank?"

"Well they certainly think a lot. Although Phyllis doesn't think much of me. We have a running dispute over inheritance tax, which is by now thoroughly academic, of course. It's her organization. More like a fundamentalist church with a military-industrial wing than a think tank. Phyllis believes she's channeling Ronald Reagan, Mother Teresa and Ayn Rand. She's about my age but not nearly as fit. Yet I'm the one with the wrinkles. Check out her face when you see her."

"She has a ranch?"

"Of course. In certain circles — you probably wouldn't know this — you're nobody unless you have cows. Actually, I don't think she does. They import these animals from Africa and then they shoot them."

"They *what?*"

"Shoot them."

"But doesn't that cost — *why* do they shoot them?"

"Sport."

"Antelope?"

"Giraffe. Elephants."

"Elephants? Diane, in Namibia..."

A slide-show lit up in his memory: Pictures from their first drive north together, through Etosha and beyond, Sheryl in her new safari clothes, and the camera bouncing around her neck. He saw her balancing on top of the car seat, her body half-way through the open roof, the elephants and their babies in the water hole. And he felt the hot air blow in through the roof with her scent on it.

"You don't have to come if you don't want to," Diane said.

"No," he said. "I want to go."

"I'll tell Phyllis we're a couple. Show her she's not the only one."

"What?"

"Nothing. Just a stupid private joke."

"When is it?"

"Day after tomorrow. Have you got somewhere to stay? I'm afraid my place is probably bugged."

"I'll find somewhere."

"Call me. Ray and Marty will take us in their plane. You'll have a good three hours to get to know them."

"Uh-huh. So the party's for them?"

"No, the party's not for them."

"Then who —"

"It's for Douglas Moreland."

But he already knew that, didn't he?

CHAPTER 41

Why was he hesitating? "Alan," Jennifer said, "what's the problem? You've sold enough of these things — don't tell me you don't know how to use one."

"Hey, Mr. Chelsea," Aurelio said, "like this!"

They were standing in the bolted, guarded and wired but otherwise untended compound to the rear of the Explorers' Club. The light was fading and the air was beginning to cool. From the northern reaches of the city came the sounds of inattentive gunfire and the occasional dull thump of a small explosion.

Inácio had flipped the trunk on his Mercedes. Aurelio was showing Vickery how to operate an AK-47.

"I know, I know," Vickery mumbled. "I was just thinking..."

"You better take it, Mr. Vickery," Inácio said, selecting a rifle and offering it to Vickery. "Not so safe now. This your best friend."

"Are these yours, then, Alan?" Colin asked. "Where'd you source 'em? Bit on the light side, aren't they?"

Vickery took his rifle and examined it irritably.

"I don't know, do I?" he said. "What do you mean, on the light side?"

"It's on the light side. Isn't it, Jo-Jo?"

Jo-Jo frowned.

"Well, yes. But the real problem is, the action is on the heavy side."

"What?" Vickery said.

"On the heavy side."

Vickery scowled at his rifle.

"Did you inspect these at the factory, Alan?" Jo-Jo asked.

"Look, I don't even know if they're mine," Vickery said. "The bloody things shoot, don't they?"

Colin and Jo-Jo conferred.

"Well, of course they shoot, Alan," Jo-Jo said. "But, in certain circumstances, it's possible to imagine —"

"Never mind circumstances. Never mind imagining. Are we doing this or not?"

Jo-Jo gave Colin a meaningful look. Vickery felt his irritation mount.

"I think we're of a mind to consider it," Jo-Jo said. "But can we just run over the batting order again? Ms. Lenehan? Starting with these girls."

"Those girls," she said, "are in and out of the Chinese embassy all the time. That's what they said, isn't it, Aurelio?"

Aurelio gave a sour nod.

"Do they specialize, then?" Colin asked. "As it were?"

"No," she said, wondering, Vickery thought, whether to humor Colin or not and then deciding to give him what he wanted. "Apparently, the money's good, they don't have to do anything they don't want to do and the Chinese guys are respectful and a lot of fun. Correct, Aurelio?"

Aurelio gave a twisted grin and shrugged.

"Ah," Colin said, doubtfully. "I mean, they're not spying or anything, are they? On the Chinese?"

"Those girls? I don't think so."

"Shame. What are they doing in the Explorers' Club, then?"

"Spending their pay-checks. Looking for business."

"They wouldn't know anything about oil concessions, would they?"

"I'm pretty sure they wouldn't."

"Pity."

"What they *do* know is where Charlie is."

"You sure it's him?"

"They described him pretty well. He's a big guy, very distinctive."

"But what's he doing moving in next door to the Chinese embassy?" Jo-Jo said. "It seems an awfully odd thing for him to be doing."

"The girls say that house belongs to the boss of some French oil company," Jennifer said. "But it's been empty ever since they lost their concession and got kicked out."

"Don't you see what's going on here?" Vickery said with a sudden vehemence. "If you want a bloody global executive management solution, there's one *right here*, staring the pair of you right in the bloody face!"

"Would you like to elaborate, Alan?" Jo-Jo asked, peevishly.

"Look. Old Charlie's helping the rebels, supposedly — right? The rebels are getting all warmed up for their attack. That's all that noise you can hear — right, Jo-Jo? And then, unless Díaz pulls the plug, the call goes out to send in the cavalry. The rebels are going to get pounded, poor bastards, aren't they? And what's the *first thing* that always gets blown up when the Yanks start shooting?"

A smile spread across Jo-Jo's face. Colin's eyebrows went up.

"Chinese embassy."

"Bloody convenient, isn't it?"

"Yeah. Better hurry," Inácio said.

"We don't necessarily have to shoot our way in," Jennifer said. "If somebody's guarding him, they're going to have to leave at some point."

Jo-Jo frowned.

"I don't see why they wouldn't just shoot him anyway," he said. "Just to be sure."

There was a moment of silence.

Vickery stirred.

"It's not just that," he said, pointing at Aurelio. "What about him? What if that house is full of kids like him? Like Bryce's house? What if his friends are in there? Or his little brothers, if he's got any?"

Colin and Jo-Jo stared at Aurelio. Aurelio backed away.

"You better go in," Inácio said. "Shoot your way."

"You make a good point, Alan," Jo-Jo said. "The only problem is, if you look at it from our point of view — well, *we're* supposed to be working for *Jason*, aren't we?"

"So?"

"Technically," Jo-Jo went on, "under the terms of our contract —"

"Never mind your bloody contract," Vickery said. "And never mind bloody Jason. You want to be a bit careful with him, by the way."

"Why?"

"I have reason to believe he's two-faced. Deceitful. Untrustworthy."

"He's a spy, Alan. All right, he sits behind a desk, but —"

"I have reason to believe he gets out from behind that desk, Jo-Jo. I'm just warning you."

"Well, be that as it may, he's still paying the bills, isn't he? I mean, if we could just get a glimpse of some kind of Chinese —"

"I'll give you something better than that," Vickery said. "Or rather, Charlie will."

"Like what?"

"Tell him, Jennifer."

Come on, he thought, make something up.

"Sure," she said. "But, first off, let me ask you this. You guys are professionals, right? And you're thinking of standing aside and letting us go in to save this man — this friend of mine, who happens to be a great guy — greater than you could possibly know — who put his life at risk to save this country of Angola, who has a lonely, sad wife and a desperately sick daughter. You're thinking of leaving this to *me?* And *him?*"

Here she jerked her thumb violently towards Vickery, causing him to recoil. "And *this* little guy?" Meaning Aurelio.

"What about *him?*" Colin asked, with a nod towards Inácio.

"I stay in the car," Inácio said.

"So you big strong guys are going to leave it to us?"

Colin had a point to make.

"Alan's quite strong."

Luckily for Vickery, so did Jennifer.

"He doesn't have a clue how to shoot that rifle."

"That's true."

"So," she said, "you're still thinking, yeah, well, it's not in our contract so we'll leave it to the three of them?"

Colin coughed.

"We were thinking about it. Obviously. Got to think before you act."

"Think away."

Colin began to speak but Jo-Jo stopped him.

"What exactly is it that Charlie can do for us?" he asked.

"I expect you two are loyal Jason-supporters aren't you?" Vickery said.

"I expect *you* are too," Jo-Jo said, looking down his nose. "*Aren't you*, Alan?"

"Not getting paid, though, am I? That's the thing. Just doing it for the —"

"So how much is Jason paying *you* guys, then?" Jennifer asked.

"It's tied to results," Jo-Jo said, gloomily.

"Well, look," she said. "Charlie has a lot of valuable information. You ought to be able to get a good price for it."

"What's it about?"

"Who's buying themselves a piece of Angola. Who's bought themselves a financial stake in the march of democracy. Who's leveraging the defense budget to pump up their portfolio."

She put her hand on Aurelio's head and ruffled his short, thick hair.

"Who's picking up the tab for this little freedom-fighter and his pals."

Jo-Jo made a face.

"I'm not sure Jason would be interested in that sort of thing."

"Not Jason. You've got to sell it to his boss."

"Why?"

"Because Jason's in on the deal. Isn't he, Alan?"

"In it up to here. Ask Charlie."

Colin and Jo-Jo looked at each other.

"No, don't start that!" Vickery said.

"Hang on a moment," Colin said. "If Jason's in on this, why did he send us here? What about the Chinese oil concessions?"

"Jason," Vickery said, "is not interested in the bloody Chinese oil concessions. He just didn't want to get found out. That's why he sent you. He had to send *someone*, didn't he?"

There was a pause. Jo-Jo squinted at Vickery.

"Wouldn't the same logic apply to yourself, Alan?"

"No. It's completely different. Here's another thing. Did Jason give you an emergency extraction code-word?"

"A what?" Colin said.

"You know — an emergency extraction code-word. It's a standard thing. You get into a tough spot, the villains are on to you, they're about to throw you to the sharks or saw you in half, depending on preference. And you use the magic code-word, and bingo! You're out of there and Jason's pouring you a glass of something cheap in the cafeteria in Vauxhall."

"Emergency extraction?" Jo-Jo said. "Code-word? But how are you supposed to —"

"Didn't give you one, did he?"

There was a short silence, broken only by the whiz and crump of a distant rocket.

"Thought so," Vickery said.

Jo-Jo looked despondent; Colin, deflated.

"Well, what's yours then?" Jo-Jo asked.

"Swordfish," Vickery said.

Colin looked at Jo-Jo as if he were going to ask him for an ice-cream.

"Oh, all right, all right," Jo-Jo said. "Let's go and get this blasted Charlie. Let's have this blasted information. I never trusted that ruddy Jason."

"Good choice," Inácio said.

Vickery removed the magazine from his rifle, inspected it for several long moments with what he hoped looked like steely resolve, and then slapped it back into position.

"Mr. Chelsea!" Aurelio said. "Number one!"

CHAPTER 42

T he Chinese embassy, in Alan Vickery's view, was a surprisingly modest affair. Located in Miramar, the same up-market neighborhood as Kellerman's house and the vast, impenetrable US embassy, it was, nevertheless, rather ordinary.

A flag-pole helped to raise its profile, but not by much. The lights were on and there were signs — music, loud voices, minibuses parked in front — of great activity, perhaps even a party.

What did all this mean? Were the Chinese oblivious to the gunfire and explosions which portended what Inácio called *confusão* on a significant and party-dampening scale? Or had they merely picked up where the British had left off — some time ago, alas — in terms of sang-froid and nerves-of-steel?

It was a very peculiar thing, Vickery mused, the empire-building spirit. It waxed and waned and came back quirkier each time. Take the Romans — all baths and orgies. And the British — tea parties, cricket and culinary enlighten-ment. And in both cases, a whole lot of earnest literary endeavor and legal codification, if you wanted to be boring about it. What about the Yanks? Hard to imagine Harlan Petty playing cricket, drinking tea or even taking a bath. As for the Chinese... Well, it would be interesting to find out. Right now, however, it appeared that the Chinese either didn't know they were about to get kicked out of Angola — or they just weren't too worried about it.

The villa next door looked empty, but of course it wasn't. Charlie languished within — cursing to himself and wondering, no doubt, why that blundering idiot Vickery hadn't come back to rescue him. Well, it wouldn't be long now. Skeptical Charlie would see Vickery in his true colors. And so too, of course, would Jennifer. Wouldn't she?

Inácio had secured access to a house on the opposite side of the street, which had been abandoned only that morning, he claimed, by an oil executive and his family, who had been flown out at the company's expense to shelter in friendly Dubai until the crisis had passed.

From the upper floor of the oil-man's house — which still smelled of burnt toast and after-shave — Vickery and Jennifer had watched a discreet patrol emerge from behind Charlie's darkened villa, at fifteen-minute intervals, to make a slow circuit of its parched, dusty grounds. The patrol consisted of two men with rifles. But, given the descending gloom and the high, concrete walls around the villa, it was impossible to say whether it was always the same two men.

Colin and Jo-Jo, claiming superior expertise which Vickery privately doubted, had set off on foot to undertake what they called a *tactical survey* of *enemy terrain*. Inácio, meanwhile, had made himself a sandwich. He offered Jennifer a bite but she declined. Vickery, quite hungry himself, had been plotting a visit to the kitchen, but it was obvious to him that Jennifer required his uninterrupted vigilance at the window.

Aurelio had dumped his rifle on the bed, an elaborate and decadent four-poster which spoke instantly to Vickery of tasteless wealth. He glanced at Aurelio. The boy had found some kind of hand-held video game and was absorbed in it.

"Shh!" Vickery said.

Aurelio looked guilty and put the game down. But he didn't pick up his rifle.

Across the street, the yard in front of the villa was currently empty. Inside the Chinese embassy, meanwhile, the lights seemed to burn ever brighter. Swaying silhouettes against the blinds suggested that — of all things — a dance might be in progress. What was it — Chinese New Year? No, completely the wrong time of year for that, even in the southern hemisphere. Someone having a leaving party? Back to Beijing with a suitcase full of rhino horn? Unlikely. Natural and uncontainable glee at the commencement, at last, of the Asian Century? No, it didn't make sense.

A red glow blew up behind one of the blocks on the tumbling slopes leading down to the bay, followed by an indifferent thump. When, Vickery wondered, did the war actually start? Would someone declare it, or had that particular nicety gone out of fashion? No, he thought. It hadn't really started yet. The participants, like footballers at Chelsea Football Club facing a crucial Euro qualifier, were just warming up on the touch-line.

But whereas rescuing Charlie first time around would have involved nothing more considerable than hacking off some chains, this time there were at least two warm, human bodies in the way. Vickery could admit it to himself privately: He didn't want to shoot anyone. Ever. He wouldn't be able to live with himself, let alone explain it to Mariella. And you couldn't count that incident up at the rebel camp because Petty had forced him to shoot and, besides, the poor bloke hadn't been hit by Vickery's bullet, he'd stepped... Well, the point was, if they had to shoot these two blokes to rescue Charlie, they hadn't really *won*, had they? It wouldn't feel right. The two blokes were just doing their job. Everybody was supposed to have a job, weren't they?

And who would do it? He knew *he* couldn't. What about Colin and Jo-Jo? Had Jason put murder in their contract? Vickery almost choked on this thought. If there were any British Government employees — or contractors — *anywhere* who were *less* deserving of a license to kill, then they were probably patrolling the streets of Chelsea even now and scrutinizing the parking permit on Vickery's Range Rover.

What about Jennifer? Vickery looked at her. Her clothes were rumpled and scratched-up as though she'd been dragged through the jungle. But then she had been, hadn't she? Or the bush, at least. Her red-brown hair was a mess, but not unfetching. And what about those shoes? They seemed indestructible. Mariella's heels fell off if you looked at them, but not these. Could Jennifer shoot someone? Vickery had propped his rifle up against the bed, but Jennifer, crouched by the window, still held hers in both hands.

Well, think about it, he told himself. Think about what had happened to her. How long was she missing-presumed-dead? Couple of months or more. What had she been through? She hadn't spoken about what had happened — not to Vickery, at least. And she did not seem like the sort of woman who wouldn't speak out, if the moment were ripe. The story about her hiding out in London was plainly bogus. But now here Vickery was, almost alone with her, with the slightly intimidating Gary and Joe, and weird old George, and Colin and Jo-Jo out of the way. This was his chance to, as it were, probe her gently. Be subtle, he told himself.

"Jennifer," he said. "What's it all about, really? I mean... What's it all about?"

"What's what about, Alan?"

"You. What are you, really? What happened to you? You can tell me now. Can't you?"

Her eyes, he noticed, though admirably green, were also bloodshot.

"I'm nothing," she said. "Nothing special. I'm just an ordinary citizen. I work in a bank."

Just an ordinary citizen. He stared into her eyes, his mouth falling open as he tried to formulate his next question. She stared back and ran the tip of her tongue along her upper lip, as if trying to settle on a decision.

"Alan?" she said.

"Yes?"

"Hold this, will you? I need to visit the bathroom."

She thrust her rifle into his hands, scrambled to her feet and rubbed the small of her back.

"Keep watching. I'll be right back."

She kicked off her shoes and padded from the room.

"You see that?" Inácio said.

"What?" Vickery said. "What?"

Inácio smiled but didn't reply.

"What?" Vickery repeated.

But before Inácio could reply, there came the sound of urgent and uncoordinated boots on the tiled staircase. Inácio's smile vanished, only to return as Colin and Jo-Jo collapsed on to the bed, causing Aurelio's rifle to slip off the pillow and demolish a model of Snow White's Magic Castle that stood on a bedside table.

"Oops," Jo-Jo said.

"Nah, he knows to keep the catch on, don't you son?" Colin said, ruffling Aurelio's hair. Vickery glanced at his own rifle, now balanced precariously against the headboard.

"So what's the situation then?" he said, trying to sound business-like.

"We reckon it's just the two of them."

"You reckon?"

"Yes."

"That's your tactical analysis?"

"What do you want, a flip-chart?"

"All right. So what do we do?"

"Well, that's what we need to discuss. Where's the lady?"

"I'm here," she said, entering the bedroom with a pained expression on her face. "It's not flushing, okay? Just so you know. I think it's broken."

Were these the words of a sniper or assassin? Vickery didn't think so.

"No, they cut off the water," Inácio said. "Could be a bad sign."

"So *what*, then," Vickery demanded, "is the plan?"

"Well," Colin said, "here's what we recommend. Someone drives the Merc up to the front gate and bangs on the horn and flashes the lights. These two blokes come to see what's going on. Whoever's in the car keeps 'em talking. The rest of us go down the side by the Chinese place and climb over the wall. Then we just sneak up behind them."

"And what?"

"Overpower them."

"How?"

"Any way you like. Doesn't matter."

"Who drives the car?"

"How about you?"

"No," Inácio said, sternly. "I drive. Nobody else."

"There you are, then," Colin said.

Vickery rubbed his forehead.

"That's it?"

"Got a better plan?"

Vickery considered the window and the clear line-of-sight that led down into the front yard of the villa.

"Not really."

"Jennifer?"

"You guys are the experts, right? What are you, Colin — ex-army? Special forces?"

"Close enough."

Supermarket security guard, Vickery thought. Night-club bouncer. Heavy metal roadie. One of those. A shiver passed down his spine.

"All right," he said. "Let's, erm, let's go."

*

The music emanating from the embassy — it sounded like Disco Night, Vickery thought — seemed loud enough to obscure the noise made by four adults and a boy climbing a wall. In addition, the racket made by Inácio at the front gates, combined with the echoing pot-shots rising up from the business district, made for a disorienting frenzy of sound.

It was perhaps because of this that Vickery was taken by surprise by the tap on his shoulder. He was last in line to scale the wall, and had been waiting for a hand-up from Colin, which he didn't get because Colin had slipped and fallen on top of Jo-Jo. There had been an unpleasant squelching sound, audible above the din.

When Vickery spun around, he found himself staring down at a Chinese gent in a suit and a puzzled expression.

"Hullo," Vickery said. "Um, speak English? Eng-lish?"

"Yes, of course."

"Right. Well, you're probably wondering..."

"Why you are climbing this wall."

"Yes."

"Why *are* you?"

Vickery wondered whether he could toss the little man over the wall and, if he did, whether this would simply serve to compress Jo-Jo even further. Verbal evasion seemed a better choice.

"Look, just bear with me a moment, will you. I can explain, if you'll just... It's — look, it's really a life-or-death kind of thing. Honest. I mean, if you knew — obviously you don't or —"

"Ah!"

"What?"

"You are Mr. Alan Vickery? From Chelsea, London?"

Vickery stared, wordless.

"Of course you are. You have come for Mr. Barclay? Good, good. Very good. My name is Li. Please follow me."

Li began to stride back towards the embassy but stopped when he realized that Vickery wasn't following.

"Mr. Vickery, please! We have the key. The French people left it with us."

Vickery glanced back at the villa wall, hesitated, then ran after Li.

"Um, Li. How do you know who I am? How d'you know about Charlie?"

"Oh, we spy on you. That's how. We spy on everybody. Have some champagne."

Bloody hell, Vickery thought.

Moments later, he found himself marveling that Chinese champagne from Ningxia wasn't half bad. Mariella would have been amazed. He stood with Li at the bar watching the dancers waltz around the bijou embassy ballroom under a large and very retro mirror-ball. That they were waltzing to techno-style disco music was a cultural oddity he didn't have the time to address.

"Let me get this straight," he said. "You have been spying on me?"

"Oh, yes. We spy on everyone. As I said."

"And — pardon me for asking, Li — have you been spying on me ever since I got to Angola?"

"Oh, yes. Especially since then."

This ought to have been disturbing news. But, somehow, the hospitable Mr. Li didn't exude very much in the way of menace. His admission, of course, did raise many interesting questions, but Vickery couldn't help feeling that if Jennifer and Aurelio were, at this precise moment and only yards away, engaged in a desperate shoot-out down to the last bullet, then his place was beside them or, at least, behind them.

"Look, Mr. Li. Don't want to be rude or anything, but I think I ought —"

"I know what you're thinking. Don't worry. Look."

He pointed to a computer screen behind the bar. It showed a set of surveillance camera pictures. In one, Jennifer and the others stood at the back door to the French villa, apparently bickering.

"You see?" Li said. "Your friends are okay. They pay off the guards. Now they argue about how to break in to the house."

"Mm."

Vickery studied the scene. It appeared that a blood-bath had been averted.

"The French people, they locked the doors, you see. When they went away."

"Ah!" Vickery said, picking up on the hint. "The key!"

"Yes, I will get you the key."

"Thanks."

Li relaxed his pose at the bar and sipped his champagne.

"You know, the French people said this was very good. Do you think so, Alan? You like to drink lots of champagne, I believe? Yes? And then, when they left, they asked us to watch their house. We didn't like to say no. They used to give us the..."

Li made a wide gesture with his hands.

"Fish?"

"No, bread. Very nice. Very fresh."

"Lovely. Can't beat good neighbors. What about the key?"

"Yes, we will get the key. But you must promise to bring it back."

"Bring it back?"

"Yes. If the French people knew —"

"Why don't you come with me?"

"And miss the party?"

"Well... All right, I'll bring it back."

"Good. Thank you. And then we will have a surprise for you."

Another one? What would it be? Mariella coming out of a cake? Secret footage from the Edgware Road?

"Fine," he said. "Give me the key."

Li took a large key from his pocket.

"Here. Remember, bring it back."

"Yes, okay, I promise."

"Wait," Li said. "You want some more champagne?"

Vickery hesitated.

"No," he said. "No thanks." He ran to the ballroom exit. "When I come back!" he shouted.

Vickery ran around to the back of the villa with his right hand held high.

"Key!" he gasped. "Key!"

Inácio took it from Vickery's hand and, smirking to himself, walked up to the back door.

Colin looked impressed; Jo-Jo, less so.

"Where'd you find that then, Alan? Under the mat, was it?"

"Next door," Vickery puffed. "Explain later. Remind me..."

"Remind you what?"

"Got to take it back."

"Take it back?"

318

Inácio had the door open. In they went. The villa was dark and full of furniture, all covered up with dust-sheets. There was no power. Jennifer was yelling.

"Charlie!"

"Basement," Vickery said, coming up behind her. "They put him in the basement, last time."

She ran into what seemed to be the main hallway. Vickery followed. There were stairs leading up but not down.

"Must be upstairs," he said.

Jennifer ran for the stairs, Vickery close behind.

"Charlie!"

Jo-Jo came up behind them, grabbing Vickery by the collar.

"Wait," he said. "Hang on. Booby-traps!"

"Booby-traps?" Vickery said. He pondered for a moment.

"Nah," he said, turning to Jennifer. "Li would have said something, wouldn't he? Come on."

He charged up the stairs, breathing heavily. She followed.

They checked three empty bedrooms and two elaborate bathrooms. Charlie was in the third, chained to a wash basin. He looked up as they came stumbling in, fixing first upon Vickery.

"You!" he said. "You again! Christ almighty! Well, at least you had the brains to bring help this time."

The others piled into the bathroom.

"Jesus! How many of you are there?"

Aurelio pushed his way to the front.

"And you brought a kid with you?"

"Charlie," she said. "It's me. Look."

Charlie looked up at her.

"Jennifer?"

He didn't seem quite sure it was her. There was a silence.

"Christ, sweetie, what have they done to you? You look so different."

"So do you."

"I thought I wouldn't see you again."

"I knew I would find you. But Alan found you first."

Charlie glared at Vickery.

"I guess he did."

"You see," Vickery said, "what happened was —"

"Whatever," Charlie said. "I owe you one. Now is someone going to get me out of this?"

Inácio produced a heavy pair of pincers from his pocket.

"No problem."

Inácio worked on Charlie's chains. Jennifer reached down to help him to his feet.

"I guess you people have arranged a way out of here, correct?" he said. "Mr. Vickery?"

Vickery took a breath.

"The first thing we have to do," he said, in a slow and precise tone, "is take the key back."

CHAPTER 43

Poor old Charlie, Vickery thought. Plucked from his lonely, darkened bathroom and thrust into the middle of a crazy, Chinese disco without even enough time to dust himself down or shake the spiders out of his hair.

As Vickery had led his victorious little troupe into the ballroom there had been a momentary break in the proceedings during which the dancers had stopped whirling to greet the new arrivals with a polite round of applause. Charlie stood, transfixed, on the threshold, staring up at the mirror ball as if he'd never seen one before. Jennifer was tugging at his arm, trying to drag him off into a private corner. No doubt they had much to catch up on.

It didn't take Colin and Jo-Jo long to relax into the scene. Nor were they slow to locate the bar. On the far side of the room Vickery spotted Inácio with Li. A heartfelt but surreptitious handshake seemed to be in progress. If he cared to think about it, Vickery felt, this would explain much. But right now, frankly, he didn't care. So everybody was spying on everybody else. So what? Huge amounts of spying went on — vast amounts. All the time. Everywhere. And what did it all add up to? How many wars were averted? Not this one, for a start. What a bloody waste of time.

He felt Aurelio jabbing him in the back. Without his rifle — they'd had to check them all at the door, which seemed reasonable — the poor kid looked like... Well, he looked like a poor kid. From a poor country. People should come and spy on him; they might learn something.

"Hullo," Vickery said. "What's the matter? Want some champagne? It's Chinese but it's all right."

"Mr. Chelsea? We go now?"

"Go?"

It was a good question. They were in a War Zone. Things had only just kicked off. It was going to get a lot more shocking and a lot more awful. They ought to flee. But they were attending a disco.

"Go to Chelsea?" Aurelio said.

"Oh, I'm with you now. Chelsea. Yes. Be nice if we could just click our fingers, wouldn't it? I suppose it's quite a decent place, really. Bit expensive. Got some funny people — but I dare say you get some here, don't you?"

Aurelio was looking up at him with a very worried expression, his little brows trying their hardest to knit themselves together but failing on account of his baby-smooth skin.

"Oh," Vickery said. "Oh. You think we're going to leave you behind. Ah. Problem. Have to think of something, won't we?"

Aurelio looked doubtful.

"No," Vickery said. "Don't be like that. We will, definitely, think of something. Trust me."

But what? And what about his little friends? Were they all still shacked up at Kellerman's place, or were they already on the march, prepared to strike at the heart of the régime and seize the levers of power, the poor little bastards?

Vickery saw Li moving towards him through the throng. Inácio had vanished — either to undertake another covert mission or to move his Mercedes.

"Mr. Li!" Vickery said, brandishing the key. "Here you go."

"Thank you, Mr. Vickery. I hope you remembered to lock up behind you. I made a promise to the French people."

"Yes, yes," Vickery said, wondering if anyone had even bothered to shut the door. "Left it as we found it."

Li beamed in apparent satisfaction. But Vickery felt compelled — one good turn and so on — to place the brutal facts before the poor bloke. If it spoiled his party, well, so be it.

"The thing is, Li," he said, "we have reason to believe it doesn't really matter. I don't know if you've noticed but it's getting a bit dodgy out there. Gunfire, explosions, that sort of thing..."

Li looked interested, so he continued.

"In fact, that house, and even your embassy here, are —"

"Oh, Mr. Vickery, we know all about that. Why do you think we are having a party?"

"What?"

"Listen."

Li waved his arms above his head and shouted something in Chinese to the dancers and party-goers. The reply came back in the form of a chant — it almost sounded as though it had been rehearsed — followed by peals of hysterical laughter.

"What did you say?" Vickery asked.

"I said, 'What is the first thing that always gets blown up when the Americans start shooting?' And they say 'Chinese Embassy.' It's a private joke. You probably have to be Chinese to appreciate it. Very funny for us. Have some champagne."

Li grabbed a glass from a passing waiter and offered it to Vickery. Numbly, Vickery took it, only to find himself flashing back to the party at Bradford Urquist's apartment where he had spilt champagne — real French champagne, supposedly — on his shoes; where he had been humiliated by Urquist in front of Urquist's entourage; and where a strange, sentimental piano melody had lodged in his brain; and where it had seemed that there really were a few strong, simple ideas that explained the world; and where, despite his humiliation, he had felt so happy that he was on the verge on stepping into that realm of entitlement where everybody had the right ideas and everybody was always right and the rest of the world was always bad and wrong and had to be kept at a distance, or at least under control. What kind of perspective-distorting geopolitical wormhole had he fallen down? Which end was the most twisted?

"So we are having a big party," Li said, "before, you know — boom!"

"Boom?"

"Then we get in the minibuses, we drive to the airport and we fly home to China. Everybody is very happy."

"But they're closing the airport."

"Oh, they will let us go. After all, that is what they want — isn't it so?"

"I suppose it is. So you know about the whole thing, then? About how the rebels aren't really meant to —"

"Oh, yes. Very imaginative, I don't think, ha-ha."

"But you're getting chucked out. It's a disaster for you, isn't it? What about the oil?"

"Yes, it's a bit inconvenient. Maybe we have to have a smarter energy policy. A beneficial side-effect, perhaps?"

"Aren't you upset at all?"

"Not really. The Americans are making a big strategic mistake. Again. You should know."

"Should I?"

"They just buy up the top politicians. With a little help from you. Very bad policy."

"Why? Worked before, hasn't it?"

"But the world is changing, Mr. Vickery."

"Is it? To be quite honest with you, I'm not so sure."

"So, for example, here in Angola, we build roads and railways and hospitals and schools. We dig up some of the mines. The Angolan people like this. We will be back one day."

"But what happens in the meantime?"

"War. I believe that is the policy. Against the terrorists."

"But there aren't any, are there?"

"There is a saying, Mr. Vickery: *If you start it they will come.*"

Vickery put his hands on Aurelio's shoulders and clasped the boy to him.

"Got to be an upside, though, hasn't there? What about democracy? The Americans love to get people voting, don't they?"

Li shrugged.

"What is there to vote for, except who steals the oil? Let the Angolans learn. Perhaps when the oil is gone."

Vickery must have looked glum because Li gave him a sympathetic pat on the shoulder and removed his empty glass.

"Oh, one thing, Li," Vickery said. "You wouldn't have buggered off to the airport and left old Charlie..."

"No, no. Certainly not. It was just much better that you release him. Poor Mr. Barclay. I think he has enough problems without ending up in Beijing. You will take care of him, of course?"

"Ye-es," Vickery said, wondering if he could actually offer Charlie anything remotely competitive.

"More champagne, I think," Li said, turning towards the bar. "Ah! Mr. Colin and Mr. Jo-Jo. I have something for them."

"Don't tell me. Oil concessions?"

"Exactly."

"They'll be very happy."

"And that reminds me! Your surprise! Come with me."

Li led Vickery from the ballroom into a long corridor lined with chairs and portraits decorated with red ribbons. Aurelio tagged along behind, sticking close to Vickery and making sure Vickery knew it.

"Not packing, then?" Vickery asked.

"No," Li said. "Stuff is so cheap nowadays."

They arrived at a closed door on an upper floor. Li tapped on the door and listened. There was a muffled groan from within.

"Could you understand that?" Li asked.

"No," Vickery said. "What have you got in there?" For a moment, Vickery fantasized that Li had adopted a pet rhino and was going to ask Vickery to care for it.

"I think we go in anyway," Li said. "After you."

Vickery began to feel that this was a surprise he might well do without, but he cracked the door open anyway.

The room was dark. There was a bed. In the bed, entangled in red sheets with a dragon motif, was a large shape.

"Go on," Li said, grinning.

Vickery edged forward. The shape writhed and groaned. Vickery glanced back. Li and Aurelio stood in the doorway, Li still grinning and now also making helpful shooing gestures.

"Go on!"

Vickery advanced. The shape rolled over on its back.

"Friggin' hell!" it said.

"Bryce!"

"Alan! Jesus! I thought that maniac Petty had murdered you."

"*I* thought he'd murdered *you.*"

"What are you doing here?"

"What are *you* doing here?"

"Me? Yeah, well, okay. Look Alan, I'm a sick man, so —"

"Sick?"

"Yeah. Friggin' malaria. I friggin' told you we were all going to get it."

"Yes, that's right, you did."

"Have you got it?"

"No."

"Well, why the fuck not? Jesus, Alan, why are you suddenly so special?"

"Never mind that. What are you doing here?"

"Don't you want to ask me if I'm going to live?"

"Are you?"

"Yeah. They gave me some stuff. But it was pretty brutal for a while there, Alan, I'm telling you."

"I'm glad you're okay, Bryce. Honest. But tell me how you came to be here. It just seems so unlikely. And suspicious. And before you say anything, I just happened to be in the neighborhood."

"Shit. You gotta nail me, haven't you? Okay, here goes. I hope this makes you happy."

"Your friend!" Li said.

Vickery smiled.

"Hope he didn't cause you any trouble."

"No!"

"Okay, Alan," Kellerman said, sitting up and wiping the grease from his face into his now overlong hair. "You may have heard talk of certain friggin' oil concessions."

"You're right. I have. Don't tell me you —"

"Well, I was supposed to be kind of finding out how much the US oil companies wanted to bid, if you know what I mean, for the concessions which are coming up for grabs when the Chinese get kicked out — no offence, Li."

"Ah!" Vickery said. "I always wondered what you were doing here."

"Hey, don't take that tone with me. It's okay for you, sitting on a friggin' mountain of cash, helping yourself whenever you feel like it. Some of us have to work for a living!"

It was an offensive remark, but Vickery decided to let it pass. The man was unwell.

"So anyway," Kellerman said, "it turns out that you Brits are trying to muscle in, and you want to know the state of the bidding. Okay, I say to myself, what does a sensible person do in a situation like this? You guys are friggin' allies, right? So maybe a little arbitrage is appropriate."

"Arbitrage?"

"Yeah, but then these Chinese fuckers — no offence, Li — come along and threaten to blow the deal unless I fake up the stats."

"About the oil?"

"Yeah. I believe the idea was to get the Americans and the Brits fighting and generally trying to screw each other. Something like that. And then Petty found out. Oh God..."

"So basically," Vickery said, "you were spying for your lot, and then for our lot, and then, finally, for *his* lot?"

"No offence," Li said.

"Oh, none taken. Right, Bryce?"

Kellerman moaned to himself.

"Is that right, Bryce? You're a triple-agent?"

"I don't know, Alan. I lost track. My friggin' head hurts. I just want to go home."

"He can come with us," Li said.

"You hear that, Bryce?" Vickery said.

"Yes."

"You're going to Beijing."

"Yes. I know. Friggin' Beijing."

"Well, exactly. To tell the truth, it's a weight off my mind. Now I won't have to tell your wife."

Kellerman groaned.

"But how did you get away from Petty?"

"One of Li's guys snuck in. Stole a chopper."

Vickery mused.

"You know what, Bryce? There's a funny coincidence. We stole a chopper as well."

"You did?"

"From FNN."

"Really? Jesus, Alan. Boy, are they going to come after you. That's hilarious. Who's we?"

"Me, Jennifer and these two other blokes."

"She's here?" Kellerman ran his fingers through his hair again. "Shit, Alan — you better get on the friggin' plane to Beijing with me. Moreland's going to have your ass. I'm serious."

"Oh, I'm not worried about old Duggie," Vickery said.

"Did you call him old Duggie?"

"Media term, apparently."

"Stop it, Alan, you're making my head hurt. Li, give me another shot, will you?"

"Sure thing," Li said, looking at his watch. "In about twenty minutes. Then we must leave."

"Listen, Alan," Kellerman said, rolling out of bed and rummaging furiously for his few remaining belongings, "if there's room on that plane, you want to be on it. Tell him, Li."

Li sucked his cheeks in as if running through the passenger manifest in his head.

"Well, we do have some spare seats. However..."

Kellerman suddenly stopped dead and pointed at Aurelio.

"Alan. That kid. Is he with you?"

"Sort of."

"Is he one of..."

"Yes, he is."

"What's he doing with you?"

"He wants to go to Chelsea."

Aurelio grinned and hooked his arm around Vickery's.

"Poor kid," Kellerman said. "I guess Mariella slammed the door on that, huh?"

"I haven't asked her," Vickery said, irritated. "We can't just abandon him. He helped us find Charlie."

"Charlie?"

"Charlie Barclay. You remember, Bryce. He used to live chained up in your basement."

"Alan, if there was anything I — never mind, never mind. Where is he?"

"Downstairs. In the disco."

"Now?"

"Yes."

"Please, we have to go now," Li said, leading the way to the stairs. "The party must end. We will have one final number. Anybody have a request?"

Back in the ballroom, Vickery spotted Colin and Jo-Jo, still at the bar, flipping through a loose-leaf binder like two choirboys with a dirty magazine.

"Got what you were after, lads?" Vickery said, sneaking up behind them.

Jo-Jo snapped the binder shut.

"Yes, Alan, thank you very much."

"Kosher, is it?"

Jo-Jo looked at Vickery and shrugged. Vickery looked at Li. Li shrugged. Li looked at Kellerman, who looked down at Aurelio. Aurelio shrugged. Vickery gave in to the mood of the occasion and shrugged too. It was, he couldn't help but feel, one of those big shrugging moments.

"So long as you give Jason something," he said.

"Don't forget you owe us anything juicy you get from Charlie."

"I won't forget."

"You better not."

"Yeah," Colin said. "Look, Alan, we're hitching a ride with the Chinese —"

"Not having a secret emergency extraction code-word, you mean..."

"Exactly."

"Probably just an oversight."

"Probably. But you won't, will you, say anything to..."

"Jason? No," Vickery said. "Not until you've cashed the check, anyway. But, you know what? Now I think of it, why don't I come with you? You never know if these code-words are really going to do the business, do you?"

Colin looked uncomfortable.

"Sorry, Alan," he said.

Jo-Jo gestured at Li, who was behind the bar, struggling to release a CD from its case.

"Yes, I am very sorry, Mr. Vickery," Li said, slipping the disk into a player and tapping at the machine's buttons. "We can negotiate the exit of certain persons with us — it is just a question of money and we have a lot of kwanzas to use up."

Li stopped, listening for the music to start.

"Ah!" he said, with satisfaction, as the first notes sounded. "But the Americans are already at the airport, and they have a list."

"A list?" Vickery said.

"I am afraid you are on it. Also Miss Lenehan and Mr. Barclay."

"But why? I'm on their side. And they weren't even expecting Charlie to leave. And they don't know Jennifer's here."

Li looked serious.

"All rebel sympathizers are on the list. And they do know Miss Lenehan is here. I wish we could help you."

The dance floor had come to life again. Vickery realized he was listening to "Dancing Queen' by Abba.

"Better use the code-word, Alan," Jo-Jo said.

"The code-word," Vickery said. "Yeah. Right. Listen, you two. You're going to do me a favor..."

"What?"

"Him," Vickery said, nodding at Aurelio. "Take him on the plane with you. Take him to Chelsea."

"Chelsea!" Aurelio sang.

Colin started to say something but Jo-Jo jabbed him with the binder.

"All right, Alan," he said. "We'll see what we can do. But I suspect he'll have to settle for Colchester or Cricklewood. Until you get back, of course."

A flicker of anxiety passed across Aurelio's face.

"Hey, don't worry son," Vickery said. "Cricklewood's practically next door. Go with Colin and Jo-Jo, and don't take any crap from them."

He gave Aurelio a gentle push. The boy stumbled forward, turned and looked back at Vickery. Jo-Jo took hold of the boy's hand.

"Look after him," Vickery said. "Send me the bill."

He felt Li's hand on his shoulder.

"Goodbye, Mr. Vickery, and good luck. We are on our way now. Here is the key to the embassy. You will lock the door behind you, yes?"

"Yeah, yeah, no problem," Vickery said, feeling dazed.

"One last track, I think," Li said. "Any request?"

"No, no," Vickery said. "Whatever you like."

Li selected a disk and put it in the machine. Then he sprang across to the entrance to the ballroom and began to direct his staff to their assigned minibuses. Amazing, Vickery thought. So calm, so patient, so polite. One day they were going to rule the world.

The ballroom emptied rapidly. Vickery caught a glimpse of Aurelio as Li checked him off against his list. The boy seemed excited but a little confused. It wasn't surprising. Vickery got a tight smile from Jo-Jo and a sympathetic nod from Colin as they filed out into hallway. He gave a half-wave in return.

"Alan!" Kellerman said, slapping Vickery on the back. "Big guy. Hey, I don't know what to say."

That made a first, Vickery thought, sourly.

"What the fuck is this music?"

"It's "Every Breath You Take," Vickery said. "By what's-his-name. Sting."

"Oh yeah. Huh. Well, I guess I gotta say *au revoir*, old buddy. Been through a hell of a lot together, haven't we?"

"Yes. But I'm still going through it, aren't I?"

"Hmm. I guess you are. But hey!"

Kellerman slapped him again.

"You're the most resourceful guy I know. You're stranded in a War Zone with the ordnance about to rain down, and you've got two terrorist financiers and a couple of top-notch traitors in tow, and —"

"Oh, you know about them, do you?"

"Petty gets stoned and talks in his sleep. And you've got Petty and Flint Gunner of FNN and Douglas Moreland gunning for your ass. And you can't even trust your own guy, Jason. But I don't have any fear."

"You don't?"

"No. Sure, *you* might. Just about now. You'd be crazy not to. But I know you'll find a way out. I got confidence in you. You're a positive thinker."

"Thanks."

"Yeah. I'll come visit you in London. We'll go to that pub you like. What's it called?"

"The Royal Fusilier."

"Sounds kind of ritzy."

"Oh, you'll really like it."

"Okay then, Alan. Be seeing you."

Kellerman gripped Vickery's hand and shook it violently with what must have been malarial feverishness. For a moment, Vickery thought that Kellerman was going to kiss him on the forehead, but it turned out that Kellerman was simply adjusting his jaw.

"One final thing, Alan?"

"What?"

"It's... It's Mariella. I..."

"What?" Vickery said. "What about her?"

"Oh... Oh, forget it. It's nothing. Bye, Alan. Take it easy."

Kellerman scooted to the ballroom exit, jumping the line and brushing Li out of the way.

Take it easy? Mariella? It was the malaria talking. Vickery watched the last few of Li's people shuffle out of the ballroom. Li slipped his notebook into a pocket, gave Vickery a high wave and vanished.

Vickery leaned over the bar and thumped the CD player with his fist until the music stopped. Then he took in the scene: The ballroom abandoned; tables full of half-empty glasses; torn paper decorations in red and gold; chairs tipped over; the mirror ball stilled; a deserted buffet.

He felt his hunger return with a vengeance and set off for the food. But half-way, he stopped and looked around, turning on his heel and making a complete circle.

He was alone.

No Charlie. No Inácio. No Jennifer.

What now?

CHAPTER 44

Díaz put the phone down. "Chinese embassy," he said, scowling. "Ka-boom." George nodded. They were sitting in Díaz's formal dining room — candle-lit because the power was out. The table was a mess; some kind of banquet had been interrupted. Díaz's domestic staff seemed to have deserted him. Roberta stood by the window, looking down over the city.

"Don't you have a generator?" George asked.

"Yes," Díaz said. "But no fuel. It's ironic, I know."

"You won't get any now."

Díaz sat alongside George at the table, pushing the abandoned plates aside.

"The Chinese got out," he said. "But it was close. They weren't expecting it so soon."

"Isn't it supposed to happen in the heat of battle?"

Díaz shrugged.

"They're getting lazy," George said. "Or they don't care any more. Either way, there's not too much time."

"Tomorrow," Díaz said. "Everything happens tomorrow."

"Today. It's past three."

"George, listen..."

They listened. The sound of gunfire had spread to most areas of the city, save the waterfront and the government district. Díaz pounded the table in irritation, causing the silverware to chime and rattle.

"Who is organizing this?"

"A man called Petty."

"If it gets much worse, I'll have to do something."

"Yes, put the army on the streets. That will help. Then you will have the Marines here in thirty minutes."

"Marines?"

"Moreland has a ship."

Díaz put his head in his hands.

"Moreland's gone."

"How do you know?"

331

"We've got radar, George. We know his plane."

"Why?"

"Why's he gone? I don't know. He's a politician. Perhaps he doesn't want to be around when the shooting starts."

"It's already started."

"Yes. Well, in the morning, we'll send the army out to secure the city and I'll make my statement."

George said nothing. Díaz looked annoyed.

"I said, I'll make my statement. On television. And radio. Simultaneously."

George glanced at Roberta before turning back to Díaz.

"What are you going to say?"

"I told you. The rebels are inconsequential. We can manage the situation. There will be no bloodshed —"

"None?"

"Not much. The oil installations are not threatened —"

"They wouldn't be."

"And there is absolutely no need — no need at all — for outside intervention."

"What about the humanitarian crisis?"

Díaz rapped the table.

"There isn't one. There won't be one."

George rubbed his eyes.

"This is what I think. You need to find this man Petty. If you can't find him, you will lose control of the situation."

Díaz stared.

"Petty? One man can... Arrange all this?"

"I believe so."

"Where is he?"

"I don't know."

Díaz threw his head back in frustration.

"Then how do we find him?"

"Ask your people if they know where Arnie Muller is."

"Friend of yours?"

"An old friend. He may know how to find Petty."

Díaz picked up the phone. George could sense Roberta stealing up behind him.

"Don't," she said.

Díaz spoke into the phone in a torrent of Portuguese. Then he rested the receiver against his collar-bone and tapped his fist against his chin.

"They're checking," he said.

Roberta whispered in George's ear.

"Please don't," she said.

"It's all right."

No, he thought, it's time to settle this.

Díaz spoke into the phone again, his tone now cautious and subdued. He put the phone down softly.

"I don't advise it," he said.

"So where is he?" George asked.

"We can't cause a scene in there. It's full of foreigners. Americans. Too dangerous."

"Where?"

Díaz shook his head.

"The Explorers' Club?"

"Yes, but we can't go there. It's impossible."

"I can go there."

"And do what?"

"Find Muller. Find Petty."

"No," Roberta said.

George stood.

"I need your car."

"The Mercedes? Forget it. There's a jeep out back. Take that."

"Thank you."

"You can stay here if you want."

"No."

"It's perfectly safe."

"You think so?"

Díaz scowled. George walked towards the door.

"But..." Díaz said. "What about..."

George stopped and turned around. Roberta stood in the center of the room, immobile. Díaz looked on, uncertain. Moments passed. Then, without a word, Roberta walked past George and from the room.

Díaz coughed.

"Good luck."

"Thank you."

CHAPTER 45

Alan Vickery roamed the empty, shadow-filled streets of Miramar like a man possessed of horrors, or a demented soul, or an avenging spirit that wasn't sure what it was supposed to avenge — one of those; he couldn't decide which.

But it didn't matter, he told himself, as his brain whirred; and huge, color-saturated, surround-sound images reeled and crashed in front of his eyes; and he marched down one rich, abandoned cul-de-sac after another. What mattered was finding bloody Kellerman's house.

What kind of fiend, he asked himself, jumped on a luxury jet to vibrant, exciting, surprisingly-sophisticated Beijing at the very moment that his house bulged with harmless, clueless child soldiers whose only given purpose in life was to sit tight until a bomb fell on their heads and they got written up in the tabloids as Africa's Terror Teens?

Bloody Kellerman, that was who. But Vickery wasn't having any of it. He was having those kids out of that bloody house. The moment he bloody well found it.

What if the kids had gone? Well, then he could calm down a bit. What if they were still there — but demanded to know what he'd done with Aurelio? Would he be able to make them understand? Could he — as a last resort — employ the international language of soccer a second time?

It seemed to him that the darkness was beginning to lift. Was the sky lightening up beyond the block-strewn hills to the east? Would all hell break loose after breakfast? He snapped into a jog. Kellerman's house — unlike everything else about him — wasn't distinctive. Twice Vickery thought he'd found it, but no. And where was Inácio when Vickery really needed him? Had he, too, scarpered for the safety of Beijing? Had he had time to clean out Vickery's safe first? And was that why he hadn't stuck around at the Chinese embassy? Obviously, you didn't expect to find good help easily in a place like Luanda, but after all those kwanzas, well...

On he went, street after street. Eventually, he spotted a patch of light in the gloom and decided to approach with caution. The glow, it turned out, came from floodlights around a large, fortified compound. It looked quite new. All the lights were on. Someone had their own generator. A big one. And fuel to run it. Then he realized he was looking at the US embassy. He hadn't seen it from this angle before, but a quick mental re-mapping allowed him to deduce the route to Kellerman's house. It would take him past the entrance gates. Well, here was an opportunity, he thought. What if he were to pop inside, declaim his ties to General Fricke, the Liberty Club and British Intelligence, in that order, and demand to know why he was being put on lists? Why not? No, he thought, upon brief reflection; it was much better that he sneak around the back.

Kellerman's house looked much the same, except that the shutters were open and there were rifle barrels sticking out of the windows. Right, Vickery thought. The kids are at home. He took a step up the driveway and then stopped. The rifle barrels swiveled to point at him. In a sudden panic, he realized that he still held Aurelio's rifle in a two-handed grip across his chest. Slowly, he bent his knees and placed the rifle on the ground.

"Hullo?" he said. "Hullo? It's me. Remember me?"

The rifle barrels twitched but there was no reply.

"It's Alan. You remember. Mr. Chelsea. Hullo?"

More barrel-twitching.

"I'm Aurelio's friend. Remember? Aurelio?"

Vickery took a step forward.

"Football!" he said, running out of ideas. "Chelsea! Goal! You remember me, don't you?"

He took another two steps forward.

"Look," he said, "I really need to talk to you. It's very important."

The door to the house opened. Two kids with rifles bounced out and took up sentry positions either side of the door. Then an unarmed group of about six rushed out and lifted Vickery off his feet. Before he had time to think *snatch squad*, Vickery was on the floor inside the house with a flashlight shining in his face and someone poking a video camera up his nose.

"Hey!" he said.

"Who. Are. You?"

"Oh, come on. You know me. Mr. Chelsea! Alan! Stop poking that up my nose."

There was a hubbub of consternation followed by a long "Ooohhhh..."

Vickery felt a sense of relief. He pushed the flashlight and the camera away gently and sat up. He was in the front parlor of Kellerman's house. The kids were exactly where he'd left them. What had they been doing? Had anyone fed them? The poor little bastards looked hungry. What about Petty's men? Where were *they?*

"All right," Vickery said, as the kids crowded around him and he realized that only half of them had boots. "I've got a very simple message for you lot. Who here speaks English?"

They all stared at him.

"English? Someone?"

Aurelio's English had been basic, but Vickery quickly began to suspect that he had been the star linguist of the group.

"Port — u — geese," someone said.

"No," Vickery said, shaking his head sadly. "That won't work. No. Sorry."

He thought for a moment.

"Look, he said. It's very simple. I'll say it in English first, and then we'll go on from there. Here it comes. Ready?"

They didn't look ready but, in Vickery's stomach, a sense of panic and desperation had begun to curdle.

"Listen," he said, loudly enough to startle the front row. "You — that's *you* and *you* and *you* — have all got to get out of here. Now. Why? Because bombs come. Bombs! You know? Bombs. Ka-boom!"

They looked at him curiously. The kid with the camera began to raise it again, but changed his mind and let his hand drop. How could he get through to them?

"It's not safe here," he said, "you've got to get out or you're all going to be killed. Out! Everybody out! Out, out, out!"

He got to his feet and, gesticulating wildly, began to mime bombs falling and exploding. Adding sound effects and picking on one child after another, he repeated the mime — bombs falling, heads exploding, limbs flying off. A wail of alarm swelled. Right, he thought; *now* they know what I'm talking about.

"Come on, then," he said. "Everybody out. Follow me. Give me that."

He grabbed the flashlight and started for the door.

"This way."

But Vickery's progress was blocked by the kid with the camera. He seemed to be offering the thing to Vickery, perhaps having misconstrued Vickery's reasons for having commandeered the flashlight.

"Where'd you get this, anyway?" Vickery asked.

The kid slipped the strap over Vickery's head.

"All right, all right" Vickery said. "I'll look after it for you. Let's move, shall we? Or ka-boom!"

In the front yard, as Vickery flicked the flashlight to and fro, trying to determine whether everyone was out, the troops formed themselves into a rough series of ranks. It was odd, he thought. Perhaps they'd had some rudimentary military training, after all.

One of the smaller ones had retrieved Vickery's rifle for him. But, just as Vickery was about to take possession, the kid snatched it back.

"Oi!" Vickery said.

The kid plucked the magazine from Vickery's rifle and threw it on the ground. Then, from the depths of his baggy trousers, he produced a new one and clicked it smartly into position.

"Yeah. Right," Vickery said, taking the rifle. "Thanks."

The troops seemed to be waiting for something.

"Right then," Vickery said. "We're all out of the house. That's excellent. Now we all just... Go. Go. Everybody go!"

He waved his arms. Nothing happened. Oh well, he thought, it was probably best to demonstrate.

"Goodbye, you lot," he said. "Get lost and good luck."

He turned his back and started walking, not really knowing where he was going. And then a funny thing happened.

After a few paces, he became aware of a rhythmic crunching sound. It was coming from behind him. Without stopping, he turned his head to look behind.

The troops were following him. They were grinning and swinging their arms. They were marching. And they were almost in step.

What had he done now?

CHAPTER 46

Dale Summers stepped down from the Gulfstream and stood on the tarmac, the last passenger to disembark. He took a deep breath. The air was frigid. Ahead of him, Raymond Priles and Martin Bazon, in step together and swinging their arms like colonels late for a meeting with the general, marched off towards the first of two waiting limousines. Diane Pennyman dawdled behind at a distance, dragging her wheeled suitcase behind her.

The light was fading. Somehow this made the landscape stretch wider and the sky loom taller. He'd never been to Wyoming before. The land here made the Carolinas seem soft and intimate.

Nor had he ever ridden in a private jet. This had probably been the most expensive journey of his life. He hated the Gulfstream. What use was it to anyone that men like Priles and Bazon got somewhere a couple of hours quicker than everybody else? The Gulfstream was noisier than a regular plane, not much more comfortable, and felt a lot less safe. He watched Priles and Bazon wait for the limousine driver to open the door for them. Okay, there was your reason, right there, he thought. The world could be too good to share. Far too good. You wanted to maintain a distance. You kept the intruders out. In southern Africa, you only saw the townships from the air — or the airport highway.

Diane waved at him to hurry up. He picked up his hold-all and his new shoulder-bag — it felt heavy and uncomfortable — and ran along after her.

Then came a lonely drive along straight, empty roads, measured out by telegraph poles. Diane didn't say much of anything. He guessed she was tired. During the flight, Bazon had kept to himself but Priles had fastened on to Diane, just riffing on and on about business and money; and then his family and his grandchildren and their various houses; and his golf course and his motor yacht — did Diane know that they sailed all the way to Barbados and back? — and then getting all dewy-eyed over what he called Diane's awful legal and financial worries. Was it all bullshit? Dale thought so. As for himself, it seemed that Priles and Bazon had taken him for Diane's employee and disregarded him accordingly.

"Where are we?" he asked Diane.

"Somewhere near Saratoga, I think," she said. "Raymond was a bit vague about it. But then that's his whole way of operating."

Dale wasn't even sure where Saratoga was. He put his shoulder bag very carefully on the floor and settled back into his seat.

They drove south for about half an hour, crossing a wide river. The land became more hilly, more forested. Mountains rose up in the distance, first on the left and then on the right.

"Nice scenery," Diane said. "But I'm beginning to wonder if this was such a good idea."

"Why?"

"Well, I can stand a good bit of humiliation. I thought at least I could show them that I'm not finished yet. But look at all this." The waved her hand at the window. "These people think big. They're not into subtlety. All the smart things I was going to say — it'll be like a gnat biting a moose."

"I think it's a good idea."

"You do? Well, good. Then I guess we don't need to find a motel."

The gates to the ranch were meant to look rustic — rough-hewn logs, horse-shoes, antlers. But underneath they were steel and high-tech. It was a pointless pretense, Dale thought. Why even try? As the limo drove up, Dale saw a security camera set at window level. The driver buzzed the windows down, presumably because the glass in them was darkened. Ice-cold air flooded in. Diane shivered. The camera took a long look at them.

Then the windows went back up and the gates opened automatically. Beyond, a paved road rolled down for a mile or more to a river valley. There were no buildings in sight. The limo powered up and swept on across a wild and empty expanse of grass and low trees.

Diane sighed.

"What does Phyllis do with all this land?"

"Everybody wants a piece of land," Dale said. In Africa the fighting hadn't even finished yet — because land was still about survival. Here, it meant something else.

"But this much?" Diane said.

"Sure is a lot."

Hadn't Diane said that hunters came here to shoot giraffe and elephant? Had he heard that right? It had seemed impossible. But now that he was here — well, maybe it wasn't. This was a private zone in which anything might happen, if you had the resources to command it. The emptiness of Namibia had a totally different quality. You could put up game fences and build lodges, but you could never impinge more than marginally on the landscape. Here, the land had been captured. It had been coerced. It had submitted.

The road crossed a smaller, fast-flowing river, and then bent to the right. They passed a stand of trees and the ranch itself came into sight. What had he been expecting? Something kind of between a southern plantation mansion and a log cabin? A real, working ranch with barns and cows? Something low, modern and Californian with the architect's picture in the hall? Well, forget about all that. Phyllis's ranch was an English country estate out of Masterpiece Theater. It was immense, but something wasn't right about it. Dale knew little about architecture

340

but he immediately felt that the proportions of the building were all wrong. The regal façade glowered and frowned — kind of like Buckingham Palace, he guessed. But the thing was too wide and flat, puffed out and swollen across its acreage like a Target or a Wal-Mart. The portico extended into the circular driveway in front of the house and was wide enough for three limos, side by side.

"What the hell is that?" Diane said.

She wasn't looking at the house. On the other side of the circular drive was a vast ornamental lake. Gliding slowly and serenely across the surface of the lake, one after the other in a wide circle in front of the house, were a dozen teetering, illuminated floats.

"I don't know," Dale said. "Are there people on those things? I can see something moving."

"I need to put my glasses on."

The limo pulled to a stop under the portico. Dale buzzed his window down and stared out at the lake. Wow, he thought. Who knew they did this kind of stuff in Wyoming?

"Okay, you want to know what that is?" he said. "I'll tell you. You see the first one? That's Noah, okay? That's his ark and he's waving at us. Looks like he's got a couple of giraffes. They're waving, also. Maybe if they stay out there they won't get —"

"Noah?"

"Uh-huh. Then the next one's Moses. That's an easy one. Nice lights. See the spotlights on the tablets? Then —"

"Moses?"

"Sure. He's waving too — look. They're all waving."

"Why is Moses cruising around on Phyllis's pond in the dark? I don't understand."

"I don't know. Kind of neat, though, isn't it? Not sure about the next one. Could be Cain and Abel."

"But why, Dale? How long are they... It must be freezing out there. Don't tell me Moses isn't cold in that dress."

"Got something on underneath, I guess."

The limo door opened.

"All right, come on," Diane said. "This is a crazy place. Phyllis must have gone nuts."

"You never lived down south, did you?"

"No."

"Well, there you go."

Diane gave him a look that seemed to him at once weary and urgent.

"Let's go in, Dale. This is..."

"Creeping you out?"

"That's the expression."

"Think it'll be better inside?"

"It'll be warmer inside."

Dale picked up his shoulder-bag and stepped carefully out of the car. His hold-all and Diane's wheeled suitcase had already been taken out of the trunk.

The limo drove off, heading back up the drive towards the public highway. They stood on the gravel. There seemed to be no one to welcome them.

"Well, let's be charitable," Diane said. "Phyllis is frail." She looked at Dale. "We're practically the same age. Did you know?"

"Yeah, you mentioned it."

"Let's see if we can get a cup of tea."

"Okay. After you."

They entered the ranch. Immediately, they were intercepted by a frightened Mexican maid. The maid summoned a short-haired young man in a cream suit and boots. Before Diane could speak, the young man held up a hand. Then he turned his back and spoke quietly into a radio handset for a minute or so.

"Mrs. Pennyman," he said, facing them again. "This way."

"Is Phyllis not expecting me?" Diane said. "I told her I was coming. She ought to write these things down."

The young man smiled.

"This way."

It was a long walk. They went up two floors. The house seemed to go on forever. Eventually, the young man located two vacant rooms.

"Looks like you got a full house," Dale said. "Must be quite a party."

"You could say that."

"So what do we do?"

"Come down when you're ready. Take the elevator — that's easiest. We're having the ball tonight. And tomorrow we'll all be watching the video feeds."

"Okay," Dale said. "How about the guest of honor? When's he getting in?"

The young man smiled but didn't reply.

"What's your name?" Dale asked.

"Todd."

"Uh-huh. So when is Douglas Moreland getting in?"

Todd looked embarrassed.

"I really can't —"

"Oh, it's a security thing?"

"Kind of."

"I got you."

Todd turned to move off.

"Hey, Todd!" Dale said, taking a ten-dollar bill from his pocket. "Here."

Todd smiled again, shook his head and walked off.

"You can cut that out, Dale," Diane said. "If anyone's going to misbehave, it's going to be me."

No, it isn't, he thought.

"See you downstairs in twenty minutes," she said.

*

Not everybody was dressed for the ball, Dale noted, as he strolled alone along the wide hallway which formed the main axis of the ground floor of the house. Diane had made him buy a new suit which he wore, self-consciously, with a plain, knitted tie. There were men in tuxedos and women in ball gowns; and attendants of different stripes in white jackets or black suits. Nobody seemed much interested in him; the only curious glances he attracted came from the staff. At intervals the hallway widened into a circular lobby with a fountain in its center. At these points, lesser corridors ran across the main drag. There was a general drift towards the far end of the main hallway where, Dale assumed, the ballroom was located.

The marble flooring, the fountains, the gilt decorations, the over-sized flower arrangements, and what sounded like piped Vivaldi — it was some ranch, Dale thought. The doors to many of the side-rooms were open. He couldn't help peering in.

In one, around a table stacked with newspapers, a group of men in suits and sports jackets sat arguing. Dale stopped and looked. At one end of the table, a tall, blonde woman of about thirty-five stood with her left hand on her hip and her right hand, index finger extended, in the face of a small gray man in a bow-tie. A dispute was in progress. The gray man cowered like a terrier with a grudge. A slack-jawed, sixty-ish man in large, red-framed glasses caught Dale looking on.

"Hey!" he said, grabbing a magazine from the table and leaping from his seat. "Did you read the new one? Check it out." He thrust the magazine into Dale's hands. "Are you with the Texas college folk? You look familiar."

"No," Dale said. "I'm from North Carolina."

"Good on you."

"Thanks."

Dale retreated. Around the table, the debate raged on. The magazine was something called The Weekly Consensus. Of course, he thought. The Consensus. He'd heard people at the embassy in Windhoek talk about it, mostly despairingly. Sheryl had said something about it once — but he hadn't really been listening. On the cover, in a small box, was a picture of the red-glasses guy, grinning and looking fifteen years younger. Underneath, a caption read "What Liberals Don't Get About Africa." Dale glanced back at what he assumed must be the Consensus's editorial team. The blonde woman still hadn't finished with the gray guy. Nobody gets Africa, he thought. I don't get it. It gets me.

He walked on. The next room housed some kind of prayer meeting. Maybe they were praying that Noah didn't catch pneumonia. He hurried past.

The shoulder bag felt uncomfortable; when he walked, it bumped against his hip, jarring the bone. He switched it to his left shoulder. It felt better, but less secure. He gripped the strap a little tighter.

Diane still hadn't come down. Dale figured her face was well-known enough — provocatively so with this crowd — that her appearance would surely create a stir. He hoped that nobody would be would tasteless enough to insult her to her face. They could leave that to the Consensus.

The tide of people drifting towards the ballroom had begun to swell. He ducked down a side-corridor, hoping to find an empty room where he could rearrange the contents of the shoulder bag. The first room he found was set up like a kind of fancy home theatre, with rows of armchairs and a large movie screen. The lighting was set low. He slipped inside and pushed the door to.

Taking a seat in the front row, he unzipped the bag and reached in.

"You know, we're not going to be ready for another couple of hours."

Dale zipped the bag quietly and looked up. A young man in a flannel shirt and a tool-belt had emerged from behind the screen. He looked like a contractor or an engineer.

"Oh," Dale said. "I thought..."

"No, sorry, guy. See, the satellite truck only just showed. We're trying to hook it up now. But we got to do the main feed to the ballroom first, you know? Get old Flint up on the big screen. Keep the people happy?"

"Oh, okay. I'll check back later."

"What's in the bag?"

"The bag?"

"Yeah."

"Just personal stuff. Why?"

"You know there's no recording equipment allowed in here?"

"Actually, I didn't know. Why's that?"

The engineer smirked at Dale and gave an amused grunt.

"You're not one of those Consensus guys, are you?"

"No."

The engineer pointed to the screen.

"Good. This is not for them. Could get kind of X-rated. Raw images. Unedited. Know what I'm talking about?"

Dale nodded.

"Don't know what you're going to see."

"No," Dale said.

"Not for everybody."

"No. Thanks. I'll check back later."

"Did you eat yet?"

"No."

"Wise man."

Dale picked up the shoulder bag and walked smartly back to the main hallway. This time, he allowed himself to be swept along towards the ballroom. At the entrance, he gave his name — his false name — and declined to check his bag. He was directed to a small table at the back of the ballroom. Diane wasn't there. The only other occupant was a shrunken, elderly man in an antique blazer and bow-tie, who seemed to wake from a deep sleep as Dale sat.

"Oh, hi, hello there," he said. "And you are?"

Dale realized that although he'd remembered to use his false name, he'd neglected to keep up his South African accent. Well, it didn't matter now. And this old man looked so enfeebled that pretense seemed like an insult to them both.

"Summers," he said. "Dale Summers. Good to meet you."

Then he saw the place-names on the table. The old man's name was Paul Zarnoff. Zarnoff looked puzzled.

"Oh, this guy?" Dale said, picking up his place-card and dropping it over his shoulder. "He's not coming."

Zarnoff seemed confused but unwilling to question Dale's identity.

"This is a fine occasion, don't you think?" he said. "And, I must say, I've seen a few in my time."

No doubt, Dale thought. The name Zarnoff sounded familiar, if also as antique as the man's blazer. Wasn't there some Zarnoff guy, in the sixties and seventies, who used to write books about sex and communism; who used to get his picture in the weekly magazines, with movie stars and boxers; who used to get into fights with people like Gore Vidal, which always ended in lawsuits? Was this the guy?

"Yeah," he said. "It's real."

Zarnoff squinted, uncomprehendingly, through his thick lenses.

"Well, I guess this ain't the top table," Dale said.

Zarnoff seemed to feel an urge to squirm which his muscles were unable to satisfy.

"I told Phyllis to donate my seat to one of those young fellows on the Fricke campaign. One likes to be able to give them a hand up. They seem very talented. So much energy. We were much more relaxed in my day."

No, Dale thought. Here's what happened: You're old and stupid and they bumped you. This is the shit table.

"That's very generous," he said.

There were three other empty places: One for Diane, one for someone called Kellerman and one with no place-card. The name Kellerman meant nothing to him.

"Oh, Paul — you're still alive. Goodness."

It was Diane's voice. Zarnoff started to get up but Diane had taken her seat before he got half-way.

"So are you, I see. I'm so glad. I'm so glad you lived long enough to see your sizeable fortune protected from legalized theft, even if you aren't. Your children must feel relieved."

"It's less sizeable by the day, Paul. And you forget — my children are not getting it."

"Then you should leave it all to the Liberty Club. I predict a death-bed conversion."

"Paul, you're such a buffoon. Phyllis doesn't need any more money. Look at all this."

Dale looked out across the ballroom. The tables — dozens of them, arranged in horseshoe formation around the dance floor — were filling; a band was taking its position on the stage, at the back of which a large movie screen had been lowered; olive-skinned waiters — an army of them — serviced the tables. The din grew louder by the moment. Dale pushed his shoulder bag under the table and placed his feet firmly and carefully either side of it.

"Who's Kellerman?" he asked.

Zarnoff sniffed.

"I'm not sure that gentleman will be able to attend," he said.

"Why not?"

Zarnoff made a sour face and stared up at the ceiling.

"So it's just the three of us," Diane said. "Fine. When do we get to eat?"

"Phyllis will speak," Zarnoff said. "And then Senator Fricke —"

"Senator-elect."

345

"— will speak, and then there will be some announcements. And then, let me see... Then we will see a special presentation from Flint Gunner. Then dinner. Then dancing. Then, I believe, the main event of the evening."

"Paul," Diane said, "what is this really all about?"

"I expect you're dying to find out."

"Something to do with MLG?"

Zarnoff smiled and formed his hands into a trembling steeple, as if preparing to pray.

"Well," Diane said, "I've got one or two things to say to Phyllis about that. For a start..."

But Dale stopped listening. A few yards away, a tall, sharp-faced man argued with a thin, pale woman who wore a tight, silvery-black ball gown. The man wore a tuxedo in an old-fashioned cut — wide lapels and double vents — and his black tie had begun to unravel. With a flush on his cheeks and a champagne bottle in his right hand, he swayed on his feet and brandished his free hand with an affronted flourish — kind of upset about something, Dale thought. The woman said nothing. Her face showed no emotion; her brow, not the slightest crease. The bony points of her shoulders twitched, but otherwise she was immobile.

The argument ended. The woman turned and walked away, slicing herself a path through the crowd like a silvery blade. Her partner rocked back on his heels, smoothed his free hand slowly over his wavy, sticking-up hair and turned with a look of table-kicking rage towards Dale. Realizing that he had been observed, he twisted his face into a grim smile, pulled a twisted place-card from his pocket and marched forward.

"Hi," Dale said.

"Yes, hello, good evening, whatever you like."

The card was flung on the table. Dale read it: "Mr. Jeremy Quentin Aylsham."

"And it's not Quentin, by the way. It's Quinton."

"Okay," Dale said.

"No, it's not okay," Aylsham said aggressively. "Oh, well at least you're here, Paul."

Zarnoff looked as though he were trying to remember if he'd ever met this boisterous newcomer.

"English, right?" Dale said.

"Well spotted."

Aylsham slammed his champagne bottle on the table, startling Diane.

"This is Diane Pennyman," Dale said.

Aylsham forgot about his champagne and stared at Diane.

"Really? Really? Is it? Paul?"

Zarnoff nodded.

"Here?"

"Yes," Zarnoff said.

"I was invited," Diane said. "And I came."

"Phyllis invited her," Zarnoff said, as if it were just the kind of crazy thing Phyllis would do.

346

"Bloody hell," Aylsham said. "Bloody hell." He stumbled to his feet again. "Mariella!" he shouted. "Mariella!" But his voice, already hoarse, went nowhere. He slumped back into his seat and gripped the champagne bottle.

"Charmed to meet you," Diane said.

"Bloody hell," Aylsham repeated. Then, apparently deciding to accept the situation as he found it, he thrust the champagne bottle in front of Diane's face.

"Want some?"

"No thanks."

"Oh. Never mind, then." He turned on Dale. "What about you? Do you want some? Who are you, anyway?"

Dale deflected the bottle gently.

"My name's Summers," he said, catching the flicker of anxiety as it crossed Diane's face.

"Sounds like a bloody butler or something. Or — what's it called? Groundsman. Gamekeeper."

"I'm sorry?"

"Like to shoot, do you?"

Dale pressed his ankles against the sides of the shoulder bag. If he pressed hard enough he could feel the cold edges of the gun.

"Not really."

"Never tried before?"

"No."

"Sure you don't want some?"

"No."

"Look. Tell you what. A bunch of us are going out tomorrow. After the show's over and they've rounded up all the dead-enders and what-d'you-call-'ems. They've got some fantastic game here. Big stuff. I'll say you're with me. Think about it, that's all I'm saying. Got anything planned, have you? Tomorrow?"

"Tomorrow?"

Aylsham looked confused.

"Yes, that's what I just said, didn't I? Tomorrow."

"No," Dale said. "I don't have plans for tomorrow."

CHAPTER 47

A top-heavy van hurtled out of a side street into the avenue, swerving directly into their path. George stepped on the brake. Díaz's jeep skewed sideways and juddered to a halt, less than five meters from the van. The engine coughed and died. On the side of the van was a truculent, red-white-and-blue logo containing the letters "FNN'.

"FNN?" Roberta said. "Who is FNN?"

"Television," George said. "American television. It's not on our satellite."

"How did they get here so quickly?"

George turned the key in the ignition. The starter made a low whine which tailed off into a soft clunk. He tried again. Nothing happened. They waited.

After a pause of a minute or so, the van's side door slid open. A small, round man in a baseball hat tumbled out and fell on the ground. Rapidly, he scrambled to his feet, dusted himself down and looked urgently up and down the avenue, fixing finally on the jeep, at which he peered warily but with an intent curiosity.

"Flint, I think it's all right," he announced, directing his voice over his shoulder towards the open door of the van. "It's just some bloke in an old jeep. Have a look for yourself."

A large head emerged from the doorway of the van. It wore a steel helmet which might have been a size too small for it. The small man pointed towards the jeep.

"It's all right. They're harmless. Look!"

"Who is that?" Roberta asked.

"I don't know," George said. "The car will not start. Perhaps they can help."

The man in the steel helmet jumped down from the van. He was at least two meters tall, George noted, and wore a heavy suit of body armor. And then he, too, stared at the jeep.

"Who's that with him?" the giant said to his smaller partner.

"Probably his wife. Why don't we ask them?"

"You think they'd know?"

"Yes. They probably live here."

"What if they're Chinese?"

349

"One of them's black, Flint."

"Oh, yeah. Okay then. You go first."

The small man approached the jeep, the giant following a few steps behind.

George wound his window down and leaned out.

"What are you, TV?" he asked.

"That's right," the small man said. "My name is Nigel. Nigel Weese. I don't know if you read the English papers —"

"English? But FNN is American, is it not?"

"Well, I'm *embedded*, as it were, aren't I?" Weese said, irritably. "It's all about economics. Look, we're after a bit of local knowledge. Local, are you?"

"Not really."

"Oh."

"What do you want to know?"

Weese looked suspicious.

"If you're not local, what are you doing here?"

"Trying to get out."

"Because of the rebels? Been terrorized, have you?"

"No, we —"

Weese turned and shouted to his partner, who loitered half-way between the jeep and the van.

"He says he's been terrorized by the rebels!"

"No," George said, "I —"

"That's my old mate Flint," Weese told George. "Flint Gunner. You must have heard of him. Very famous. Very highly-paid."

"No. But our car will not start. Perhaps you and he could help push —"

"Love to help," Weese said. "But, unfortunately, what with the way our schedules are..."

He shrugged.

"Your wife's probably stronger than me. And Flint's contract, well..."

"That man," Roberta said. "He looks so strange. I don't think he knows where he is. He has a head like a..."

"Mallet," Weese said, rolling his eyes. "Everybody thinks so. Except him. Anyway. I'll get to the point. Statues. We want statues. Know any good statues?"

"I'm sorry?" George said.

"Statues. Male, obviously. Preferably of a military appearance. We've got a tank organized, and we're all ready to go."

"I don't understand."

"If you could just point us in the right direction."

"You want to see a statue?"

"See it, pull it down, chop its head off, pay people to dance around it, whatever. Yup."

George looked at Roberta.

"Yes," she said, after a pause. "I know of one."

"Marvelous. Who is it, then?"

"Aghostino Neto."

"Aggo... Care to spell that for me?"

Roberta spelt out the name of the first president of the independent republic of Angola.

"And where can we find this chap?" Weese asked.

"Follow the coastal highway to the south. You will not be able to miss him."

"South. Brilliant. And his job description? What would you say? Dictator? Communist? Evil tyrant, by any chance? Marxist?"

"Marxist, perhaps. But some people would —"

"Flint!" Weese shouted. "We've got a good one!"

He turned and scuttled back to where his partner, Gunner, stood waiting. There was a brief, excited conversation. Then Gunner strode back to the van and leaped inside. The van began to move. Weese ran alongside. An arm as thick as a small tree reached out, grabbed Weese by the collar and hauled him inside. The van spun around to the south and roared away.

George slumped in his seat.

"Neto," he said. "How tall is that monstrosity?"

Roberta flashed a smile.

"I don't know. A hundred meters. More. I think it is the strongest building in Luanda."

George laughed.

"And still it is not finished."

"They won't destroy it, will they?"

George opened the door of the jeep.

"Not with one tank. I think we must walk now. I"m sorry."

*

D ale wasn't surprised to find that Zarnoff had got the evening's running order wrong. Phyllis Ann Curtin did not speak in person. Nobody explained why. Instead, they were shown a movie.

It was *The Life of Phyllis*, more or less, and it lasted half an hour. The last ten minutes dwelled on Phyllis's personal crusade against the Death Tax and related evils like defense cuts and the European Union. These evils were handily personified in the form of Diane Pennyman, who — hypocrisy of hypocrisies — was practically a billionaire herself and took vacations in France, where the family farm had been taxed out of existence.

At the conclusion of the movie, teams of boys and girls dressed as farmers went from table to table collecting money.

Aylsham's laughter boomed across the ballroom.

"Awfully clever, these PR chaps. Absolutely skewered you, didn't they?" he said, looking at Diane.

"Well, if you're going to twist the facts like that —"

"But you do support the Death Tax, don't you?"

"Yes, but —"

"Well, then?"

"Paul," Diane said, turning to Zarnoff, "we used to have civilized debates in our day, didn't we?"

Zarnoff made a face.

351

"Look where it got us. These young people have the right idea. They're impatient. We were too tolerant. If you know you're right, well then — just do it. I believe that's the way they think."

"No bloody talking-shops," Aylsham said. He had finished his Champagne and was attempting to summon a waiter. "Facts on the ground. Boots on the ground. That's the stuff. Leadership. Steadfastness. Resolute... Resoluteness? Resolution?"

"Resolve," Diane said.

"That's it — resolve, thank you. No turning back. No nay-sayers. No diplomatic solutions. Devotion. Not changing your bloody mind once you've started. Democracy and free markets. Fundamental values. Not complicated, is it? If they don't get it, knock the stuffing out of them until they do. Waiter!"

Dale closed his eyes and allowed himself to drift back once again to the farm in the desert, to Spruitfontein. There he was, on the kopje with Jay, listening to all that stuff about the Resistance, and then Jay's confession, if that was what it really was. Then two white streaks from nowhere in the evening sky. The machine itself too small to be visible. Its operators hundreds or perhaps thousands of kilometers away. Technological scars for ancient rocks. Ashes, and no rain for years. Jay's words — *you try so hard*. And Sheryl, with the stuffing knocked out of her.

He got to his feet.

"Excuse me," he said. "I need to go find someone."

"Dale?" Diane said. "Who..."

Dale began to make his way to the ballroom exit. Behind him, he could hear Aylsham's question and Diane's reply.

"Funny chap. Something the matter with him?"

"There's nothing the matter with him."

As Dale left the ballroom, Senator-elect Wallace Fricke mounted the stage to a roar of triumph and devotion.

The private viewing room was empty. But in the hallway he saw the main doors to the residence flung open and a procession enter. The procession swept down the hallway towards the viewing room. In its midst and beaming like a sure-fire champ on the way to the ring was a wide-shouldered man in steel-framed glasses. His hair was swept back as if blown by the wind and his jaw, half-set into a grin of self-amused rectitude, seemed to precede his passage by a fraction of a second.

Dale ducked out of the way and watched. Then, realizing that he'd left his shoulder bag behind, he rubbed his eyes and returned to the ballroom.

*

Vickery's troops had followed him all the way back to the Chinese embassy. There was no shaking them. But the embassy — or, rather, its remains — were occupied. Vickery and his army lay down behind of a pile of crushed concrete and brick and peered over the top.

The FNN van idled on its own in front of the building. It looked as if Gunner and Weese had found themselves a story.

352

Flint Gunner, in a steel helmet and body armor, clambered from the van and strode over to the camera. Nigel Weese, in a grimy safari jacket and FNN baseball hat, followed, his hands in his pockets.

"This the school?" Gunner asked.

Weese looked uncertain.

"Could be," he said. "Could very well be."

"Jeez. Look at it."

"Like a bomb hit it," Weese said.

"Yeah. Okay. The kids... They're all..."

"Gone. Yes."

"Nige?"

"What?"

"We *are* going to find a statue, aren't we? You know I get a bonus if —"

"Yes, yes. Don't worry. Don't know why that woman sent us down there."

"That wasn't a statue."

"No. More what you'd call a towering colossal monument of abstract design."

"Maybe she's with the terrorists."

"Maybe she was having a laugh. Are you ready?"

"You said it's clean in there, right?"

"Yes."

"Okay. Then I think I'm ready."

Weese took a moment to survey the scene.

"Wait a minute," he said. "Can't be too careful. Don't want any nasty accusations. Just need to verify the facts on the ground a bit. Before we go on the record, as it were. Have you got a screwdriver?"

"What?"

"For unscrewing things."

"Ask the crew."

Weese scampered over to the FNN van, returning with a large screwdriver and an expression of ruthless determination. He approached what was left of the embassy perimeter wall. The object of his attention was a small, brass plaque. Kneeling by the wall, he attempted to unscrew the plaque. The screws wouldn't budge.

"Must have got welded or something," he called out to Gunner. "With the heat."

But Gunner was studying his notes. Weese frowned and inserted the screwdriver between the plaque and the wall, forcing it down with his heel. Then he put both hands on the screwdriver, both feet on the side of the wall, and pulled. The plaque came away. Weese fell backwards.

"Ow! Bugger."

Gunner grunted with impatience.

"We okay to go now?"

"Not quite," Weese said, flinging the plaque off-camera. "One more thing."

He limped into the front yard of the embassy and stood under a splintered tree, looking up. Caught in what remained of the branches was a fragment of red cloth. Weese put his boot against the trunk of the tree and kicked. The tree shivered. Unfurling itself gracefully, the fragment of cloth revealed a large, yellow, five-pointed star.

"Ah," Weese said.

He kicked again. The flag unraveled further. Four smaller yellow stars appeared.

"How'd that get there?" Gunner shouted. "The hell is it?"

"Just a mo," Weese said. He raised his arms and began to jump. But the flag was hopelessly out of reach. He kicked the tree again, to no effect.

"You're not gettin' it," Gunner said.

Weese glared.

"No. All right. Hang on."

He began to climb the tree.

"Don't fall," Gunner shouted. "We didn't insure you."

Weese was too occupied to reply. He edged out on to the branch which led to the flag. He was half-way along when the branch bent suddenly and the flag dropped.

"It's down!" Gunner yelled.

"Yes," Weese said. "But, if I'm not mis—"

The branch snapped and Weese tumbled.

"Ouch," Gunner said, ambling over to where his partner lay writhing, "that's gotta hurt."

Weese groaned.

"You better get cleaned up, old buddy. You got black stuff all over you. You're okay, right?"

Weese muttered something.

"Say what, Nige?"

"The flag..."

"What flag?"

"Get rid of it. That. Over there."

"Sure. If that's what you want."

Gunner picked up the flag and threw it behind a pile of rubble. Then he walked back to the camera. With a grunt of pain, Weese rolled on to his hands and knees and made a slow, undignified exit from the yard.

Gunner removed his helmet and smoothed his hair.

"Okay, let's roll," he said.

Bloody media, Vickery thought. It was true what people said. He crept away, wondering if the troops would creep too, or stay to watch the show.

*

Dale glanced up at the giant screen in the ballroom. Flint Gunner stood in front of a ruined building. His jaw was set in a configuration which Dale read as compassion-in-the-face-of-brutality.

"To see it now, you wouldn't think so," Gunner said, "but this used to be an elementary school."

Aylsham shook his head slowly.

"Terrible, isn't it?"

Gunner glanced over his shoulder, as if he couldn't believe the story he was about to tell and needed to remind himself it was really true.

"But that was before the terrorists came." He clenched his famous jaw. "Let me show you around."

Microphone in hand, Gunner stalked off towards the building, pausing twice, unnecessarily, to beckon to his crew and urge them on. He stopped in the middle of what had been a large room and wiped the back of his hand across his mouth.

"We can only imagine the horror of what took place here, just a few hours ago," he said.

Zarnoff wagged his finger at Diane.

"There is no justification for the slaughter of children," he said sternly. "None whatsoever. That's why we never advocated it. Not once in sixty years. Never. Except to defend freedom."

Diane closed her eyes.

"We will probably never know the full truth of what happened here," Gunner said, a tremble in his voice. "But it seems safe to say that the terrorists came in through there..."

Gunner pointed randomly off-camera.

"...and forced the children and their teachers over here..."

Without looking, he gestured vaguely at the empty space behind him.

"And we know what happened next."

Dale stared at the screen. Where was the blood? Where were the bullet holes? Where were the bullet casings? Where were the bodies?

Gunner knelt and picked something up from the floor. It was a scrap of brightly-colored paper. He held it up to the camera, his head nodding with suppressed emotion.

"They were in the middle of their weekly art class. This is Flint Gunner, reporting live from the battlefront, in Angola, Africa."

"Bloody barbarians, the lot of them," Aylsham said, loudly. "Waiter!"

*

A lan Vickery had never, in his entire life, considered joining the military. Despite what people like General Fricke said, you couldn't be an entrepreneur in a uniform. You needed a suit. Unless you were one of those computer twerps. So it was ironic — Phil was one for irony and he would have savored this — that the military had joined Vickery.

He had acquired his own private army. It was the sort of stuff that lawn-chair warriors like Aylsham fantasized about. Well, all right, Vickery's army consisted of a scruffy bunch of underfed kids, half of whom seemed, frankly, a bit daft in the head, but they had attitude and they had rifles.

Precisely why they had chosen to anoint him their leader — and how long this exalted status would last — Vickery had no idea. But for now, as the sun rose above another bright, fresh, hope-filled Angolan morning, and as he marched — crazily, defiantly — at the head of his potty platoon down towards the commercial heart of the city, he felt a sort of loopy, heart-fluttering contentment. It was as if there were nothing that couldn't be accomplished with a splash of resolve and steadfastness and a bunch of teenage gunslingers; and it was nothing to do with feeling light-headed on account of lack of food.

Plus, he'd saved these kids from certain death, hadn't he? Up to now.

The warlike noises of the night had quietened. But for a distant pot-shot or two every couple of minutes, it could have been a Sunday morning in Surrey, without the lawnmowers. It was amazing, Vickery thought, how quickly you adjusted to circumstances. He wasn't even flinching. And look at those kids — tumbling along behind him, jumping on each other's backs, laughing and goofing around; distant gunfire was nothing to them.

All the same, as they approached the edge of the city center, and Vickery started counting the burnt-out cars and smashed windows, the sense grew in his mind that this was, really, just the quiet before dawn — except, of course, that dawn had been hours ago.

What was his plan? It was simple. The army made it plausible. All Vickery had to do was find the way to Díaz's house. Díaz was obviously some kind of government bigwig. Assuming that his seat at the cabinet table hadn't already been hijacked by General Freaky, or Muller, or — God help everyone — Petty, Díaz would be in a position to guarantee Vickery and his young followers safe passage or, at least, sanctuary. Wouldn't he? Course he would. Furthermore, although no cash had passed directly from Vickery's hands into Díaz's, well, come on...

Vickery had to admit, however, that he was confused about which side Díaz was actually on and, indeed, how many sides there actually were. That was partly the fault of German George — obviously one of those Teutonic hair-splitters — with his fake rebels and his factions. But this didn't matter because Díaz was just as confused. That much had been obvious. Confronted with Vickery and his brigade of middle-schoolers, Díaz could probably be persuaded.

But to clinch the deal there was, of course, nothing like cold, hard cash. And that was why Vickery, in a moment of four-star decisiveness, suddenly took a sharp left down an alleyway he was fairly sure led to the Avenue of Fidel Castro. He was fairly sure because he could see the FNN helicopter parked on a distant rooftop. What were the odds that Jennifer's CIA Resistance chums would have parked anywhere else but Vickery's office? It was so convenient. By now, of course, they had probably spirited the two American bankers away to safety and booby-trapped the helicopter. Did he feel used? Did he!

Speaking of which, there was a good chance that Inácio had cleaned out the office safe. But it was still worth a try.

Vickery strode on along the alley, reaching the half-way point before realizing that something was wrong. The troops had fallen behind him, their chatter now subdued. He stopped and looked around. The troops pointed to the far end of the alley. Vickery looked. All he could see was a small heap of rags. But there was rubbish everywhere in Luanda. What was the problem? Then, slightly puffed, he took a deep breath through his nostrils, which gave him his answer.

Oh right, he thought. Yes. They said it was a very distinctive smell, didn't they? Well, it was. And you knew right away. It got up your nostrils and sort of stuck there, filmy and dank and sweet and fetid. Perversely, his light-headedness evaporated, leaving only a tightness between the temples.

356

"Come on," he said, without turning around. He began to walk. The troops followed.

There were four of them — he was pretty sure it was four — and they were about the same age as the troops, as far as he could tell. The walls of the alley were scored with bullet hits. Vickery remembered Petty's camp and the landmine explosion. That had shaken him — but not like this. He held his hand over his mouth. Why? The question floated through his brain and it infuriated him. Stupid, stupid, stupid, he thought. Don't be such an idiot. Stop asking why, why, why. What are you, a politician? You bloody well know why.

He felt the troops jostle him from behind. Off-balance, he stumbled forward. Something cracked and splintered under his foot. He looked down. It was a pair of glasses. He didn't need to pick them up to tell they were brand-new, gold-plated, light-reactive, super-expensive, bifocal, vision-correcting, granddad specs. Half an age ago, they had fallen from his very own nose as he peered down at urchins from an MLG balcony.

"No, wait a moment," he said, trying to hold his ground as the troops pressed against his back. "Hang on. Don't you see? This is so —"

But the troops refused to linger. Vickery found himself swept along, stumbling and tripping, then running and dodging until he and his comrades piled out into the brightness and vastness of the Avenue of Fidel Castro, and Vickery fell in a heap in the middle of the road and the troops picked him up and patted him on the head.

Get a grip, he thought. Assume command. Why not?

Taking but an instant to recover his military decorum, Vickery left his army in the lobby and, like the inexperienced commander that he was, scuttled unaccompanied upstairs to his office, hoping that he would find his forces waiting for him on his return.

The door to the office was locked. With trepidation he tapped his rifle butt against it three times and waited. No one answered. Inácio didn't bounce out and offer him a cup of tea. Petty didn't jump out and demand to know if he was having fun yet. There was no sound at all. It was eerie. He fumbled for his key, unlocked the door and pushed it open a crack with his foot. Then he poked his rifle into the gap and made a series of short stabbing motions with it, the idea — not a good one, he knew — being to warn any lurking looters, bandits or squatters that he meant business.

But the office turned out to be empty. He wandered in and carried out a cursory inspection. The power was off, the phone was off and the water was off. He was still one chair short of a quorum. Everything was normal, in other words. The safe, far from being smashed, empty and possibly defiled, as he had imagined, was intact, locked and sat smugly in its original position. He sat before it on the floor, spun the dial and opened it up.

Had he misjudged Inácio? Like a mini-bar in a posh hotel, the safe had restocked and tidied itself. Dollars to the right, kwanzas to the left, and plenty of both. Vickery shook his head, even though there wasn't anyone else there to see him do it. Money did funny things when you started a war. It went crazy, rushing here and there, flinging itself on people and ending up in the most unlikely places. Well, some of them weren't so unlikely.

But who cared how the money had got into his safe? The issue was how to remove it. His pockets weren't big enough. Well, he thought, what was the point of having an army if you didn't use it? This inspiration seemed about to kick off an interesting train of thought but he stopped it dead in its tracks and bowled back down the stairs to the lobby.

His army was waiting for him.

"Right," he said, pointing and imitating the tone of voice of a sergeant-major from a black-and-white British war movie. (You didn't get British war movies any more — why was that?) "I want three volunteers." He surveyed his troops. Some of them wore little more than football shorts. Others had acquired those camouflage cut-off things with baggy pockets. He selected the latter. "You, you and you. Follow me. The rest of you stay here and keep guard."

There was a confused interlude of muttering and shoving, which culminated, to Vickery's pleasure and surprise, in the three volunteers being flung forward by their comrades.

"Excellent," Vickery said. "Come on, then."

He turned towards the stairs and started to run but almost immediately felt someone tugging at his jacket. Not only that, but the troops had begun chanting his name — Vick-ry, Vick-ry! Which was odd because he hadn't introduced himself — except, of course, as Mr. Chelsea. He spun around and collided with the volunteers, who were right behind him.

"Ouch! Sorry lads. Hold on a moment. What's the —"

But immediately he saw what the matter was. It was Inácio. He was running towards the building and calling Vickery's name. Spotting Vickery, he began to wave his arms. Vickery folded his and waited.

"Oh, hullo," he said, as Inácio arrived, out of breath and drenched in sweat. "Funny seeing you here."

"No," Inácio said, gasping, "not funny. Not funny."

"Funny," Vickery said, "as in you showing up just as I'm about to empty the safe."

"No, no. Not that. You don't understand."

"Don't I? What happened to you?"

"Me?"

"Left me in the lurch, didn't you? Like Jennifer and her old mate Chas, the grumpy git. Talk about bloody ingratitude. And the bloody Chinese wouldn't take me because I'm on a bloody list!"

Inácio was gazing with a kind of exasperated bewilderment at Vickery's ragged regiment.

"But what are you doing with these —"

"I'm taking care of myself. Which I should have done from the beginning. What happened to you?"

Inácio mopped his brow — irritably, Vickery thought.

"My family. I have to take care of my family. What do you think? You come here, you start a war. What do you expect me to do? I need take them away. Out of the city. What are you doing to these... These children?"

Vickery thought for a moment.

"Family, eh?" He thought some more. "Family, is it? Well, I suppose that's reasonable. As for these kids — well, I rescued them, didn't I? From bloody Kellerman's house. Which has probably been blown to bits by now. And then they just sort of —"

"And you brought them here?"

"Yes. Why not?"

"This building is not safe. This building is a target."

"A target?"

"You must go now. Now!"

"Yes, but..."

"Now!"

"I know, but... Look, Inácio. The safe — it's full, you see. And I thought —"

"No, listen, please! This whole area is dangerous. You *must* go now. They tell me you are here. And I think, such a crazy, crazy guy, okay? But I like you. So come, please." Inácio turned to Vickery's army and shouted something which caused them to flinch and to back away but not — quite — to flee.

"All right, all right," Vickery said, wondering if an ordinary office block would really be some kind of special target. "Tell you what. I'm just going to make a quick dash, okay? A quick dash."

He turned and bolted for the stairs. The volunteers followed. The whole thing was a blur of stair-leaping and trouser-stuffing and it was over in what seemed like seconds. With their hearts pounding and their pockets bulging, Vickery and the volunteers tumbled from the building to see the rest of the army, half a furlong away, taking the Avenue of Fidel Castro at a brisk gallop.

"Come on, lads," Vickery shouted, "race you!" The volunteers sped past him, leaving a light trail of kwanzas which Vickery didn't bother to collect. As he watched the volunteers recede into the distance and as his heart began to pound in his ears, Vickery noticed an object approaching from far end of the Avenue. It was silvery and cylindrical, and rather fast, and it had chosen to travel at about thirty feet above street-level.

Actually, it was really bloody clever, he thought as it whooshed past above his head, how the thing managed to steer itself down the street like that. Pretty bloody amazing. And there was a roundabout at the end of Fidel Castro, as well.

Then, seconds later, as he lay on his back with debris falling all around him and the wind knocked out of him, he saw the FNN helicopter topple from the roof of his building — or where the roof used to be — and come crashing down into the street. Look at that, he thought. Collateral damage. Always happens.

*

"Y ou're very kind," he said, his voice amplified above the din. The applause and the cheering swelled. "I don't deserve all this." All across the ballroom people began to stand. "Gosh," he said. "Isn't it just great to be among friends?"

Dale stood. Aylsham was already on his feet, banging his hands together with a sweaty, alcoholic passion.

"Isn't it great that we can do this together?"

There seemed to be no doubt about it.

And Douglas Moreland had a life fit for celebration — this much was clear from the movie which had preceded his glory-stroll to the center of the stage.

Working parents — hard-working and uncommon, but also the very root and stem of the heartland, hardy and restless and ambitious for their third-born. (What of the other two?) A father who moved where his job took and him and made his own way up in business, if not far. Modest houses, modest automobiles — or so they looked now. Mother worked, not always successfully, for the conservative candidate. Adversity, but not much, Dale thought, given the times. Young Doug — as he was known then, although he always preferred Douglas — in stills from Little League. No home-run? Deferred gratification, always. Douglas the young man enduring deferment — no fault of his own. A commendable record in the National Guard. A hand-written note from his commanding officer, and that lucky break into politics. State representatives' offices — lowly work; a look at The Law, but Business is preferred; the nation experiences a short economic downturn; congressmen's offices; a radical voice in agency after agency; and then a lucky break — the CIA is recruiting and Africa cries for help. A soft blanket of secrecy. Trials but ultimate triumph in the eighties. Drift, decadence and moral decline for the nation in the nineties, but corporate glory for Douglas. Then, in the second decade of the new century with all its terrors and alarms, the renewal. Respect. Recognition. And vindication.

"He'll run one day — trust me," Aylsham said.

Dale sat down. Moreland began to speak. His words sounded relaxed but there was a tightness in his voice. Perhaps it was those jaw muscles.

The speech went on but Dale stopping listening. There was a different movie running in his head, now. When Moreland finished, Dale joined the happy mob which followed him from the ballroom.

*

D íaz didn't seem happy. As he looked from Inácio to Vickery's army to Vickery, the expression on his face transformed itself from conspiratorial irritation through affronted standoffishness to slack-jawed incredulity. Vickery didn't hold it against him; he was a man under pressure. Inácio had said so.

They stood in front of Díaz's house. Díaz stared down at them from a balcony, almost as if he were acting the part of the incensed nobleman in one of those outdoor Shakespeare things that Marie-Thérèse liked to drag Mariella to.

Ignoring Vickery, Díaz started into another heated exchange in Portuguese with Inácio. Vickery's troops amused themselves by rearranging the flowerpots in Díaz's courtyard.

This wasn't going too well, Vickery thought. Bumping into Inácio had seemed like a stroke of luck. For one thing, he knew the way to Díaz's house; Vickery, dazed from the wholly unexpected cruise missile attack on his office in the Avenue of Fidel Castro, had been about to set off in the wrong direction.

Inácio put his hand on Vickery's shoulder.

"He says 'Go away. Try the British Embassy.' And he says to leave his flowers alone."

"What?" Vickery said. "Try the British Embassy? He must be bloody joking. Look, tell him from me... No, wait a minute. He speaks English, I've heard him. Oi! Díaz!"

Díaz scowled down from his balcony.

"Listen," Vickery said. "You owe me. I practically emptied the till stuffing envelopes for all your bloody pals and cronies."

"Envelopes? What envelopes? What are you talking about?"

"Don't be like that. Come on, then. How much do you want?"

Díaz waved his arms as if trying to swat an invisible mosquito.

"Go away!"

Vickery pointed at one of the troops. "See him?" he said. "See his trousers?"

Díaz made a gesture which involved tapping his forehead and wiggling his hand.

"I said, see his trousers?"

"What about them?"

"Full of dollars. Or kwanzas, possibly. Some of them have got dollars, and some of them —"

"I don't want your money. Go away."

"You've got to offer us protection. It's your job."

"No, it isn't. I can't. I don't want to."

"We haven't got anywhere else to go. I was at the Chinese embassy. That blew up. Then me and the lads here were at Bryce's house. That's probably blown up by now. And then we went to my office and that blew up. Bloody cruise missile. Have you ever seen —"

"What do you think is going to happen to my house? I've got to do my broadcast, then I've got to get out. I'm going to a hotel. I suggest you —"

"I can't do that. I'm on a bloody list, aren't I? I wouldn't be surprised if you are too. What broadcast?"

"Go away!"

"What broadcast?"

"To say we do not need foreign help..." Díaz paused. "It might work."

Vickery rolled his eyes, in a deliberately exaggerated fashion.

"Where'd you get that idea?"

"It's my idea."

Vickery folded his arms and waited.

"All right," Díaz said, gloomily, "it's George's idea."

"George!" Vickery said. "What are you listening to him for? Listen to me! I'm the bloke on the inside, aren't I? I work for old Duggie and MI6 and the bloody Resistance, more or less. Is he here now, old George?"

"No."

"Where is he?"

"Gone. Looking for a man called Petty."

"Oohhhh..." Vickery said.

Díaz gripped the balcony railings so hard his knuckles turned white.

"What do you mean, oh?"

Vickery turned to his troops and made a swaggering gesture which involved putting his fists on his hips, nodding, and grinning a lot. This seemed to catch the troops' attention. They put down their flowerpots.

"Vickery! What do you mean?"

Vickery turned back to the house. Inácio, he noticed, was watching him with a queasy smile.

"Sent old George after Petty, did you?"

"No. It was his idea."

"Who's with him, then?"

Díaz hesitated.

"Who's with him?"

"A woman."

"A woman? What — just the one? Not Jennifer?"

"No, not her. I think her name is Roberta."

"Right. I see. So they're going to take out Petty, are they?"

Díaz said nothing. Vickery helped himself to a flowerpot. The troops, attentive now, followed their leader's example.

"Thing is," he said, "I happen to know a lot about old Harlan. Extensive dealings, I've had. Used to know him way back in Brooklyn. Or Queens, possibly."

"Did you? How long —"

"He's what we call a hard bastard, Harlan. Don't know what the American is for that. So old George..." And here Vickery shook his head with what he hoped looked like great sorrowfulness. "Well. Obvious, isn't it? Doesn't stand a chance."

Díaz shuffled from one foot to the other on his balcony.

"So?"

"Probably end up telling Harlan you sent him." Vickery dropped the flowerpot. It shattered. Díaz looked shocked.

"I know how to deal with Petty," Vickery said slowly, "and — in case you haven't noticed — I've got my own army."

"They're a bunch of kids!"

"Yes," he said, returning Díaz's stare. "But this is Africa, isn't it?"

Díaz frowned for a moment, then turned his head, as if being hailed from inside the house.

"Well?" Vickery asked.

"Do you know where Petty is?"

"Course I do," Vickery lied.

Díaz glared down at him. Vickery, using the side of his foot, began to sweep up the mess from the broken flowerpot.

"All right," Díaz growled. "Come inside."

Vickery signaled to the troops. They dropped their flowerpots and formed a scrum at Díaz's front door. Vickery glanced at Inácio. Inácio smiled back in a crazy, happy sort of way. Always one step ahead, Vickery thought.

When Vickery entered Díaz's office, the deputy minister had shed his sweat-soaked polo shirt, while retaining his jeans and sandals, and was in the process of stripping the wrapper from a brand-new dress shirt. In front of Díaz's desk stood a battered TV camera on a tripod whose broken leg had been repaired with sticky tape.

D ale stole into the viewing room and sat at the back, tucking his shoulder bag under his chair. Nobody challenged him; everybody was too busy watching the screen, where a tall, elegant, dark-haired man sat at a large desk. He looked a healthy but worn-out fifty-five years old and wore exuberant clothes — a smart, double-breasted suit, French cuffs, gold cufflinks, a voluminous and colorful silk tie — but he looked weary and, underneath the weariness, angry. Behind him was a single, creased Angolan flag.

The picture buzzed, flickered and split, on occasion, along the diagonal, which had the effect of separating the man's mouth laterally from the rest of his head. The audience in the viewing room laughed. There were about seventy people in the room, Dale guessed. In the front row, with his entourage, was Douglas Moreland. Moreland wasn't watching the screen. He was reading newspapers. He held his newspaper high, his head inclined upwards. Dale could see the flash of his wrists as he ripped through the pages.

On screen, a series of rough captions appeared. Dale caught the name "Díaz". He leaned forward and spoke into the ear of a woman sitting in front of him.

"Who's Díaz?"

The woman turned her face to him; she looked excited.

"Oh, hi! He's like the... Excuse me one moment."

She flipped through a stack of papers on her lap and ran her fingers down a list of names.

"Oh, okay — he's deputy minister for internal security."

Dale nodded.

"Important?"

The woman made a face.

"Kind of. Kind of not."

"What's happening?"

"Oh, he's just going to ask for our help, that's all."

"Military assistance?"

"Oh, sure. It's all right here."

She tapped the papers on her lap. Dale noticed that the smile on her face had frozen.

"Thanks," he said. "Sorry to bother you."

"You're welcome," she said, after a pause.

From the screen came a blast of thin, brassy music. It cut off abruptly, instead of fading, and Díaz began to speak in Portuguese.

*

A lan Vickery sat on the floor with his back to Díaz's bookcase. Inácio sat alongside.

"What's he saying?" Vickery asked.

"He talks about the history of Angola. Don't worry — he's going to repeat it all in English."

"How do you know?"

363

Inácio smiled.

Four of the troops slipped into Díaz's office and, setting their rifles down quietly on the carpet, joined Vickery and Inácio at the bookcase. Díaz flashed them a look of annoyance but kept talking.

The troops were eating from small bowls. Vickery, ever conscious, like all the best commanders, of the welfare of his men, had ordered the doors to Díaz's kitchen to be flung open. His final command, before the stampede, was "Bring me a sandwich." This order had yet to be fulfilled.

Díaz talked on, his hands folded together on the desk in what Vickery took for fireside-chat mode, Angola style. His voice was low, steady and well-modulated. A bit more animation, Vickery thought, and the man could be a Brazilian talk-show host. He was going to need a new job. But, below the desk, Vickery could see Díaz's toes twitching nervously in their sandals.

*

The Explorers' Club didn't want to admit Roberta, but when George shouted that he was looking for Muller and Petty, the doors opened.

The club was packed with foreigners. Most of them seemed to have been there all night. Some were sleeping on the floor. A hardy few were still drinking. The main power was off. The club's standby generator was churning somewhere in the background. It wasn't enough to run the air-conditioning and the atmosphere was consequently thick and foul. But it was sufficient to power the two TV sets which were suspended above the bar. One, tuned to FNN somehow — since when did FNN broadcast in Africa, outside of the American bases? — showed Senator-elect Wallace Fricke standing on a stage in front of a wall of flags, apparently addressing a dinner-dance. The sound was turned down. On the other TV, Díaz was making his speech. A small group of Portuguese-speakers were listening, wearily.

"Muller's not here," Roberta said. "I don't see him. Let's go."

"We'll wait for him."

*

Moreland rose from his front-row seat and turned to face the audience in the viewing room. Behind him, Díaz continued to speak, looking, Dale thought, sadder and more bitter as he went on. Moreland put his left hand on his hip and, with the right, pointed randomly into the audience with his rolled-up newspaper. He looked like a game-show host seeking a volunteer to come up on stage.

"Anybody here speak Portuguese?" he asked.

Laughter rolled across the room.

Dale leaned forward to his neighbor. She was laughing too.

"Why's that funny?"

"I don't know," she said. "I guess because the guy's been talking already for like ten minutes, and..."

364

"Do you know him?"

"Who?"

"Douglas Moreland."

"Not really. He comes to our office sometimes."

"What office is that?"

The woman started to speak but then stopped, her mouth half-open.

"Oh, I'm sorry," Dale said. "Really. I shouldn't have asked."

"What's your name?"

"Dale."

"Okay. So Dale, are you with —"

"I'm with Diane."

"Is that your wife?"

"No. I don't have a wife."

"Then —"

"What about *him?* Does *he* have a wife?"

Stop it, he thought; if you frighten her any more, you'll have to leave.

"Mr. Moreland? Of course..."

"What does she do?"

"She's in politics. How come you —"

"She must be pretty tough."

"I guess so."

"Sorry to bother you again."

"That's okay."

The woman turned away. For a minute or so she sat still — very still, he thought. Then she made a show of organizing her briefcase, stood and slowly walked away.

So what, he thought. What did it matter now?

*

Alan Vickery hadn't really expected to get his sandwich; he hadn't expected it any more now than the time he and Mariella rented that villa on Mallorca and the cook didn't show up. He could, of course, have gone down to the kitchen himself, but he didn't want to miss Díaz's performance — or let Inácio out of his sight again.

But then the study door cracked open and there it — the sandwich — was: Thrust through the gap and clasped tightly in two small, brown hands. Vickery nudged Inácio. Inácio took the sandwich and handed it to Vickery. Vickery leaned forward and made a thumbs-up gesture, which he hoped the sandwich-bringer was able to see.

The contents of the sandwich were mysterious. Vickery didn't care. He closed his eyes and bit deeply. And it was at that moment that Díaz decided to switch to English.

*

365

D íaz had been shrunk to a small box in the top-right corner of the screen. He continued to speak, inaudibly. In the center of the screen, instead, was a rectangle containing a sharply-rendered, moving view of city streets as seen from directly overhead. The streets could have been those of almost any large southern African city, but Dale knew it was Luanda. Below the moving cityscape were boxes in which numbers updated furiously and meaninglessly. Around the edge of the rectangle were the familiar icons of modern office life: The network drives, the recycle bin, the start button.

Douglas Moreland sat at a table to the side of the screen, operating a laptop computer. Two aides peered over his shoulders. Moreland moved his mouse over a series of buttons to the right of the moving city, as if preparing for something. Even from the back of the room Dale could see the creases in Moreland's forehead. The man was concentrating. The room was silent — but for Díaz, mumbling on at low volume in his cell in the corner of the screen.

Dale had worried that the woman he had frightened away would return to expose him. But there she was again, standing at the back of the room, arms folded, watching.

The forward motion of the image slowed and became circular. The picture zoomed in to show the roof of a large house. Moreland drew a hollow square over the roof, which now seemed to revolve on its own within the frame. The square locked itself to the roof. Moreland looked up at one of the aides. The aide nodded. Moreland clicked on a button. The button turned red. Moreland took his hand away from the mouse and positioned his fingers carefully above the keyboard. Control, alt, delete, Dale thought, or some such combination — for irreversible operations only.

Once more, Moreland turned to his aide. Again, the aide nodded. Moreland leaned forward and pressed his fingers to the keyboard like a concert pianist beginning a sonata. There was a delay of perhaps five seconds. Then, silently, the explosion filled the frame and the roof of the house vanished.

Somebody began to clap. Dale looked; it was the frightened woman. The rest of the room joined in. Moreland stood, beaming, in acknowledgement. Dale stared at the woman, at her suit, her briefcase, her long fingernails. She smiled back at him, still applauding. Was she no longer afraid of him? Apparently not; she sat in the empty seat beside him.

"Wasn't that amazing?" she said. "I've never seen that before."

"I have," he said.

"Really? You know, we work on software. We just took over this little company. But it's just, like, data-mining. Kind of boring. To get at their financial networks, you know. It's nothing like *that*. *That* would be something, wouldn't it?"

"It *is* something."

"Do you... Do you, like, have any plans for when this is all over?"

"When it's all over?"

"You know — like, tomorrow?"

"No. None at all."

"Okay. So why don't I give you my card? Here you go." She held out a business card. Dale took it. "I have to go to a presentation now — you know, like new bosses and all that."

"New bosses?"

"Yeah, they're like these real big-shots, Raymond Priles and Martin Bazon? Couple of really sharp guys."

"I've met them."

She seemed surprised.

"Really? Wow. Well, take care."

"I'll take care. You too."

She smiled and slipped out of the room. He looked at the business card. Cheryl with a C, he read. Same but different.

Moreland's aides had shut down his laptop and packed it away in a steel case. Díaz had been returned to full-screen status, still speaking in Portuguese. Dale slipped his feet either side of the shoulder-bag and dragged it out from under his chair. Would now be a good time? What about a new life with Cheryl-with-a-C? No. But now wasn't a good time, either, and Díaz had just begun to speak in English.

*

Speaking in English was a good idea, Vickery thought. But was anyone watching? Had Angolan TV signed the necessary paperwork with CNN, the Beeb and the rest? Was old Duggie blocking all transmissions?

"This is a moment for calm reflection," Díaz said, wearily. Under the table, his toes twitched away uncontrollably. "We must not make a crisis where there is no crisis. We must not start upon a road from which there is no return."

It was great stuff, Vickery thought, even if Díaz's tone of voice suggested that this wasn't exactly what he'd been saying in Portuguese. Now, if only he would get to the point...

"This nation has suffered much. And we have learned that war is not the solution to our problems. We cannot prevent the things we fear through war. The only thing that war prevents is peace."

It was a good line, Vickery thought as he munched on his sandwich, but possibly not original. Inácio yawned and rubbed his eyes.

"Angolans can work together," Díaz said. "We *must* work together. This is our country. It is up to us."

Vickery thought of the MLG briefing he'd attended just after his arrival in Luanda — the one where he'd lost his glasses and heard the explosion that killed that computer bloke. He thought of the oil men, the money men and the security men splashing their cash in the Explorers' Club. He remembered the breakfast he'd eaten at the vast and not very Angolan MLG compound in the southern hinterland. And he thought of Petty's training camp and all the cash he'd handed out to Díaz's circle of privilege. And he wondered: Was Díaz's heart really in this? Had he given up already? Was he, instead, hoping to be installed as puppet or figurehead number three, after the first two, as per usual, had bombed out?

"I urge all parties to exercise restraint. All parties. There will be change in Angola. But it must be peaceful change."

Vickery took another bite of his sandwich. Had Díaz really lost his nerve? If so, what then?

"All parties must come to the conference table," Díaz said. "All those elements who have taken to the streets. All parties. All interested parties."

Elements? Parties? The elements were fake. And the interested parties — who were they, exactly?

"And, of course, we welcome the assistance of our friends in the international community."

One of Díaz's sandals came loose and flew across the room. The troops flinched. That was it, Vickery thought; it was time to intervene.

"Tell them you don't want to be another bloody War Zone," he said.

Díaz froze. Then he turned his head very slightly out of alignment with the camera, staring into nothing. He swallowed.

"What?" he said, softly.

Vickery finished his mouthful.

"I said, tell them you don't want to be another bloody War Zone."

"Don't I? Don't we?"

It was deer-in-the-headlights time, Vickery saw.

"Course you bloody don't. Do you want me to tell them?"

"Well, I..."

"Because I will, if you want."

Díaz seemed paralyzed.

"Hold that," Vickery said, handing the remains of his sandwich to Inácio, who was now wide awake, to say the least.

Vickery jumped to his feet, positioned himself behind Díaz and put his hands on Díaz's shoulders.

"Right. Now listen," he said, speaking directly into the camera. "I've had enough of this. And it's really beginning to get on my wick. So I'm going to put everyone straight about a few things. And I'm not a bloody politician, so you might have to put your hands over your ears now and then. No, no, no. Forget that. Just bloody well listen, will you? This is important."

*

Roberta nudged George. "Look," she said. "Look at the TV." George looked. The crazy Englishman was leaning over Díaz's shoulders, his face flushed, his suit torn and his hair sticking up all over.

There appeared to be something red in the corner of his mouth — blood? He was wagging his finger at the camera. Díaz looked stunned and helpless.

George groaned.

"This, I think... May not be so helpful."

"What is he doing?"

"I don't know. I don't think he knows. But perhaps we should admire him, yes? Just for a moment?"

*

T he room had fallen silent. Moreland rose from his seat in the front row and stared at the screen. Behind him, others stood. There was a scraping of chairs; people were running to the front to get a better view. Someone turned the sound up. Dale pushed his shoulder-bag back under his seat and stood. He couldn't see, so he edged out into the aisle.

A crazy man had Díaz by the throat and was shaking him — or so it seemed at first. Actually, Dale realized, the intention was really to encourage Díaz, not to throttle him. Díaz looked straight ahead into the camera, his mouth open, his eyes blinking. His companion, meanwhile, ranted into the camera in a low-class English accent.

"For a start," the Englishman said, jabbing his finger at the camera, "these so-called rebels or terrorists or what-have-you. It's a complete and utter load of total bollocks, isn't it? There aren't any bloody rebels. NO BLOODY REBELS! Want me to spell it out for you? N-O rebels. Ask matey here. Oi!"

He shook Díaz by the shoulders.

"Are there any rebels? Speak now!"

Díaz blinked and shook his head slowly, a fixed, wide-eyed expression on his face.

"See? And he's the bloody minister for security and fuck-knows, isn't he?"

Dale remembered his last conversation with Jay. He'd said something about a crooked businessman from London who was running guns to Africa. Was this the guy?

"It's fake. It's bogus. It's a bloody put-up job. They're just a bunch of kids, that's all they are. Like my lads over there."

A glance off-camera.

"They give 'em guns and tell 'em they're all going to be rich. Fucking oil millionaires. What a fucking rip-off. They send 'em down here — and half of them haven't even got bloody shoes, by the way — and then what? Boom-bang-a-fucking-bang, blood and guts everywhere, oh fuck me let's have a bloody régime-change, shall we? Have a bit of fucking stability, that's what we want, isn't it?"

A pause for breath. Díaz's face had turned a dark red and had begun to twitch. Moreland snapped his fingers at his two aides. They ran to him, pushing the crowd aside. He took a cell phone from one of them and held it to his ear.

"We're not having another bloody War Zone here, we're not having it. We don't want any bloody foreign intervention. We don't want any coalitions or joint fucking task forces or NATO-led fucking peace-keeping forces or any crap like that. We don't want to be fucking invaded, in other words. Tell them."

Another shake for Díaz.

"Tell them!"

Díaz blinked, swallowed and raised his head. With as much dignity as he could muster, he removed the Englishman's hands from his shoulders and then brushed at them, as if to remove dust or crumbs.

"Yes," he said. "This is true. This is all true. The so-called crisis here has been manufactured by agents of foreign powers. Angola is a country rich in oil. That, of course, is one motivation. There may be others. In the name of the government and people of Angola I say this. We do not seek foreign assistance. The government is stable and secure. Any foreign military intervention will be met with resistance. I repeat: We do not seek assistance. We are completely enabled to assist ourselves —"

The Englishman interrupted.

"Actually, that's bollocks. They're as corrupt as hell — and I've seen some places, haven't I? But that's not the bloody point, is it?"

Díaz broke into a pained smile and shook his head.

"And I'll tell you another thing. This whole bloody racket. I'll tell you who's responsible."

Moreland stepped closer to the screen, bent his head forward and removed his glasses.

"Bloody Arnie Muller. He's one. Bloody Bryce Kellerman, he's another. Well, all right, I've got to feel a bit sorry for him, because he's got malaria, hasn't he? But they're the ones who conned me into this. And all those fucking stuck-up, we're-better-than-you, over-religious, fucking dodo-brains in the bloody Liberty Club. Harlan Petty, he's another one. Bloody psycho. Blew up that computer bloke, what's his name? Tom something. Ah."

A long pause.

"Yes, well, if Jennifer's listening... If she's listening... Well, what I mean is, I'm sorry. I'm really fucking sorry. For everything. Honest. Really. She'll know what I mean."

Moreland replaced his glasses, turned his back on the screen and spoke again into his phone. But the Englishman hadn't finished.

"And then there's bloody Douglas Moreland, or old Duggie as some people like to call him, don't they, Nigel? Thinks he's going to rule Africa. Got another think coming, hasn't he? Yes, folks, yet another bleeding psycho."

Moreland removed his glasses and began to polish them.

"And MLG. Military Logistics Group. Write it down. They're the ones who're going to run the bloody government, build the bloody bases, cash in on the bloody contracts and steal the bloody oil. Have you got that? Write it all down! Thank you. All right. Now I'll show you what it's really all about. It's about these poor bloody kids. Come here, lads..."

The Englishman beckoned. Two thin, nervous boys appeared. There were rifle magazines tucked into their waistbands. They stood either side of the Englishman. He released Díaz and put his arms around the boys' shoulders.

"And let me just tell you something else about this whole War Zone crap. It's really fucking stupid. What a fucking waste. Think of the money, it's diabolical. Look at these kids. What have they got? Nothing. No homes, no jobs, no school, no water, no power, no medical... You name it. Now, I ask you..."

Moreland finished speaking into his phone. He began to stride from the room, the aides falling in behind him and the crowd parting in front. As he reached the door, he stopped and turned.

"Oh, good gracious, damn it! Cut that off!"

He swept from the room. Dale gathered up his shoulder-bag and began to push his way towards the door. On the screen, the picture switched to FNN. The man in the red glasses was talking to a tall, blonde woman.

"…And so a new government would really give the Angolan farmers the incentives they're looking for to get out in the fields…"

Dale pushed his way out into the hall. But Moreland was gone.

CHAPTER 48

"No, no. Stop!" Díaz said. "Stop!" Vickery took no notice. There was a great deal to be said, he felt, on the subject of his troops and their welfare, and he was going to make sure he said it.

"It's pointless!"

"What?" Vickery said. "What do you mean? I was just getting started."

"The connection has gone. Look. Look at the camera. Nothing. It's dead."

"Someone cut us off?"

"Yes."

Petty? That was Vickery's first thought, but he kept it to himself. Petty — blowing up TV stations, toppling transmitters, hacking through cables.

"Oh. That's a shame. There was so much... But I suppose we got our point across, didn't we?"

"Our point?"

"Yeah, course we did. Gave them something to think about, didn't we? Think twice before invading now, won't they?"

Díaz said nothing, but rose from his seat and began to remove his jacket, tie and shirt.

"Met with resistance — that's what you said."

Díaz rolled his eyes.

"Did I?"

"Yes. So when are you going to unleash it?"

"Unleash what?"

"This resistance."

Díaz retrieved his sweaty polo shirt from the floor and slipped it over his head.

"We've created a window of opportunity," Vickery said.

"A window?"

"Yes. Get your people out. Mobilize 'em. They can go and find Petty and... And send him home, can't they?"

"You said you knew where Petty was."

"Roughly, yes. Approximately."

"So why don't you take your little army and deal with him yourself?"

373

"Well, I... What are *you* going to do? Aren't you going to organize the resistance?"

"No. I'm going to hide. Goodbye."

Díaz pushed past Vickery and stepped over the troops' rifles.

"But what about your family?" Vickery asked.

"They're in Lisbon."

"Ah. Well, good thinking, I suppose. But..."

"Goodbye, Mr. Vickery."

"But what about safe passage for me and the lads? What about sanctuary?"

"What about them? This is Africa, Mr. Vickery. Good luck."

A few of the troops had spread themselves out across the floor. Díaz stepped carefully over them, shook his head at Inácio and left the room. His footsteps echoed down the marble staircase, speeding up as he went.

Vickery felt torn. On the one hand, his TV address — had it actually gone out on the air — had been a cracker; enough to deter even old Duggie — at least for a while. But, on the other hand, he wasn't sure what to do next. Bold action was required; the troops would expect nothing less. Going after Petty was an option. But that might be too bold.

He felt a tap on his shoulder. It was Inácio, returning his sandwich.

"Oh. Thanks."

He chewed thoughtfully, hoping that a plan of action would come to him. And it was while he was chewing that they heard the first explosions — huge, floor-shaking, window-rattling explosions, at regular intervals of twenty seconds or so.

"What's that?" Vickery said, flinging the remains of his sandwich on to Díaz's desk. "What the hell is it?"

"Ah, yes," Inácio said. "Bombardment."

"Bombardment?"

"Naval bombardment. I think we should go now."

"Where?"

"Explorers' Club. Safest place, now."

The Explorers' Club! Full of westerners and therefore exempt from bombing, probably. And German George was there; perhaps he would know what to do. But what about the troops? Would they pass the dress-code? And how would they get there?

"But how do we..."

Inácio held up two sets of car keys. Fifty seconds later, Vickery found himself at the wheel of Díaz's escort truck, fighting to keep up with Inácio in Díaz's Mercedes as Inácio spun the car through the empty but rubble-strewn streets of the city center and the bombardment boomed all around them. In the back were the troops, none of whom, it turned out, could drive.

*

A banner across the top of the FNN screen read "Situation Room Africa." Vickery's TV performance, to George's regret, had been cut short. The bombardment had started just minutes later; a testament, George felt, to the power of Vickery's oratory. He listened to the blonde woman on FNN.

"Initial reports say that Angola — that's a country in south-west Africa — has requested military assistance. An alliance of left-wing rebels and terrorists has threatened foreigners in the country, including a group of US students who are studying wildlife in the area. Administration sources tell FNN that, while there are no US forces at present in the region, the threat is being taken seriously and forces may — that's *may* — be redeployed from the Gulf of Guinea. Little is known about the terrorist groups, but intelligence sources say it was only a matter of time..."

"George."

Roberta took hold of George's wrist.

"Students?" he said. "What students? What wildlife?"

"Muller."

Arnie Muller stood by the bar, gazing up at the FNN screen, a beer can in his left hand, a pistol on counter in front of him.

Roberta whispered in George's ear.

"Look at him. Let's go."

"Go where?"

"Anywhere."

She was right. Díaz, with Vickery's ardent support, had said *no* to foreign assistance; *no* to military intervention. That message, reversed, had travelled, in minutes, from Díaz's study to the FNN Situation Room. Angola *had* requested military assistance. And it was already receiving it. Now, it mattered little what George did, or what Petty did — or Muller.

"We can try the hotel."

The atmosphere in the room had changed with Muller's arrival. A space had opened up around him and the noise had dropped. The voices from FNN, thousands of miles away, blared out, slightly distorted. George pushed his way gently through the crowd, leading Roberta towards the exit.

When they were level with him, Muller turned.

"Where are you going, George?"

"We're leaving, Arnie."

"No, no, no. Wait, George. Don't you want to ask me where Harlan is?"

"No."

"No? Someone told me you did. I don't know, George. He's everywhere. What a guy!"

George pushed Roberta towards the exit.

"No, no, George — I said wait. Wait! Did you get your little chat with Mr. Douglas fucking Moreland? Did he mention me? Did he remember me?"

George shrugged.

"You see, there's no gratitude. Is there, George? You shouldn't expect that from these people. It's what can you do for us now, that's all that matters. I said that to Harlan, but what does he care? Mr. Harlan fuck-brain Petty. He's a true believer. What about your friends, George? Did you find them?"

"What did you say to Petty?"

"He gave me this." Muller waved his pistol. The empty half-circle around him grew larger. "And fifty thousand fucking dollars. How long's that going to last?" He finished his beer and threw the can behind the counter.

"What did you say to Petty?"

"Your friend Fernando — man, he really pissed Harlan off, you know? I said, you want to know where he lives? Fernando? Give me a couple of those fucking bundles. Two hundred K, it's worth it. He says, fuck you, Arnie, you're history. They talk a lot about history, these people. Have you noticed that, George? Total bullshit."

"What did you —"

"I said, listen, Harlan — don't you want to know who's holed up with Fernando? No, it's not fucking George. I wouldn't waste your time. Who's Douglas told you to watch out for? Hey? Who's the Ace of Spades? Who's the fucking Queen of Hearts — or is it Diamonds? Who's the Jack of Clubs?"

"You told him where they are?"

Another series of explosions shook the Explorers' Club. What were they meant to destroy? How many targets could there be?

Muller laughed.

"George, did you see that idiot Vickery? What the — that man is seriously fucked. For God's sake. I split my sides, I did. What's he doing with those kids? He'll catch something."

"Arnie. What did you tell Petty?"

"I said a hundred. He said fifty. Like anybody is counting."

"What else?"

Muller laughed.

"I went to Fernando's house, George. What a dump. I saw them all there. Trying to fix that broken-down plane of his, it's pathetic."

"Petty's going there."

"No, George, the fucking terrorists are going there." Muller laughed. "After they finish off the biology students. It's so fucked-up it's funny."

George turned his back on Muller and edged towards the exit, pushing Roberta in front of him.

"Don't look back," he whispered in her ear.

"George, don't go," Muller said. "I need someone to talk to. We're both finished. It's all over. It doesn't matter any more. We can have a drink and talk about the early days. I don't want you to go. Stay here, you hear me?"

They were out of the door and half-way down the stairs.

"Run," Roberta said. "He's crazy."

"No. Come on."

At the foot of the stairs, Roberta's foot came loose. George knelt down and helped her adjust it.

"George!"

Muller was at the top of the stairs.

"You can't go. There's nowhere for you to go."

"We're going back to Swakopmund."

"You don't belong there. It's a ridiculous place."

"Goodbye, Arnie."

Roberta was back on her feet. The door was four meters away. George turned his back on Muller and pushed Roberta gently ahead as he began to walk.

"You don't deserve any more than I do, George," Muller said. "You know that."

"That's not true, Arnie. I have things here that I love. You don't. You never did."

George unfastened the door and kicked it open with his foot. Gently, he guided Roberta though.

"Wait for me outside," he said. Then he turned to face Muller.

*

When Dale returned to his table in the ballroom, he found Zarnoff asleep and Aylsham explaining to Diane how he intended to buy into MLG, despite the fact that it wasn't a publicly-traded company.

"You have to be invited," he told Diane. "They want the right sort of people."

Dale smiled at Diane. She looked relieved to see him.

"Did you find what you were looking for?"

"Not quite."

He sat and glanced up at the video screen. The words "FNN Alert" spun into the center of the screen, flashed three times and then spun off again. A gasp of tentative interest floated across the ballroom.

Gunner, in full body armor and helmet, appeared on screen, standing in front of a heap of smoking wreckage. Behind him, a six- or seven-floor building had been half-demolished. But this time Gunner wasn't alone. He had a side-kick, a shabby man with knotted hair who was only about two-thirds as tall as Gunner, but just as wide.

"We had to bring you this," Gunner said, "because it shows you what the fight here is really all about."

Gunner removed his helmet and beckoned to his partner, who had been poking around in the wreckage with something that looked like a golf-club. The partner looked up, realized he was on camera and straightened himself up, which didn't, to Dale's eyes, make a hell of a lot of difference.

"I know that chap!" Aylsham said, with a high-pitched squeal of delight. "It's old Nigel. Must be braver than he looks. Well done, that man!"

"Nigel?" Dale said.

"Nigel Weese. Newspaper chap. One of the best. Always see him on TV — you know, What The Papers Say and all that. Got his finger on the pulse. Seems to have taken to this Flint chap. Odd couple. In some ways."

"How come he doesn't have armor?" Dale said. "Or is that just because he's braver than he looks?"

Aylsham looked confused and shrugged.

"What you're looking at," Gunner announced, "is the smoking wreckage of FNN's Eye Over Angola. Nigel — can you show FNN viewers the... That's it."

Weese pointed his golf-club at the detached door of what had apparently been a helicopter. The letters "FNN' and "TV" were still visible.

"Now this helicopter," Gunner said, "was in our possession until a few days ago, when it fell into the hands of the terrorists. And for more information about what happened next, I'm going to turn to my junior partner here. His name is Nigel Weese, he's from the Times of London and he's an expert on terrorism here in southern Africa."

Weese looked as though he were chewing on something unpleasant.

"Yes, thank you, Flint. Actually, I'm not your... And I'm not with... Never mind. No, Flint, you see, this helicopter was actually recaptured from the terrorists —"

Gunner looked excited.

"Special forces?"

"Oh, I expect so, yes. Anyway, it was being flown off for repairs and servicing and what-have-you when the terrorists spotted it — and you can see what happened."

"Uh-huh. And what happened, Nigel?"

"Well, Flint, they saw the FNN logo. They saw the word 'TV' which we had specially painted on. And they knew they had to stop us."

"Stop *me*."

Weese flinched.

"Yes, *you*."

"They are actually — if you can believe this — targeting the news media."

"That's right, Flint."

"They don't want America to know the truth."

"No, Flint. Nor the rest of the world, neither."

Gunner turned to the camera.

"I guess I should make it clear to our viewers that although this is, obviously, a highly dangerous situation, we do not take unnecessary risks with the safety of our crew. Nigel?"

"Yes, Flint?"

"There is a building here which appears to be in a state of collapse."

"Yes, Flint."

"What can you tell us about it?"

"Well, Flint, I had a good look around — as you suggested — and I would say it's going to fall down at any moment."

Gunner's face darkened.

"Oh!" Weese said. "And it was obviously being used by the terrorists as a base. We found money, documents, telephones, computer equipment... Furniture. There was a lot of evidence. It was pretty obvious. Yes, they were using this building, or part of it, as a base or training camp."

"Training camp?"

"Yes, that's right."

"In an office building?"

"Yes. We're finding that more and more. It's a very disturbing development."

"I'll say."

Aylsham tapped his forefinger on the table in front of Dale.

"That man knows what he's talking about."

"Oh, sure," Dale said.

"And what happened to the building?" Gunner said.

"Well, either the terrorists blew it up," Weese said, narrowing his eyes for extra shrewdness, "or we did."

"Special forces?"

Weese nodded.

"Probably, probably."

"Glad those guys are on our side."

Weese tapped his golf club on the ground and stared off to one side.

"And Nigel," Gunner said, "I guess there's a story attached to that golf club?"

Weese raised the club and examined it, as if he'd been looking for it all morning and was surprised to find it had been in his hand all along.

"Yes, Flint. There is indeed."

Weese looked grave.

"You want to share it?"

"Flint," Weese said slowly, running his fingers along the shaft of the club, "let's just say I made a promise. I made a promise that we would never let Angola, ever again, become a place where a man had to risk his life — and his family — just for a simple game of golf."

Gunner stared, grim-faced.

"Oh — oh, I got you. I guess that says it all. Back to you in the studio."

The picture reverted to the panel discussion. Heads were shaken.

"What was all that about the golf?" Aylsham asked.

"I have no idea," Dale said.

"I suppose there are some things they can't tell us."

"I guess so."

*

Whether or not Inácio was relying on Díaz's satnav to find the way to the Explorers' Club Vickery couldn't say. But he found himself once again on the Avenue of Fidel Castro, spinning Díaz's truck around the rubble which used to be his office. In the back, the troops held on tight, like children on a roller-coaster — even though some of them weren't even *this* tall, and were thus ineligible to ride.

But when Vickery drew level with the smashed helicopter, he saw something that made him hit the brake pedal in a hurry. Behind him, the troops collapsed into a heap. Ahead, the brake lights on Díaz's Mercedes came on, followed rapidly by the reversing lights. What Vickery saw was Nigel Weese. He was standing in the middle of the road, waving his arms.

Vickery jumped down from the cab, leaving the engine running.

"Alan! I thought it was you! What are you doing here? This is a War Zone now, you know."

"Not yet it isn't."

"What are you doing with this truck? What have you got in the back?"

Vickery looked at the truck. One by one, as they struggled to their feet, the troops raised their heads and shoulders — or, in the case of the younger recruits, their heads only — above the steel sides of the truck. Weese stared.

"Alan," he said. "Whose army is this? Is it yours?"

"Never mind whose army it is, Nigel. What are you doing here?"

Weese pointed.

"See that?"

Vickery looked. Emerging from the FNN van parked on the far side of avenue was the mallet-headed giant who, along with Weese, had invaded Vickery's study in Chelsea and spilt wine on his carpet.

"Me and Flint are covering Operation Safari Freedom," Weese said.

"Operation what?"

"I know it's a terrible name, but we can't change it — they've done the graphics."

"Never mind the graphics, Nigel. Listen to me."

"Right-ho. What is it then, Alan? We'll put the army thing on one side, shall we?"

"Nigel."

"Yes?"

"Did you see Díaz's speech?"

"That?" Weese laughed heartily. "Bloody hell, Alan — that was quite a performance you —"

"Did it go out on the air?"

"Yes, of course. Up to a point."

"Up to a point? What do you mean, Nigel? Was the world watching — that's what I want to know."

"The world? Not really, Alan. Don't worry, though — it was seen by the people who really matter."

"What about the Beeb?"

Weese shook his head.

"CNN?"

"No, Alan. We're the only ones here, you see. Me and Flint. FNN."

"So it went out on FNN?"

"Yes, Alan. But..."

"But what?"

"Well, we're running two feeds, aren't we? There's one for our regular audience. And then there's another one which is a bit more exclusive."

"Which one was I on?"

"Well, Alan, far be it from me to cast aspersions as to the nature of your average FNN viewer — especially with Flint bearing down on me as he is now — but, between you and me, you're a bit X-rated as far as they're concerned."

"So who saw me?"

"Well, let's see. There's some of your chums at the Liberty Club; the MLG people, of course; old Duggie; maybe even our own glorious PM. So you're pretty famous, Alan. With the people that count. Congratulations."

"What about the invasion, Nigel? Did I stop it?"

Weese doubled up with silent mirth.

"I'm sorry, Alan. Excuse me. The answer to that — well, just look up a moment, will you, Alan?"

Vickery looked up. A formation of five military helicopters thundered in from the direction of the bay and swooped over the avenue.

"Nigel," Vickery said, a note of steel entering his voice. "Things are not what they seem. They're not even what you seem to think they shouldn't seem. Do you want to know the truth about what's going on here? I'll give you the biggest bloody scoop you've ever had."

"The truth?" Weese scratched his nose. "That's a tricky concept, isn't it, Alan? Bit hard to figure out on the ground, as it were. Take you and your army, for example — what's that all about? In our business we have to figure things out in advance. Got to give the audience a story it will understand. And then stick by it. Can't keep chopping and changing. Lose credibility like that, wouldn't we? Watch out — Flint's coming."

Vickery looked. Gunner was marching towards them. Inácio, standing by the open door of the Mercedes, caught Vickery's gaze and pointed towards the truck.

"But Nigel," Vickery pleaded, "don't you want to know what's really happening?"

"I know what's happening, Alan. Operation Safari Freedom is happening. And history will prove it was the right decision."

"No, it won't."

"Who put you in charge of history?"

Gunner came to a halt at Weese's side. Vickery saw himself reflected in Gunner's shades. It wasn't a flattering image.

"Hey," Gunner said. "This is the guy who stole our chopper."

"No, Flint," Weese said. "Alan *borrowed* our helicopter. The *terrorists* stole it."

"Oh, right."

Gunner pointed at the troops.

"Who are they, Nige?"

"Well, we were just discussing that, actually, Flint."

"They could be terrorists, Nige. They're not wearing uniforms."

"Yes, well, it all rather depends on Alan here, doesn't it? Look, Alan..."

"What?"

"You ought to be thinking of Mariella and that lovely daughter of yours — what's her name?"

"Sara. Why?"

"What you could do, you see, is surrender to us now. To me and Flint. Right here and now. Won't take a moment. You see —"

"Surrender?"

"Yes. Because then, that way, you could probably avoid some of the unpleasantness, so to speak, that, otherwise..."

Vickery studied Weese's face. It had contorted itself into a million mendacious creases. Gunner's face was a blank.

"Surrender to *you?*"

"And Flint, yes. Mainly Flint. Get the cameras out and do a little rehearsal, shall we?"

Vickery began to back away. Out of the corner of his eye, he saw Inácio jump back into the Mercedes.

"Is he surrendering?" Gunner asked.

"Not entirely," Weese said.

"So what are you saying, Nige? Is he with us, or..."

Vickery climbed back into the truck and slammed the door.

"I'm afraid I'd have to say no at this point, Flint."

"Guy's a jerk, Nige."

"Up to a point, Flint. Up to a point."

Vickery threw the truck into gear and roared away, all but ramming the Mercedes in the process. And as he tailgated Inácio all the way down the Avenue of Fidel Castro, he wondered where his wife and daughter were. Then he imagined them getting together and discussing the question of whether he ought to place himself in the detestable hands of the vile Weese, and then going on and taking a vote. What might be the result of such a poll?

*

T he steel gates to the compound at the rear of the Explorers' Club were shut. Inácio pulled Díaz's Mercedes to one side and jumped out. He must have seen something that Vickery couldn't — something to the rear of the compound — because he stopped and stared for a moment. Then he rattled furiously at the gates.

Drawing closer, his knuckles white with the vibration of the gear-stick, Vickery could see that the gates were chained. Inácio turned and waved at Vickery to stop. Vickery shifted down a gear and glanced in the rear-view mirror; the troops were holding on as tightly as ever. Well, he thought, he'd always wanted to do something like this, hadn't he? Phil had talked him out of it the time those crooked Spanish developers bribed the mayor to confiscate his land. But now... He pressed the accelerator to the floor.

With a sound like a ten ton truck bursting through steel gates — it was just as he always imagined it would sound — Vickery and the troops crashed into the compound and skidded to a halt. The first thing Vickery saw when he opened his eyes — and it wasn't a welcome sight — was Muller.

Muller stood in a corner of the compound. He held a rifle across his chest. Beyond him, on the ground, was a small, indistinct shape. Muller glared at the truck — not surprised, not hostile, just vaguely put-out. It was as if the phone had rung at an awkward moment. He didn't seem to recognize Vickery.

Vickery opened his door and began to climb down, but Inácio blocked his way.

"No," he said. "Wait. Something bad here."

Muller walked towards them. Vickery stopped his engine and leaned out of the window. Muller made a circle of the truck and, fetching up beneath Vickery's window, shoved Inácio aside with his rifle butt.

"What is it with you?" he said.

"What's what with me, Arnie?"

"Get out of the truck."

"I was going to. Give me a chance."

Vickery climbed down from the truck; behind Muller's back, he could see Inácio edging away slowly towards the Mercedes. From the direction of the city center came the sound of three large explosions.

"You hear that?" Muller said. "They're taking care of the opposition parties. The Communists, the leftists..."

"Arnie," Vickery said. "You're looking a bit... Are you sure you're all right?"

Muller glanced over his shoulder, swaying and almost losing his balance as he did so.

"Yes."

The smell of alcohol on Muller's breath carried a punch that Vickery had never experienced before — not even in the gents' at the Fusilier.

"Perhaps you ought to go and lie down."

Muller said nothing. Vickery thought he saw something move in the corner of the compound.

"We're looking for old George," Vickery said. "Do you know him? German bloke?"

Muller stared up at the troops.

"Where'd you get *them?*"

"They followed me."

"Where'd you get the truck?"

"It's Díaz's."

"That fuck-brain. You really finished him, Alan. By God, you did."

Muller began to laugh, rocking on his heels and supporting himself with his rifle. Vickery tried again.

"He said George was here. Are you sure —"

Muller snapped his rifle to the horizontal and fired. There was a sharp cry. Vickery saw Inácio drop in the dirt.

"Arnie!"

Vickery snatched at Muller's rifle. Muller kicked Vickery's right leg out from under him. He fell on his back, the pain piercing the entire right side of his body. Muller fired his rifle at the side of the truck. The sound of the bullets deflecting was like a hammer striking an empty oil drum. The troops ducked. Vickery felt a hand on his right ankle. Muller began to drag him through the dirt towards the entrance to the Explorers' club.

"Arnie, for fuck's sake..."

"Shut up. You're going to see George. That's what you wanted."

Muller let go of Vickery's leg. Vickery could see the double doors which led into the Explorers' Club. The steps leading up to the doors were wet. There were footprints — dozens of footprints. Muller kicked the doors open. From his position on the ground, Vickery could see little. The lobby was full of flies.

"There he is, the old bastard," Muller said. "Get up. Take a look."

Vickery rolled on to his left side. Over by the wrecked gates, Inácio lay still. The troops, Vickery presumed, still cowered in the truck. Couldn't they see his predicament? Couldn't they... Do something? Or was this just another thing he'd got completely, totally, hopelessly wrong?

"Go on, get up," Muller said. Then he reached down and picked something up. "Here," he said, dropping the object in front of Vickery's face. "There's a souvenir for you. Greetings from Angola."

The object was an artificial foot. It was covered with blood. Vickery eased himself up on to his left knee.

"Oh Christ, Arnie. What have you fucking done?"

"He did it to himself, Alan. There's a lot you don't know." Muller put his boot against Vickery's chest and pushed. "What I am saying? You don't know *anything.*

You're just a greedy, fucking clown. What makes you think you can come to a place like this? It's fucking pathetic, man. You can't survive here. You're not entitled to. I sweat my entire life away... So that people like you..."

Muller began to sway on his feet again. Vickery glanced into the corner of the compound. Again, he thought he saw something move.

"What have you done to her, Arnie?" he said, softly. "Have you done... Anything?"

"I've got to take your car, Alan."

Muller staggered off towards the corner of the compound. Once there, he bent down and grabbed with his free hand. Vickery struggled to his knees. The pain was intense. Muller began to drag a body towards Inácio and the Mercedes. But it was a live body. It was George's Roberta.

Vickery stood, putting all his weight on his left leg. Roberta could see him — she could see him, but she didn't make a sound. Why not? He didn't understand. This was beyond his experience; pain, desperation, humiliation, shame, panic and, from time to time in the sleepless depths of night, self-disgust — all old friends, of course. But what he felt now, a combination of horror, loathing and pity — was new to him. He stumbled forward.

"Arnie!"

Muller, one-handed, fired his rifle again at the side of the truck. Bullets zipped above Vickery's head.

"Arnie!"

Muller ignored him. Vickery lifted his right foot off the ground and began to hop. Yes, he thought; this was stupid, it was pathetic — but he was fucking hopping mad, wasn't he? Let Muller shoot him. He was past caring. This was just... Too much, too much. Line in the dirt, wasn't it? For Alan bloody Vickery? Yes. Line in the bloody Angolan dirt.

Muller drew level with Inácio. Let him be okay, Vickery thought. Let him be okay. Not dead, not dead. Give him a bonus for not being dead, that's what we'll do. He hopped behind the truck and paused for breath. Then he began to jump. On the third attempt he got a grip with his good foot and hauled himself up. He peered over the side. The troops, as one, looked up, eyes wide.

"Please, lads," he said. "Need a bit of help here. Come on. Please?"

For a moment, the troops stared at him. Then, like a little camouflaged tidal-wave, they swarmed over the side of the truck. Vickery dropped from his perch and rolled in the dirt. He could hear the troops shouting. A single rifle shot went off. Vickery rolled on to his knees and crawled around the rear of the truck.

The troops had Muller face-down on the ground. They were kicking him — but not, Vickery noted, with great enthusiasm. Roberta lay on her side in the dirt, watching in silence. Inácio, to Vickery's heart-popping relief, was sitting up. His white shirt had turned red under his left arm. Vickery got to his feet again and limped towards the troops.

"Thanks, lads," he said. "Thank you, thank you. Everybody all right?"

As Vickery approached, the troops backed away from Muller, leaving him prone and exposed. One of the troops — the little one with the camera — offered Vickery his rifle.

"What?" Vickery said.

The kid pointed at Muller and pushed the rifle into Vickery's hands.

"What? No, I didn't mean..."

He felt the rifle in his hands. Something made him point it at Muller. There was no way — no way — he was going to shoot Muller. It was impossible. He knew this. And yet...

Vickery dropped the rifle, fell to his knees again and threw up his sandwich.

"Arnie!" he said, wiping the phlegm from his lips. "Take the bloody car. Take the bloody car and go. Now!"

Muller rolled over and began to wipe the dirt from his moustache.

"The car?"

"Take it and go. Fuck off now, before I change my mind."

Muller sat up and scowled at the troops. The troops raised their rifles.

"Go on, Arnie," Vickery said. "We're waiting, you bastard. Take it. Keys are in it."

Muller stood and began to walk backwards towards the car. When he reached the gates, he turned and ran. Vickery realized that he'd never seen Muller move so fast. The Mercedes started up. It lurched backwards through the gates and then scorched off in a cloud of dust towards the bay.

Vickery approached Inácio.

"Had me worried, you did. Had me really worried."

"Yes. I worry also."

"How bad is it?"

"Let me see." It was Roberta's voice. "I have experience."

Vickery hopped out of her way. She was on her knees but was more mobile than he was.

"Um, what about you?" he said, looking down at her. "Are you..."

Roberta looked up at him.

"Did Arnie..."

"I am not harmed," she said.

"Right," Vickery said. "But... The club? Where is everyone?"

"They all left."

"Oh."

"We shouldn't stay here."

"No. Well, the truck still has half a tank. If the gauge..."

Roberta shuffled forward and looked inside Inácio's shirt.

"Your friends..." she said to Vickery.

"Friends?"

"The American woman?"

"Oh, right. Her."

"And the others. Muller told Petty where they are. They are at the house of George's friend. Do you know Petty?"

"Yes."

"We should warn them."

"I suppose so."

Roberta buttoned up Inácio's shirt.

"This man is not so bad. We should go."

Vickery glanced towards the doors to the Explorers' Club.

"Yes, but..."

Roberta sat up and said something in Portuguese to the troops. The troops began to climb back into the truck.

"But what..." Vickery said. "What about..."

"George? George is dead."

"Yes, I know. Shouldn't we..."

Roberta pointed.

"Would you please bring my foot?"

"Yes. All right. Hang on."

Vickery retrieved Roberta's prosthetic foot. He tried to wipe the blood from it with the sleeve of his jacket, but it was no good. He limped back and handed it to her. She fastened it to her leg and stood.

"Thank you," she said.

"Thank them," Vickery said, gesturing towards the troops.

Roberta didn't reply. She loped over to the truck and began to climb up into the passenger seat. Vickery helped Inácio to his feet.

"Sorry about the car," he said.

Inácio shrugged.

"It's war, I suppose," Vickery said. "Everything gets messed up, doesn't it?"

Inácio nodded.

*

The situation, for once, was clear. Jennifer and the others were holed up in Fernando's house. Muller had told Petty they were there. Petty was a homicidal psychopath with an interest in politics. Something had to be done.

You want me to drive? Inácio had asked. No, Vickery had replied, I'm getting the hang of it now. And this bloody truck as well.

And so Inácio had climbed in the back with the troops and Roberta sat with Vickery in the cab, clinging to her seat as the truck flew through the frightened, empty streets of the city and distant guns boomed.

But the streets weren't entirely empty. Swerving on to a wide highway leading south along the coast, Vickery found his way blocked by the FNN van. It was driving down the center of the road, apparently at full speed. Vickery bit his lip, shifted down and hit the accelerator. The truck lurched forward.

Vickery ducked to the right and pulled alongside the van. He could see Weese bouncing and nodding in the passenger seat. Weese's window was up; the bloody van was air-conditioned, of course. Vickery yelled.

"Nigel!"

Weese turned and registered Vickery's presence. There was a delay of about a second before his vacant air turned to peevish irritation. He buzzed his window down.

"What is it now, Alan? Changed your mind? Want to surrender after all? Well, as it happens, this is not really a good —"

"Slow down!"

"Can't."

"Why not?"

"Got an important appointment."

"Slow down!"

"Sorry, Alan. Duggie's orders. More than my job —"

"What orders?"

"Top secret. Bugger off, Alan. You're being very tiresome."

"Where are you going?"

Weese seemed to be staring past Vickery at something.

"That woman — who is she, Alan? She sent us on a bloody —"

"It's Petty isn't it? You're going to meet Petty?"

Weese's face froze. Up went the window.

"Nigel!" Vickery yelled. "Stop the bloody van!"

Weese turned away and held his hand up to the side of his face.

"Right," Vickery said. "Hold on, everyone."

In the rear-view mirror, he caught Inácio's glance and made a sharp, stabbing gesture. Inácio seemed to get the message; he got the troops down on the floor of the truck. Vickery dropped back behind the van and shifted down again. The gearbox screamed. He took a deep breath and put his foot down hard. The truck surged forward, this time to the left of the van.

Díaz, Vickery reflected in a moment of Zen-like clarity, might not know much about public speaking, but he knew how to choose a set of wheels.

Wrenching the steering wheel to the right, Vickery slammed the truck into the side of the van. The van wobbled but corrected itself. Vickery slammed again. The van, like an editor confronted with an insistent proprietor, instantly took a new line and veered off the highway, careening down a side street and bouncing across a vacant lot of grass and rubbish on to the beach. Here it bumped and slewed to a halt, up to its axles in the sand.

"Gotcha," Vickery said.

Roberta stared at him — not understanding, of course. Vickery smiled, put the truck into gear and pulled away.

"Which way now?" he asked.

Roberta pointed.

"Ah. Not far?"

Roberta shook her head.

*

F ernando's house lay next to a corrugated strip of dirt that he appeared to use as a runway. Vickery took a short-cut across a patch of waste ground and bumped up on to the strip. The house was visible at the far end. But so were three pickup trucks and a jeep. In front of the house, Fernando's Land Cruiser was on fire. Vickery braked and threw the truck into neutral. It grumbled and clattered to itself.

Three pickup trucks and a jeep. Just sitting there. Not the postman, not the dustman. Who, then? Petty? Petty and his *irregulars?* And were they waiting for Weese and Gunner? What did it mean?

"What do you think?" he asked Roberta.

She blinked and widened her eyes, but said nothing.

Vickery stuck his head out of the window.

"Inácio?"

Inácio leaned over the side of the truck.

"What do you think?"

"I think this is the man you were looking for."

"Yes, but what..."

"We can turn around..."

"Right..."

"Or stay here and watch..."

"Uh-huh..."

"Or..."

"Or what?"

"That's up to you."

Vickery reflected. After all, the troops really weren't his private army. The military option always had consequences, didn't it?

"What about the lads?"

"They understand. Now."

"Right."

Vickery ducked his head back into the cab. It was all very well being a big decision-maker, he thought, when all you stood to lose was money. Or face. Or an election, possibly, one day. What would Mariella advise if she were here? That he'd got himself into this situation and he would jolly well have to cough up however much it cost to fix it? He put the truck into gear.

Slowly, as the truck rumbled down the strip, the pickups and the jeep came into focus. There was Petty, in his hat and boots, slouched in the jeep with his hands folded behind his head and his feet on the dashboard. The sun was high now. It glinted off the guns on the pickups as they swiveled in Vickery's direction.

Vickery pulled the truck to a stop directly between Petty's jeep and the house. Petty stared at the truck through his sunglasses but didn't move. Then, with exaggerated resignation, he stretched his arms, adjusted his hat and climbed delicately out of the jeep. Vickery cut his engine. Petty approached Vickery's window and stood, silent.

"Hullo," Vickery said.

For several seconds, Petty didn't react. Then he spat on the ground and removed his sunglasses.

"It's you again," he said.

"That's right," Vickery said.

"You again."

"Yup."

Petty tapped his knuckles gently against Vickery's door.

"Nice truck you got yourself here."

"Not bad."

"See, the thing is, Mr. Vickery — or maybe I can call you Alan now, huh? I guess we know each other pretty good?"

"If you like."

"See, your truck — and, you know, I'm not saying it's not a mighty fine vehicle, in its way, but it's kind of in the wrong place. It's kind of in our way."

"We're not staying long."

Petty jumped up on the running board and looked into the cab.

"I see you got yourself a new friend. Where's Mr. Fischer?"

"Who?"

"You know, George — the kraut guy."

"Something happened to him."

"Did it? Shoot. Maybe somebody put him on a list."

Vickery felt a spurt of bravado; Petty was mocking him.

"I'm on a list."

"Yeah, you ticked some people off. And you let my fuckin' lion out. But nobody really cares about you. What's in the back?"

Vickery could see in his mirror that Inácio had got the troops down and out of sight.

"In the back?"

"Yeah."

"Nobody. Nothing."

Petty jumped down from the running board and replaced his sunglasses.

"All right, Alan, old buddy. Let's move it, shall we?"

Vickery hesitated.

"Harlan?"

Petty removed his sunglasses.

"What?"

"What are you waiting for?"

"I'm waiting for you to get the heck out of here, Alan."

"No, apart from that."

Petty looked down and muttered something to himself. Then he looked up again.

"Okay," he said. "Why shouldn't I tell you? We're waiting for our friends in the media. That's what we're doing. We're sitting on our asses 'til they decide to show up."

A note of asperity, there, Vickery thought; possibly even derision.

"Well," he said, "it's lucky you mentioned that."

"Why?"

"Because we just passed Flint and Nigel. On the road. Back there."

"You *passed* them?"

"On the side of the road. Must have got a flat tire, or something."

"A flat tire?"

"Or something."

Petty snatched a radio from his belt and brandished it in Vickery's face.

"You know what? If this crapola worked, maybe they'd have let us know, don't you think? Not yours, are they?"

"Radios? Don't think so."

"Aw, shit."

Petty seemed agitated. Here he was, all ready for a prime-time onslaught on Fernando's house and the cameras hadn't shown up. Plus Vickery's truck was cluttering up the frame. What was stopping Petty from going ahead anyway? Whose production values was he laboring under?

"Harlan?" Vickery said.

"What?"

"How's the coup going?"

"It's not a coup, Alan. You know that. It's a mutually-sanctioned preventive intervention to safeguard democratic freedoms. And it's going great."

"And old Duggie really wants to see the highlights, doesn't he?"

Petty coughed.

"Did you say *old Duggie?*"

Vickery nodded towards the house.

"He wants to see this, doesn't he? Live footage, as it were?"

Petty folded his arms.

"You get yourself and your truck out of here right now, Alan. You hear me?"

"But you can't get stuck in until Flint and Nigel get here. Because old Duggie will be cross if he misses the show."

Petty said nothing.

"Must be frustrating."

Petty began to back away, raising his arm in a threatening manner.

"And it doesn't look right with us in the way, does it?"

Petty turned his back and began to march towards the nearest of the pickups.

Vickery started his engine. Then he pulled the truck forward and to the right and shifted into reverse. With the engine screaming, he let the clutch out. The truck lurched backwards, flattening Fernando's gates — which were really nothing compared to those at the Explorers' Club, to be honest — and shunting aside the smoking remains of Fernando's Land Cruiser. Vickery steered sharply to the left to avoid an ancient Cessna with no propeller and fetched up with a crunch against the wooden rails of Fernando's porch.

Petty had taken charge of the machine gun on the first pickup. The truck had withstood Muller's rifle assault but this, Vickery knew, would be something else. He turned to Roberta.

"Might be safer in the back."

Despite herself, he thought, she laughed.

*

Dinner had come and gone. Neither Dale nor Diane had eaten much. Zarnoff had sipped away two large glasses of brandy and was now asleep. Aylsham had eaten Dale's Mississippi mud pie, in addition to his own. How did he stay so thin? Now, fortified with wine, he had gone in search of the thin, pale woman who had discarded him earlier.

The dancing that Zarnoff had promised hadn't started. There was no music; instead, the FNN Situation Room special boomed and chattered, on and on. How exactly, Dale wondered, would the dancing be scheduled? Between the air-strikes and the beach landings? During a lull in mopping-up operations?

But why was his mood sinking like this when all the news was good? The British Prime Minister had promised full and unconditional support. Stocks linked to MLG had been uprated by all the major investment banks. Religious groups were collecting Bibles to send to Angola. Senator-elect Wallace Fricke, an expert on the region, had reassured Congress that ordinary Angolans would reach out, in their traditional way, to liberation and stabilization teams, were any to be sent. The President had asked the American people to pray for Angola. Dale hoped that they would. And the government of South Africa, having disowned an earlier accusation by one of its elder statesmen that an invasion was in progress, had been warned by the Vice President that foreign interference in Angola would not be tolerated.

There was no such place as Spruitfontein. It had not been smashed and incinerated. Sheryl had never been there. He, Dale, had never knelt in the ashes. No such things ever happened, ever.

Lie upon lie, Dale thought. They fell like rain, almost a force of nature, and after a while you were soaked through and up to your knees. Not much later and you were underwater, swimming through mud, your ears full of distorting echoes. To cleanse your senses and open them to the truth you needed to stand on the South Atlantic coast, turn your back to the wind and listen to the desert.

"Dale?"

Diane was speaking to him.

"Dale?"

"I'm sorry?"

"I think I've had enough. I thought I might get to talk to Phyllis, but I guess that's not going to happen. I think it's her loss. Shall we leave now? Dale?"

But Dale was on his feet. Moreland's aides had approached the top table. Now their boss was striding from the ballroom.

"No. I'm sorry. I can't go yet."

He snatched up his shoulder bag and hurried towards the exit.

*

"Get in the truck!" Vickery yelled. In his mirror, Vickery saw Jennifer emerge from the house. The he heard the tailgate clatter down.

"Get in!"

Gary and Joe appeared at her side.

"Who the hell is it?"

"Jennifer!" Vickery shouted. "Get in the bloody truck! Harlan's about to do his bloody nut!"

"It's him," she said to Joe. "It's Alan. What do we do?"

Joe looked at Gary. Gary shook his head.

"Get in the truck!" Vickery yelled. "Harlan's not supposed to murder anyone until the bloody TV get here! Duggie's orders. Come on!"

"What difference does it make?" she said.

"Okay, okay," Joe said. "No — no, this is crazy. Alan!"

"What?"

"Are you sure?"

"Listen. I know the two bastards very well, and it makes perfect sense. Get in the truck!"

Joe shook his head.

"Shit. Okay, in you go, Jennifer. Gary — get Charlie and Fernando."

"What about you?"

"Jennifer, if we all get in the truck, they're going to follow us, aren't they?"

"I can't leave you. You never —"

"Me and Gary, we'll attract their attention. Soon as you're out of the way. Looks like we're meant to be the stars of the show anyhow."

"Alan's got — he's got an army."

"Nice kids. No match."

"Now would be good!" Vickery shouted.

"What's going to happen to you?" she said.

"We're going to resist."

Vickery saw Charlie and Fernando drag Jennifer towards the truck. All three climbed in. Vickery revved the engine.

"Any more?" Vickery yelled.

"That's it," Joe said.

"Not coming?"

"No."

"Right."

"Hey!" Charlie said. "Look — that kid's got my camera!"

Vickery put his foot down. The truck hurtled back down Fernando's dirt strip. Forty yards ahead, Petty's pickup blocked the way. Vickery hit the brakes.

"Get down on the floor, if I were you," Vickery said to Roberta without looking. He heard her shuffle off her seat on to the floor. The truck bumped forward in first gear.

Petty twisted the machine gun this way and that, as if its mounting were rusty and he were trying to loosen it up. He kept adjusting his hat. Petty wasn't sure, Vickery thought. He wasn't sure if he was really going to do it — to spoil the show and offend his boss. Was he succumbing — possibly for the first time and in a small but important way — to doubt?

Vickery shifted up a gear. The pickup began to back up, slowly. Vickery accelerated. Then, from just above his head, came a sound like fireworks exploding in a dustbin, and he realized that Inácio, one step ahead as ever, had marshalled the troops up to the parapet and ordered them to fire. Petty ducked into the back of the pickup. The pickup spun around and tore off into the brush by the side of the strip. Vickery accelerated. A cloud of dust rose up around the truck.

At any moment, he thought, Petty's machine-gun would tear into the back of the truck. How tough was the poor old beast? Would the bullets slice through truck's sides and rip into the troops? And Jennifer? What would he find back there when he stopped? And Petty's gun — had he seen it before with so-and-so in Naples or what's-his-name in Budapest? Let it be as *crapola* as the radios, he thought. Crapola! Please!

But all he heard, as the truck skidded off the end of the strip and bumped down a bank of weeds and litter towards the main road, were two single rifle shots, close together. And he realized that Gary and Joe were the stars of the moment. Not him. Them.

Back now on the coastal highway, the truck roared north towards the city. Did Vickery know where he was going? Did he have a plan? What kind of plan could he possibly have?

Passing the FNN van, Vickery let out a blast on the horn, followed by two more. Then he heard a hammering on the roof of the cab.

"Stop! Stop here! Stop!"

It was Jennifer's voice.

He hit the brakes and the truck skidded to a halt. She leaned over the side.

"Alan — we need to get on TV."

Vickery shook his head.

"No, no, Jennifer. I see where you're coming from, but it won't work. Trust me. I've tried it. Complete washout."

"No, *you* trust *me*, Alan. This is something else. We've got to do it. We've got to do it now."

"To tell the truth, I'd rather just run away now, if it's all the —"

"No, come on — this is for Joe and Gary. It'll make a difference."

"Will it? Really?"

"Where are you taking us anyhow?"

Vickery considered.

"All right, bugger it, come on then."

Vickery left the engine running and jumped from the cab.

"Inácio? Keep the bloody seat warm, will you?"

Jennifer straddled the side of the truck, dropped down into the sand and began to run towards the FNN van. Vickery caught up with her.

"Flint and Nigel — they're probably going to be a bit funny about this. It was me who —"

She stopped running.

"You put them in the sand?"

"Yes. They wanted me to surrender."

"Okay. In that case..."

She ran back to the truck.

"Charlie! Toss me that."

Charlie looked at the rifle he was holding.

"Yeah, that!"

She caught the rifle as it dropped towards her and ran back to where Vickery waited.

"I'm not going to argue with them," she told him.

Gunner had seen them coming. As they advanced on the van, he dropped the plastic bottle he'd been holding and began to run along the beach. Weese called out to him.

"Flint! Don't panic, for Pete's sake, it's only old Alan!"

Gunner kept going. Jennifer stopped and looked down at her feet. Then she pulled her shoes off, flung them aside and raced ahead. Vickery, taken up in the excitement, did the same.

Now Weese looked worried.

"Who's that woman, Alan? What's she doing with that gun?"

"Never mind who that woman is, Nigel," Vickery said. "Where's the crew?"

"In the van. Where'd you think?"

"Tell 'em to get cranking."

"What?"

"We're going on air."

"What — again?"

"Yes. Whatever you've got, turn it on."

Jennifer stumbled to a halt at Vickery's side. Weese looked nervous.

"Who are you?"

"You know who I am, Nigel. Look at my feet. I'm not wearing any shoes. Do what Alan says." She poked him in the gut with the barrel of her rifle. "Because I'm mad as hell and —"

"All right, all right, I know the rest," Weese said.

"Tell them Flint's got an urgent update."

"Have to start the engine, okay? For the generator." Weese leaned in at the van's window. "Um, guys? We're going to do another segment now. From the beach, yes. What? Flint? Well, it looks like he's gone for a bit of a run."

*

T he screen showed the deck of a large ship. Not a navy ship; it looked like something else — something too brutal to appear in Pentagon accounts. Three large helicopters were being prepared for takeoff — or so it appeared to Dale. But nobody was watching. The crowded viewing room was in an uproar. Moreland stood at the front, his back to the screen, arguing with his aides.

Dale looked for Cheryl, but couldn't find her. He approached a girl with a clipboard.

"What's happening?"

"I'm not sure — they're saying like Flint Gunner's been kidnapped or something."

"Who by?"

"The terrorists, I guess."

"Bad news."

"Yeah."

Dale pushed closer to the front of the room. There was a sheen of perspiration on Moreland's face. Something was beginning to leak out of his hair.

The screen went blank. The noise in the room dropped to a murmur. Moreland stopped in mid-sentence and turned to face the screen. For perhaps twenty seconds it remained blank. Then there was a blur of movement and a new picture snapped into focus: A beach, an ocean. The room fell silent.

Into the frame stepped a shoeless woman with red-brown hair. Her clothes were stained and wrinkled. The wind blew her hair, knotted and heavy, into her eyes. She brushed it aside. In her hands she held an automatic rifle. She moved a little closer to the camera. A man joined her, diffidently. He wore a ragged business suit and was unarmed; Dale recognized the crazy Englishman from earlier.

"I hope you can hear me," the woman said. "I hope everybody can hear me. I hope Douglas Moreland can hear me. I hope the Resistance can hear me. You better had, guys. I hope Dale can hear me."

Dale pushed closer to the screen.

"Here's the message," Jennifer said. "The code book. Forget it. They know all about it. Do what you have to do. Shut everything down. Find a new way. Keep doing what you're doing and good luck. This is for Gary and Joe. And Sheryl. If Dale's out there... If you're out there, Dale... It's for you, too."

Dale edged further towards the front, ending up six feet behind Moreland. He unzipped the shoulder bag.

"As for you, Douglas," Jennifer said, "I guess if anybody hears this you will. All I want to say is, well, I won't forget what you did. Neither will they. You know who I mean."

The silence in the room seemed to intensify.

"I guess that's all I have to say," Jennifer said. "No — wait..."

Another man entered the frame — large, red-faced, in jeans and T-shirt. He handed Jennifer a small video camera.

"Read what's on the screen," he said. "Fast-forward for the next page. Alan — give the kid some money, will you?"

"You bought a camera?"

"It's mine. I bought it back. Please?"

"All right. I suppose you know... Oh! One last word from me for old Duggie. You're not going to rule bloody Africa, mate. It's going to rule you."

The Englishman disappeared from the frame. Jennifer began to read. Names, dollar amounts, corporations, banks, account numbers, shipping companies, investment houses, serial numbers, addresses — Dale recognized some of the names but the rest made no sense to him. But somehow he felt sure that someone, somewhere had just clicked the red button.

"Why are we listening to this?" Moreland demanded.

The people nearest to him recoiled.

"Why is this allowed to happen? Why are these people permitted to do this? Why is no action being taken? I thought I saw a ship. I thought I saw helicopters. Did I see them? I think so. Of course I saw them. Where are they?"

He pushed his aides aside and made for the exit. Dale blocked the way. Moreland put his hand on Dale's chest.

"Out of the way."

Dale resisted.

"You don't know me, do you?"

"You're in my way."

"I just want to know if it was you."

"If what was me?"

"The farmhouse. In Namibia."

Moreland said nothing. Then he raised his hand and ran it through his hair.

"Was that you?" Dale said.

"Farmhouse?"

"Yes."

"Do I know of any farmhouses? In — where was it?"

"Namibia."

"Namibia?"

Dale reached into the shoulder bag. Moreland struck him on the neck. And he fell.

Was the gun still in his hand? It seemed to be, but then something punctured his wrist and his arm was in spasm. Was he on his stomach now? Yes, face-down. Could he see anything? Only the floor. Was there a weight on his back? Yes, and more weight. What could he hear? Shouting, screaming, and Jennifer's voice at a distance, reading names from a list.

He closed his eyes and let go.

*

A lan Vickery purchased Charlie's camera for an uncounted quantity of kwanzas and ran back to the beach. Jennifer was reading from the camera, which seemed strange. Charlie looked on over her shoulder. Weese sat in the sand grinning, which also seemed strange. Fernando, meanwhile, had somehow dragged himself out of the truck and now stood at the edge of the Atlantic, looking out to sea. This, under the circumstances, was odd.

"Nigel!" Vickery said. "What's so funny? This is going out, isn't it?"

"Oh yes, Alan."

"Not encrypted or locked or anything?"

"Nope."

"You haven't pulled a cable out anywhere?"

"It's wide open, Alan. Anyone can pull it down off the satellite. I fixed it."

"But..."

"I don't mind embarrassing old Duggie, Alan. He's a pain in the arse. Wouldn't say that if Flint was here, of course."

"Nigel, you must know that Jennifer here probably has a pretty bloody amazing story to tell if you —"

"Yes, I dare say she does, Alan. But it would be the wrong story, wouldn't it?"

"It'd be true."

"True but wrong. Shame. How long is she going on with this, by the way?"

"Well, I..."

"It's just that, if you look over there..."

Weese nodded towards the ocean. Vickery looked. Close to the horizon he could see a half-dozen small, square objects, strung out in a line.

"What are they?"

"You must have had a deprived childhood, Alan. Amphibious landing craft. Used to get 'em in your Cornflakes. Oh — and then there's *that.*"

Vickery turned around. A small helicopter in camouflage colors swept towards them from the direction of Fernando's house, slowed and descended towards the road to the rear of the truck. The troops took cover.

"Who could this be, I wonder?" Weese said.

Jennifer stopped reading and looked. The she turned back to the camera and started again. Charlie picked up her rifle. Fernando turned and shielded his eyes from the sun. Then he began to walk towards the road.

A tall, thin man in a dark-green jump-suit and wrap-around shades emerged from the helicopter. He was wearing shiny, black dress shoes, which was definitely strange. Fernando walked towards him. The man waited. Fernando stepped up on to the road. The two stood face to face. Then Vickery saw them shake hands.

"All right," he said. "Jennifer, come on. I think the bloody Cavalry's here. Nigel — you're a bastard but you're all right."

"Same to you, Alan."

Vickery ran up to the road.

"This," Fernando said, "is Mr. Jay Percival. And, for once, he's in the right place at the right time."

CHAPTER 49

I t had felt like a victory. But, from the air, all the physicalities of power — the childish hegemony of facts-on-the-ground — were all too apparent to Vickery.

Weese stood on the sand, waving. Behind him, half a mile from the beach, a line of military landing craft bore down on him. Vickery wondered how he would explain Gunner's absence.

On the other side of the coast road, behind the hill, Fernando's house burned out of control. Three pickup trucks and a jeep drove slowly away along the dirt strip.

Smoke drifted between the blocks of the city and out over the encircling shanty-towns. Downtown was empty but the blacktop highways and the red-dirt roads out of the city teemed. People were moving out — by truck, by motorcycle, on foot.

To the south, a convoy of trucks had begun to emerge from the airport. Chinook helicopters lined up along the runways.

Below, on the coast road, a solitary truck drove south at speed. Vickery had handed over command of his little army of boys to Inácio. Had the kids seemed relieved? Maybe so. But they'd given Vickery a noisy send-off. Vickery had hugged Inácio like a brother. He'd tried to persuade Roberta to join them on Jay's helicopter, but she'd refused. Vickery had made Fernando promise to take care of her.

Now they flew south along the coast, barely above the waves, beach after beach. Fernando, it turned out, had been incorrect. Jay had come for Gary and Joe and, once again, Vickery was given to understand, had arrived too late.

Charlie sat beside Vickery, paging through names and numbers on his camera as if he felt he had to memorize them all. His face was slack, his mouth half-open, his eyes restless. He was trying to figure out what had happened to him, Vickery thought. And good luck to him.

Jennifer waited until they were well clear of the city, then she climbed into the empty seat beside Jay — yet another spy, presumably. Jay rummaged under his seat and handed Jennifer a dirty headset. Vickery found another one under his seat.

"So where are we going?" she asked.

Jay tapped at a gauge.

"See how far we get. Might make it to Namibia."

"How did you know where we were?"

"These resistance guys — they have someone at the NSA. They weren't happy about using me but I was all they had."

"They still don't trust you?"

"Not quite. Got their principles."

"They need a new network. Moreland knows how it works. I was just on TV. I told everybody."

"You did? On TV? That's great."

Below them, the shore stretched on, empty. Once in a while they saw a fishing boat or a cluster of huts in a circle of red earth.

"I'm sorry about Gary and Joe," Jay said.

"We'd have been there too," she said. "If Alan hadn't shown up."

Yes, Vickery thought — there *was* that.

"What happened?" Jay asked.

"He had this truck, and these kids — and he just kind of outwitted that guy Petty."

"Petty?"

"You know him?"

"Yeah. We all know him. How did Alan outwit him?"

"It's hard to explain."

"What's he doing here, anyway?"

"It's hard to explain."

Very true, Vickery thought.

"Where'd you get the helicopter?" Jennifer asked.

"That's easy. Stole it from MLG."

Vickery sighed a sigh of pure pleasure.

"They'll miss it."

"Tax write-off."

"Do they pay tax?"

"Good point."

"So you think we might make it to Namibia?"

"Maybe."

"What then?"

"You say the network's down?"

"One way or another."

"That could be a problem. But don't worry about it."

Jay had a good attitude, Vickery thought — for a spy.

"One thing..." Jennifer said.

"What?"

"What happened to Dale?"

"I believe he went home."

"To do what?"

"Whatever he wanted."

"Like what?"

"Guy like that — who knows?"

Vickery leaned back in his seat and closed his eyes. The noise and vibration of the helicopter carried him off into a half-sleep of boy-soldiers, and stolen helicopters, and explaining to Mariella that none of what had happened was really anything to do with him.

When he awoke, Jay's voice was in his ears.

"Look down."

He saw the mouth of a wide river and its cloudy breath, billowing out into the Atlantic.

"That's the Kunene."

On the far side of the river, the big dunes began.

"And that's Namibia."

"We made it?"

Jay tapped the fuel gauge.

"We're running on fumes. Get ready."

CHAPTER 50

J ay was searching for something. He flew low above the waves, his attention
now on the fuel gauge, now on the line of the tide along the beach. A fierce
wind blew; the down-draft of the helicopter blades added little to the foam.
The coastline, as far as Vickery could see, was empty: Nobody to hear the waves;
nobody to hear the oscillating whine of the helicopter on its last throatful of fuel.

"What are you looking for?" he asked.

"A skeleton."

"Oh."

"Got to be one soon. Hope it's a good one. We're on the reserve tank. Not
much in it."

They were twenty feet above the waves, Vickery thought. It might well be
survivable. Then he saw a dark shape in the water.

"What's that?" he said. "Up ahead?"

It was a dead ship, lying on its side, two-thirds in the ocean. Its blackened ribs
scorched in the sun.

"Well spotted," Jay said.

"Thanks."

"We're on plan B, by the way. Plan A was north to Congo, but it's too hot there.
Just so you know."

Jay brought the helicopter lower.

"Here's what you do," he said. "Jump into the water. Stay in the water. Walk
along to the ship. Get inside. Stay there. Stay out of sight."

"What about you?"

"I need to park this thing a couple of blocks away. I'll come back here when I
can. If I'm not back by... Shit, you'll figure it out."

"We stay in the ship?"

"Yeah. Get these guys in there. Stay out of sight, if you can. No tracks on the
beach, okay? Very important."

"Okay."

"Wake the other two up. Charlie might need some help."

Vickery roused the two bankers and pointed at the water. Jennifer got the idea quickly; she was first out. Charlie strapped his camera high up on his chest and followed. Vickery gave Jay one last glance, but Jay didn't look away from the fuel gauge.

Then Vickery was in the water, up to his thighs. It was like ice. The sun scorched his face, the light blinded him and his ears were full of the sound of the waves and the helicopter. Then the helicopter was gone. He squinted into the light. The dead ship came into focus and he began to wade towards it.

How many ships like this were there? What had happened to their crew and passengers? There was nothing here. No settlement. No water. No roads, not even dirt roads. Only the dunes. Was there a more desolate coast anywhere in the world? But Jay had brought them here for a reason. What were they hiding from?

Inside the ship, the air was still and hot but the water just as icy. The waves boomed against the skin of the hull and scoured its sand-blasted bones. The ship was a corpse, but it would never be allowed to rest.

"This doesn't seem like a good idea to me," Vickery said in Jennifer's ear. "What if Charlie here slips and gashes his leg?"

She shrugged.

"What are we supposed to be doing?" Vickery said. "Waiting for a bus?"

"I don't know, Alan. We're keeping out of sight."

"Where are we, anyway?"

"This is the Skeleton Coast."

Vickery nodded.

"Not kidding, are you?"

They fell into silence and the rhythm of the waves took over. Jay did not return. Charlie, Vickery thought, looked sickly. The tide was advancing, not retreating; he could find nowhere to stand or perch where his feet were not in the water.

The sea rose and still Jay did not return. Then, the booming of the waves modulated and deepened, becoming a powerful and pulsating beat, which then rose up above them.

Vickery waded waist-deep over to a hole in the hull and looked up. A single military helicopter — an Apache, he thought — tore along the line of the beach and directly over the wreck. He could see its sharp projections and its ugly protuberances clearly, but not its pilot. It reared up from the beach and turned inland, into the dunes.

He moved his position so that he could see. The helicopter stopped at a distance of perhaps half a mile. It flew slowly in a tight circle, as if inspecting something on the ground. Then it backed away, flying in reverse, and stopped again. A thick line of white smoke drew itself from the pods beneath the helicopter to the ground. The helicopter swung around in an arc of about ninety degrees. There was a second line of white smoke. No sound reached his ears; the wind and the waves obliterated it.

"What's happening?" Jennifer asked.

He retreated from his viewpoint.

"They're looking for us."

The helicopter returned to the beach and made another pass. Its sound receded. Then it came back for a third pass and hovered above the dead ship for what seemed like minutes but was probably only thirty seconds. Vickery caught Jennifer's glance. He looked up and mimed the firing of an arrow from an enormous bow. She smiled. The helicopter made another circle above the wreck and moved slowly away to the north.

For an hour or more they waited. The helicopter did not return.

"What about Jay?" Vickery said. "Do you think we ought to..."

"I think we ought to wait," she said.

They waited. The light began to fade.

"I don't see how he could hide," Vickery said. "Where could he hide?"

"I don't know."

"Perhaps we ought to get out now. Look at Charlie..."

"Maybe," she said. "But —"

"Hey, people."

It was Jay's voice.

"Time to come out."

Vickery waded across to the hole in the hull and stumbled up on to the beach. Jay was covered, from head to shiny shoes, in sand.

"You're covered in sand."

"I had to hide, too."

"But your tracks..."

"The wind."

Vickery stared at him.

"Beetles do it," he said.

*

A lan Vickery lay in the warm sand with Jennifer at his side. The light would be gone soon, he knew, and the air and the sand would turn cold. They had no shelter, nor any food or water. And no radio or satellite thingy — not that it would have been safe to use one, presumably.

Jay's helicopter had been destroyed — another write-off for MLG. On the brighter side, Vickery's legs had begun to thaw out and his trousers were drying nicely. Charlie looked like he might survive. He claimed his camera was dry and undamaged, which Vickery felt was bloody nice for him, and no more than he deserved.

Jay had said they should wait there in the dunes. Since, as far as Vickery could tell, dunes was all you got here, that was fine by him. Nobody was going back inside the dead ship, no matter how many warplanes darkened the sky. Jay's plan was to wait and see what turned up, apparently. He called this "Plan B".

But Vickery had something else on his mind. He had a few things he wanted to say to Jennifer. Some things he wanted to get off his chest. Not a confession, exactly; not a full and comprehensive explanation or rationale; not a plea for understanding — he thought she probably understood him pretty well, alas. And, more to the point, so did he, now. What he had to say was... Well, he knew what he meant and so would she.

"Jennifer?" he said.

"What is it, Alan?"

"Um, how would you like to walk across to that dune over there?"

She made a face. Was she going to make this difficult for him?

"What's wrong with this dune?"

"Nothing. Only I... I thought we could have a private word."

"We could?"

"Yes."

"Okay, then."

He followed her to the dune — it wasn't the one he meant, but it didn't matter. They were all the same.

"So let's hear it," she said, sitting on the cusp of the dune. He sat down beside her.

"It's just that I've got a few things to say. To you."

"So you said."

"I'll start then, shall I?"

"Sure."

"Right. What was that?"

"What was what?"

"Thought I heard a noise."

"Come on, spit it out. I'm all ears."

"Well listen, then."

"Alan —"

"There it is again."

"What?"

"I don't know. It sounds like — well, it sounds a bit like Bryce. You know — my former associate. When he laughs, he... But he's in Beijing."

Vickery turned around and peered into the thickening gloom. The dunes had begun to merge into a single foggy carpet, stretching off into nowhere. He strained his ears and his eyes; there was *something* out there somewhere.

"Oh my God," Jennifer said.

This, Vickery knew, was what American women, and Mariella, said when they got excited. But, this time, Jennifer wasn't wrong. Emerging into hazy visibility were two — no, four — large, lumbering animals.

Vickery wasn't sure he was up to comprehending this spectacle. He made an effort. But all he could come up with was that these must be the legendary lost wildebeest of Angola, perhaps attended by sad lions, come to his rescue; and that, riding upon them, were none other than the former King and his Queen.

This was complete rubbish, of course. What he was looking at were four camels — this was a bloody desert, after all, wasn't it?

And it wasn't the former Queen of Angola, it was his own bloody daughter, Sara. And it wasn't the former King, it was just some bloke she'd brought with her, whose name was Brian, according to Jennifer.

Vickery realized that Jay had stolen up alongside him. The man had a way of moving.

"Plan B always looks stupid on paper, Alan," he said. "Spies like you ought to know that."

CHAPTER 51

Alan Vickery removed a fresh bottle of gin from the cabinet in his study and ventured out again into the January sunlight. He crossed the lawn, where the fountains now lay dormant and deactivated until further notice, and ascended to the top of the rockery — sorry, rock garden — where General (now Senator) Wallace Fricke had given his famous "Dark Times" speech.

Then, approaching the pool, he passed the spot where — irony of ironies — he had accused Jeremy (now Lord) Aylsham of making improper and typically sneaky advances on his daughter, Sara (formerly Zara). Lowering himself back on to his seat at the pool bar, he handed the bottle to Derek (always and forever Spud).

"Here you go, Spud."

"Thanks, Alan. Lovely. Top-up, Ronnie?"

And it was in this very pool, Vickery recalled, that he had sneered at his friends for their ignorance of the world of politics, averring, if he remembered rightly, that this was the reason they were stuck on this bloody island. Well, life was dripping with such ironies, wasn't it?

His ears were still ringing on account of that phone call from Jason. Vickery and Jennifer and the others were in the car, in Johannesburg, on the way to dinner with the affable but long-faced Walter Gabo (some kind of ANC-connected big-wig).

You listen to me, Vickery — if you ever set foot again in the bloody Yoo-Kay, I'll see to it that...

And so on and so on.

Well, empires fell, didn't they? In the end. Every one. His was no exception. First, Pest Control: Sued into bankruptcy by a minor but vengeful government department. Then, Loans and Financial Services: Toppled due to multiple irregularities. Well, you could audit the bloody fish shop on the corner and find irregularities, couldn't you? It was all a question of who had the power to do what to whom. It was politics. And then Property: The foreign stuff was owned obscurely enough to escape but, in what Jason liked to call the Yoo-Kay, the rush to call in Vickery's loans had resembled two-pints-for-the-price-of-one night at the Fusilier.

And, lastly, his Atlantic Affairs Institute: Now the personal plaything of Jerry touch-my-robes Aylsham, newly relocated from Paddington to Mayfair and gorging itself, no doubt, on Liberty Club dollars. Well, good riddance.

Vickery sniffed and cast his gaze down towards the far end of the pool.

"Well, at least take your bloody jacket off," he said. "And stop looking so bloody miserable." This, of course, was advice he could have given himself.

"Bothering you, is it?"

"Yes, Phil, it is."

Fat Phil sat on the edge of the pool. He had removed his shoes and socks and had rolled up his trouser legs. But that was as far as he had gone. He looked like an owl which, having been told to take a bath, had decided it wasn't going to.

"You're not the only one, you know," Vickery added.

"So how did she break it to you, Alan?" Derek asked. "How did she inform you, as it were?"

Vickery groaned. *Inform* was the word, he thought. No rows, no tears, no pleas or showdowns. Not even any discussion. He had been *informed*.

"You won't believe it, Derek. She sent her bloody lawyer round. It was 'Sign here, mate, or else.'"

"You should have chucked him in the pool, shouldn't he, Ronnie?"

"That's what I would have done."

"Me too."

"How," Vickery demanded, "can you be chucking people in my pool when you're always bloody in it yourselves?"

"Alan makes a good point, Derek."

"As always, Ronnie. Had to give her half, did you, Alan?"

"Half? I wish. More like three-quarters. They had all these reasons. I couldn't be bothered to argue. Frankly."

"Money isn't everything, Alan. That's something Derek and me have learnt."

"Yeah, that's right," Vickery said. "Isn't it, Phil?"

"If you say so, Alan."

"What I don't understand," Derek said, "is why Mariella prefers that posh git to you."

Vickery ground his teeth and reached for the gin bottle.

"Happens all the time," Ronnie said. "These posh girls. They do like a bit of rough —"

"Especially if he's loaded —"

"Yes, Derek, loaded is often a crucial factor — but after a while, well..."

"The novelty wears off."

"Course it does."

"They revert."

"Exactly. They revert. It's not Alan's fault. They revert. To type, if you want to put it like that."

"Nothing anybody can do."

"Nothing."

"Bugger all."

Vickery gulped down half a tumbler of neat gin. Then he grabbed a lemon slice and sucked on it.

"Shut up, you two. It wasn't like that at all."

Or was it? Vickery pictured Aylsham and Mariella — or Lord and Lady Aylsham, as they now were — wandering into the study in the Chelsea house, spotting the wine stains on the carpet and blaming him while Weese and Gunner got away without a stain on their what's-its, ha-bloody-ha.

"Well, at least you've still got this place," Ronnie said. "You got a bargain, Alan. What was the name of that bloke? Rock star, wasn't he?"

"I forget," Vickery said. "Think he's dead now, anyway. Hounded him, they did. Wouldn't keep quiet, would he? Wouldn't knuckle under. Poor bastard."

"I thought you didn't like him?"

"No, he was a right evil — I mean, he wasn't very nice, was he? All the same..."

There was a moment of silence, but it wasn't, Vickery knew, in honor of a fallen musical idol.

"So why'd they make that bloke a lord?" Derek said.

"Services to something," Ronnie said.

"Services to what?"

"I don't know, it's always services, isn't it?"

"Or back-handers or loans."

"That would be *financial* services, then."

Vickery sent a wave of water splashing along the edge of the bar. Derek and Ronnie lifted their glasses clear.

"Oh, shut up, the pair of you," Vickery said. "I'll tell you why he got that. Because he's got no fucking brain, right? Right, Phil?"

"No fucking brain," Phil said.

There was a pause.

"No," Derek said. "But he's got Mariella, hasn't he?"

Vickery closed his eyes and counted to five. When he opened them again they were moist, but it was just the humidity — that was all it was.

"Have you seen the papers?" Ronnie asked, changing the subject.

"No," Vickery said.

"Well, you say he has no brain, but he was right about one thing."

"What?"

"Angola."

"What about it?"

"Well, it *is* another War Zone. It's official."

Vickery took another gulp of gin.

"Apparently, they got there just in time," Derek said.

"So?" Vickery said, sensing the futility of trying to explain to his friends what had really happened but wondering if he ought to do it all the same.

"So you must have had a narrow escape."

Vickery thought of the cruise missile slicing into his office; of the Chinese embassy, pummeled almost to dust; of Petty and his machine-gun, which, Vickery now felt certain, wasn't the least bit *crapola*; and of the dead ship on the beach and the attack helicopter thumping overhead.

"Not really," he said.

"Tragic, though, isn't it?" Ronnie said.

Vickery took a deep breath.

"I'll tell you this, Ronnie. Luanda — bloody pearl in a jeweled what's-it. Potentially, I mean. Someone like you could have made a fortune. And the rest of the country — tragic is right. It's incredible. If someone just went round and dug up all the..."

"Dug up all the what?"

"Never mind. Doesn't matter. Who wants another drink? Both of you? Phil?"

Phil looked distracted, rather like an owl which, spotting another owl, had decided it didn't like the look of the newcomer's beak.

"Who's this, then, Alan?"

Vickery lifted himself half out of the pool and looked. Strolling down the garden path was a small, tidy man in a light-cream suit and one of those hats which a certain type of posh Brit still wore in hot places.

"I don't know. Another bloody lawyer, probably."

The man approached the pool, collecting a folding lawn-chair on the way. He positioned the chair carefully by the side of the pool, sat, crossed his legs and removed his hat.

Vickery panicked. He vaulted from the pool, shook the water from his hair, and ran towards the house.

"Alan, come back! Jason's not here. You're perfectly safe."

Vickery stopped and turned. Richard smiled.

"That's right. I'm not here in any official capacity. Nothing I do is official any more. Come along. Introduce me to your friends. I'm new in the neighborhood."

"Derek, Ronnie and Phil," Vickery said, returning. "What neighborhood?"

"Well not Barbados, in actual fact. Not quite my thing. Not that there's anything wrong with it. No, I've got a little place on Nevis."

"Nevis."

"It's another island."

"I know."

"Thought I'd drop in on you. Don't mind, do you?"

"Depends, doesn't it?"

"Who's this, then, Alan?" Derek asked.

"Richard," Vickery said. "Don't know his last name."

"We were on first-name terms from the beginning, weren't we?" Richard said. "Why don't you offer me a drink?"

"Help yourself."

Richard poured himself a gin but then looked lost.

"Pass the bloody tonic, Derek."

"Right-ho, Alan. Here."

What did Richard want, Vickery wondered. Here Vickery was, minding his own business, keeping his mouth shut, staying out of sight, doing what he was told. What more did they want?

"I trust you've got plenty to keep you busy, here?" Richard said.

"Yes," Vickery said. "I have."

"Yes, that's right — you've got that club of yours, haven't you? Well, good luck with it. No travel plans, I suppose?"

410

"No."

"Very wise. And you've got everything you need here."

Except my wife, Vickery thought. Except my daughter. Except my businesses. Except my hard-earned earnings. Except my bloody freedom.

"I feel the same. I'm retired, now. Just like you."

"Like me?"

"Mm."

There was a pause.

"So," Ronnie said. "Were you with Alan in Angola?"

"In spirit, yes," Richard said. "In spirit."

"Shame what's happened. You'd think someone would have predicted it."

"Yes, you would, wouldn't you?"

"Or done something to stop it. But, then, I suppose these things happen. No point trying to blame anybody."

Richard said nothing. He looked at Ronnie, then raised his glass and drank.

"Well, Alan," he said. "I've got some pleasant news for you. That lovely daughter of yours — Sara, isn't it?"

"Where is she?"

"Still in Africa. It's better if I don't say where. Still with Mr. Callaghan. Brian. I haven't always seen eye-to-eye with him, but one has to admire him in certain ways. And they do make a lovely, if unconventional, couple, don't you think?"

"Couple?"

"Yes, couple. Married couple."

"Married! But he's... How do you know?"

"Communication networks can be quite resilient these days."

"Yes, but he's..."

"A little older. But they're obviously very fond of one another."

"Yes, but..."

"You should be happy. Her mother isn't, alas."

Well, there was always that. And Derek seemed happy.

"Congratulations, Alan. How about a toast?"

Vickery nodded and they drank a toast to his only daughter, twenty-three years old, lost in Africa and hitched to a fifty-something, left-wing journalist of no fixed employment.

"Cheers," he said.

"And I thought you'd like to hear about Inácio," Richard said. "He wanted me to pass on his regards."

"How'd you know about him?" Vickery said. "I thought he worked for the Chinese?"

"Not exclusively."

"What Chinese is that, Alan?" Derek said.

"Sush, Derek. So where is he, then?"

"He and your little band," Richard said, "are conducting operations along the Angola-Namibia border. Quite successfully, so far."

"What operations?"

"I really can't say."

"Huh. So you and Inácio... Well, well. What about that Fernando bloke?"

"He's still flying. Whether one should call that good news, well..."

"And Díaz?"

"Who's Díaz?"

"Just shut it, Derek."

"Picked up by persons employed by MLG. Not heard from since."

"Oh. Something he said?"

"Or something you said."

Despite the heat, Vickery felt a subtle chill run down his spine.

"But we mustn't be downhearted," Richard said. "It's not over yet."

"What isn't?"

"History. Not by a long chalk."

This seemed so obviously true that Vickery wondered if perhaps there might be a hidden meaning. Richard was one for hidden meanings if anyone was.

"It looks like you might need another one," Richard said, picking up the gin bottle, which was, in fact, only two-thirds empty. "Shall we take a stroll?"

"All right."

Vickery, in his dripping trunks, padded down the garden path after Richard and followed him into the study. Richard glanced up at the laughing rat and raised his eyebrows.

"Yeah, I know," Vickery said. "Long story."

Richard smiled.

"She's all right," he said. "Walter and his people are looking after her. She wanted to be remembered to you."

"Ah," Vickery said. "Good. Good."

"As did Mr. Barclay. He says he'll never forget the time the two of you first met."

"Right. Good."

Here, Vickery realized, was an opportunity to get something off his chest.

"Um, Jennifer. There were things I wanted... We were sitting in the sand, and then, of course, the camels came, and..."

"You had things you wanted to say to her."

"Yes."

"But you didn't get the chance."

"No. So I was wondering —"

"I'm afraid you'll never see her again, Alan."

"No? Oh."

"But I'm pretty sure I know what you wanted to say."

"You are?"

Why bother being surprised? Was there anything Richard didn't know — apart, just possibly, from what had happened to Díaz?

"Yes. I'll pass your sentiments on. In the most delicate terms, of course."

"Right. Of course."

Richard took a second look at the rat.

"Curious. Look, Alan, I came here to give you these..."

Richard took an envelope and a card from his pocket and handed them to Vickery. "...And to ask you a question."

Vickery examined the postcard. It was from Shanghai and depicted a children's zoo surrounded by skyscrapers. The writing on the back was indecipherable, except for the signature — "Aurelio". Vickery looked at Richard.

"No, I can't read it either, I'm afraid. But I gather he's doing well."

Vickery opened the envelope. It was a bill from Kellerman.

"I wouldn't bother paying that if I were you," Richard said.

Vickery sighed.

"So what was your question, then?"

"Politics, Alan. All over now, is it? Finished, are we?"

"Yes."

"Completely? I'd just like to be sure."

"Completely."

"It's not that we're ungrateful for your efforts — latterly, that is."

"Course you're not."

"No."

"Good."

"So that's all settled, then?"

"Yes."

Richard took a deep breath and stretched his arms.

"Well," he said, "I ought to be going. It's a busy time. So much to do. Say goodbye to your friends for me."

"You said you were retired."

"I am."

"So what —"

"It's the impulse to intervene, I suppose. To interfere. Never goes away. I suppose I just can't resist. Goodbye!"

Richard waved his hat and stalked out into the hall. Vickery rubbed his knuckles across his forehead. Had he won? Had he lost? It was hard to say, overall. Had he been on the right side? Yes, in the end. Could he point to the instant in which he had crossed over? Not quite. Did it matter? No.

And what remained for him? He couldn't say. Perhaps, in time, it would become clearer. Would Richard ever visit again? Probably not. If Vickery went to Nevis, would he find him? Daft questions, really.

And if Muller called again, trying to seduce Vickery into peddling more guns — this time in central Asia because the Russians were *so much more realistic* about these things than the Americans — then he would tell Muller that letting him drive away from the compound behind the Explorers' Club was the worst decision he'd ever made. This might not be true, but it was something to relish in the saying.

He sidled up to the drinks cabinet and extracted another bottle of gin. Then he began to walk slowly back towards the garden. But, half-way, he stopped and put the bottle down on an occasional table imported by Mariella from Barcelona. With a lump in his throat, he took down the laughing rat from above the fireplace, turned its face to the wall and propped it up against the mantelpiece.

Then he collected the gin, tucked it under his arm, and stepped out to re-join his friends.

Also by Rory Harden

Who thinks he has an answer to the Greater Persian Question? Who's going to save a nation on the brink? What's going down in the Libyan desert? Why all the motorcycles? What's the deal with the iguanas? And, most of all...

Who is John Dolt?

Ever thought you'd make a good dictator?

Rory Harden

THE POPULIST

"Smart, funny, thrilling–and subversive."

A fortuitous encounter in the bathroom section. Menacing objects in the African sky. A secret and luxurious fortress in the Costa Rican jungle. A strike of all the really productive people. A private army on the streets. An honest man thrust into the seat of power.

Also by Rory Harden

Who really won the Presidential Election? What's the true purpose of the Chinese moon landing? Who's building big in Madagascar? Who's on a mission to *disrupt?* America won't be the same again. In fact...

Will it even be America?

A third-party candidate to be US President. An exclusive hedge fund with *consistent* returns. Naval conflict in the South China Sea. An underground battle over secrets. Unrest in Hong Kong. A destitute woman with nothing but the key to unlimited power.

About the Author

Rory Harden lives in London with his wife, Nancy, and two adopted cats, Spike and Monty. He enjoys travel, books, music and computer programming. And he plays guitar and bass – not too badly, sometimes.